HOW NOT TO MAKE MONEY

HOW NOT TO MAKE MONEY

A NOVEL

RAJ KUNDRA

AND

ARGHYA LAHIRI

RANDOM HOUSE INDIA

Published by Random House India in 2013
Second impression in 2013

Copyright © Raj Kundra and Arghya Lahiri 2013

Raj Kundra and Arghya Lahiri have asserted their right
under the Copyright, Designs and Patents Act, 1988,
to be identified as the authors of this work

Random House Publishers India Private Limited
Windsor IT Park, 7th Floor
Tower-B, A-1, Sector-125
Noida 201301, UP

Random House Group Limited
20 Vauxhall Bridge Road
London SW1V 2SA
United Kingdom

978 81 8400 397 0

Typeset in Dante MT by R. Ajith Kumar

Printed and bound in India by Replika Press Private Limited

For sale in the Indian Subcontinent only

CONTENTS

PART ONE
THE BOYS

Dirty Deeds Done Dirt Cheap
—AC/DC

CHAPTER

2 THE BOYS

1.1

There were ten minutes left until they'd start the run back from Calais and Mike was watching the seconds tick away on the café clock while JD kept his face buried in *The Sun*. When you were running two hundred thousand pounds worth of contraband into England, there was only so much you could do to keep from getting caught, and once you'd done that there was fuck-all else to do. If they felt Customs coming down on them once they were moving, there'd be options, but they wouldn't know what those options were until the last second, the last chance. So what was there to talk about?

'Mike?'

'Yeah?' Mike looked out of the window, through the collected grease of years, at a sky that darkened towards a singular grey.

'It says here that a bunch of Arabs spent fifty thousand pounds in one evening at a place called the Doxy.' JD's head emerged from the paper. 'Can you fucking believe that?'

Mike shrugged. 'It's their money.'

'I wonder how much that is in camels?'

Mike laughed through the side of his mouth and JD

grinned back at him. He shook his head and looked down at *The Sun*.

'Fifty thousand pounds,' he said. His voice was soft. Mike winced. JD was setting himself up for one of his monologues. He looks like a violin-playing Jew, and not a Punjabi misfit from Heston, thought Mike. JD had mournful basset hound eyes, hair that went every which way and Satan's grin. It was an attractive, sharp face. But it wasn't distinctive. JD had learned that trick very early in their association.

They could both effortlessly disappear into crowds. It was a skill that they'd possessed since their childhoods. Profit always ran in the mob, at their end of the street. JD was better at it because he was brown, and because he was smaller.

Mike had to work harder at it. He was taller, bigger, memorable because he was weather-beaten. He had a hard face, but one that people identified with. Mike looked like someone everyone knew. Mike drained the last of his coffee.

JD glanced at his watch. It was verging towards half past. He swung around and waved at the waiter for the bill.

The two men exited the café, both pulling on leather gloves. They walked around the corner to a small white van. Mike reached into his pocket for the keys. Above them, the night was on the move, descending, restless, like black ink seeping through cotton. The streetlamps were already beginning to hum. The wonder of it, JD thought, was this little stretch of Calais, removed from the clock tower that served as the dead centre of the town by only a handful of streets, and was quiet enough for him to catch that hum. He turned around the other way—he could see the top of the enormous glass dome that formed the entrance of the Cité Europe mall. *That*, he knew well enough. He had spent a large part of the previous twenty-four hours moving in and out of it.

Mike was already in the driver's seat, waiting. They always picked ordinary-looking vans. But every single one of them had the living hell tuned out of it.

'Let's roll,' JD said, the grin still on his face. 'It's a nice enough night for it.'

Mike turned the van around, waited at the intersection and turned right, heading back towards Cité Europe.

~

Mike drove quickly but unhurriedly, as if he spoke the van's language. The two of them had once outrun a tail on the M25, taking the off-ramp into a series of country roads that JD had never seen, and had never seen again. That was the fastest he'd seen anyone drive, and Mike had done it with the tach red-lining, barely touching the brakes. There were three turns, JD remembered, where he was certain that they'd finally run out of luck—the rear end of the van fishtailing like it was on snow. On each of those turns Mike had literally *talked* the van back onto the road, laying fifty or sixty feet of rubber every time. His shoulders never tensed. His grip on the steering wheel remained light and relaxed, with Mike still laid back in the absurd position he always put the driver's seat in, almost horizontal. They'd lost the tail in about twenty minutes and had come to a halt at a pub—The Traveller's

Rest—with their tyres still smoking. JD had opened the door and vomited, mostly out of relief. Mike had just grinned. It was only later in the pub that his hands began to tremble. JD had forced him to drink two whiskys and had driven them home with changed number plates. Shortly after that, they had altered their model of operation to the present one.

JD shifted in his seat and crossed his right leg over his left. As he untied and redid his shoelace, swearing under his breath because of the gloves, the van joined the motorway proper. They were clear. On the other side of the road, the traffic into Cité Europe was beginning to build up. They were now out of the town limits.

'Do it,' Mike said, not taking his eyes off the road.

JD reached for the rucksack lying at his feet, pulled out two packets of chewing gum and tossed them onto the dashboard. Mike grunted a single short laugh.

'Never forget, huh?'

'It's a charm, bruv. You respect the luck. Only then does the luck respect you.'

'Did you come up with that? All on your own, JD?' Mike asked.

'There's more I can come up with,' said JD. 'If you like.'

'Please spare me.'

JD took three cell phones from the bag, his bashers on this trip, all of them identical. Each had a tag of paper taped to the side, neatly numbered, the sequence running 1-2-3. He picked up the phone labelled '1', pulled off the label, and dialled.

Ritual came with the territory. It made them what they were—successful smugglers in a business that afforded very little success. This was the climax to their weekend. This had been the climax to most of their weekends over the past five years.

If Brian disconnected after a single ring, it meant they were going through with the run. And they were running the single largest amount of contraband they had ever attempted. The moment they entered the inspection bay before boarding the train across the Channel, everything went on hold. Decisions, if they had to be made, were made in seconds. Maintaining a winning percentage in this business required a combination of intelligence, intuition and pure balls.

The game had three stages. The first, and most basic, was sourcing the goods. Depending on the size of their shipment, this might indicate either a day-trip to Calais or a longer visit. For the current stock, JD and Mike had made the trip across on Saturday morning, yesterday. In turns, they ran Cité Europe ragged, while the other visited a number of smaller shops in and around the Town Hall. They were always careful, never buying too much from one location, always paying cash. This morning they had driven into a warehouse they rented in a poorer quarter of Calais. Brian Nash, the driver of the stock van, had driven across the Channel at a pre-arranged time, parked his van in the warehouse (he had his own key) and left to get breakfast. There, JD spent approximately an hour in absolute concentration, transferring the goods to Brian's van. It was all about the packing: the central core of cigarettes and booze was surrounded equally on all sides by boxes and boxes of packed drinking glasses. JD had a friend who serviced baggage X-ray machines at Heathrow airport, and he'd picked up this little nugget after feeding the guy a few pints. Carbon confused the scanners. It had worked for them thus far. The glasses guaranteed nothing. Just that the Customs guys would think *once* before they unpacked everything.

When he was done, JD would replicate the set-up in their own van. Inevitably, he would use more boxes this time around because he was compensating for weight. He needed to make up the difference, the weight of the contraband, with more glasses. The vans needed to be identical, with one crucial difference in the belly of the beast.

While JD was working on Brian's van, Mike spent the hour washing down every square inch of their own, obliterating any possible fingerprints. This was central to their current method of operation; once JD was done with Brian's van, he would wear gloves for the rest of the trip. Since the opening of the Eurotunnel, Customs had clamped down very hard. The tax on booze and cigarettes on the Continent made bulk-buying very attractive, and the tunnel invited large-scale racketeering.

The guidelines allowed for personal use—around three thousand two hundred cigarettes, and proportional quantities of booze, one hundred and ten litres of beer—on a single trip. Anything above was contraband. Mike and JD typically moved between seventy-five thousand and a hundred grand worth of stock on any given weekend. A bust meant seizure of the van and immediate arrests. Or occasionally, they got tails once they landed in England, Customs trying to uncover the London base for a suspicious van. But since that narrow escape on the M25 about two years ago, they had perfected their method.

A hired driver drove the van with the actual stock. He was the straight guy. His party line was simple. He was just the driver. If anything was found in the van, it had appeared there without his knowledge. All of the drivers were drilled about this and their stories never changed, which is why they held up under interrogation. They were making this trip because it was a chance to make extra cash on the weekend, but beyond driving the van, they had no idea. JD had set up a string of small companies, all virtual, in order to aid this paper trail. They alternated between companies on runs. Every driver was packed to the gills with the correct paperwork and ID. And while they had had the occasional bust, no one had ever gone to prison on their account.

If the van carrying the stock was busted at Customs, then that was the end of the run, no way around it. But being alongside the van when it was seized allowed Mike and JD to bring contingencies into play much earlier—a lawyer on permanent retainer in London, and an additional two hours in which to sort out the story of the fictional company which had ordered the shipment in the first place. The moment the affair was settled, the company in question was shut down. The driver was handed a one-time bonus and never used again. However, if they left the disembarkation bay with a tail in Folkstone, Mike and JD would attempt to run interference. But interference was always a risky business, with very little margin. Twice, caught in traffic snarls, they'd had to order the driver of the stock van to simply park it and walk away. The third factor in the game was the distribution of the stock, once they got back to their warehouse in London. This was the easiest part, usually done inside of a couple of hours of reaching London. On a couple of occasions, they'd had to lay low for a week before selling the stock simply because the heat was too great on the streets. But once they were in London, holding down the stock between themselves and their friends and family was never difficult.

Getting there was the hard part.

~

The phone rang once. JD felt his heart rate crank up a notch. Just a notch, but enough to indicate they were into the business end of their weekend.

It was a wait of a second and a fraction longer. The call was firmly disconnected. JD brought the phone down and turned to Mike.

'Green. We go.'

Minutes later, they turned into the embarkation bay.

~

Traffic was light. Very few commercial vehicles were waiting to board the 16:34 Calais–Folkstone, but the private cars still numbered in their hundreds, people heading back to England after the weekend. The sky had darkened further; this was storm weather. Mike had driven this route enough times to see there would be snow. Just ahead of them, to their right, stood Brian's white van. The sticker running along the side-panel read, 'Glad Handlers'. Mike shook his head. He'd left the naming of the companies to JD.

The 'Glad Handlers' sticker was the only thing that differentiated the two vans. And Mike had one just like it tucked behind his seat.

Customs Inspectors were making random stop checks and guiding drivers to inspection bays. Mike had driven them through, as he did on almost all of their runs, so that they were just behind the stock van. It allowed them the small luxury of monitoring the van across a queue. At this point in the game, it was all they could do.

'What d'you reckon?' asked JD. Ritual.

'We're getting through, bruv. Even if it kills me.' Also ritual. A Customs official approached Brian's van. Another was making his way through towards them.

'*Bonjour Monsieur. Anglais? Francais?*'

Mike lowered his window, welcoming the Customs official making his way towards them but also trying to listen in on the conversation to their right.

'*Anglais,*' answered Brian. 'Please.'

'Of course,' replied the official. He was English, young, fresh-faced, not more than twenty-seven or twenty-eight. Well, young for a Customs official. Most of the dogs, thought Mike, were right old bastards around forty—grim and relatively hard, at least when it came to commercial vehicles. The face the tourists saw was always much prettier.

To their right: 'Your papers please. And kindly park the van for a random check.'

'Sure,' said Brian, pulling out his set of papers from the glove compartment, neatly filed away in a waterproof transparent document holder.

Another Customs official arrived at their van. Mike presented their papers. Mike Hamilton, twenty-seven, London. The official asked him what he was carrying. Mike explained that he was carrying along some drinking glasses, earning some pocket-money over the weekend. His friend, pointing at JD—Jai Singh Dewan, twenty-six—who waved at the official like an enthusiastic tourist, was simply along to keep him company.

The line behind them began to grow. The official looked at their passports, handed them back and waved them through. He turned to the next car in the queue.

Mike pulled away slowly, a careful British driver on the Continent. Next to them, the official was looking at Brian's papers.

'You're carrying glasses for Kudos International?'

Mike winced. JD grinned. And they heard Brian say, 'Whatever the documents say, guv. I'm just the driver.'

'Okay. Please wait while we X-ray the van.'

~

Ten minutes passed. They were in the queue of cars inching forward, waiting to board the train. Mike had become utterly still, his eyes on the side-view mirror. The only movement was his jaw, grinding the chewing gum relentlessly. JD could tell Mike was starting to suspect they were in the shit. The longer Brian's van failed to join the queue, the more likely that four months of money pitched into the game tonight had simply been blown apart by stupid chance. And JD always handled stupid chance better than Mike.

'Relax, Mikey,' he said, trying to find a way to draw Mike back. He knew where Mike was headed, and what would happen when he got there. The rage came from some deep, unknown well. It was as fundamental to Mike's nature as his bull-head, the set of his jaw and his eyes.

There was no reaction, not even a flicker.

JD tried again. 'Come on now, Mikey. You know the glasses always beat the X-ray. And even if they don't, it's fine. We'll get the next game. Brian's cool. He's sorted. We're fine.'

Mike turned to him and JD was taken aback by how old Mike suddenly looked. 'You know how much is on this run, right?'

He knew. In the van behind them was more than twice the amount they had ever attempted. They were doing it because it was Christmas. And winter was easier. Darkness helped.

Mike turned back to the mirror. 'It's mine, Jai. We worked for it. Three years we worked on this system—just for this one game. If we run home, we're clear for six months, maybe a year.' His voice was flat. 'They're not getting their fucking hands on it. Not on mine.'

JD sighed. He registered the use of 'Jai'. Still, he knew better than to argue with Mike. He couldn't call Brian until they were on London side; it would look too odd. He sighed again, and twisted the rear-view mirror so that he could look at the ramp leading up from the inspection dock.

~

Another five minutes. A light rain had begun to fall, thunderclouds streaking across the Channel. They had turned off the overpass and gone down the ramp to the platform, now second in line to board the train. The light traffic behind them had built into a flood of cars.

'This is taking too fucking long,' Mike said. 'This should take ten minutes, tops.'

JD was almost as worried as Mike now, but he kept it to himself. One of them had to remain calm, and Mike had clearly decided it wasn't going to be him.

'It's a Sunday, Mike. It's busy. Tourists. Amateurs trying to get shit across. That's all.'

Mike shook his head, his eyes still on the side-view mirror, when, as they the turned onto the train, they both saw the Glad Handlers van turn onto the ramp.

'What did I tell you?' JD whistled, slapping the dash. 'Dollars, baby! We ran another one past the frogs. We're landing this motherfucker.'

Mike shook his head again. 'Too long, JD. Something's not right.'

JD said nothing as they pulled into the dirty yellow neon of the train. When Mike parked the van and switched off the ignition, he had that same bleak, almost haunted look. JD tried one last time.

'Mike, if he didn't clear the fucking scan, he's not on the fucking train. And if he's on the fucking train, he's cleared the fucking scan. That means we're fucking flying home free.' Each 'fucking' was punctuated by a light stabbing of the seat between them. All JD wanted was the *possibility* of hope. Because, if Brian hadn't cleared the scan, why the fuck did they let him on the train? That question had nasty implications.

Mike turned to JD. 'We're not home yet, bruv. Not yet.'

1.2

JD tried the radio, picking up mostly static and bad pop music. Christmas week meant that each song was worse than the song that preceded it. JD looked at Mike, he was radiating tension, reduced to monosyllables. There was more here, more than just money. This was a suicide run. If it fucked up, they would be blown clean out of the water.

It had taken him twelve seconds after they'd rolled onto the train to work out exactly what was going on.

He watched the reshuffle. He saw the possible permutations. And he thought he knew where they were headed.

If he was right, this had become a three-man game in a hurry.

The question was: what could he do *now*?

~

Mike fixed his eyes on the steering wheel. By the time they got off the train in England, they'd be in extra time. What was the play now? The game had been fixed—he could bet his life on it.

He looked at his watch. 'Seventeen minutes.'

'Two minutes to fame, Mike. It's time to get the fat-suit on.'

Mike forced himself to slow his breathing. His mind began to clear. What were the elements? The stock, the weather, the uncertainty about what awaited them once they disembarked. He groped for answers and he cut it off at the knees. Sometimes there weren't any answers. Sometimes the only answer was to stay in the game and stay open. He didn't like it, unlike JD who thrived in situations where every decision was improvisation. But he didn't have a choice.

Two things were possible at Folkstone: one, a straight bust. In that case, however much it fucked them up, Mike and JD would still be able to drive away with the precious time it would take for them to put things in motion. The loss of the stock would be colossal, but they'd probably walk away with no arrests.

But, as much sense as the straight bust made for Customs, Mike didn't think that that was what they needed to worry about. With the amount of stock they were carrying, it was risky for Customs to have let them get on the train in the first place. That they had indicated that they were after a much bigger prize. Something, somewhere, had tripped off an alarm. Mike was prepared to make two more guesses on the strength of this one—

First, that Customs knew *exactly* how much stock they were carrying. This wasn't a carload of arsehole tourists trying to get lucky.

Second, that if they didn't make the bust at disembarkation, then JD and Mike had been fingered, and Customs was setting them up for a full-blown opera. That meant at least two tails and a rolling base, followed by a reception in London. First they'd nail the transport, then the warehouse. All parties involved. In one fell fucking swoop, Sir.

If Mike's guesses were right, outrunning Customs was no option. Shaking off the tail in this weather was impossible. He couldn't even ask Brian to attempt it. It wasn't about the stock—stunt driving on a night like this would get you killed.

The only ace up their sleeve was the fact that they were on the train with the stock van. The dogs didn't know that Mike and JD were *in* the game.

The train slowed. They were minutes away from disembarkation. People who had been out stretching their legs began returning to their cars.

JD reached for the chewing gum. 'Someone dynamited London for this run,' he said. 'If they don't bust us here, it's a trick. And we're fucked if we try running in this shit.'

'You mean dead.'

'Right. The question is: where are we staging the Schillachi?'

Mike thought about it. His head was now completely clear, and he was cold straight through to the bone. JD was right. It *had* come to the Schillachi, to their big play. It was about the staging area. And balls. And a degree of luck.

But they might be able to create luck. The night was right for it. All they needed was location.

'Maidstone,' he said.

～

No one stopped the Glad Handlers van when it rolled off the train and onto the M20, and after trailing behind it at about two hundred metres for ten minutes, Mike and JD knew why. The rolling base was a big blue movers' van with twin industrial antennae. They might as well have stuck a neon sign that flashed 'Coppers' on the roof.

Mike stuck to the second lane. He drove slowly, with care. Traffic was thin. More than half the cars that'd gone through the tunnel had pulled off within minutes of being on the motorway. On the radio, between each song, jockeys were telling people to get off the roads and stay home. The van bucked and skidded under a seething, swirling mess of sky that was a dozen shades of black.

Establishing the two tails was almost as easy as spotting the base. The first was a blue Ford Focus that stayed unwaveringly behind Brian's van, maintaining an even distance of about a hundred metres.

'He's good,' Mike said. 'Fucking copper he might be, the lad's relentless. See how he holds his distance? He figures what Brian'll do before he does it, so he never has to back off or catch up.'

JD slid his window down a bit, spat out his gum and replaced it.

'The lead driver's shit, though,' Mike continued, indicating a white Peugeot with a tilt of his chin. 'The weather's fucking with his head and he's panicking. Can you see it?'

JD nodded.

The Peugeot driver had sped out from the shoulder of the M20 just seconds after Brian had passed, and without paying attention to the speed of his target. Mike had spent three minutes watching him work his way back with a grin on his face. He'd clearly been ordered back. But dropping back was a little difficult when there were no other fucking cars on the motorway and you were driving in the middle of a shitstorm. And, twice, he'd slowed down when confronted by open stretches and high wind. Both times, he'd been ordered back up. It made Mike feel a little better—Customs were having to alter the script too.

Mike and JD both knew that the guy driving the Peugeot was the probable fracture line on this operation, though they committed to nothing yet. They were simply picking up their threads, sorting them, bunching them up. The play was so close and just out of reach. They'd have to will themselves to it.

'They bugged the van in Calais,' Mike said.

'Sure,' JD agreed. 'But it'll be a surface tag. Nothing on the inside.'

Mike noticed his grip on the wheel had tightened and relaxed it. Time. What they needed was more time.

'Make the call,' he said.

JD looked at him. 'You sure?'

For the first time since they'd gotten on the motorway, Mike took his eyes off the road and the rolling circus ahead of them and looked at JD.

'Aren't you?'

JD didn't bother replying, just pulled the phone marked '2' from the rucksack, then paused. He grinned like a teenager. It was the oddest burst of sunshine, and Mike felt for the first time that evening that he might enjoy himself hugely in the next thirty minutes or so. JD dialled Brian's number.

'Hiya, mate. How do you do?'

The tail-lights of the Glad Handlers van ahead of them lit up once, briefly.

'Can't complain.' Brian was calm, unruffled. JD felt a rare wave of affection for him. It was a real pity that they weren't going to be able to use him after tonight, however it turned out. 'What's the score, then?'

The Glad Handlers van slowed, almost imperceptibly.

'Three-zero, it looks like,' said JD. 'The off-side's leaking. Where are you?'

'On the M20.'

'On a night like this? With Hurricane Liam blowing? You'll catch a chill. Or an over-turning. Nah, I'm serious, man. Get off the road.'

'I might actually take that advice. Could use a bite to eat.'

JD looked at Mike for confirmation. This was their first play England-side and it had to be on the nail. Mike nodded without hesitation. 'Maidstone,' he mouthed.

'Maidstone,' JD said. 'Nice big services. Costa's, Wimpy's, even a bloody Travel Inn, and I think that there's a restaurant. Wait out the storm and I'll see you soon. We'll get a drink or something tomorrow.' He disconnected.

Mike let the van out, touched sixty, and then nudged it towards seventy. The snow was coming down thick and fast now. The cambering, designed to protect from run-offs, had become a shute on a sled run. The back end of the van, with the extra weight of the glasses, kept drifting out, upwards.

It defied gravity at these speeds. But Mike kept the hammer down, the tach permanently red-lining, and always a gear lower then he needed to be. The promise of the heavier power was all that was holding them onto the road.

JD fought the urge to light a cigarette. It was important that the van was sterile by the time they hit Maidstone—in the last three minutes that had become the most important factor in the game. He looked around once, then again, trying to see if there was anything that gave them away. But it was a surface scan, he was in deep thought. He was very close to having chalked out a plan for the rest stop at Maidstone and he was examining it minutely, coming up with a contingency at every turn. The play dictated his role, as it dictated Mike's, and he was just thankful that it fell right into the realm of things he was good at.

Two minutes down the road, they blew past Brian and the rest of the cavalry. Mike dropped his pace, making it more reasonable in plain view. As he passed Brian, he dipped his headlights once. Brian remained rock-solid behind the wheel, giving no sign of having seen them, but as they cleared the lead car and began to pull away, his headlights dipped once.

~

Maidstone was better than they'd hoped. There were a number of cars in the parking lot. The restaurants and the shops were jam-packed. JD doubted whether the rest area had seen business like this in a long time. It boded well.

They parked out towards the very edge of the lot. All the slots closer to the two buildings were already occupied but Brian would see their van clearly from the off-ramp. And the choice of slot made it impossible for the two tail cars to park behind the vans—they would be forced much further into the parking lot. Both Mike and JD were reasonably confident that no tail would park right alongside the van, not if the Customs guys had to remain in the cars. Which left the blue van, and that was where they needed luck to turn their way the slightest bit.

Mike turned off the ignition. Both men looked around the parking lot, checking to see if any CCTV cameras had sprung up since the last time they'd passed through and, seeing no obvious signs, they waited for a moment in silence. They had never attempted what they were about to try tonight. The hand didn't even matter. They were now dealing only in bluffs.

Mike pulled out his rucksack. Looking around, he checked the parking lot once again and pulled out three rolled-up paper tubes from behind his seat, the largest about two feet long. He placed the tubes in the rucksack, careful to not bend them in any way.

JD looked at him, his eyes glittering. 'Fuckin' crime's supposed to be easy. That's the attraction, see? For people like me. That it's easy. Instead…' He thought about it. 'Instead… this.' Then he laughed, easy and relaxed. 'The 'Hail-Mary' play, they'll call this one. You tell me, Mikey—can you feel hands of God?'

Mike looked at JD. 'Around my neck, you mean?'

'Come on, then. The least you can do is buy me a cup of coffee.'

They ducked into Costa's with their heads low against the wind and their collars pulled up—two ordinary guys finding shelter from the storm.

~

As they waited over cups of coffee at a booth near the large shop-front window overlooking the lot, twenty-three cars pulled into the lot. JD counted them without even being aware of it. The conversation in the coffee shop was loud. It felt almost like a pub. People were forcing life and warmth into the place. Mike and JD added nothing to it, just sat and watched.

Brian's van pulled in first. Without hesitation, Brian pulled into the last row on the outer perimeter, two spaces from their white van, and began to walk toward the coffee shop. As he did, the Ford Focus pulled in. Again, Mike admired the driver. Parking next to the target van would have been stupid. Instead, he did the best he could, parking two rows further in, pulling into the first available space, but now between the Glad Handlers van and the block that housed the restaurants. His passenger was on a cell-phone, perhaps asking the Peugeot driver where the fuck he was— Mike figured the silly twat had overshot the off-ramp. There was a moment of indecision in the Ford. To wait in the car in weather like this would look ridiculous and clue the target. The passenger got out and headed towards Costa's.

Okay. Coffee to go was the first fallback. Then one would need to use the loo. The checklists were holding. And now it was time to set them on fire.

Brian walked into the shop completely ignoring Mike and JD, took a stool at the counter and bought a coffee.

As the Customs guy making the coffee run walked across the lot, two more cars pulled in, and behind them, the blue movers' van. One of the cars parked in the closest available slot, two rows away from the building. It was an old red BMW, in pretty good condition. A middle-aged man in a corduroy jacket locked the car with a remote and walked briskly towards Costa's.

JD had his mark. Still, he waited. Now, so close to the pitch, timing was everything. And the pitch turned on the blue van.

Mike and JD watched it circle the parking lot once and then turn out again onto the off-ramp. Customs clearly believed that the base was too much. It would park on the off-ramp. If there was a problem, they could always flash IDs away from the glare of the parking lot.

In his head, JD heard a faint sigh as the last card kissed the baize, stopping just in front of an outstretched hand. He turned to Mike.

'Call me. And keep the line alive. I'll buy you a couple of minutes.' Getting to his feet, JD looked back at Mike. 'Just pray the reception holds.'

'And if it doesn't?'

He held his palms out, toward the ceiling. 'Hands of God, Mikey.' With that, he headed for the counter.

Mike gritted his teeth. He absolutely hated it when JD left him playing blind. He picked up his phone and dialled.

JD breezed towards the counter, his synapses on fire. As the BMW owner walked through the door—'The Professor', JD had named him—JD's phone began to ring. JD swore. He was fumbling for his phone when he bumped into the man.

'Bugger—sorry—can't find the bloody—ah! Sorry!' JD said as he fished the wrong phone from his left pocket. The Professor waved away the apology. JD had a distracted, disarming smile on his face. With his right hand, JD clicked 'TALK' on the ringing phone in his right pocket, and tucked the BMW keys he'd lifted from the Professor's jacket under the phone. He looked at the phone in his left hand, scowled, and then answered before it could ring again—as if it had been ringing in the first place.

The illusion was perfect. It had taken four and a half seconds.

'What *now*, love?' His voice was harried and loud. Someone at the counter turned to look at him.

Mike watched from across the shop, doing his best to not laugh. He could hear JD through the phone in his pocket.

'Well, that's not my problem, is it?' JD said. He rubbed his eyes and wandered to the take-away line, where the Customs agent had his back to him. 'You'll fucking *not*!' he snapped at the phone, turning, and caught the elbow of the Customs guy ahead of him just as he picked up his two cups of coffee.

Wearing the hapless expression of an idiot, JD took one neat step back and watched the coffee curve out of the Customs guy's cups, rise up, turn, and splash all over the polished floor. The Professor caught some on his trousers and hissed in pain, pin-wheeling back and getting tangled with two people in the line behind him.

Dominoes! JD thought. Because each of the Professor's victims knocked back two of their own, and then the shoving and toe-crushing spread through the line and out to the rest of the shop in a chain reaction that pleased JD so much he wished he could stay to watch the rest of it. He had caused this effect. It was utterly logical, it was order—it only *looked* like chaos.

The shouting was just beginning when he walked out to the parking lot.

He moved like a man who suddenly didn't care about the weather at all, heading straight into the middle of the lot, yelling into his cell phone, unaware that it was snowing. He wasn't really sure what he was saying. He was simply rushing to occupy the rough centre of the triangle between the blue van, the Ford Focus and the BMW. He was working purely on intuition. If this didn't work, then he'd have to figure out another option, but he felt fairly certain that he'd already arrived at the last one possible—the last second, the last chance.

The perfect play.

He walked, craning for a glimpse of the blue van. He was almost at the BMW now. If he crossed beyond it, he didn't know if the play would work. Behind him, he heard the door of the coffee shop opening and the rising voices. Someone called out to him. He was abreast the Beemer now. He thought, Fuck *me*!

'Hey!' from the coffee shop. 'Yeah, you!' JD stopped, beginning to turn back. As he turned, he caught the hazards of the blue van in the corner of his eye.

In that eternity, before he completed his turn, he asked himself the one question that he always asked himself, and that no one ever knew he asked.

Do you believe?

There was a white roar in his head, a soundless explosion. JD triggered the BMW remote in his pocket four times in rapid succession, hoping that the remote on the cell phone signal, amped by the radio frequency between the blue van and the Focus, would be enough to cause something, anything, a minor distraction that allowed Mike time to move.

Nothing happened.

Then the parking lot exploded.

Anywhere between sixty and a hundred alarms screamed out at once—the blare of the sirens deafening, the lot suddenly a blinding display of Christmas lights. The man in the Ford Focus froze.

People began to pour out of the coffee shop and the restaurants. JD waited until he could feel the buzz of a gathering crowd behind him, could hear their voices getting louder and closer. He shouted above the din as hard as he could and pointed at the man in the Ford.

'It's this guy!' JD yelled. 'His radio did it!'

As the mob surged out onto the parking lot, JD saw Mike

merge with it and then peel off toward the darker outer perimeter, even while the Customs guys were trying to pull out their IDs.

~

Mike could've done a manual change on the licence plates; he had that much time.

Instead, he slapped three stickers onto his van—the 'Glad Handlers' logo, and two licence plates. Mike now had two identical vans. He crossed to Brian's van—now his—knelt by the rear bumper and felt around as if he was looking for a set of spare keys. His hand brushed against the bug on the first attempt. He pulled it off and quickly attached it to his own van. As he walked over to the driver's side door of the stock van, he ripped off the original 'Glad Handlers' sticker.

On the off-ramp, the dogs scrambling from the blue van didn't give him a second glance. No sticker, no cigar. A minute and twelve seconds after he had exited the coffee shop, Mike was back on the M20.

Only the wind chased him into London.

1.3

Mike waited till he was about ten minutes out of Maidstone and well into the country. No tails, no blue moving van. His head yammered. London. Something had gone off in London. He wanted a face. And he wanted to break that face.

He found what he was looking for, a small cul-de-sac, with only one farm in the distance. Mike swung the van around in a U-turn and killed his lights. The world had been airbrushed with silver. He felt like he was stepping into an X-ray.

It took him barely a minute to change both the number plates. As he worked, the plan sorted itself out. He decided on Bayswater, one of their two fallbacks. And he had to move the stock tonight, all of it. If he could keep it together, smart and efficient, he'd put the motherfucker away in a couple of hours. Eight-thirty, he estimated, he'd be done.

~

The first few minutes in Maidstone were a riot. The double-doors of Wimpy's had shattered, and no one knew how. As the crowd surged over the parking lot, a few people had completely forgotten about the snow and ended up on their arses.

JD, in a moment of genuine sympathy—this was, after all, between them and the dogs—slipped into the crowd and deftly put the keys to the Beemer back in the Professor's pocket. JD turned away and for the first time that day, though they'd been within yards of each other for an hour or so, looked Brian straight in the eyes. He grinned. Brian smiled back. Brian would have to wait this out; he had to be here if and when Customs wanted to look at the van.

More than half the cars in the lot were still wailing. Mobs had gathered in two different spots. The first was around the Customs guys. Their radio seemed to have been the single element that had sparked the chaos. And regardless of their IDs, they weren't the police. On the pavement outside Wimpy's, a different argument was pulling more and more people into its orbit. The employees of Wimpy's were looking at their front doors shattered across the curb and around the feet of the people who'd probably broken it. An expectant audience now lined the parking lot, roughly three hundred people, watching and waiting. The Customs guys were going to get their comeuppance, and the argument outside Wimpy's was going to turn into a brawl.

This was where JD had to wait out the bluff, the first time in over an hour where he didn't know what he would do next. It depended on when the coppers showed. If they were here in the next five minutes, he was done. If they weren't he'd have to find a way to stall Customs. He was up for it—he was Pro-Am when instigating riots.

But there was such a thing as pushing your luck. He'd done well. Now it was time to see if the game would reward him.

JD gravitated towards two big, amiable-looking black guys who were standing near their own car. He'd noticed them because they were two of the few people not hurrying, but mostly because they were so amiable-looking. He checked again. Brian was back in Costa's. Out in the parking lot, someone was pushing their way through to the two Customs guys. The blue movers reveal themselves, thought JD.

Then, without even being aware of a decision having been made, he turned to Black Guy #1, and said, 'But they'll keep blaming the immigrants—always the immigrants. Immigrants setting off fucking car alarms.'

Both men turned to him, Black Guy #1 raising an eyebrow. They were big guys. And even though it was a light comment, it wasn't to be taken lightly. JD just grinned back.

It was a magic grin—Mike could have told them. It made JD look like a fourteen-year-old. It told of a companion, of revolution and of stories over beer in the light of a warm fire.

Black Guy # 2 burst out laughing. It was hard not to. A young Indian kid had popped up out of nowhere to reel off a wonderfully casual racist pronouncement.

'Your car go off?' asked Black Guy #1.

'Nah, mate. I hitched a ride in and the guy took off when this shit happened. I figure if a fight breaks out, I'm with the two of you.'

Black Guy #1 smiled, extending a massive hand.

'Alistair,' he said. JD shook the hand. Then he turned to Black Guy #2 and extended his own hand.

Black Guy #2 was still grinning as they shook. 'Kenneth,' he said.

'I'm JD. It's a pleasure to meet you boys. Trust me. Us immigrants is gotta stick together.'

'You know what happened?' asked Alistair.

'Someone was saying it's that copper's radio,' said JD.

'But why would a bunch of coppers drive around in December in the middle of a storm, setting off car alarms?'

'They're Customs, actually,' JD replied. 'And now we get to stand here waiting. Life used to be simple, man. And we didn't used to have to stand around and wait for people to tell us what to do. I mean, look at us—ice forming around our testicles, waiting for someone to tell us what to do.'

Kenneth started laughing again and JD turned his grin on him. 'I like you, bruv. In time I could grow to love you.'

'What do you do, kid?' asked Kenneth.

'Me?' JD thought about it. 'I drink, man.'

'No, really, man,' said Kenneth, struggling to keep a straight face.

'I'm telling you, man. I *really* drink,' JD continued. He was starting to get a little worried. The coppers should have been here by now. 'You can check it out. Conduct a few tests. Two per cent blood in my alcohol count. And when I was six, I wanted to be white.'

Alistair was now grinning as well. JD didn't need a second invitation.

'We got to fuck these boys up good,' JD said. 'Make them *really* earn that Christmas bonus.'

Alistair looked at him. 'And how are you going to do that?'

'Well, that's the tricky bit, isn't it? Me, I'm waiting for a sign from God. I admit I haven't got much experience in the rioting business, but that's not entirely my fault, is it? I mean, think about it. You've got your anarchists, your football hooligans, your skinheads—now how's a Paki supposed to get ahead in that field?'

Kenneth turned away from JD and doubled up. It took a moment for the people standing around them to realize that he was actually laughing. And that he was laughing so hard that tears stood out in his eyes. He gathered his breath and let out an hysterical howl.

'You talk some *shit*, boy!' he said, putting his hand on JD's shoulder. 'But it's good, man, it's good!'

'You're a treat you are,' JD told him, then switched his attention to Alistair. 'But what makes you such a tough audience, bruv? This is some of my best banter!'

Alistair merely snickered, but it sent Kenneth into another fit.

JD was looking at both men, but he barely saw them. His eyes swept the parking lot. He filed away every detail. Mr. Blue Mover, clearly the authority figure, looked like he was under some real strain. He had expected a nice easy bust. Instead, his tails had sparked off a revolution in a parking lot.

He was a pebble on a hilltop, thought JD. One push and this thing could spiral badly out of control. He waited, squeezing the last millisecond out of the beat, knowing that what he wanted the most was to see someone break Mr Mover's nose.

JD turned to look for Brian and he saw cars with flashing lights pull in off the motorway. Enter: The coppers.

He allowed himself a tight smile. He'd done well, but there was a part of him that was disappointed, all the same.

The chatter in the parking lot dropped into a deep buzz as more people noticed the cops. Multiple conversations became a single one, all at once.

Mr Mover had been trying to impose order on the scene. Now, he just backed away slowly as the police cars moved in and crunched to a halt on the outer perimeter of the lot. Coppers emerged in a hurry—a pair headed towards them and a pair towards Wimpy's. JD caught it in the corner of his eye and turned to Alistair.

'But there's your sign from God. No rioting today.' He grinned. 'Come on. The least I can do is buy you guys a cup of coffee.'

~

Mike made good time. He followed the A20 almost all the way home. Somewhere near Blackheath Hill, he pulled over and bought himself a pack of fags. He didn't smoke much, but he figured he'd just fob off the packet to JD later that night. Outside the newsagent's he found a dustbin and finally got rid of his gum. It felt like spitting out a wad of tissue. He was killing time. There was no tail. There were barely any human beings in sight.

He was very, very tired. Every once in a while, there would be a stunt like the one they just pulled. A mad scramble, every nerve jacked up. When they were younger, it was part of the charm. Now, it just exhausted him. Mike could feel it in his bones. He felt heavy. With age. With terminal exhaustion.

All this just to go scurrying around like a rat. Like a bunch of lepers, banished to London's underbelly.

Mike flicked the cigarette away, watching the comet-trail of sparks. He shrugged and got rolling.

Mike didn't even have to wait at Royal Chelsea, didn't even have to park. Gary was waiting on the sidewalk, watching the traffic. Mike slowed and Gary—small, dark and wiry—climbed into the van. He wore a tan overcoat that was too big for him and his short hair glistened from the rain. His face was square and bony, mostly jaw. He was the antithesis of JD: Still, coiled, monotone. Only the eyes gave him away. He touched Mike on the shoulder and nodded. Then he smiled. They were already moving. Mike knew where the garage was. Down Pont and onto Bayswater. It was more posh than the neighbourhoods they normally haunted, but tonight it served them well to do so.

'What happened?' Gary asked. 'You skip a tail?'

Mike told him in quick, short sentences. The play. The opera. The Schillachi.

Gary frowned.

'Schillachi?'

'1990 World Cup. Little Italian bugger. Looked like a serial killer. Came out of nowhere—'

Gary had started nodding as soon as Mike had mentioned the World Cup. He completed Mike's sentence for him.

'—and won the Golden Boot.'

Mike was a little surprised that it already felt months behind him, like it had happened to another person. They drove in silence for a few minutes while Gary went through it in his head. He laughed out loud.

'They'll be talking about this one for years. You buy that boy a drink. On me.'

'If I know him, no one's going to have to do him anything tonight. Everyone just needs to get out of the way,' Mike said, smiling a little.

Gary shook his head. He pulled out his phone and paused, looking at Mike.

'You want to spread this out? Or is a single drop okay?'

'It's your call. If the buyer's good, if there's no heat from him, then a single drop's fine.'

Gary thought about it.

'We'll split it,' he said. 'We'll spread it around networks we know, so there's no heat, but we'll spread it.' As he spoke, he hit one of his speed-dials. The phone rang once, as far as Mike could tell.

'J. Stock's in. This is important, so listen up: stock's very hot. Get 'em in. Quick. And a stagger, three deep. Like the tide, bruv.' It wasn't an order or a request. Things would just happen.

'Javed's still working with you?' Mike asked as he pulled the van around into Bayswater. Gary grunted. Then smiled again.

'Sometimes people get a glimpse of the other life, you know? And then they grow up. Start to get responsible. And they move up with you. There—' he said, pointing to the garage.

Mike guided the van towards the door that Gary had indicated, driving slower now. Gary pulled a small remote from his pocket, triggered the door, and the van pulled into the darkened bay. Gary disappeared into the darkness, the overcoat whispering. Neon lighting sprang to life overhead. Mike didn't know what they used the garage for, but it made him pause. He didn't know how many pies Gary had his fingers in. He was reasonably sure that drugs were a part of the business. The garage could become anything it wanted to. Tools hung from hooks, neatly ordered to size and function. It felt like a hospital, sterile and clinical.

Mike got out and opened the double doors at the back of the van. Gary simply stared for a moment, confronted by the neatly stacked boxes of drinking glasses.

'JD?' he asked.

'JD,' Mike agreed.

'One day, he'll be running rings around all of us. If he ever gets it together. Come on, first one's in ten minutes.'

~

It took the coppers about twenty minutes to impose some semblance of order on the scene. Somewhere within that span of time, the Customs agents, no longer in charge of the scene, discovered that the van that they had tailed down the

M20 was parked in a different space. There was a conference. Then there was a conference with the coppers. And then the dogs made their first move in Maidstone. They came for Brian, still parked at his stool, reading *The Guardian*.

JD sensed most of it. The conference happened out of sight, and the dogs approached Brian behind his back at Costa's, but it moved around JD—he was the supernova.

Brian strolled out to the van, hands in his pockets. Even though the mob outside had mostly been broken up by the arrival of the coppers, Brian's walk, with a dog for company, was enough to switch the spotlight back on. People who had been making their way back to the coffee shops and restaurants stopped and slowly started to drift back towards the parking lot.

JD watched as much of it as he could without advertising his investment. It helped that most of the coffee shop was watching, too. They turned around on their chairs. Even Kenneth and Alistair dropped the conversation. This particular evening was taking on the air of an Italian soap opera. One table, a bunch in their twenties, got up and moved over to the window.

JD never had a clear line of sight through the second go-around, but saw it through a constantly shifting scrim of bodies, like he was trying to find a friend in a crowd. He searched for the group of Customs officers and coppers, and Brian, slightly to the left, driving them mad because he was so casual about the whole thing. JD just wanted the visual. He knew what was going to happen. He knew they were clear, had known it from the moment Mike left.

They asked Brian what was in the van and JD saw him shrug. He didn't know, and he didn't care. The Customs guys pointed out that the van was parked differently. Brian smiled benignly and said 'Sure' while shaking his head. He might as well have spat in their faces. They asked him for the paperwork. Brian produced the full set.

It left only one thing. JD knew it would turn on whether they cracked open the back right here on the parking lot, or whether they hauled Brian off. If they opened the van up in front of the coppers and everything was in order, there was no way back for Customs.

It went better than he'd factored.

The lead agent—the blue mover—stepped forward. It seemed like he was going to eyeball Brian, but Brian took a smooth step back. There was no way he could commit to the process. Not yet. He was still the hired driver, still unaware of what the hell was going on.

The conference was done. The blue mover wanted the keys, and Brian coughed them up.

They went through the wall of drinking glasses faster than JD could believe. It had taken him thirty minutes to pack the glasses that morning and they were through to the core in about a minute and a half. Then everything stopped.

The wait was long enough for JD to wonder, briefly, if Mike had actually driven off with the wrong van. There was no reaction at all, from anyone. Not from the two agents whose arses were sticking out in the cold, not from the coppers standing around, and not from Brian, who slouched, hands still in his pockets, like he was in the line at the bank.

Time spun out, everything and everyone suspended, waiting
for a revelation.

A single bewildered face emerged from the van. It said
something, and was clearly asked to repeat it. It said it again.
More silence. A loud, remarkably articulate scream of '*Fuck!*'
from Mr Mover, and they were done.

A few of the people standing outside clapped. There was
a louder cheer from inside the coffee shop. The blue mover
stalked off and sat in the Focus. The cops were unsure of
what to do next, as were the remaining Customs agents.
Brian, still the hired driver, still unsure of what the hell was
going on, now committed to the process. He was, after all,
standing around in the middle of a parking lot in Maidstone
in the worst weather imaginable, surrounded by cartons of
drinking glasses, like he was some sort of conceptual artist.

Who the hell was going to help him repack?

~

In Costa's, JD finally gave. He'd been at his best for close to
an hour and he was done. He could see the coppers helping
Brian load the boxes, and he knew that Brian would probably
have to leave his details and make a statement to the police
at some point tonight. But that was admin. This was a wrap.

He had reached the end of the alley, had run into it full-
tilt. He needed to get home and he needed something cold
to take care of the noise in his head. He'd need a lot of it.

JD never knew whether he telegraphed it or not. Within
minutes of the climax, Alistair asked JD whether he wanted

a ride into London and JD accepted with real gratitude. On the way out, he insisted on paying for the coffee like he'd promised. He climbed into the back seat and settled in, wrapping his leather jacket around him as tightly as he could. The heater would take a while to come into effect, and the inside of the car was bitingly cold. He would hitch to Tottenham Court Road and then take the Central line into Notting Hill Gate and walk the rest of the way down. It would be a relief to be alone for a while.

~

Mike and Gary worked quickly and efficiently. There would be no repacking tonight, no chance of any of the booze or cigarettes going back with Mike. Regardless of profit, they were dumping all the stock tonight. The rain continued outside, a soft, distant murmur.

Ten minutes after they had started, a buzzer sounded from within the house. Mike liked the precision, the scope of Gary's arrangements. They might have been sitting in a fortress. Gary walked across and opened the door that led into the house. There was a tall black man and two smaller men— they looked Iranian to Mike but he wasn't sure. The two smaller men were carrying folded duffle bags. Conversation done, Gary walked across the room and quietly sat down at a worktable. He pulled out his cell phone and started punching keys. To Mike, it looked like he was deleting messages.

There was some haggling, but they were both realistic. Christmas was around the corner, and Mike needed the stock gone. It worked for both of them. The black man nodded and then turned toward the door. The two men slipped forward out of the shadows and quickly put away the selected stock, booze and fags distributed equally across the two bags, careful to cushion the bottles. The black man counted out the money and Mike folded the notes into his jacket. It was done in less than two minutes.

The process repeated itself twice, in exactly the same way. The only difference was that the other two buyers were Mr. Patels from the off-licences on corners somewhere nearby—clientele that Mike was more used to dealing with on a regular basis. During each interval, Gary and Mike chatted—regular, everyday conversation between men who hadn't seen each other in a while.

It took thirty minutes to unload the whole stock and the Calais run seemed to Mike like something that had happened to other people who broke the law on the weekends. All that remained was two bottles of Courvoisier. They had sold everything else. It was a tidy profit, although much less than they'd been expecting. Saved by the T-shirt sales, thought Mike. He couldn't remember where it was from. JD would know. JD *lived* on obscure rock 'n' roll trivia.

The phone in Gary's pocket beeped once. He pulled it out and looked at it. Then answered it by pushing the 'Accept' button and holding it to his ear. He didn't utter a word, just waited.

'Okay.' He hung up. 'Your boy's here.'

Mike looked at his watch. It was a quarter to nine. God, but they'd been perfect tonight.

'Thanks again.'

Mike picked up one of the bottles of Courvoisier and held it out. Gary gently knocked it away.

'Not before the first.' Gary stayed sober during peak season. It made sense. They weren't dealers, they were businessmen. It was a small but crucial difference. Mike nodded. He put his hand into the pocket of his jacket, reaching for the wad of notes that had accumulated over the last half hour. Gary laughed out loud.

'I'd do your face in. Don't be a cunt.'

Mike shook his head, smiling a little himself.

'Thanks,' he said.

'Fuck it. Give my love to your mum.'

Gary walked across to the garage door. Mike picked up the two bottles and carried them into the cab. He started the van. Gary pushed the button and the door rose silently, letting the night back in. JD stood in the driveway, holding a white plastic bag from an off-licence. He raised his hand and Gary raised his in return. Mike backed the van out to the edge of the driveway and stopped. JD climbed in, dripping wet.

'It's colder than a lesbian's left tit,' was his only comment as the garage door descended and Gary simply disappeared from view. JD turned to Mike. 'Come on, Mansell. It's back to hell for the likes of us.'

1.4

It could have been eight minutes or fifteen. The silence rested easily between the two of them. JD roused himself as they pulled into Heston. He took out his phone and made a quick call to their lawyer. Lawyer was a bit of a stretch, thought Mike, although Sumit Sen was, technically, a lawyer. What he was, really, was their hatchet man. He pushed most of their paperwork, both legitimate and dirty. He was a jerky, nervous Bengali with thick glasses and he operated through charm, low cunning and an army of contacts. Anywhere, any time, Sumit could always find them a button man. They paid him obscene amounts of money, but they did it because they could make phone calls like this one.

JD gave Sumit his instructions. 'Kudos International' was to be shut down first thing tomorrow morning, and the paper trail needed to disappear completely. The conversation was brief. Sumit could, if in the mood, bang on for hours. Not that it wasn't fascinating. Sumit had a number of fingers in the lower rungs of the entertainment business and he usually recounted his experiences with great relish.

Tonight, however, Sumit listened, made his notes and disconnected.

It was as if the aftermath of the Schillachi was slowly infecting everything they touched this evening.

~

They pulled into their warehouse a couple of minutes later. It was in a darker, dingier corner of Heston, but it served their purpose. They had quick access to major arteries, it was within walking distance of where they both lived, and it was cheap. How could it not be? Heston itself was now a darker, dingier version of itself. It was rotting from within, collapsing back into London as it had mushroomed from it.

Someone had once asked JD about Heston. Even Jimmy Page got the fuck out, he had said. He worshipped the devil and even *he* got the fuck out.

'Warehouse' was a term. Their office was a converted garage. The garage door led into the bay. Worktables lined both sides, with tools and collected junk dating back years. Along one wall, and under most of the space below the tables, were boxes and boxes of drinking glasses. There was space for two vans to park. The bay continued onto a raised concrete ledge that ran the width of the garage. They had built a softboard partition that ran across the platform and divided the space into three rooms; one for storage, a small office and a pantry.

They hadn't spent much on it. The paint was flaking and they waged an almost constant battle with rust. The only things they were careful about were the lighting, the windows, the safe in the office and the security system. Because of demand and supply at odd hours, they sometimes needed to leave cash in the office or have it waiting there. Even Mike had given up trying to keep it neat. Too many people moved through the office, too many people occasionally crashed in the small cot, too many people dropped by to use the phone. And regardless of what they did, they couldn't get rid of the smell—stale cigarette smoke and car exhausts, packing tape and takeaway meals. It smelt of a place where the tide turned, of transit.

Mike, who had spent half an hour in another garage just a little while ago, looked at their warehouse carefully. Heston. Chelsea. It was a class thing. Even crime was a class game. Oh, yes.

They parked and sat in the stillness. It was the first pause in hours and it felt unnatural. Mike broke the silence by yawning unexpectedly. It was a jaw-breaker. Mike heard his tendons creak, and the yawn seemed to go on forever, getting wider and wider until it decided to suddenly quit. JD snorted laughter.

'That's why we only let you out of the cage twice a year.'

They climbed out of the van. Mike took out the packet of cigarettes he'd bought and handed them to JD.

'Want to smoke one?'

They smoked in silence, drawing it out at leisure. When they were done, Mike turned to JD. He needed confirmation. It was ritual.

'That was the Schillachi?' he asked.

'That was the Schillachi,' agreed JD. He was tired but he grinned at Mike as he said it.

Mike stood there, thinking about it, writing it up in his head. He dropped his cigarette and ground it out on the floor. He shook his head at JD, smiling.

'Get out. Before I throw you out.'

As they locked up, Mike handed the Courvoisier to JD. JD raised an eyebrow and Mike nodded. JD shrugged, impressed.

They stood on the pavement a minute. It was very cold, although it had finally stopped raining. But the temperature had driven people indoors. It was quiet, even for a Sunday night. The silence was broken by a loud boom, as another plane swung in towards Heathrow. Windows shivered, then chattered and then began to rattle. In this neighbourhood, the windows that had broken because of the sonic boom stayed broken.

Mike thought of physics experiments in school. Iron filings on a piece of paper, jittering as students shook the paper about, forming clumps along lines of force. Everything served something larger. And so on.

'I'm probably not coming in tomorrow,' JD said without turning from the street in front of him. 'My mom's got me going to some engagement.'

'That's fine. I think I gotta couple of things myself. If there's anything, I'll call.'

'Fair enough. G'night, mate.' JD turned and began to walk away. Mike watched him go.

'Jai,' he called.

JD stopped and turned back. Mike looked at him.

'Don't let it get too wild, man. We did good today.'

JD considered it. He nodded. 'We did do good. But this native's getting restless.'

Mike laughed softly. JD raised his right hand, the one with the Courvoisier and made a slight tipping motion. Then he turned and he was gone. Mike tested the lock one last time, pulled up his collar, and began to walk.

~

JD moved steadily, hunched against the wind, head down as his thoughts swirled. He slowed a fraction as he approached home. One can of Foster's was already dead, the second was in his hand. The alcohol was settling fast. It mixed with JD's empty stomach, his exhaustion, and his relief. It hit hard. JD burped. It was small, minor, but he felt his stomach move all the same. He knew the signs. He was going to get drunk tonight. Between the sixth beer and the first drink, clarity would arrive like a bomb. JD killed the second can and tossed it onto the pavement. He reached for the third. Even for him, he was on record pace.

He turned the corner onto his street. Anonymous two-storey houses, each a carbon copy of the other—every detail, every life interchangeable—ran along both sides, extending all the way up the hill. The houses crowded in, squeezing out the night. It was dirty here. There was shit on the streets, plastic and paper bags, and rubbish littered most of the front gardens. There were clumps of cigarette butts where kids had trampled them before their parents could see them smoking.

There was spit, red paan stains, the works. It stuck out from
the rest of Heston like a sore thumb. There was colour, true,
but much of it was tired, rundown, as if it had been fading for
decades and the street had finally settled into the yellowing
sweat-stains of middle-aged decay.

JD was thankful for the bitter cold. Normally, at this time,
on his way home, he could expect to be stopped at least three
times—friends, family friends, acquaintances. He wanted no
conversation tonight. He paused on the pavement outside
his house. Only one light was on, in his parents' bedroom.
That would be his mom. He let himself in the front door as
quietly as he could.

On the way to his room, he knocked on the door of his
parents' bedroom. Once he'd reached the age of eighteen,
he had made a deal with his mother. She would stop waiting
up for him as long as he let her know when he was home,
regardless of how late it was. There was no response to his
knock. He looked in. His mum had fallen asleep, book in
hand, on her side of the bed. She still had her glasses on. His
father was fast asleep. JD shook his mother's shoulder. It only
took a couple of seconds, she had obviously just drifted off.

'I'm home, Mom. Go back to sleep.'

She opened her eyes, a little startled at first. Then she
sighed and nodded. In the light of the single bedside lamp,
she looked old and vulnerable. JD felt something move, small
and light, somewhere in his chest. He didn't know what it
was, but he suddenly felt overwhelmed by sadness. His eyes
hurt. Gently, he patted the top of his mother's head.

'Take off the glasses, Mom. Go to sleep.'

'Okay. Okay.' Then, in Punjabi: 'Have you eaten?'

'I will, Mom. Just go to sleep.'

He waited until she took off the glasses. Then he turned and headed for the door. As she turned off the light, she said, 'If you got wet, you take a shower. And you get out of those clothes.'

'I will, Mom.'

He softly closed the door behind him.

~

When JD sat up with a start, it was three in the morning, and he was beyond wrecked. It took him half a minute to realize where he was; the alcohol dragged his eyes shut, and pain throbbed behind them. He winced in the light, and nothing he looked at made sense. His desktop was a mess of wires—he'd jerry-rigged his computers since the age of seventeen—and now everything was spinning so much the mess looked like it was alive. He hit 'Pause' on the CD player and AC/DC stilled. The sudden silence made his ears ring.

The room was icy. JD had a vague recollection of going downstairs to drink some milk almost two hours ago. When he'd returned, the room was blue with smoke and it stank. He'd opened the windows, to let in some air. Which made sense now—he'd smoked every cigarette he had. Beer cans lay around the room like discarded bullets. The bottle of Courvoisier was half empty. There was no glass. He'd been drinking straight from the bottle.

JD got up slowly. He dropped the headphones on the

carpet and shuffled to the bathroom. He took a long piss, staring at the pot with fierce concentration. As he worked to maintain his focus, a quantum of self-disgust asserted itself through the dull pounding in his head. The smell hit him just as he was zipping up, and his stomach lurched. He dropped to his knees.

A minute later, when he was sure it was over, he flushed again and backed away from the pot. He looked in the mirror. This is no way to live your fucking life, he told himself.

It was ritual.

~

Mike bought chicken and chips from the chip-shop around the corner from his house. It was run by a family of Polish immigrants who struggled with the language and with central heating. Late at night, around here, if you were lucky, you could have an experience that left you feeling like you were in a ghetto somewhere far from England. A desperate mix of languages, races, colours—an army of poor people trying to understand that you wanted Rizla King-size papers. There was something deeply unsettling about life here. You could almost taste the violence in the air. He paid, picked up the packet and threw in his salt and vinegar. Then he wrapped it up again and went home.

He liked this walk home, though. He liked being alone. He liked to keep his memories fresh. He knew that he was walking through a warzone. Heston was a bare-knuckle fistfight in disguise. Asian people flocking to the cheaper neighbourhoods. And the white people, elderly, not so well off, clinging to houses and storefronts. White people of a certain generation were soft. They depended on inheriting the idea of a nation—one that had been based on robbing a large part of the world. Brown people worked harder. They kept their heads down. But distant cousins slept on floors, people came over on tourist visas and simply disappeared, and everyone was shitting out kids.

Home was a small, functional flat that he had bought the year before. The kitchen opened out into the hall and there was one bedroom. He had moved out of his childhood home when his mother went to Nottingham to live with her new boyfriend. He hadn't seen his father in twelve years.

Mike finished his meal, rinsed the plate and pulled a can of Coke from the fridge. He drank it, scanning through the scores, the television on mute. Sheffield Wednesday were doing badly, never having recovered from the hammering in September. Chelsea continued to float, and United were running away with it—at least leading up to Christmas. There was no fucking justice in the world. He finished his Coke, brushed his teeth and went to bed.

Mike woke early. The weather was better, although still cold. There was at least the distant promise of sunlight. He fixed a cup of tea and read the papers for the next couple of hours. He had woken up with something turning over in his mind and he wanted to follow it.

On his way to Brian's garage, he tried JD's phone. There wasn't anything particular, but it was habit. There was no answer. Mike wasn't surprised—he had seen the signs of the approaching bender last night, in the silence on the way home from Chelsea. He knew that the only way JD was going to stop was when he fell over.

Brian spent his weekdays working for a courier company, delivering packages throughout London. He was normally on the 'urgent' routes simply because his knowledge of the roads allowed him to cover more distance in a day. Mike walked up to the front of the office building and waited. In a moment, Brian saw him and began to walk towards him, unzipping the front of the jacket. It was beginning to warm up nicely.

'Breakfast?' Mike asked.

While they walked, Brian filled him in on the events of the previous night. The bust at Maidstone, and the statement he had given to the coppers. As an added precaution, he had simply driven the van home in case the dogs tried to tail him again. Everything was in order; they were home and dry.

Both of them ordered sausages and onions in baguettes at a hole in the wall around the corner. Brian leafed through the copy of *The Sun* on the counter in front of him, perusing the usual gallery of tits. Mike slid an envelope in front of Brian. He opened it and counted the notes. It held seven hundred pounds.

'What's this for?'

'For last night. A bonus.'

Brian smiled. He nodded and then pocketed the cash.

'Thanks, but I'd have done that for free.'

Their baguettes were ready, so they began to walk back towards the office. Someone spotted Brian and shouted; his van was ready. It was time to go. Mike considered his

options and decided that plain-talking was all he was good
for. Brian rolled up the tissues that had held his breakfast and
patted down the corners of his mouth. Mike reached out and
touched his elbow.

'How did they know, Brian?'

Brian looked at him.

'How did the dogs know?' Mike looked at Brian. '*All* of it.'

'You sure?' Brian asked. 'Really, really sure?'

It was Mike's turn to consider what he was asking. And
the question wasn't to be taken lightly. Because it placed
them in opposition to something or someone. They just
didn't know who.

It changed the game.

Mike nodded. 'I'm sure.'

Brian frowned. Mike knew what he was doing, he had
been doing it himself for the last fourteen hours, asleep or
not. Brian was casting back through the last couple of weeks,
ever since the play had been set, trying to see if there was
anything—a stray remark, something that he had heard, two
unconnected events that might just make sense now.

A small breeze swept past them, picking up newspapers
and trash. Mike waited patiently. After a moment, Brian
looked up. Mike knew from the look on his face that there
wasn't anything that had leapt up at him. Brian shook his
head.

'No, Mike. I don't know. There's—I'm not sure. I sure
as hell don't remember anything. Nothing big. Nothing
in neon.'

'No sweat. If there's anything, just give me a call.'

Brian was quiet for a long moment.

'Mike… we're just not that big. Not for us to be fingered,' he said.

'I know. I'm not saying that it's—fuck knows—fucking sabotage or anything. But we were sure as fuck fingered. Nothing else explains the size of the opera. Two cars and a base?' Mike watched the expression change on Brian's face. 'I know,' he said. 'When you think of it like that, it changes a lot of things in your head.'

Brian turned and headed towards his van. Mike stood on the pavement and watched him go. He had voiced the suspicion that he'd held in his head since they'd gotten on the train yesterday. In the light of day, it didn't sound as ridiculous as he'd thought it might.

Which left him his second meeting of the morning. He turned and walked, deep in thought.

~

'Stop.'

Aziz Basrai laughed. He laughed out loud. He was moving too fast, for no reason except that it was all he knew to do. He had parked the car a good ten minutes away and he'd sliced through Canary Wharf at a pace just short of a run.

He had a meeting, yes. The meeting was important, yes. But he was early. When his mind wandered, he walked quick. Had done, ever since he'd been a kid.

He slowed. Even though it was winter, he would start sweating in a minute or two. Fifteen years in England, but a brisk walk still brought on sweat. He couldn't go into this meeting sweaty. His hands were jammed into the pockets of his overcoat. The muffler hung loose, like someone had thrown it onto to him as he ran.

He looked at his watch. Still eleven minutes to go.

Aziz knew that he'd be judged on when he walked into the meeting. He was going to be judged on everything this morning. This was a callback. But it was a callback at ten on a Monday morning, at a fairly exclusive bistro in Canary Wharf.

There was a business card at the end of this cup of coffee.

Aziz found a bench and sat down. He looked across the small stretch of water for a moment. He lit a cigarette with a Zippo. The Zippo's casing was dull, worn smooth over years. There was a small inscription on the left hand corner. It said, simply: 'aziz', lower case, unobtrusive. Aziz ran his thumb over the inscription, nodded and pocketed the lighter.

He used to collect business cards when he was a kid, he remembered suddenly. He'd pester the people who'd come home—it didn't matter if they were guests, relatives or insurance salesmen. In the eighties, not that many people even had business cards in Karachi. But he collected them like stamps. It didn't matter if people were from the same company. He built sets—business cards ordered by company, by title, by grandeur, by bad spelling.

Aziz grinned. There had always been a tic, some sort of habit; that became a charm. He'd been eerily self-contained as a kid. But he'd needed one idiosyncrasy to hold on to. The business cards had been followed by a stupid survey. When his father finally managed to emigrate to England, Aziz had

spent a couple of months asking people how much money
they made. He kept careful records, and he compared answers
continually. He had to wait years to discover that he'd been
performing some demented statistical analysis. And well, at
that. He was careful about it, but it was inevitable that his
mother would find out. He got smacked across the mouth.

There had been a raft of things. He couldn't remember
them all. A pair of sneakers. Boris Becker's Wimbledon
streak. His meticulously organized collection of nudes and
sexy photos of actresses culled off the internet. These things
were innocuous enough when he stumbled upon them, but
they quickly became things that regulated his life. Because
they brought him luck.

He knew it was ridiculous. But that wouldn't stop him
from lighting up just before an important meeting, with that
particular Zippo. Over the years he'd understood that if he
got some things right—very right, in his case—in the eyes
of the world, then he simply didn't have to explain himself.

Aziz stood up. Another minor coronation waited inside
the building across the way. He was relatively certain of this.
In itself, it wasn't a major thing. But it made the months to
come easier.

He flicked the cigarette away and began to walk.

~

When JD awoke it was close to eleven in the morning. His
head ached and his mouth felt like someone else had been
doing terrible things with it while he was asleep. He could

feel the quivering come from a place deep inside of him. He wondered why the house was so quiet. Then he remembered that his parents were out. He was expected at the engagement himself. It was a neighbourhood thing.

He stepped into the shower, turned it over all the way to 'H' and stood there for a couple of minutes. Then he flicked the knob to 'C' and stayed under the icy spray as long as he could—it drove the air out of him like a punch to the stomach. By the time he was dressed, he was good as new. He was going to go downstairs, feed the hangover and then head across to the Chaddas'.

He paused for a moment on the riser. The house was a ghost town this morning. It felt like a photograph fading before his eyes. Mostly, his mother gave the house its vitality. She made it real, made it three-dimensional, made it the home he came back to.

JD turned and went back to his room. His suit lay on the bed, waiting to be pulled on. It was cut sharp. But it never fit him quite right. In a suit, he always looked like someone had picked him off the street and shoved him into something against his will. Or like he'd just stepped off the boat wearing something that was so out of whack that it was almost back in fashion.

He pulled out the little metal box that lived in the drawer. Swan Filters had once run a promotion where you had to collect a bunch of Swan cards and then you traded them in, along with some change, for this nifty little box.

He rolled himself a joint. He took his time and he made it with care. He and Mike had once thought about going into the joint-selling business together, peddling packs of perfectly rolled joints at nice premiums. They abandoned the plan when Mike, after an afternoon of watching JD make the pitch and the accompanying demonstration, pointed out that profit margins were likely to take a hit if JD smoked every joint he rolled *because* he'd rolled it so well and it would be a shame to let it go.

Plus, he'd have been really bored.

JD lit the joint and went back out to the landing. He settled on the top step, holding an empty cigarette pack as the ashtray. He very rarely smoked weed at home. He very rarely smoked weed before he'd had breakfast. And he very rarely smoked weed when he felt the crash coming.

Spitting into a strong headwind, he thought. He *really* didn't give a fuck this morning.

He always woke up feeling guilty after a drunken night. He couldn't remember the things he'd said and done, even if he'd been on his own. It was worse after nights like the previous one. The crash came easier after you'd set off a hundred car alarms in a parking lot on the M20.

For two hundred grand? Some bare minimum of profit after Mike's distress sale last night?

As he saw the smoke drift away, the house came rushing up the stairs. JD saw himself from afar, watching from the other side of the abyss. Some of it was the dope, no doubt. Paranoia feeding depression, holding hands. But it was feeding a fear that stalked him. He felt like the house—fading into sepia-tinged ordinariness. This was what awaited him. An empty house. An empty life. Like Nik Chadda, whose engagement it was this morning. String of white girlfriends. Fell in love, even. Marrying a girl that his parents had picked.

Then kids. Then a mortgage. Then a second one.

An all-consuming bitterness that would spill out in pubs after two beers, joining the sewer stream of similar stories.

He stubbed out the joint, trashed it in the bin. He quickly ate the breakfast that had been left out for him. He went upstairs and put the suit on. He didn't bother looking at the mirror on his way out.

He paused for a moment on the pavement. His head was still swimming. The world was shimmery—not quite in focus. He felt nauseous. The aftertaste he got from dope was always sickly sweet. Nothing he did would get rid of it for about an hour. He was out of cigarettes. He'd simply have to soldier on for a bit until he could bum a cigarette at the engagement.

'Fucking idiot.'

He shook his head. He'd forgotten to air out the house. He sighed and tramped back in, knowing he'd have to open out the windows and waste at least half a can of air-freshener. He wondered if he should smoke another joint while he waited.

~

'So you came to England when you were ten?'

Aziz nodded.

'Your English is fantastic.'

'Well,' began Aziz 'it better be'. He paused for effect. Fuck it, he thought. Work the crowd.

'Innit?'

Both Keane and Russell burst out laughing. They liked

him. Aziz already knew that they coveted him—the approach had been theirs and theirs alone. He'd been in a holding pattern after his Masters', biding his time.

But the soon-to-be-shop-Paki got race humour. That was a bonus.

Stop it, Aziz told himself. You're moving too fast again. He liked Keane. Liked him very much. Keane had been the one who had called him. There had been no job application. Aziz hadn't filled out any forms. This was a recruitment—a trade. Lexington Brothers had gone shopping for new talent that would take them into the new Millennium.

Aziz had done the first meeting. Then the interview and another meeting with Keane. This was the first time he'd been introduced to one of the partners. Michael Russell was a bit of a legend. He'd been a once-in-a-generation lawyer in his thirties. Then he'd become an equally remarkable money machine.

Fuckin' due diligences, thought Aziz. What a thing to dedicate your life to.

This morning was the fairy dust exercise. Keane summoned Aziz to a ten o'clock meeting at Canary Wharf. Best cup of coffee in London, Keane had told him on the phone. As a surprise, they dry-cleaned the legend and plonked him on a chair opposite Aziz. He was supposed to fall onto his knees in gratitude and awe and take whatever they gave him.

Good coffee, expensive restaurant, and a blinding light of the profession. It wasn't a race thing, though. Not exactly. It was a size thing. Intimidation as aspiration. Lexington would have done it to anyone in Aziz's place—black, white, yellow, brown, red.

Who the fuck do these guys think they are? Man United?

Their food arrived. Omelettes. A Panini. Aziz had asked for a muffin. He sipped his coffee. It *was* good. But it wasn't the best he'd ever had. There was an Illy in Bayswater, with a very attractive Italian woman behind the counter. There, a cup of coffee was like drinking sin.

Aziz used the moment to look out of the window. He saw a bastard grey world, drained of colour. Cold, it was. Business districts like quarries. A demented Garden of Eden. Steel and glass temples, throbbing to the rhythm of counting machines.

The redevelopment of the docklands had been another of those secret charms; a good luck badge. Whispers floated for years. He was already well enmeshed in the country when the tenders went out, and contracts were signed. People around him thought it would never work. The Jubilee line was a joke before it became a convenience. And so much of it happened out of sight. He'd been a kid, head down, charging through school. But it was happening. It was possible.

A Pakistani kid going to school based his hopes on the construction of a business district that had absolutely nothing to do with him. Yet, he got things right and people left those strange beliefs alone.

'You've been on scholarships since you were twelve?'

Aziz smiled at Keane. Keane shrugged slightly, as if to indicate that he was simply doing his job. It went without saying that he was good at it. Aziz nodded.

Russell looked up. 'I hope you don't mind us digging

through your past. As you've no doubt realized, this isn't, um… what you'd call a *standard* interview.'

'I'm flattered,' said Aziz. He sat still, hands linked on the table in front of him. He seemed to be looking at the glass of water in front of him.

'Scholarships all the way through to your Masters' in Law at Oxford,' Russell continued. 'Trainee Solicitor with Barrington Fletcher. You talked them into letting you get the Masters' degree while you were still working there?'

'Yes. Yes, I did.' Aziz's voice was almost at a murmur. He had half a smile on his face. Russell groped for the tone of the next question. He wanted a reaction, a big smile, a shrug, something. Keane simply waited. He had seen Basrai retreat to this place before. But Russell was his boss.

'Do you like working at Barrington Fletcher?'

'Oh, yes.' Aziz looked Russell in the eye and grinned. The question hadn't surprised him as much as the immediacy of his answer. Aziz thought of Miles Barrington as a father figure. He was a good man, a fine lawyer and a person who understood where the world was heading. Unlike the man across the table from him.

'Why would you want to leave?'

'Miles has what you might—' Aziz looked Russell straight in the eye '—term a slightly, um, conservative view of succession.' Aziz grinned. 'You know. If you're fifty five, married, two kids, a mistress and a bad heart. *Then* you might qualify for Associate Partner.'

Russell looked at Keane and then grunted. He flicked through the pages of the folder in front of him.

'You've done a bunch of very strange little jobs.'

'The wills?' asked Aziz. 'Tax returns?'

'Yes. All very... nominal. A few divorces. That sort of thing.'

Aziz thought about it for a moment.

'Well, it was practice.' He paused. 'It's also how we're brought up.'

Russell closed the folder. He folded his arms across his chest, leant back on his chair and looked at Aziz for a long moment. Aziz knew what he was going to say before he said it.

'I know you wanted partner. That it was your only condition. But you're only twenty-five.' Russell waited for an objection. There was none. Only the same level gaze.

'However, we do think it's only a matter of time.'

Russell reached into his inside pocket and pulled out a very expensive leather card wallet. He teased out a single card and handed it to Aziz. It was like being handed a piece of solid silk; an off-white amulet, a mag-card that would open doors all across town.

'Associate Partner. First man in over a hundred years to make Associate Partner before the age of thirty-two.' He paused. 'And you can call me Mike.'

Aziz shook Russell's hand. He turned to his left and shook Keane's hand.

'No more of that small stuff, eh?' Russell laughed.

Aziz smiled. His hand rested on the business card. He hadn't looked at it yet.

'We'll see,' he said. 'We'll see.'

~

JD couldn't escape that feeling of being hemmed-in. He cut across four streets to his destination. Twice, he went through the gardens and backyards of people he knew. No one cared, really. He turned onto the Chaddas' street, feeling like the earth was revolving just a little bit faster today.

Two vaguely familiar uncle-types waited at the corner. They were both wearing overcoats, stamping their feet to try and stay warm. They were both holding purple plastic glasses with tea in them. One of them waved at JD—he waved back, but he stayed on his side of the street. These guys were family, but they weren't particularly close. That's why they had been dispatched to the end of the street. They were there to welcome people. They were also mainly there because people tended to get lost in Heston. Here, 'look for the two Sikhs standing at the corner' was a legitimate direction. On a winter's day, at least.

Where the hell would we be without cell phones? thought JD.

He glanced around and crossed the street, avoiding an abandoned sofa on the pavement. Those things tended to smell like urine and burnt hair. JD looked at the sofa-owner's house as he walked. The house looked like a face that had been battered. Leaking eyes. Mushy around the edges. Crooked teeth.

There was either a hard-luck Asian family in there, barely clinging on, or there was a baleful white face. Above the age of sixty, usually. Terminally bewildered. This was the crud collected at the bottom of the melting pot that everyone just ignored, like the dumpsters behind fine dining restaurants. JD was somewhere in the middle of that stew—he occupied the space between his parents and white faces. The English he spoke sounded right. He understood the pools and Marmite and what standing in a queue meant. But he'd been in too many fights, had escaped too many serious injuries to forget the fact that he was brown. Usually, it was white people who wouldn't let him forget that fact. And when that happened, that's when brown people would remind you that you *were*, in fact, brown.

Meanwhile, both teams were desperately poor. Race was actually a money thing, yeah? That was his big life lesson. And the neighbourhood looked it. It was worse at night. Half the buildings were condemned—boarded up windows with tarpaulin whispering all night. Armchairs on street corners. Everything bathed in this sick-fuck yellow.

My evenings, thought JD, seen through a spray of vomit.

He shook his head once as he neared the Chadda house. Depressed was one thing. He needed to walk in with a smile on his face. At least for the first five minutes.

JD paused outside the house. People had tried here, they really had. He felt grudging respect. The décor went across three houses—to the left and the right. The neighbours had given up their gardens for this afternoon so that there was a sense of a real lawn. Guests wouldn't have to clamber over the buffet table to say hello to someone they hadn't seen in five years. They'd strung up lights. It would look nice at night, glittering like a little corner that had been made to feel special.

The smell of food from the house was divine and JD's stomach rumbled. His mother would be in there somewhere, elbow deep in batter as the women sang and cooked and teased the bride. These were also the times, thought JD with a grin, when it didn't matter that you lived in Heston. His parents had carried home with them. When they were surrounded by their own, when they felt safe enough, they could recreate home wherever in the world they were. It was some kind of magic. And it was a magic he'd never possess. That was the trade-off for the accent and Marmite.

People waved at JD from the window. JD waved back. He was about to step into the garden when he noticed a familiar person sauntering towards him. JD turned back to the window and indicated that he'd be there in a minute. He waited on the pavement for the familiar face to cross the distance between them. JD couldn't believe the shade of red the man was wearing—a plastic tracksuit? Was that it?

JD sighed. Multiculturalism also made you believe that you were black. And that you were a rapper.

'Dink,' he said.

'Jai, hey, hey. Hiya.' Dink always sounded like he'd been running; every word was breathy, as if he was about to cough at any second. Dink held JD's gaze—he was sharp, but he was broadcasting from a long way away. One corner of his mouth twitched. The tic was faint. A lot of people would have missed it entirely.

'Long way from home, Dink,' said JD. It wasn't a question.

'Hey. Hey, hey. What-ah, what are you talking about?'

'Dink,' JD's voice was gentle, 'this is an engagement. I know these people.'

'Fuck you, man.'

JD had known Dink long enough to know that he'd managed to piss him off. He'd touched a real nerve. Which probably mean that he was coming down. Maybe Dink didn't have anything planned. Maybe this was simply an innocent stroll, three and a half kilometres from home.

Maybe things were just coming to a head today.

JD looked at Dink for a minute.

'If a single car goes missing, if a fucking stereo's nicked, if anyone even so much as turns a mirror, I'm gonna tell Mike.'

Dink looked at JD.

'Fuck you, man,' he repeated. His voice was hoarse. He had tears in his eyes.

JD looked down, at his shoes. This fucking morning, eh? It was all too much.

When he looked up, Dink had already started walking.

'Dink,' he called out. 'Dink.'

Dink stopped and turned. But he wouldn't approach JD.

JD pulled out his wallet as he walked over to Dink. He counted out two hundred pounds.

'Go get what you need. And buy those two clowns at the end of the street a couple of cans of beer.'

'I don't need your money, man.'

'No,' said JD. 'No, you don't. Merry Christmas, though.' He tucked the money into Dink's hand and turned towards the house. He felt a little better, and he was hungry.

~

JD walked into warmth and good cheer. He could smell

cinnamon frying in butter and ghee, an aroma he had always associated with food for special occasions. He grabbed a couple of samosas off a passing tray—no servers here, only relatives. The aunt in question let him eat the samosas and then handed him the plate. He'd been enlisted good and proper.

He'd missed the exchange of the rings. People were settling down to the real work; eating and drinking. The older men had occupied a corner of the living room. The house was humming. JD had been to enough of these through the years to know how the afternoon would go down. Someone was going to get pissed and talk too much. There would be an argument and one family, at least, would storm out at some point. Teenagers would drift in and out like ghosts. Upstairs, in bedrooms and bathrooms, there would be desperate snogging and fumbled, incomplete oral sex.

He wasn't planning on staying long.

JD drifted between the hall and the dining room. He was aiming for the foot of the stairs. It was the safest vantage point. He could spot a gap, avoid relatives and further samosa duty, and check in with his mom. He heard someone begin to come down the stairs in a hurry, heels like gunfire on the wooden floor and turned, just in case it was someone he needed to avoid.

The woman was tall, taller than him in heels. She was in a saree that hugged every curve. For nine yards of silk, thought JD, it didn't cover much. The saree drew attention to the woman's midriff—the knot was low, so low—and the drape of the fabric pulled your eyes up to the blouse. JD had seen bikinis that revealed less. He wondered, briefly, how the fuck she'd managed to trek across to the house for the engagement in that saree, in the dead of winter. And then he wasn't thinking of anything much.

Her midriff was the colour of light coffee. She glowed with a golden sheen under the lights. The saree was an electric blue. She turned the corner, hair open, flying out behind her.

For a second, JD couldn't breathe. And then everything jumpstarted with a roar. There was something lodged in his throat—he could almost taste it. He felt a deep, low pulse at the back of his neck.

It wasn't the body, although the body was a large part of it. She was taller, thinner, much more angular than the women he liked. She moved like she was a challenge, a weapon in a sheath that barely contained her. But it was mostly her face. She could have been Italian, or Eurasian. She was fair, and black-haired, and she was a step away from being beautiful. Instead, the face was sensual, with light eyes and full lips. It was a proud face. And it was an ageless face—she could have been twenty-one or thirty-five. He couldn't tell and he didn't care.

She stopped three stairs above him. She'd been looking through JD, like he didn't exist, on her way down. She looked at him for the first time. She might have been looking at a 'Stop' sign on the street. JD swallowed. There was a faint popping sound and he could hear his heart hammering away.

The woman simply stared at him. The lips parted slightly. JD could see the gloss on them, like a promise. Her eyes narrowed. JD felt the sharpened focus.

'Uh…' She let the word trail away. She was amused. An eyebrow arched. JD saw a slight sneer.

'You're in the way. Do you mind?'

JD couldn't remember the last time he'd been dismissed like this. She had evaluated him and hadn't found much. He felt like a poor little commoner, getting spat on by a princess. It was the thought of spit, standing in front of her, with his head thinking some *very* odd shit, that did it.

He was instantly hard; all the way. He had never been this aroused in his life.

JD grinned and stepped aside. The woman shook her head once and moved past him. JD sniffed the air as she moved past him, trying to memorize her scent, warm, rich, exotic, like expensive liqueur. He watched her back as she walked away. He wanted to run his tongue along its length.

JD had never felt the wet, blind need for a woman, outside of the movies. This girl had slipped past his defences, his rationality. He wanted—*needed*—to take her to bed. He'd do it right now. All she had to do was snap her fingers.

He didn't know whether it was the dope. His head had cleared up all the way. Certainly, all the blood was headed in another direction. JD shuffled around at the foot of the stairs for a little bit longer, walking around in small circles so that he wouldn't be embarrassed when he walked into either room. He pretended to play with his phone. When he felt like he could walk without having an accident, he pocketed the phone and walked into the living room.

JD was looking for Nikhil Chadda, to show him that he'd attended, when he saw another familiar face. A white woman, not yet fifty, incongruous in this gathering, by herself. She seemed to be looking at the men gathered across her, and the beginnings of the bridge game that would go on for a good three hours. JD's father was there, drawing up a score sheet on a pad, confirming and writing down partnerships. But the woman looked through them. There was an aura around her that no one would breach. She sat on her own island.

Of course no one would really approach her, thought JD. They believed that it would bring bad luck. Her being here today was a bad omen. Except—no one had thought of telling her, of explaining to her something that was utterly alien to the lady in the armchair.

The lady must have sensed that someone had stopped to look at her. She looked up and located JD. JD raised a hand in acknowledgement and smiled at her.

'Hey, Missus T,' JD mouthed from across the hall.

It took Julia Tipnis a moment to gather herself. JD could see her try to identify who was waving to her. Then she smiled. It was a great smile, one that JD remembered. The smile made her look ghastly.

'Hello, Jai,' she mouthed. She nodded. She looked suddenly delighted.

Uncle T wouldn't be here, thought JD. It was busy season. That was one of the reasons she was sitting all alone. Her only son, Jimmy, had killed himself just over a year ago. She was a white woman who had married an Indian man and they had been happy. She still hadn't gotten over Jimmy's death and none of the fucking cunts in the kitchen had had the decency of informing her that she had been invited to this gathering as a matter of form. Her son had killed himself, so she shouldn't attend the engagement of one of his peers. It was bad luck.

Mrs Tipnis gestured to him to come sit down. JD made a sad face and shrugged. He held up the serving platter and pointed at it. He tried to look as put upon as he could. He definitely wasn't thinking about the girl he'd seen three minutes ago.

'Sorry,' he mouthed. He genuinely was, too. He would've gladly gone across and spent the next half hour talking to her, but he just didn't know what they'd talk about except Jimmy. And he wasn't ready for that.

Julia Tipnis smiled. She nodded once, gravely and slowly settled back in her armchair. JD turned to look at her as he stepped into the hallway. The tide was in again, and she was back on her island.

As he moved towards the kitchen door, he saw one of the junior cousins ambling by, a kid he'd bossed around once upon a time. JD had a reputation and he wasn't averse to using it occasionally.

'Oi.' He grabbed the kid by the arm. The gesture was affectionate, but also meant business.

'Yeah, Jai?'

'There's a girl here. Blue saree, looks like a model. What's her name?'

'My name's Pamela.' The voice came from behind him.

JD closed his eyes for a second. He'd been blindsided twice in four minutes by the same woman. The signs were ominous. He turned.

Pamela had one foot on the first riser of the staircase. Her right hand was on the banister, and her left hand held the pleat of the saree, pulling it up, making the stairs easier. She looked like a statue.

She wore the same air of dry amusement. She looked him up and down once, like she'd remember this time.

'Pamela,' she repeated. 'Pam for short.' She paused before the last word, just for a fraction, and she caressed it. She made sure that JD knew that she was looking down at him.

JD didn't know what to say, mostly because this woman, at this present moment, wanted absolutely nothing to do with him. Plus, looking at her was disconcerting. It was as if she knew, by looking at him, every filthy thing he was thinking and he just didn't measure up. The hard-on was back. Mrs. Tipnis was a distant memory.

Everything that JD fell back on in situations like this, his charm, the sideways view of the world, the fact that he was some sort of a demented genius, his sense of humour and that he wasn't doing too badly in the world, thank you very much, counted for nothing.

He opened his mouth with no idea of what he was going to say. Fair enough, that was half his waking life. But he really had no control over what emerged, which was rare.

'My mom has the same name.' JD started shaking his head as he said it. He heard the snort from junior, behind him.

Pam pursed her lips and JD *really* had to go sit down somewhere.

'That might be interesting,' she said. And then she was gone.

JD did another circuit with the phone, trying to calm down. He was even more off-kilter now, confused by lust. He called himself a fucking idiot, put the phone away and then noticed that he was still holding the serving platter.

~

JD found his mother. He waved his hand in front of her face. She swatted it away. He waved the serving platter around and put it down on the kitchen counter. Four hobs were going at once, all cooking different things. She looked him up and down; a swift appraisal. She thought about saying something. Then she turned away, but not before JD saw her lips clamped together, turning her mouth into a thin line.

'I suppose last night got late.'

She'd found him passed out in his room a few times this past year. Almost invariably, he was fully dressed, with his boots on, on the floor of his bedroom. They kept it between themselves. She'd wake him up, pester him until he either lay down on his bed or showered and changed his clothes and left for work again. He'd normally get an earful the next day, but she never told his father.

'Almost,' JD muttered. He wasn't quite thinking about his drinking. His mother looked at him a little more carefully.

'What happened?'

'Nothing.'

His mother sighed. 'Great. I'll find out in another three months.'

'Mom.' His voice was sharper than he intended. This

time, she really looked at him. The oven was between them and he saw her through the steam and the heat rising off the hobs. Her look was a mixture of anger and fear, of exasperation and love. But it was a face he knew well. And maybe exasperation and love went together.

~

JD left the kitchen just in time to hear a burst of applause, then laughter. He was genuinely puzzled. He couldn't think of anyone who was invited to this morning's function who could make an entrance like some homecoming hero. Certainly not in the living room—that was the senior crowd. Indians of a certain age wouldn't be impressed if the Pope walked in. Has to be an oldie, he thought. Someone I don't know, or someone I've forgotten. Clutching a can of beer, JD wandered out into the hallway.

He first saw the back of an expensive overcoat. The person wearing the overcoat was hugging Nik's father. The old man was delighted. He stepped back and held the face of the man who had been hugging.

'You came,' Mr Chadda said. 'You came.'

'Don't be silly, Uncle.'

JD heard the voice and shook his head. He grinned. This completed the surreal morning, all right. No question.

Aziz Basrai turned and caught JD's eye as another of the seniors reached out for him. He nodded and winked. I'll be with you in a second, the gesture said. JD nodded and went back into the kitchen. Aziz would come and find him when he was ready. He stood over the sink and drank his beer. He could still hear the swarm outside, as everyone came up to Aziz to see him with their own eyes, to talk to him, to touch him.

It's like Jesus came back three days early, thought JD. His parents would be in that line too. JD's parents adored Aziz, as did most of the families on the street. Aziz was what every immigrant family hoped their kid would turn out to be: a genuine success, academically brilliant, climbing the ladder rapidly and on his own terms. He had entered the English game and was winning.

Aziz was an enigma even for someone like JD because JD was, essentially, English. At a stretch, he was British Indian. He had been born and brought up in England. Aziz, on the other hand, had moved to England when he was ten years old, when his father, after years of back-breaking work, pulling double-shifts and attending night-school after night-school, had managed to save enough to bring his wife and son over to England from Pakistan.

Aziz had been an alien in ways that JD couldn't even imagine. It transcended the colour of his skin. It was everything. His language, his references, his understanding of the world and how it worked. It must have been the biggest fucking shift that ever hit him, JD had thought once. You take a kid who's ten and then you rip him away from everything he knows and you land him on an island where it rains all the fucking time. And then you say to him: Go on, son. The world's yours for the taking.

It was a blue miracle that Aziz hadn't grown up a ganja-scoring, sex-obsessed, bleeding-heart liberal on the dole.

When they had become friends, Aziz had told JD about walking down the streets his first summer in England, reeling from the amount of female flesh casually lying about in parks, getting sun, drinking beer and smoking cigarettes. 'I had a hard-on for three straight months,' Aziz had told him.

They had become friends because their fathers had been bridge partners. It was the only luxury that their fathers allowed themselves; they didn't go to the movies, or to football games, or to the theatre—they didn't even watch television. But every Wednesday, rain or shine, they played bridge, starting from seven in the evening until two in the morning.

Aziz went as far back as JD could remember, even further than Mike. And even though he was a year younger than JD, Aziz was at every signpost through the years—the first stolen bottle of booze, the first pack of condoms, fights over football, the lies to his parents about his extracurricular activities. Aziz had been more than a back-up; he was a brother, the other half of the equation, elder in experience if not in years.

By the time JD had scraped through his 'A' Levels, he was already working with Mike, running cigarettes from France in his backpack at the weekends. Aziz, on the other hand, had been a straight-A student, and he had been on a series of scholarships since the age of twelve, all the way through to a Master's in Law at Oxford. Oxford Law on scholarship was the Holy Grail, especially if your grandfather came from anywhere *near* the subcontinent. When your family breached Oxford, that was payback; it was the ultimate fuckoff to a lifetime of gritting your teeth so that your kid could get one foot through the door.

JD had wandered back to the hallway. He watched Aziz as his thoughts ran. He wasn't paying attention to what was being said. But watching Aziz work the room like a politician, it dawned on JD how much he'd missed him. It had been months since they'd seen each other. Even longer since they'd *really* talked.

The senior room was hanging on to Aziz's every word. They thought they were being indulgent but they were being dazzled. Aziz was the Insider, who has also an Outsider, one of them.

Fucking double-agent, bruv, thought JD. He was one of ours, although he didn't live here any more. What he was, though—and JD knew this in his bones, though they had never discussed it—was someone who belonged everywhere, and belonged nowhere. He was the island Julia Tipnis wanted to be.

Meanwhile, Aziz was still effortlessly pulling rabbits out of the overcoat. JD caught the remainder of the shtick over another burst of laughter. Even Mrs T was smiling.

'I'm telling you, they're all circus monkeys, every single one of them. He's wearing dark glasses inside a movie theatre—*at night*—and he's trying to convince me that the only way that we're going to be able to show legitimate expenses is if he buys an S-Class. And I'm trying to tell him that, sure, okay, but you have unpaid taxes going back three years, and you've missed alimony payments for the last nine months and they're going to be climbing all over your back.'

Someone said something.

'He says to me, I'm not giving that woman—well, that's not the word he used, but you get the idea—I'm not giving that woman any more alimony. She uses all of it for nose jobs.'

JD turned to leave. He heard his mother ask a question but couldn't make out what it was.

'Third wife, aunty. In these cases, it's always the third wife.'

JD went into the kitchen. He leant against the sink, arms folded, waiting. He waited for the Prince to come see him. Aziz looked in through the door half a minute later.

'Hi-ho, Caesar,' said JD softly. 'We who live normal and boring lives salute you.'

'How are you, Jai?' asked Aziz. They grinned and hugged.

'I'm okay, A. I'm all right. It's been a while.'

'It has. Too long, yaar. We're older and not much wiser.'

Aziz stepped back and looked at JD.

'It's not like you to be hiding in the kitchen,' he said.

Aziz could do boardroom speak, he could do living room engagement chat—the seniors out there were used to having gossip delivered to them in a certain way—and he had yet another voice for JD. He could switch between them effortlessly and in three languages.

'Need new stories, Aziz. Plus, you called on them, you spoke, and they came. You know?'

Aziz snorted. 'Yeah, I didn't think mid-level movie star stories would get you hard. What's up? Customs steal your Christmas spirit?'

JD looked up sharply. Aziz frowned.

'I was kidding,' he said. 'What the hell *did* happen?'

JD thought about it. Thought about telling him. About the previous night. About this morning. He came to an abrupt decision.

'Let's get out of here. This place is driving me nuts.'

'The engagement?'

JD simply indicated the space around him with his hands. Everything, it said. The engagement. The street. Heston. Fucking London. Then he grinned. He'd missed this man.

'Let's get out of here before the girl's father stabs Nik in the back and gets you engaged to his daughter.'

'Mate, we hit that age. It's gonna happen to you, if it hasn't already.'

'Then, while we can…'

Aziz nodded. He turned and left the kitchen to make his goodbyes. When you get to be like him, thought JD, you can just put in an appearance at an engagement and disappear. Don't have to put in the full shift.

Aziz wrapped it up neatly, not two minutes later. At the door, he paused and then, with shy pride, handed JD's dad a business card.

'I got the offer this morning,' he said. It sparked off another small swarm. The card was handed from person to person. People clapped Aziz on the back. Elders near the back, or the ones still sitting, had the news relayed to them. More murmuring. People *eyed* him. It was really a bit like knowing a movie star. JD saw the younger lot make an appearance. He saw Pamela somewhere in the background. Much like him, she wasn't looking at Aziz as looking at everyone around him.

JD watched his parents admire the card. I will never be that son, he thought, never could be. I triggered a hundred car alarms in a parking lot on the M20 last night. But it isn't enough.

And he no longer wished to change it.

They walked onto the street and JD, through force of habit, turned left, heading back towards the warehouse, until he heard Aziz whistle. He turned. Aziz nodded to his right and JD looked at the brand new Golf GTI. JD raised an eyebrow.

'You think I got into law because I care about justice, JD?' asked Aziz. His English had switched again, up a gear, closer to what Aziz spoke on an everyday basis. It was International Boardroom, without inflection or root. JD looked at him carefully. He had missed the clothes in the kitchen. Aziz wasn't wearing stuff off the rack. There was understated elegance here. It was the package. At a meeting, you'd be buying into the man, into the hair that looked like it was on the verge of being too long, but never quite was.

'Fucking hell, Aziz.'

Aziz didn't reply, just tossed JD the car keys. JD caught them and looked at them.

I am the reason that that car hasn't been nicked, he thought. How d'you put *that* on a business card? He breathed out and shook his head.

'That's not me,' said JD. 'It's the other bloke. That's the guy who's going to strip your car down and look at its nipples.' He threw the keys back. 'I am, however, going to fuck with your music system.'

~

The two of them found the remains of a park. The grass was dead, walls covered in graffiti, and there was broken glass, used condoms, cigarette butts and needles underfoot. It was council estate hell. Or maybe it was just noon on a Monday.

'You still smoke?' asked Aziz. 'I only ask because I haven't seen you inhale three in the last twenty minutes.' JD's first big, reputation-making play had been the fact that he smoked in front of his parents. Even Aziz didn't smoke in front of his father.

'I smoked all mine last night. I was hoping that you'd ask.'

Aziz gave him a cigarette and lit it with the Zippo that he'd had for as long as JD could remember. It was a gift from his mother or something equally absurd.

'Don't I get a business card, too?' JD said as he drew on the cigarette, looking straight ahead of him.

'What happened last night?'

JD told him about the game. Even two days ago, telling Aziz about the Schillachi would have been a victory march. They had come a long way in less than twenty-four hours.

'I've never felt older than nineteen, you know,' said JD. 'It's like we stay somewhere, one particular age, for years. Then we slide forward. Or we're forced forward.' He exhaled loudly. 'I went from thirteen to nineteen. And I've been at nineteen.' He looked at Aziz.

'Until this morning.'

JD pulled on the cigarette. Ashed it. Fumbled with it. Pulled on it again.

'You're having one of those days,' said Aziz. His tone was thoughtful. He wasn't looking at JD, his gaze was fixed on the grass at their feet.

'I'm having one of those lives,' said JD. 'I had a theory growing up. About Mike, actually. When we went into business together—when I stopped just carrying for a friend?'

Aziz nodded.

'I actually still believe this to be true. You're only ever ready for something up until a certain point, yeah? I believe this like a fucking formula. It's between forty and sixty-five per cent. Of being *ready* for something. Anything. Job interview. Sex. Talking to a girl. Fighting your father. Running contraband.' JD looked at Aziz once to see if was still listening. 'More than sixty-five per cent, and you've waited too long. That train has left. And any less than forty and you're kidding yourself. When—' JD's voice was urgent, but he stopped himself.

'When do you throw yourself off the edge of the building, A?'

It was Aziz's turn to look at JD sharply. JD just sat there, eyes dark, looking into the heart of something only he could see. He hated this. He hated this conversation. He hated that he was having this conversation with this man. Maybe he hated this man too.

Most of all, JD hated how ordinary it sounded.

'I don't want to be a passenger on the train, Aziz,' said JD. 'I don't want to be driven somewhere. I don't want to sit there waiting. Because waiting is worrying. And I've seen what it does to people, right? It makes 'em old. It presses down on them. All our fathers. Their lives gone, ripped out their hands. They didn't choose this, you know. But the world fucking rail-roaded them outta their lives.' JD looked down at his hands.

'Even if I'm going to crash, I'd like to do that on my terms. Okay? My own fucking terms.' JD fell silent. Minutes passed. Traffic was distant, the world had been dialled down. All he ever wanted, really, was to throw on his superhero cape and get out under the lights. He wanted to give his weird head full reign, because he just couldn't shut the fuck up. He wanted to be the exception to the rule. He wanted to be the reason for the new fucking rules.

JD sighed. Then he grinned.

'All done, Father,' he said. 'I'm sorry. It's been a, uh, *heavy* twenty-four hours. How are you?' He looked at Aziz. 'Congratulations, bruv. I'm sorry. I really didn't mean to piss on the parade.'

Aziz looked at JD once and nodded. He looked distracted. After a moment, he looked away. JD's phone beeped once. He disconnected it without looking. Aziz was playing with the Zippo relentlessly, snapping it open, flicking the flint-wheel and watching the flame, then clicking it shut and repeating the process.

'What's with all the preamble, A? Tell me what's on your mind.' JD's tone was gentle. For the first time in a very long time, despite Aziz's success and his confessional from three minutes ago, JD felt like he had to be the older one in the relationship.

Aziz pulled out his phone, switched it off, and put it on the bench between them. For a moment, he simply flicked the

Zippo from one hand to the other, picking up speed, making it look like a magic trick he might show kids. It was sinuous, graceful and compulsive. His eyes never left the lighter. To JD he looked like a man with a set of keys, trying them on a single lock, one after the other. Finally, he looked up.

'I have a game for you,' Aziz said softly. He looked at JD, a smile twitching at the corners of his mouth. JD looked like he'd smashed his thumb with a hammer, a perfect 'O' of surprise on his face.

Somewhere, a bird chirped. It was the only sound, apart from his own heartbeat, that JD heard. The guy inside of the system—the guy who'd made it, the guy JD admired more than anyone else he knew, even more than Mike—was looking outside. And he was looking at JD.

'Huh'. But in spite of his surprise, something about this felt familiar to JD. Aziz had known for years, from the very beginning actually, what he did for a living. JD had never imagined that their paths might cross, but here they were. Aziz was making too much money to be coming to JD unless it was something huge. So, it was also something illegal. Illegally huge? Hugely illegal? Whatever it was, there wasn't even a decision. The decision had been made a decade ago, over turns on a Gameboy. His friend had come to him with an offer and he was in.

JD never once asked himself if Aziz had, indeed, come to him this morning to make that offer.

JD closed his mouth and turned to Aziz.

'You're promoting me to white collar.'

Aziz nodded, the slight smile still on his face. 'What've I been telling you for years, JD?'

'That's where all the real money is.'

Aziz shook his head. 'No, man. That's where *all* the money is.'

~

'What do you know about VAT?' asked Aziz.

'Value Added Tax,' said JD. 'What do you want to know?' He felt a single knot of tension—the good kind.

Aziz leaned forward slightly. He made as if to pick up his phone, still on the bench between them, but decided against it. Instead, he let his fingers rest on the phone.

'So it's a tax, obviously, and as always, is levied on the cost of the item itself—let's say were talking phones. Right?'

JD nodded.

'Right. Now, in EU regulations, there's a small provision regarding the import of high-value items. It exists to allow quick passage of goods. Like this phone.' Aziz slid the phone towards JD. 'For example,' he said 'let's say I buy this phone from Mario in Italy; I don't pay VAT.' Aziz pulled the phone back to himself. '*But*. I then sell this phone in England...' He waved the phone at the ruins of the park. 'And I charge VAT. At seventeen-and-a-half per cent.'

Aziz set the phone down between them again and waited. JD's eyes narrowed. He looked at Aziz and then at the phone. He had more than an amateur's understanding of the cycle of taxation within the economy. He made his living from it.

'But VAT moves down the economy.' It wasn't quite a question.

Aziz nodded. 'That's right. So I buy from Mario, no VAT there. Then I sell the phone to, say, *Mike* in England. I charge Mike VAT. Mike wants to make a profit of one pound, so if he sells the phone on, the price he charges is what he paid, plus a quid, plus VAT. Then Mike sells it on to… your dad. And then your dad takes his profit, charges VAT and sells it to the next guy. And all the way down the chain, until it gets to the bloke who takes it home and uses it to call his mates. It's a question of where you get in.'

JD thought about it for a whole minute. He could see a shape here, he understood the basic premise. But he had been building checks for as long as he had been building games. It made him very good at what he did. And Aziz's little scenario was throwing up all sorts of alarms.

'I don't get it, A. I mean, I get it, but I don't *get* it.' He smiled. 'I'm not an effing lawyer.'

'You're looking at it wrong, Jai. It's not the dummy game you've been running. It's a straight hustle. It's a straight rip-off. No stunts. It's simply a question of where you position yourself.' Aziz looked him in the eyes. There was no smile now.

JD watched him closely. He already had dozens of questions. Only a handful of them had anything to do with VAT. He was watching a man cross over. JD didn't understand why, and he was fairly certain that Aziz didn't understand it himself. Not fully.

'Here's the thing,' Aziz went on. 'You're looking at two

inherently different systems that have been force-fitted on top of each other. The first's about the European Union. The second's about the Union Jack. In 1992, governments should have changed over to a clearing house system. They didn't, and that's our window.' Aziz waved JD off as he started to ask a question. 'Couple of minutes. It's not difficult, but you need to know this.'

JD shrugged and looked at the ground, his forehead creasing.

'The guy in Italy doesn't charge me VAT. I *can* and will charge VAT in England. That's legal. Here's what I want to do. I want to bring in my goods, price it more competitively than anyone out there, charge VAT on it and not pay the government.'

JD's frown deepened.

'Aren't there reclaims? As in, the guy who buys from you will ask for his VAT reclaims? So that he pockets *his* profit but...' JD made a vague circling motion with his hand. 'The VAT continues to move down the chain?'

'Reclaims. Sure. Every three months.'

Aziz paused for just long enough.

'Who says you have to be there when they come for the reclaims?'

Slowly, JD nodded. 'So you're legit.' Aziz nodded. 'With a VAT number and everything.' Aziz nodded again. 'And you just disappear in two—'

'—two and a bit months,' Aziz finished.

JD looked at his hands for a moment. He sat up and took Aziz's phone from the bench. Disassembling it in seconds, he put the pieces between them on the bench, then put them back together again.

'Thoughts?' asked Aziz.

'It's a straight rip-off, all right,' JD said. The distaste was visible on his face. 'It's a brown-skin *typical* Paki rip-off.' He bared his teeth in a grim smile.

Aziz shrugged. 'A Communicator's three hundred pounds, JD.'

JD snorted. 'That's fifty-two pounds, fifty pence per phone.'

'Beats the hell out of skipping tails on the M20 to make a tenner on a carton of Gauloises Blondes.'

JD thought about it, about the dodge from the previous evening, and seven years of running with no end in sight, grasping at every opportunity, the stakes rising silently every time they'd made the Calais runs these past three years.

Here it was. Fucking white collar, brother.

He grinned.

'I'll call Mike. Let's see if he wants to buy some phones.'

~

Mike had called Gary while he was walking towards The Rose and Crown, after he'd left Brian's garage. It was pretty much the same conversation. Had Gary heard something? Or seen something? Gary made much the same point as Brian: Mike's outfit wasn't big enough to get fingered. Besides, for two hundred thousand?

But the objections were delivered in a quiet manner, as

if Gary was reminding both himself and Mike that this was something that they needed to bear in mind. Mike allowed for it. Gary told him that he'd call him back.

Next, Mike had called a cousin who worked for the police and asked to meet for lunch. This was a not a request he made often. Their relationship was a strange exchange of currency: Mike's cousin, Adam, was very aware of what Mike did for a living and he chose to turn a blind eye to it, but occasionally they traded information that they thought might be beneficial to each other. Still, Mike hated to be this open, hated the sense of obligation, because this time he had nothing to offer in return.

Mike had gone to an all-day-breakfast and sat there for the better part of an hour, waiting for Adam to show up, rehearsing his questions.

The phone rang. Gary had nothing concrete, but three days before the Calais run, two of Gary's associates had received a combined six phone calls. There was a query on the streets for a large quantity of tax-free Gauloises Blondes. Gary and Mike drew three inferences from this. One, word was out that a shipment was coming through that was large enough to be interesting. Two, there had been a rough fix on the date that the shipment was going to come in. And three, they knew it was coming over the Channel. He thanked Gary and hung up. Adam showed not ten minutes later.

They talked while they ate. It was a business meeting.

'What do you want to know?' Adam had asked.

Mike played it absolutely straight again, not beating about the bush.

'Fences. Contraband. That general area. Anything in the last couple of weeks?'

Adam nodded, broke a yolk with his fork and began to spread it over his fried eggs.

'Are you looking for a specific bust?'

'I'm not sure, Adam. I'm just fishing.'

Adam broke off a piece of toast and mopped his eggs with it. 'And I'm guessing that I shouldn't ask why.'

Mike was silent. It wasn't a big deal, but his cards were on the table. Adam shrugged.

'Last Tuesday we pulled a guy out of one of the council estates. No big deal, some shouting, some furniture being thrown. Disturbing the peace sort of thing. Neighbours'd had enough. Guy by the name of Freddie. Goes by the name of 'Fingers Freddie'. The surname's not important, is it?'

Mike shook his head. His face showed nothing. He knew the name, he knew the man. There was a payoff here. A small, grimy payoff.

'The PC called it in. Fingers has a record, long, but not distinguished, so the PC pulled a little search. A couple of ounces of ganja, some E on the dresser. Enough. We squeezed. It didn't take much.'

Mike grunted. So it went. A cunt got high and had it out with whichever skank he was scoring with that weekend. Five days later, the shit hits the fan in London. So it went.

'He babbled in about four minutes at the station,' Adam said. 'How he was working as a fence for the Suburb Collective. How it was the only job he could get because prison time meant no one else would hire him. How he was just holding the stuff we found, how he had *no idea* what it actually was. But we heard the magic words. The Suburb Collective.'

Mike nodded. The Collective people were one of their bigger customers—they distributed through Heston. They weren't half bad. But they weren't very particular about who worked for them, and what they were on.

'Neat little package,' Adam continued. 'Christmas shipment. Over the weekend. Booze. Fags. Everything. Single van. Probably Calais. It was on the wire by Tuesday evening. And the Customs boys were snapping at the bit. Some people,' he paused, looking at Mike carefully. 'Some people have been fucking them over for too long. It seemed perfect. Poetic, almost.'

Mike continued to eat in silence, his jaw tightening. They weren't the fucking Boy Scouts, no one had to pretend they were friends, but there were unwritten rules everyone respected. Otherwise, they'd get torched, all of them. And if the Collective knew that Fingers had been hauled, and that the weekend's game had been fixed, common business sense dictated that you got on the wire. Fuck courtesy. Business sense. Meanwhile, him and JD had driven to France with their dicks hanging in the wind. The more he thought of it, the angrier he got.

Neither said another word while they finished lunch. Mike took care of the bill. After a moment, Adam leaned across the table.

'Keep better company, Mike.' He got up and left the café.

Mike watched Adam go. He had found the knot that

had bothered him and he had unravelled it. It hadn't taken much because it wasn't much. Last night's heroics seemed absurd in the face of what he had just heard. He fought the impulse to walk down to the Collective's warehouse and go to work with a sledgehammer. He wouldn't kill anybody, but that was about all he could promise. Mike got up abruptly, the voice that ran things inside of his head churning. He could stay away from the Collective, maybe, but he'd find a fight somewhere else tonight, walking out of some pub. Violence would follow him like his shadow until he found something to break.

He paused outside the café. He needed to find neutral ground. He tried calling JD, only to have JD reject the call. Mike gritted his teeth. The fucking universe was moving in only one direction today, and he could feel the heat rising in his throat. He understood the kind of mindless frustration that drove men to buy guns and hose down shopping malls, but he couldn't let that be what moved him. He had to focus the anger, make it useful.

He walked into the nearest newsagents', bought a pack of Bensons and went back to the sidewalk, deliberately surrounding himself with people. He lit a cigarette. Standing there, he tried to work his way to what they'd do next, knowing but not believing that the game that they'd run for three years had just been blown sky-high. But his thoughts kept getting drowned out by a rush of blood he could actually hear. The joints of his fists throbbed with that rhythm. The need to cause harm was quickly becoming a physical reality.

An irritating chirp got through the white noise in his ears.

It took Mike a minute to realize it was his phone. He pulled it out. It was JD. Mike waited for a long moment, standing on the pavement in the weak afternoon sun, then swallowed and answered the phone.

What JD said next meant that Mike could put aside the violence for a while. But only for a while. And then it would be worse than he'd ever imagined.

The first of the three legendary meetings of the Heston Principle occurred on Monday, 27 December 1999 at the warehouse that Mike and JD rented. It had been a week since Aziz and JD had had their conference on the park bench. The date was precise—Customs finally managed to track it down three years later because the papers towards incorporation had been filed the very next day. It was unglamorous, a fifty-minute run-through of details at seven o'clock on a bitterly cold evening.

The three of them looked at the model for a while, although there wasn't much to look at.

The stock came in from the EU. They sold in England— at a price that gave them an edge in the face of regular, legitimate, competition—charging VAT. They disappeared before the reclaims. That was the model. It was that simple.

The only thing that had changed was the other side of the equation. No longer peddling their wares in the dead of night from the back of a van, Mike and JD were dealing with legitimate retailers for the first time. They needed genuine paperwork, documents that would enable invoicing and receipts, and they needed real banking. It was a new system and regardless of its simplicity, there were checks and balances.

The simplicity had Mike worried. He and JD had spent years coping with the pressures of real crime—the kind of crime the police chased you for—and he knew how to outrun them. The fact that he couldn't feel any danger in this made it all the more dangerous. This new system was criminal, but where were the dogs? Who would be chasing them now, and how could they outrun what they couldn't see?

The easy, perfect logic of the system made Mike's jaw stiff. If only there wasn't so much fucking money in it. The trick to this game was in reaching the Zen of a learned, rhythmic boredom. There was no jazz, only the pattern to be mastered: shuffle, cut, deal, shuffle. They had to become a metronome—precise, functional, *small*.

And, therefore, Mike worried about JD. The figures made sense to JD; it was the only reason that he had agreed to the new game in the first place. But JD had been struggling with his distaste for this game the entire week. There were no suicidal riffs, no desperate creativity to offset the monotony of the setup. JD was a genius at the contraband system because every Calais run was a war with the dogs, it was fucking personal. That was the release that let him get through the rest of the week. This gig offered no release. The irony was, Mike thought that JD might have a real flair for it if money alone could be enough for him.

There was going to be trouble.

It was Mike who broke the silence.

'If it's that simple, why is no one else doing it?'

Mike was the only one at the table. Aziz was leaning against the back wall, arms crossed. JD paced the platform outside, smoking continuously.

Aziz cleared his throat. His right hand pulled the Zippo from his pocket. He began to flick it open and shut. If he played poker, thought JD, that fucking lighter would be a dead giveaway.

'I think the larger import–export world *has* thought of it. It's too simple to miss. There are hundreds of guys out there like me. You know? Who can look at something on a page and understand the implications of it in the real world, in practice?' Mike nodded. 'But it's risky. That's the thing. Because you have to appear and disappear all the time. You sell and then you fold. You have to be visible—you're peddling the stock. There has to be someone a vendor sees, a voice and a face at the other end of the deal. And you have to be big *enough* otherwise something, somewhere down the chain, will fuck up. A payment will go begging, paperwork won't be complete, you'll stay in three days too long for one more play. But if you're really big, then it's a huge risk. Because a fold becomes multiple—through all the levels. If you're too big and customs stops you once, then *everything* stops. It's a double-edged sword.'

JD chimed in from the door. 'What he's saying, Mike, is that no one runs this at a major level because no one has ever thought of it as purely a scam. You know, not skimming off the top occasionally, but structuring all of it so that the whole thing is centred around playing VAT?'

Aziz grinned. Mike smiled but he wasn't done yet.

'Still,' he said, 'the size thing's a valid point. How do you do that? Get big enough and still stay little?'

'It's in the set-up, boys,' said JD. His voice was soft. And Mike knew JD had it— whatever it was. This meeting was in the bag. They'd be done in the next twenty minutes.

'How?' asked Aziz.

JD took a moment. He drew on his cigarette, walked back into the office, crushed the cigarette out in the ashtray on the table and sat down. He closed his eyes, once, like he was making sure he could remember every detail from the scene in front of him. Then he looked up, first at Mike and then at Aziz, eyes gleaming.

'You're right,' he said, turning to Mike, 'the fold *is* the difficult bit. The fold is necessitated because the vendor you sell to will file for his reclaims every three months. That's your horizon, because it's the only thing that can chain you to your game. We know this much. Right?'

Both Mike and Aziz nodded. Mike let his eyes wander in the office as he picked up details. He was trying to make the connections as JD spoke because he knew that it would be he, Mike, making the big calls—fixing the balance of the actual run—in less than a week.

'It's unlikely to be a problem even if there are reclaims. Because we'll be gone before then. And that's what I'm telling you. Even if the turnover of stock's constantly bringing the dogs around, *because* we keep disappearing—and it will show up, boys, eventually—we have to disappear in multiple ways, multiple times.'

This time, only Mike nodded. Aziz was unconvinced. There was a difference between being able to see something on a page, thought Mike, and knowing how to make that tick in this world. It wasn't about *beating* the three-month loop. It was about rolling with it. JD had a real gift for the statistics of a scam, for the factors beyond blind luck and Hail Mary stunts. He lived on probability, covering his bases in the way he loaded a game. And when he was good, he could occasionally render luck unimportant.

Aziz, on the other hand, was about to get JD-ed.

JD looked at Mike again and grinned, then transferred his gaze to Aziz, still leaning against the wall.

'You build your system around the quarter. Let's say that we're bringing in something at a hundred pounds from Italy, and that we're selling it at ninety-five-plus-VAT. Just as an example.' JD held out his hand and counted off the points on his fingers.

'One. You can only make something like this work if you're working high-value merchandise, otherwise the margins don't make sense. Two. The merchandise has to be small, otherwise the fold doesn't work. Chips, calculators, watches, mobile phones. And three. The only way you beat the dogs on the fold is by running at least three parallel import companies. You start up all three within two weeks of each other. You load two of them equally. The third, you take the foot off. It's a buffer. Nothing through it. Stock passes through the other two, as much as you'd like, as much as we can afford. If God is kind, nothing happens.'

JD paused, lit a cigarette and checked. He had their attention, all right.

'You fold the first one in an even two months. The moment you do that, the moment you put the first one to sleep, you start the process up top again. Three more companies, load two, the third's the buffer. Ten days later you kill the second company from your first group. And between a week and eleven days after that, you kill the buffer from the first group. You already have three companies running. Everything repeats itself. The only difference this time out—the second time—is that you don't kill the buffer. You make one run through it, completely legal, declaring everything. It does business. You declare the taxes and you let it sleep. At the end of the year, given that fate leaves you untouched, you have six loops of making eleven pounds on every hundred pounds, tax-free, a blizzard of companies that spring up and vanish, and three beautiful companies, completely fucking legit. You could start farming out tax write-offs if you'd like. All bases covered. Tight little knot. Sexy in every way. Bob's your uncle.'

There was a moment of silence. Aziz shook his head once and then pocketed the Zippo. It said much for the room that it wasn't a eureka moment. No one pounded the table. It was a good system. The percentages were covered from all angles, from practically all the hits both possible and probable. The tax write-off coverage thrown in for a bonus was an especially nice touch. But there wasn't much to be said. JD had just found an interesting way for them to run a simple game.

'I do have an uncle named Bob, you know,' Mike said, after a minute.

Aziz burst out laughing. They were done. They just needed to sort out the finances.

~

Between the three of them, they had a hundred thousand pounds that they could throw away on spec. And it *was* spec, at least for the first three months. Not that Mike or JD could strictly afford to lose their shares on a spec run, but every time they invested in a new system, ritual dictated that they think of it that way. So they would load the system as JD had described and they would run the first three-month loop.

Each of them had a to-do list. Aziz was going to hold down his job at Lexington Brothers. He had quietly accepted the associate partnership. He already attracted a silent rush of clients. They would only multiply over the next few months. Even Michael Russell knew—within a week—that Aziz had been right all along; he was on a fast-track to full partnership. It was a matter of months.

Aziz's clients were almost exclusively Asian, mostly Indian and Pakistani. Anyone who controlled about five million pounds, and had any dealings that were even slightly grey, flocked to him because he walked both worlds. He was the cream of the British legal system, but he was also a Pakistani kid who had never turned down a single request on his street while growing up. He had drafted wills for families who only had a small newsagents', he had advised on divorces, he had a wealth of knowledge when it came to investments and realty, and he knew the tricks when it came to beating Inland Revenue. Aziz understood—you didn't need white explanations. He could pull a favour, get a conversation, anywhere. He always knew somebody who knew somebody else who had a cousin who knew someone who could help. He was a walking assistance directory.

If Aziz had been interested in a burgeoning law practice alone, he could have left in three months and set up shop. But he needed to keep the job over the next three months because Mike and JD were essentially unemployed and they'd put most of their savings into the first run. They needed the money Aziz earned, and they needed the intangibles, the ability to pick up the phone and dial Rome, looking for the right kind of exporter.

Mike and JD had the next couple of weeks to do two things: set up the first six companies, and find the banking that they needed. It was here that Aziz genuinely surprised them for the first time. While setting up the banking, he suggested, they needed to cultivate a handful of crooked bank managers. Not obviously corrupt guys, but people who could be swayed to look at things in a slightly more flexible way. They needed a soft stance. When they rolled hard, the first thing that Customs would do was tighten the leash on banking privileges. It was the institutionalized response: Customs would take measures they had taken before, when faced with similar situations. They would target the volume of cash, believing—rightly, Aziz added—that if the cash flow was restricted, a mis-step would follow. So they needed bank managers who could help. And if they had the right bank managers, those managers would provide the tellers and auditors. That kind of thing had its own momentum.

Mike was the only one unsure of what to make of the information.

'I don't think that you can actually find managers like that.' Mike paused. He didn't do delicate well. 'With all due respect, it's not your part of the world. This kind of thing is very difficult to find here. We've spent decades weeding it out.'

Bugger, thought JD. That's a first meeting for you. Racial stereotypes on a Monday evening, right after tea, just before the pub. It was an unnecessary complication, another crack in the ever-widening circle that had been just Mike and him a week ago.

Aziz looked at Mike and smiled.

'Everyone, within certain limits, has a price,' he said. 'All you have to do is understand that limit—what a person would *not* do. And you have to find the price. It doesn't matter where in the world you are. That never changes. And we're not asking them to steal, we're not asking them to make money disappear. All they have to do is, when the time comes—if it does and it will—is do us a favour. Because all we will ask them is whether or not they want to do us a favour.'

'And if they don't want to do us a favour?'

'You should think more highly of people. You know, it's my high opinion of people that's gotten me where I am today.'

Mike smiled back. 'It's not where you are that worries me,' he said. 'It's where we're going.'

Mike wasn't quite sure about the first part, either.

~

They started with a hundred thousand. Ten for admin, for running the office and for miscellaneous expenses—JD's 'pint money'. Ninety thousand for the actual stock. The more they looked at it, the more mobiles suggested themselves. There was a constant demand for them, and there was a rapid turnover as people looked to upgrade. They settled on the Communicator—the Nokia 9110i. At three hundred quid a pop, they were looking at an initial run of three hundred phones, with a profit of about forty quid per phone. They would take three pounds each per phone, with one pound going towards the office and the rest would go back into the system. At the end of the first run of the loop, they'd have enough profit for thirty more phones to enter the game. It rolled from there.

JD was the last to leave, locking up behind Mike. He smoked in silence, reviewing the strange week they'd had. He knew that VAT wasn't the Holy Grail. It wasn't the Ultimate Game, the game that he'd been searching for ever since he had started in the business. *That* one would be once in a lifetime; a complex, intricate, minutely assembled system that reacted with speed and intelligence from *within* the system, self-perpetuating, the perfect machine. It was why he was in the business. And this wasn't it.

But it was a good game all the same. It had the dim pleasure of detailing done well, and it called for care. And, somewhere, the money murmured.

White-collar. Fucking hell. Miracles were on the move, Christmas was still in the air. It suited him well. It suited him just fine.

~

For all of Mike and JD's experience with incorporation, they weren't retailers, and this was still a new game. They had moved up in the world. Even the most basic VAT scams were more complex. Aziz was right; this is where the big boys played.

They needed to get a VAT number, something that took months to process. But it was also possible just to buy an existing company, one that had a VAT number but wasn't trading. These companies went for five thousand quid each and VAT numbers changed hands all the time.

JD's three-company stagger, so fucking neat in concept, was an expensive habit. It meant fifteen thousand pounds up front, which inflated their initial budget straightaway, and then fifteen thousand pounds every three months. JD insisted on it. But it meant that they were opening hard, and that they were running hot from the very beginning. It had to be a blitz.

~

Five days before the first meeting of the Heston Principle,

Mike and JD climbed into Mike's battered Ford. They'd split eight cans of Foster's in the warehouse. Now they were looking for a snooker hall. It was Mike's year to choose the locale.

Growing up in Heston, they'd had to go about five miles, in any direction, before they found good snooker halls. JD grew up in snooker halls that were single-owner-run. Those snooker halls were dungeons. They were, always, magically, bigger than they seemed. Tables in pools of light, set against a backdrop that vanished. When frames got serious, JD felt like he was on a platform that rose up from pure black. Everything you saw was a shade of baize.

The air smelt of cigarette smoke, stale beer and grease. Grease covered every surface except for the tables themselves. Shoes would stick to pavements for a good hour afterwards. Playing snooker for hours on end would leave him feeling like a vampire, JD remembered. He would surface and blink in surprise at the fact that it was only two in the afternoon.

JD played snooker seriously for two years, between the ages of fifteen to seventeen. He started because it intrigued him. It was like playing Tetris with curves, in 3D. He liked the concentration involved in break-building—it was real-time strategy that had to evolve over the course of a few hours. It was about attempting to order chaos.

Plus, it was just a fucking game. No one cared, really, if you won or lost. Nothing was at stake. He wasn't dealing with expectations; his own, his parents, the world at large.

He started to get good around thirteen. Because he obsessed over it. He dreamt it. And he didn't mind getting his arse handed to him by good players if it meant that he was going to, eventually, get better. By fifteen, he was playing snooker because it enabled him to buy hi-tops and remote-controlled cars. He built the biggest slot-car racing rig he could imagine. And he bought all the tech junk—computer hardware—he needed. He played snooker because his parents and their peers didn't understand what he wanted. His appetite was alien. He spoke a different English.

Around seventeen, the casual bets started to end in fights. They were minor scuffles, some kicking and punching, knives being pulled. It wasn't a big deal. By the time you got close to your A-levels, if you weren't prepping for Uni, you were getting other kinds of vocational training.

But the fights weren't strictly necessary. People hustled at snooker halls all the time. They bet on frames. They bet on games of darts. They bet on matches on the telly. They bet on 'Countdown'. They bet on the next person to walk in through the door. The bets were usually moderated by an immensely fat man, usually called Don, usually an ex-darts champion.

JD would set people up, take their money and then start taunting them. It was cute at first. A seventeen-year-old kid, going off like a rabid dog after he beat someone at a game of snooker. But it got old soon. The owners spoke to him. Then the Dons spoke to him. JD alternated between charm and profanity. He was too good to keep away, too much of a spectacle. However, he was pissing off too many patrons. So street law took over.

He was ambushed in an alley as he left the snooker

hall. The first time, they broke his cue. He'd saved up for three months after he'd started hustling to buy that cue. JD bounced into the same snooker hall three days later. He asked for the bet, picked up the first cue he could spot and stayed on the table for the next hour and a quarter. The next day, he went to see Mike. He wanted to see if Mike would occasionally accompany him to some of the seedier joints, bring some balance to proceedings.

They'd known each other for years. They'd been friends for years. They were neighbourhood bruvs. Mike's mom, Joan, worked two jobs. They'd been dirt poor ever since Mike's father skipped town. To this day, JD didn't know what his name was, and whether the old bastard was still alive. Mike was inducted into JD's family one afternoon when he called on JD and JD's mom discovered that a packet of crisps had been his lunch for three days straight. Her lips clamped together in a familiar tight line as she made him a quick sandwich. She didn't know whether he'd eat Indian food. That turned out all right. He'd been eating Gujarati food since he was eight. Families around the area liked him. He was a tough kid but he was fair. He was too poor to be racist. And there was no one around for him to absorb prejudice from. His elder sister was already out of the house, living with an aunt in Bristol. She saw education as her only way out. Mike, on the other hand, had been making pocket money from little games and plays since he'd been ten. Nicking stuff. Running courier for the Indian bookies in the area. Peddling a little weed.

And then his friend Gary told him about contraband.

JD had helped Mike set up the first string of virtual companies. He'd still been drifting back then; snooker game to snooker game, discovering alcohol, already a chain smoker. He'd done it as a favour to a friend, and because mostly what he was interested in doing was making the computer talk. He wasn't interested in programming, and he thought hacking was for pervy little shits who couldn't have fun in the real world. But he liked to know what his computer was doing, liked to know how he could get it to do things.

They escaped a particularly nasty fight together after another snooker hustle, through luck more than anything else. A stock-boy in a Chinese restaurant opened the service door at a fortuitous time. And JD and Mike had run through the restaurant, through the waiters and the guests and a couple of tables. Four fat old fucks had given chase, trying to beat JD out of the money their friend had lost. Mike and JD gave them the slip, doubled back, ambushed the four fat old fucks and had themselves a merry Friday night.

Mike watched JD get drunk after that fight. JD alternately raged at the old fucks and at his father. His father was too old, too staid, too fucking Indian. He—JD—had been born handicapped, that's what he was. Then he got maudlin.

'What d'you want, Mike?' he'd asked. 'Out of life?'

Mike had watched him carefully. In the years that followed, there was no indication that JD remembered that particular conversation. JD never alluded to it and they never talked about it again. Then again, JD had a phenomenal memory—drunk, bombed, while he had diarrhoea, it didn't matter.

'What do *you* want?' asked Mike. He was surprised that he'd resorted to simply turning the question around. These things never actually got discussed. Ever. Between anyone.

'What the fuck does everyone else want?' asked JD in return. He was silent for a bit. 'To be able to pull. Like this,' snapping his fingers. 'The villa, the swimming pool, the fucking sports car. My own private jet.' He grinned at Mike. 'The full Keith Moon, y'know.'

Mike was surprised at how sad the response made him. In the end, even the wild ones were reading lines off some predetermined script.

'Fuck that, though.' JD's voice was soft. Mike looked up at him. 'What I want, Mike, is to get out of my own head. That's all. I want this,' JD tapped an index finger against his temple 'here.' He was pointing to his palm with the same index finger. 'Relevant.' JD thought about, eyes glittering in the way that Mike would become familiar with. 'Burn it down. Don't care if I don't win.'

'But I want that chance.'

JD looked at Mike. Mike nodded to himself. He took a deep breath

'I want to retire,' he said.

'What?' JD was deeply amused. Mike was eighteen. JD himself was seventeen.

'Nah. Not like that.' Mike was grinning. 'I want to put something away for Billy, you know?' Billy was Mike's nephew. 'If he wants to play football, or learn the fucking violin or be some poof chef, it shouldn't matter.' Mike looked down at his hands.

'I just want to put away enough money for a few years, you know? Like, maybe five. Then I want to go and get level two and three coaching.'

'You missed level one, bruv.' JD had a vague recollection of a conversation when they'd been kids. Mike, football manager. Someone else wanted to be a rapper. And someone a professional fluffer.

'No,' said Mike absentmindedly. 'I got level one last year.' He looked up and saw JD's look of surprise. 'Only your dad knows,' he said. 'I told him not to tell anyone.'

JD was silent for a bit. Then he raised his can of beer thoughtfully.

'Here's to retirement, mate. And to getting out of my head. Now those,' he grinned 'are worthwhile ambitions.'

Mike had gone to see JD the next day, well after two in the afternoon, allowing for the hangover.

'Fuck the snooker, hustling guys for twenty pounds and then having to hit some stupid red balls for the next three hours. Come and work with me.'

JD thought about it and nodded 'yes'. He went in to work the very next day. It was December, and there was money to be made on cheaper smokes.

They rode in on the cue-stick, he'd tell people later. Like a *very* fucked up cavalry.

And once every year, somewhere in December, they'd find one day to go play snooker.

It was a ritual.

~

They played snooker for a couple of hours. They didn't discuss Aziz or the offer he'd made. JD told Mike about the engagement, about Aziz entering like the theme from 'Dallas' was blasting in surround sound.

'You're a lucky fuck,' JD observed. 'No one pushing you to get married. Making all those fat white girls shriek their own names.' He'd been drinking steadily. He never played snooker sober any more.

'I didn't know you had a thing about fat girls.'

'Fuck you. I'm sure it's a wonderful three minutes for both of you.'

'Hey, twenty times in an hour isn't so bad. Get two in and variety's the spice of life.'

'I'm serious here, Mike.'

'So am I.' Mike grinned. 'Your mother wanted me to have a chat with you. "Tell him that we're not growing any younger".'

JD looked horrified. Mike relented, mostly because he didn't want JD picking another fight when he got home.

'Well, she *could've* said it.'

'Best of five frames' descended to 'hit it as hard as you can'. They listened to all of 'Back in Black'. They put away a couple of pints each, as well as a nasty bacon burger. At some point in the afternoon, someone Mike didn't know came looking for JD. He was a pasty little white guy. The bag he passed to JD clinked as JD put it away. JD gave him some money and he fucked off. Mike looked at JD.

'Cough syrup,' said JD, chewing his burger. 'For Sudeep.' The name was familiar to Mike but he couldn't place it.

'Sumit's brother,' said JD, after watching Mike trying to work it out. 'Long story,' he said, before Mike could ask a question. 'I'll tell you about it some other day.'

And that was it really it, thought Mike. Mostly, they still had stories to tell each other, in spite of having grown up in the same neighbourhood, in spite of being friends, in spite of working together. It was the best evening either of them had had in a long time.

JD brought up work once they got back in the car.

'What d'you think?'

Mike was silent. He'd been thinking about Aziz's pitch, on and off, for three days. It tired him out, just thinking about it. There was a lot to do. He didn't know if he had the energy for it. Whether he had the imagination for it.

He'd put some money away. Six months worth, maybe. And he could find a job. He had enough hours working with youth teams to apply for level two.

And maybe the Schillachi was a sign. The perfect play as the perfect party blow-off. It was time to get off the streets, to trade in the edge for a whistle and the warmth of a childhood dream.

All this ran through his head in the space of a second. He looked up. He was about to start speaking when he looked at JD. JD's head was against the glass and there was a distant look in his eyes.

'Give me three months, Mike. I can't do this on my own. Aziz isn't someone I've been running with since I was thirteen.' He paused and grinned. 'Come and work with me, Mike. Three months. Then we'll see.'

Mike shrugged. This wasn't even about choice.

'V-A-T,' he said and started the engine.

~

Nothing much happened for the next two weeks.

~

Once the civilized world was satisfied that the year 2000 hadn't made their computers die or rise up against them, January got underway and everything began to fall into place. They had their paperwork, their six companies, and they had the deals lined up. The three men had found the rhythm of their working relationship, and each was comfortable with it.

Mike and JD, meanwhile, let the aftermath of the last Calais run happen to other people. The Schillachi had become an instant legend on the street and the blowback was savage. The dogs turned the heat up on the streets and on the docks until they'd reversed the ratio—where one in three runs used to get busted, one in three now got through. They didn't bother scanning vans at spot checks, just tore them open and dug in. All over London, contraband runs in booze and cigarettes lay in ruins. Fences, and then entire distribution networks, were folding. They hadn't seen anything like it in ten years.

It had nothing to do with Mike and JD any more.

They met with Aziz early in the evening in a pub just off Tottenham Court Road on Sunday, 11 January. It had been two weeks and a day since the three of them had last been in a room together. With a bit of help from Sumit, they had covered a lot of ground. The first small lot of Communicators waited in an Italian warehouse for an order to start the first of the trails through the Continent. But Mike had refused to put the first deal through.

'We *could* just as well have gone on Friday,' JD said, eyeing Mike innocently over the rim of his pint.

Mike put down his beer. It was one of those moments where JD's buzz outmanoeuvred his logic and things that should be left unsaid got hazily spoken. Mike leaned closer over the table.

'What's your rush?'

'What's my rush? Where's yours? We're ready, bruv. Everything's set. I'd have thought you'd be excited.'

'Excitable people are liable to make mistakes.'

'We're doing it. You know we're doing it. So why not just *do* it?'

'Fuck off, Nike. In the first place, I was never going to start it on a Friday. I don't want anything moving over the weekend when we can't check on it. You ever see an Italian drive? If some cunt with delusions of Formula 1 puts his van into a fucking canal with our merchandise, I didn't want to wait all weekend to find out. So I ask you again, JD, what's your rush?'

'The first loop, man. I want to *see* it.'

'That's why I want it to happen in plain view—during the week.'

'Then we go tomorrow.'

Nothing on Mike's face moved except his lips. 'Maybe.'

'Keep everything where you can see it.' JD smiled and took his pint to the bar where, through his usual charm, he'd convinced the pub owner to surrender control of the CD player when they'd come in around four-thirty.

'No, I'm not going to play The Specials,' he told the owner with a glint in his eyes. 'Childhood sap. Rubbish. That's just what they'll be *expecting* me to play.'

Watching from the table, Mike laughed quietly and closed his eyes.

'If there are repercussions,' Aziz said, 'we won't know about it for another three months, whether we'd launched on Friday or not.'

Opening his eyes, Mike said, 'I'm used to working in cash under the table. If I'm going to do a lot more business with the banks, I'd rather do it when they're open. Call it instinct. Call it what you like.'

The sad cheerfulness of 'A Message to Rudy' began to flow from the speakers as JD slid into the booth beside Aziz. Both men looked at him.

'What can I tell you? I'm a sentimentalist at heart.'

They burst out laughing. They didn't talk about work again that night.

They told old war stories and they listened to music they liked and they drank.

And they talked about money. It was right there. It was so easy—easier and easier as the night went on. They thought of it as luck, as a gift that had fallen into their laps because that was just the way that the game—all games—worked.

You could never pretend ownership, but you could feel lucky.

They watched the pub fill up and they infected the other patrons with their cheer. The three of them seemed somehow brighter than their surroundings and people saw that. It was an occasion made for JD and he jumped into it, happily rolling out the old banter and taking song requests, never once failing to laugh appreciatively when someone made the wretched pun on JD and DeeJay.

When he slid back into the booth, there was still the glint in his eyes but the rest of his face was slack and his mouth ready to slur. He drained his pint and then looked up at Mike. 'I gotta go home, Mike. I gotta go break some copyright laws and fight with my dad. I gotta go.' But he didn't move, didn't even attempt to get up. The ever-present cigarette burned in the corner of his mouth and his eyes didn't leave Mike's. Mike turned to Aziz and saw the flat gaze on his face.

Mike looked down at his pint and the pale-gold promise it held at its bottom. He saw the old game, so lovingly assembled, such a faithful mistress for three years, that they had dismantled because, always, they were searching for a better way to do the same thing. He saw the garage in Gary's house in Chelsea, and the promises it held with its gleaming tools—cars could be stripped and heroin cut and bodies vanished. It was the same thing, all of it. It was a vacuum to be filled, and an empty stage where they made their stand. If they so wished.

It's all I'm good for, thought Mike. The next action, the move forward. One more fucking play. He looked up.

'Okay, boys. We go tomorrow. Let's try not to get fucked.'

PART TWO
THE GREAT GAME

*'Now the only thing a gambler needs
is a suitcase and trunk'*
—The Animals

*'Yeah, I've got a tombstone hand in a graveyard mine,
Just twenty-two baby, I don't mind dying
Snakeskin shoes baby, put them on your feet,
Got the goodtime music and the Bo Diddley beat
Who do you love?'*
—George Thorogood and The Destroyers

*'The hippies wanted peace and love.
We wanted Ferraris, blondes and switchblades.'*
—Alice Cooper

2.1

It was the ten minutes between being asleep and being awake, Valerie Stewart decided, that was the silly season. Every damned day. Between reaching over a still-snoring Ken to bash the alarm on the head, and finally sitting up to go downstairs and put the kettle on. But it was also necessary season. She spent the rest of the day trying to reclaim those ten minutes. In those ten minutes, disconnected thoughts, the fragments of dreams and grocery lists were all equally important.

Val had spent most of her working life trying to remain in silly season. Detached, calm, taking in the world with the gaze of a child. That place where grim patience took you past the books in front of you to the horizon beyond. Thirteen different things had to run together in your mind, like a current gently swirling under a bridge. And day after day she dropped small pieces of bread into that current, waiting to see which way the pieces got pulled, and whether the pattern repeated itself or whether it was only a random accident of Fate.

There were always patterns, Val had learnt.

Val rose at half past six every weekday. She put the kettle on, showered, drank her first cup of tea and walked down to the newsagents. She bought two papers, read them over her second cup of tea, then woke Ken, ate some breakfast cereal, and got dressed for work. She kissed Ken goodbye as he groped about with his first cup of tea and she picked up the two slices of bread that had been left in the oven overnight and stuffed them into a small zip-lock bag. It was an old habit, one she had learned from her mother. It had been a ritual from when you couldn't buy breadcrumbs at the nearest Sainsbury's.

She left the house at ten to eight, as she had for years now. She was short and lean, and she walked with purpose. From behind the scarf, the face was essentially kind, the eyes bright. Her hair, almost completely white, had been cut as short as a schoolboy's. It made her look like a benign pixie. Every day, unless the rain was too troublesome, she would go to the park at the end of the street and spend ten minutes absentmindedly breaking off bits of bread and throwing them out to the pigeons, who had grown used to her appearance every morning.

It was a Monday, so she thought about the weekend that had passed. She and Ken made it a point to stay in on Sundays, sleeping late and walking down to a small café around the corner for breakfast at about noon. For three pounds fifty, they made back the cholesterol count they had held at bay over the week. Sunday was a day to read the newspapers for hours, to catch up on correspondence, to attempt to stave off the coming week and then give up somewhere around four in the afternoon, and start to prepare for Monday mornings. Val sometimes worried about what retirement would do to that. Ken could easily clock another ten years if he wanted, being a year younger than Val and a career academic. Her clock would run out when she hit fifty-eight. That was just over five years away. For the past two years, she had considered retirement very seriously but hung on for two reasons. One was the pension. Although she and Ken were decades past money being a major bone of contention, she would much rather control her financial stake in their relationship, thank you very much. The second was the fear that without her job, old age would come rushing through the door like an uninvited house-guest and refuse to leave.

She had graduated with her Master's in Mathematics from Oxford at twenty-three, on a scholarship, and within a week of graduation she had fallen into a job. It came the way things did back then—her father knew someone who had a friend. There was an opening in Internal Audits and she had said yes. A job was a job, and a gap year was a luxury.

In fairness to Val, she had thought of it as a slightly longer term stop-gap arrangement. The job meant security and she would ultimately return to a PhD or to teaching. By the end of the first year, because of her languages—she had French and German—she was part of a much smaller unit of auditors who were tracking down illegal tax shelters originating from the UK through Europe. It was a job that sounded far more glamorous than it actually was, a team of six in a room off Belgrave Square looking at statements and account ledgers all day. But it was more interesting than Treasury accounting, more interesting than fertilizer audits in the West Country.

There were always patterns, Val had learnt. Patterns that confirmed that there was nothing out of the ordinary, and patterns that told you that someone, somewhere, was trying to get away with *something*. There were always patterns.

In 1973, Val was enlisted into the Cold War. Her team of six had been too successful in too short a time to go unnoticed. They had found three massive tax shelters, and had begun to discover ways to appropriate them, even if the money remained out of reach legally. Without much preamble, the team's hunt for tax shelters had morphed into a system dedicated to the manoeuvring of Cold War funds on the Continent and across the Iron Curtain, as well as tracking the movement of money that wasn't theirs. They chased every trail that M16 sent their way, whether it was the Russians or the Cousins—twice they'd even tracked Nazi money that had appeared from out of pre-war Germany. With the rise of OPEC, Val's department finally added counterfeiting and terrorism to their purview.

They had been hounds. A pack of hounds, trained and turned loose, hunting because it was what they had been bred to do until it became their only impulse.

By 1974, Val's first marriage was over. She became head of her division in 1976, and had even spent a manic three months working out of the M16 headquarters, living in the cipher-room, trying to buy her country inch after bloody inch as the world struggled for balance.

By 1981, Val was too senior and knew too much. She had earned a reputation of being mercilessly thorough. She had the patience of an executioner and the ease of a fine scrum half—she made the target come to her and she almost always found the right break. But the murmurs said she was ungovernable. She had seen too much good work wasted, too much research become useless. She preferred action. And she had seen too much to have any respect left for anyone in the upper echelons of power. Her disdain had begun to show; unhappy and overworked, the department stumbled through the eighties with bone-weary indifference.

By then, Val had found Ken and gradually restored colour and light to her personal life. She came to her job with her usual, natural professionalism and although the fire had dimmed, her experience and greater detachment left her as good as she had ever been. She knew she had burnt too many bridges to ever dream of real career advancement. As the fires of the Cold War slowly died out across the world, she had become, in the lexicon of the Administrative Services, a janitor. She went where she was needed to sweep up. As soon as she restored normalcy, she was shipped somewhere else. This, too, had become a pattern.

Val was rigid about only two things: she would not leave London, and she was damned if she was going to let her pension go. She didn't care that it was going to be as small as it was. She just wanted to see it happen.

She had been transferred to a new posting in mid-1998. She was now attached to Customs and Excise, having made the trip across from Inland Revenue. She understood that she was, in essence, being put out to pasture. Even five years ago, it would have brought on the sort of showdown that she had become infamous for—one of Val's turns. Instead, she had gone quietly, understanding that it was perhaps for the best that she slowly learn to envisage a life without the job. In the past few years, she had discovered grace.

Val finished the two pieces of toast and continued to break thin air for a few seconds before looking down and realizing that her hands were empty. She carefully put the zip-lock bag into her purse. She looked at her watch. It was two past eight, time to go into work. Two pigeons from her flock wandered closer. They pecked hesitantly against her shoes in the hope that there was something left. She looked down at them.

'Shoo,' she said.

~

It was two weeks into their first run before any of them understood what was really happening. Where they grew up, getting rich wasn't supposed to be this easy. This game had a kind of lairy momentum, a mad charge like Palace's 1990 FA Cup run. It was JD who figured it out first, so it was JD who spotted why they were, indeed, fucked.

He'd come home one night, swiped his dad's scientific calculator, and calculated until three-thirty in the morning:

Three runs a week split over two trading companies while the third company lay untouched. They bought mobiles at three hundred and sold at two ninety plus VAT, retailing at three hundred and forty. From this, they kept three pounds each as profit and one for the offices and pumped the rest back into the system.

JD started with three hundred mobiles. In two weeks, he'd pulled out eighteen thousand pounds for the three of them. But the ninety thousand pounds in the system had become one hundred and thirty-three thousand pounds and suddenly there were four hundred phones circling in the system.

JD punched in more figures. At the end of thirty-six runs through the loop—three runs a week for three months—there would be 4,725,720 pounds circling through the system. *Aside* from their profits.

The number didn't completely floor him. Four mill was great PR, but it always became phones the next morning. The way to do it would be to cash out around two million (somewhere around loop thirty, he saw in his untidy scrawl) and just fucking run.

Just run.

That was where the knot was, the knot that he'd missed completely.

He got up, washed his face, lit a cigarette and picked up his phone. He had to wait three rings, two more than standard.

'Hello?'

'How many pints have you had?'

JD heard Mike sit up.

'I'll call you back.'

The phone rang three minutes later, enough for Mike to dunk his head under the tap and get a cup of tea. JD had gone through the projection again. He wasn't sleepy any longer.

'Go.'

'Okay. I'm looking at a projection for 14 March.' 14 March

was the day they were scheduled to kill the first trading company.

'Yeah.'

'Here's the good news. The three of us have got thirty-six grand a head. There's four and a half million pounds in the system. That's fifteen and a half thousand phones the next morning, allowing for our profit.'

'What's the problem?'

'What's the scam, Mike?'

Mike was silent for a minute.

'We're pocketing the VAT we're charging,' he said. He wasn't hesitant, but he was worried.

JD breathed out. He was livid. They should've seen this at the very beginning, all of them.

'That is the scam, yes. And what are the potential dog-fucks? How are they going to come sniffing around?'

'If.' Mike was rocketing down the path, looking for possible factors six months away. '*If* there's enough profit posted by the vendors we're dealing with, *if* their numbers are off the charts and they're consistently pulling higher, then we might get a visit from VAT officers. Because we've pocketed the VAT on all those deals.' He paused. 'But if they come around to the office, even if they're carrying a summons, we won't be there. We'll have been gone months ago—another office, another address, another company.'

'They will come eventually, though, right?'

'I think so, yes.'

'Because the numbers will only go up. We know that already. Because the demand's been fucking unbelievable, because we're undercutting every legitimate fucking exporter!' JD had been picking up speed. He ended on a shout.

'JD, what the fuck are you getting at?'

'Who are you going to *deal* with when we get to the new office, Mike?' The question was calm, and utterly triumphant.

'I—' Mike stopped himself. They were going to go back to the same guys who had been such excellent customers the past two months, the vendors who were allowing them their magical profit. Except that, with each successive fold…

'How's it going to look, Mike, when we keep reappearing as a different company every three months, and every three months the dogs come around asking for the company we just killed? The Indian guy and the tough-looking yob? Coming and going, different disguise every three months. And the VAT officers, they *ask* love, they keep asking for the last disguise. Those two. Those two. Same two. Two fucking scam artists.'

There was silence. Mike nodded to himself.

'I'm going back to bed,' he said. 'Meeting tomorrow?'

'I should fucking well hope so,' said JD and hung up.

Disappearing wasn't difficult. Coming back had suddenly become the big problem. There was a voice at the other end of every phone call, a face that nodded and smiled and haggled every time a deal went through, someone who signed the cheques they were cashing, or, at the very least, a guy who had made the ATM run so that he could get a payment across to them. Fucking *people*.

~

The boys met in Russell Square the next morning, Mike and Aziz on a bench with JD pacing before them. They were only concerned with the possible fixes.

'The first thing is to slow it down, take the foot off the pedal,' JD said. 'We'll cap it at a million circling through the system. That's roughly three thousand phones. We'll still pull our profits out. At loop twenty-four, that'll be twenty-four thousand each. We each keep fifteen grand and drop nine back in.'

His hands stuffed into his jacket pockets, JD paused as if there'd been a question. His breath frosted as he went on. 'We've still got a staff to pay, and three more companies with VAT numbers to buy within the next month and half.'

'That leaves eighteen runs over ten weeks,' Mike said. 'Now how do you reckon we're going to cover our asses with the vendors so that the folds don't have them getting up our asses every time?'

JD looked to Aziz, who said nothing, and continued, 'We're going to have to spread it thin. Thirty phones here, twelve there, door to door if we have to.'

'Then we may as well get back into smuggling,' Mike said. 'Peddling little contraband packages in the grey market, only now it's telecom instead of booze.'

JD smiled. 'Yeah, at ten times the profit and no bloody weekends in bloody Calais. Aziz, can you and Sumit work the phones to find us some quasi-legit traders?'

Aziz nodded, still saying nothing. Even for Aziz, he was being exceptionally quiet,

'We'll need to drop our rates a bit and bargain like

motherfuckers...' JD stopped again, looking at Aziz, and felt a real pang of remorse. Aziz had come to them with the loophole, and their design and execution had a fundamental flaw. 'Look, Aziz, I—'

Aziz waved JD off, shaking his head. 'Nah,' he said. 'I should have seen this coming, up top. It's not that. It's a spec run and I'm pretty sure we'll figure. I'm just trying to see how we can pull the cash out in white. That's the trick, I think.'

It was a promising idea. If they could take the profits, make them legal, and then rejoin the stream... it was a big if.

JD thought that it would just delay the inevitable. The white money would re-enter the system again but it didn't change the problem. The *problem* wasn't going anywhere. The problem was the fold. The fold made them the money, and the fold was going to hamstring them every time out.

~

Mike covered amazing ground after the emergency meeting in Russell Square. He never pushed, never coerced, never tempted. He was just a guy who showed up, sold some phones and disappeared. Fifteen phones. Twenty-seven phones. They spread it thin, almost invisible.

But the inevitable problems occurred. Because quantities were smaller, vendors were less inclined to pay up on time. With the vendor payments lagging, it was harder to get the stock in on time. Which meant that the vendors who hadn't paid were fucking it up for the ones who had. And that fucked it up for Mike, JD and Aziz, because creating demand was a continuous process of delivering on promises—you brought stock in on a Friday because of a promise you'd made to a vendor three Tuesdays ago. And you'd made *that* promise because you didn't want him to going to someone else, not when he'd been so good about paying on time.

They needed a nice injection of cash to keep things flowing smoothly, to grease the loop. Someone, JD decided, needed to pay them. Pay them up front. And pay big.

JD made his decision on his own, two weeks into February. By then, they had an intricate database of mobile phone vendors through London and most of the large cities in the UK. He found Cleartone, a relatively new London firm that had a reputation for being supremely disorganized, and having money to burn. He'd had his eye on them since January and—with the annoying chop and change haggling they were swamped in—it had been too much of a temptation. JD blitzed them three times in two weeks, selling them six hundred phones, then eight, then a thousand.

It sorted out the cash flow for a while, almost to the end of the quarter, and made all the other gritty little deals less of a nuisance. Just like JD thought it would. It was a good play, JD thought.

On 14 March, as per plan, without the slightest indication, they killed the first trading company.

~

On 14 April, the three original members of the board paused. The phones came in and went out, but all three of them watched the day pass like the whole scam depended on it, since it did. It was three months since they'd launched, and the original group of vendors would be seeking their reclaims on the VAT. Reclaims that were now lining their pockets. If the dogs sniffed anything, it would show now.

A week slid by. Nothing. Not a whisper. The volume of phones they brought in from the EU began to rise again.

At half ten on the morning of the 24th, JD's mobile rang. He didn't recognize the number and he hesitated for a second. Unknown numbers were rare. Mostly because Mike and he were the ones who did the calling, pushing the phones on the market.

The unknown number stared at JD from his mobile for another three seconds.

'Yes?'

'Jai Singh Dewan?'

'That's right.'

'I'm calling on behalf of Cleartone.'

Someone had taken the trouble to trace his personal mobile number. Shit was adding up in all sorts of wrong ways here.

'Yes?'

'Cleartone,' the caller repeated. 'Clear. Tone.' The man's voice was crisp with fury. 'We bought some phones off you, mate.'

'Uh. Just a minute, sir.'

'Sure. Mate.'

JD leaned back in his chair. He hooked a drawer with his foot, pulled it open and then pushed it shut. He ruffled through some papers on his desk. He had all the figures in his head. He was simply trying to decide what to do. Face-offs with the dogs on the M25 didn't prepare you for this.

'That would be three orders? Twenty-four hundred pieces in total?'

'Bang on.' The caller waited. 'Mate,' he said.

'What seems to be the problem?' JD had the earnestness right, the desire to please, like all the boys who ran shops on the street he lived on.

'Think about it,' the caller said. 'I'll ask again tomorrow.' He hung up.

JD looked at the mobile for a while. Not so good then, he thought.

There was only one decision to make. Did he deal with this on his own? Or did he call Mike?

The decision to blitz Cleartone had been his. Therefore, so was the fallout.

~

There was no follow-up call the next day. JD hadn't expected one. The theory here—and he'd seen Mike pull this stunt a dozen times—was to let the other guy stew in the *anticipation* of the call. JD activated Sumit and they began to gather a Cleartone file. What he uncovered, and the facts were just about as easy to gather as it must have been for those boys to access his phone number, wasn't pretty. It didn't faze him. But, for the first time, the concept of fucking due diligence had been underlined for him.

On the morning of the 26th, JD's phone flashed 'private number' and he answered right away. This time, he was ready.

Within a minute, JD said, 'So what's the trouble, sir? Where are you going to do better than two ninety plus VAT? Three hundred forty quid per unit's a steal.'

'It is at that, mate,' the caller agreed. 'Especially when you're walking away with the VAT.'

'Well, now, there's a troubling allegation. I assume you'll be taking your concerns straight to Excise? I mean, obviously if you've been defrauded the exchequer would recognize you as the injured party and you'll still have paid ten quid below wholesale for each phone. It sounds to me you're making out just lovely.'

'Perhaps. But I reckon I can do better.'

So Cleartone wanted to pay even less for the phones than they already did, they still wanted to charge VAT, and they still wanted their reclaims.

It was his scam, his and Mike's and Aziz's. And these cunts wanted in.

'I'll have to speak to my partners.'

'Jolly that, mate. Take a week.'

JD clicked off. Then he scrawled 'Gary Block' on the pad in front of him and underlined it. Gary Block, whose garage made so many things disappear.

~

On 2 May, JD's mobile rang for the second time in an hour. He simply looked at it for a moment. He was still breathing hard, still trying to climb down from the previous phone call. When he saw who it was, he knew that the word was on the streets for sure. His last threat had been good for that much.

Here we go, he thought. Another example of how quick the fucking world had changed. Contraband was a cinch. Bloody VAT was evolving before his eyes like a virus. On the third ring, he answered, steeling himself for what was bound to follow.

'Yeah, Aziz.'

Aziz was ridiculously polite, like he was discussing the weather with a stranger. That, in some ways, thought JD, was absolutely true.

'Who are Cleartone, Jai?'

JD could've stalled, turned it into another argument. But it was time to reestablish the inner circle of the game.

'They're a London vendor I blitzed three times in February.'

JD heard Aziz leaf through papers at his desk. He didn't have to look very far.

'Twenty-four hundred phones. A hundred and twenty thousand pounds of your foot on the pedal. Or was it someone else's idea that we slow things down a bit?'

'That would be me.'

'Well, I suppose it was a fine idea for other people. When did they call you?' Aziz paused, made sure that he was asking the right question. 'The first time?'

'Last week. The 24th.'

'Last week,' Aziz mused. 'So much for the three-company

filter. Basically anyone with a free half hour could get your personal mobile number.'

'It's a laundering front. They're turning black money. If they were going to be fucking monitors then they would've gone straight to Excise.'

'Do you think I care?'

JD was silent. He had nothing to say.

'I'm going to ignore the fact that you didn't come to either Mike or myself last week. Call it your executive decision. That's your fucking business. But—' For the first time, Aziz's voice began to rise. 'When Cleartone called back this morning, and both you morons started trading threats, d'you reckon that you might have mentioned it to either of us at some point?'

'How did you know?'

'Fuck! It doesn't matter!' Aziz stopped himself. When he spoke again, he sounded calmer. 'We're all plugged into the same networks, JD. When you throw out the names of Chelsea drug dealers with Russian connections, people start to panic. It isn't exactly the norm in tax scams.' Aziz paused again. 'You're going to get all types here. These guys aren't legit traders. And they'll come after you *because* they aren't legit. Because they get their reclaims anyway.'

'I understand that,' JD cut in. 'That's what got me so pissed off, man. We're not nosing into any of their games, but they want to shove in on ours. You can pull scams without being a cunt about it.'

'You weren't to know that they were dickheads,' Aziz agreed. 'But you didn't deal with it. You can't pull smuggling stunts here.'

JD bit his lower lip. Hard. Deliberately. He was furious.
'All right.'

'It's not all right. It's about patience, Jai. We both know
that. But this is the thing, and this is what I'm trying to say to
you: patience doesn't come naturally. It's like anything that
matters, anything that makes a difference—you have to work
at it. You have to hold the pose, the posture, whatever you
want to call it. Hold it. Pretend to be patient. Every day. Live
it until it's real. And then, maybe, if you're ready, if you've
earned it, it will be real. And if it comes, it's because you're
been ready for it your entire waking life.'

JD continued to prod the wound in his mouth with his
tongue. He kept scraping away the layer of tissue that was
trying to stem the flow of blood. He felt sweat running down
the back of his neck. Patience would have helped, sure, but
no philosophy was going to fix the fundamental flaw in the
design of the game. He was *sure* of that. *Everything* was about
the game. Aziz was right that he'd been impatient, but his
impatience had shown off a crack in the very basis of the
system. They had to go back to the system.

What was the difference between what they were doing
here and what they had been pulling out in Calais? That was
the question. Fuck patience.

Calais had been a closed system, a closed loop. So how did
he sell phones to the world at large and make that a closed
system? How did he close the loop?

'Jai, are you there?'

'Just thinking.' JD grinned. He didn't know it, but the grin
was stained a pale red. 'About what you said.'

~

In the end, Mike took over. Aziz wanted to make a payment, hand over a fat chunk of flesh to make sure that Cleartone kept the information to themselves. But once JD had had his arse handed to him to Mike's satisfaction, he could see that his friend had a point. It was the principle of the thing.

Cleartone had about as much style as they had class, Mike observed. They had a cookie-cutter storefront on Tollington Road next to a Burger King, both of them housed in the Holloway Road Nag's Head shopping centre. From his parking space across the street, Mike could see most of the office through the glass front. Rows of young men sat at long tables without dividers, tapping at laptops and chattering into headsets. They looked eager and clean and yet somehow nervously arrogant.

Dotcom cunts.

But none of them were his man. The director, a lawyer named Daniel Terry, was fifteen years older than any of them. Mike had watched him come out of and return to his back office twice in the half hour since he'd parked, comparing the face against his memory of the printout Sumit had given him, which he'd then shredded. For a money launderer, Terry didn't mind plastering his own face all over the Cleartone website. He probably thought of himself as just a very cunning entrepreneur, like so many of the cheap little internet thieves Mike had read about.

The lads started shutting down their machines and filing out at a quarter to five. By a quarter after, the front office was empty. Having already checked the parking lot for a back door, Mike knew he was covering the only way out.

He slipped on his gloves. If Terry wasn't out by six, Mike decided, he would go in. Going into Terry's office wouldn't have quite the same effect as what Mike was hoping to do, but it would do.

Popping the glove box, Mike took out the short flathead screwdriver and slid it tip-first up the left sleeve of his leather jacket. He didn't know if he'd have to use it or not, but working in daylight called for more options than a late night job.

At ten of six, he came out of the back office again, a man as tall as Mike and about one-and-a-half times as wide. He pulled on an overcoat. Mike started the car. When Terry stepped out onto the sidewalk, Mike saw that the printout hadn't done justice to the sculpture that was Terry's hair. It was the latest, a shiny black, swirling tribute to male preening and product, angled just so about the ears.

Like Russian nightclubs, you never knew how truly ugly and absurd some things were until you saw middle-aged fat men in them.

Terry turned and locked the storefront door. When he started walking west toward Holloway instead of east to go around to the parking lot, Mike turned off the ignition and got out. He let Terry finish the block to Holloway and turn south before he started trailing him at roughly twenty metres.

The underground station was dead ahead two blocks but it would only mean more time if Terry went in. Mike had set aside plenty of that this evening, as much as it took, and it was simple to watch someone from the next car when they didn't know you.

Mike noticed something about Daniel Terry's shoulders as he stalked the man, the easy confidence with which they were thrown back. Despite his girth, he still managed to lead with his chest. Being fat hadn't beset Terry late in life, he'd always been that way. He'd always been the biggest bloke in the room, had never worked at it, had never even tried to shape it into anything but brute mass.

Mike had known lots of that type—the bloated, cackling fuckers who always sat too close to your date at the pub. Rugby bullies.

Quickening his pace, Mike's fingers curled around the handle of the screwdriver as Terry closed in on the underground entrance. He was twenty feet from it at most when he turned left and pulled open a door. Rapid male voices blared out of it and flashing neon bathed Terry's face for an instant before he went in. Mike winced and let out a breath.

'Sports bar.'

There were six TVs in cages along the ceiling above a horseshoe bar at which sat maybe a dozen men, not a girl anywhere—it was early yet, and Mike was glad for that. The voices that practically vibrated in the wood countertop when he took a stool towards the middle of the horseshoe weren't those of the patrons but of the dozen commentators dangling above their heads. Mike quickly eyed all the matches—the most recent was from three days ago.

Terry was sitting seven seats to Mike's left, in the corner of his vision. He was alone but it seemed he could strike up a conversation with anyone in the place easily enough. They all dressed alike—Mike picked out four men in blue shirts with white collars—and they all had that hair.

Day traders.

The pint came and he fought the temptation to down the whole thing in a few gulps, promising himself not to drink more than half of it in the next twenty minutes. This wasn't to be a fight, it wasn't to be done drunkenly with joy and abandon. Well, definitely not with abandon.

Six minutes later, Daniel Terry headed towards the bathroom. Measuring his breath, Mike let the handle of the screwdriver drop fully into his palm, counted ten seconds, and went in.

The bathroom was empty except for two feet in one of the stalls. The stall door was closed and the feet were facing the toilet.

Shy boy, thought Mike.

The bathroom door had a lock on it, but Mike left it unlocked. If someone tried the door, he wanted it to stay shut but to still give a little. That would confuse anyone who tried it from the other side, without triggering the suspicion a locked door that's usually unlocked tends to. Mike had had the same plan for Terry's office, or for any door they might find themselves behind, just the two of them.

He crouched, pulled the screwdriver from his left sleeve with his right hand, and slammed it expertly between the door and the jamb. It would give at a hard kick, but it would take a hell of a lot to make a law-abiding citizen kick a door. And this wouldn't take that long.

Mike went to the sink and ran the water until Terry

emerged from the stall and stood behind him. Mike looked up into the mirror and smiled.

'Hello, love,' he said, and threw his elbow into Daniel Terry's face.

Terry's nose gushed as he stumbled back and Mike stepped into him, driving a right hook into his stomach before he had any chance to catch his footing. As Terry doubled over, Mike stepped around him, grabbed his throat from behind, and dug his thumb into the pressure point behind his ear.

With his left hand, he twisted Terry's left wrist behind his back and guided him to his knees.

'Think it about it,' he said quietly.

Terry said nothing, gasping for air, and Mike glanced at the doorknob—steady.

'I'm not choking you, by the way. It will take you a minute to get your breath back. I'm not stopping that. Not yet.' Mike put more pressure on Terry's wrist. 'In the meantime, think about it. Who am I? Why am I here?'

Mike gave it a few seconds.

'Ph-phones?'

'There we are. Now. We all know what we all do and the—'

The doorknob twisted and the wood creaked against the screwdriver jammed in it. There came a knock and a confused, 'Hello?'

'We've had an accident in here and I think it's jammed,' Mike called out, tightening his grip on Terry's throat. 'Just stand back, okay?'

'Right, er…' The voice trailed off.

'Well, since I haven't got time for speeches about unspoken codes I'll just assume you take my point. Besides, it's not much of an unspoken code if we speak about it.'

He could see Daniel Terry's face turning a brighter red. He could feel the man's pulse through the leather gloves. He had just a few seconds left. He leaned close to Terry's ear.

'Next time you get the notion you're a member of fucking Parliament,' he said, 'just remember: you're not even safe taking a piss.'

Terry passed out and Mike rolled him onto his back. He pulled the screwdriver from the door, sleeved it, and opened the door.

'I think this man's had a heart attack!' he told the man on the other side of the door. Then, to the rest of the bar, he shouted, 'Is anybody here a doctor?'

Patrons were rushing to the bathroom as Mike slipped out of the bar and headed for the underground. He'd come back for his car after dark. Well after.

I'm giving myself three more months, he thought. This gig has things to recommend for it.

~

JD found himself in a store, absently looking at jackets and boots. He'd seen the 'Sale' sign out of the corner of his eye and wandered in automatically. JD had been stockpiling jackets and boots ever since he'd had money to spend. It was compulsive.

Ordinarily, he hated shopping, but jackets and boots were different. He had shitkickers and hiking boots, MC jackets and dusters. They could take wind and cold and rain. They were anti-shock, anti-melt, anti-slip. A habit was a habit, and here he was feeding it.

But the store was a bust. There was nothing here. Besides, there was too much going on in his head for him to focus on anything. He found himself trying to find a fix for the game they were running. He'd found himself doing that almost constantly since his bollocking from Aziz three days ago.

JD swung around, meaning to leave, and his eye fell on a white guy of about twenty-five or so, who was examining a gas cartridge camping stove with great concentration. JD shook his head. The guy had never been in a field in his life, he could bet on it. He'd seen the type before. They were usually part of the drug crowd, and camping equipment made it easy for them to operate out of garages. There had been a growing storm about how weed was being cut, about how they were getting lit, night after night, on something that was essentially bits of ground glass with a measure of cannabis thrown in for the smell. But it was always fucking hilarious, finding a solicitous ganja-growing fuckwit trying to blend into an outdoor goods store. The most exercise this guy ever got was probably a walk down the hall to take a long piss while wondering about where he was going to order food from.

The guy must've felt someone looking at him. He turned to look over his shoulder, trying to be as casual as possible, and was startled to find JD staring straight at him, grinning widely. JD kept grinning until the guy looked away nervously. He looked back at JD, this time a quick, untidy peek. JD was still there, like a statue, the smile spray-painted onto his face,

impossible to ignore. The guy had had enough. He dumped
the stove back on the counter and bolted. He was going so
quick, still sneaking glances at JD, that he walked straight into
the two men walking into the store. And then the grin was
wiped off JD's face and he looked on, unbelieving.

They were larger than life, the two men walking in
through the door, like they had been six months ago. They
still moved like they were bookends, like they were props.
And they were still the same Punch and Judy combination,
the strange, loveable marriage of size, reggae and the Spurs.

'It's a sale, man—' began Kenneth as the white guy
bounced off him. Kenneth didn't even notice him. It was
Alistair who saw JD first. Kenneth saw the look on his face
and turned. JD was standing by the rack with the jackets,
shaking his head, the grin having returned full force. He
began to move towards them. Kenneth's rumble went
through the store.

'It's dat crazy boy.' He enveloped JD in a bone-crushing
hug. It had been a May like that, a May where you hugged
strangers who you liked a great deal.

The three of them moved out of the store in minutes,
in search of a pub this time, capping the second meeting in
the way they should have capped the first one. For the first
time in days, VAT was the furthest thing from JD's mind. But
after a few pints and many stories, it began to sneak in again.
Because, based on the experiences of the past few weeks,
who was to say that they wouldn't be needing bodyguards?

2.2

It was a Monday, and Mondays had their rituals.

Val got her cup of tea and spent twenty minutes typing out her resignation with two-fingered ferocity. She printed it out and then signed it, 'Valerie Jean Stewart' in her neat, angular handwriting, then she put the letter in an envelope addressed to Wexler, and sealed it. She would leave it in the first drawer in her desk, and there it would stay until Friday evening. If she made it through the week, she took the letter home with her and she and Ken would read it before heading out. She always threw it away the next morning.

That first Monday, five years ago, she'd really meant to resign, but writing the letter had been a sobering and oddly calming exercise. Simply putting down the words had cut through the frustration that had provoked the resignation in the first place. Val saw that, most of all, she was still better off with the job than without it because the job kept her in line. It was necessary balance. And, therefore, the letter belonged in the bin. But the letter was a reminder, a clamp on her stubborn mind. So she put it in the drawer as a flag, something she would see a half a dozen times every day.

Val dropped the letter into the drawer. At ten minutes to nine, most people on her floor weren't even in yet. But her clock ran her. She cast an eye over the stack in her 'In' tray and pulled out the thickest file first. It was the end of the month, and she was on her rubber-stamp tour of monthly and quarterly files.

The first file—the thick one—was the VAT review.

~

JD was roaring drunk, sitting in his bedroom. He'd been a good boy. It had been seven months since he'd ridden this particular train, all the way back to when they blew up the booze game with the biggest motherfucking Schillachi anyone could remember. They had been the guys who had done that, him and Mike.

And here they were, along with a whiz-kid, hotshot immigrant lawyer, trying to be some sort of half-arsed businessmen, walking around and around a system that could blow the roof off the city and they couldn't find a way in. They were sitting on a goldmine and they were drawing nothing but small retailers out of Southall. It was fucking brutal.

JD had lived with it for weeks and he had finally driven himself into a fit four days ago. When JD went quiet at meetings, Mike shook his head at Aziz to let it slide. He knew the geography, Mike did. There was a rumble in the distance and JD had no idea whether it was a good one or a bad one.

In the end, JD had taken a surprisingly rational decision:

he hadn't gone into work for the past two days and he'd switched off his phone. If there was an emergency, Mike knew where to find him.

He'd been drinking steadily for about thirty hours. It had been scientific, thought JD with a grin. He found a level around four in the afternoon yesterday and he'd let the flag hang there, doing just enough for maintenance. His room was like a tomb. It was like he'd dropped in through a crack in the world, as if the world had been bleached of his personality. *This* was impotence. This was his worth dissipating before his eyes. And it pulled him deeper, like a bed of sand while castles crumbled, washed away by fucking time.

He sat at the desk, smoking, trying to force a game for the first time in his life. He pulled out his phone, his cigarettes and lighter, and discarded packets of chewing gum and ranged them across his desk. They were his pieces, elements in the system that he was trying to control. He sat there with a pen and he followed the chain over and over again. We bring in the phone without VAT, we sell the phone with VAT, we disappear. And we can't come back. How's that? All in spite of the three-company stack that Mr Magic dreamt up.

Try as he might, he couldn't close the loop. He couldn't insulate them from the outside world.

Fucking people.

The focus wavered and then finally went at about ten. JD had thrown the kitchen sink at it and there had been nothing. He turned to the Jameson's and let the balance go. He felt old and used. There was nothing left but to drink it down and go to sleep.

JD tipped his chair back. This was a game he'd played since he was a kid. There was a point, if you were careful about the balance and you stayed still enough, where the chair would stay upright on its own. He knew the chair, and he knew the carpet, but it always took him a few attempts, going back and forth. Inevitably the chair went too far back, or JD didn't go far enough and the chair would thump back onto the floor. But it was immensely satisfying every time. JD never thought about it much, but he suspected that it was because it was something you could do easily, if you were careful, if you were concentrating. It didn't depend on anything else. The chair, the floor and the man in the seat. Nothing else.

He shook his head slightly, smiling. It was a closed loop.

JD was holding his pen in his right hand. He began to flick it between his fingers, turning it over and over until it was a blur, like he was Cozy Powell at the end of a hook in Donnington—waiting while the band kicked and held—before he hit the cymbal and they went again. He had gotten very good at it, like it was a magic trick. He could make the pen disappear.

He hit top speed and the pen flew out of his hand. It struck the door and ricocheted under his bed.

JD frowned. The pen hadn't gotten away from him in a long time. Retrieval was going to be a bitch. He got off the chair and shuffled toward the bed, aware that he was moving like an old man, and finding it hilarious. He knelt next to the bed and tried to peer underneath, then stretched out and lay on the floor, his stomach to the ground, one cheek on the carpet. He looked around owlishly and finally located the pen, snagged it on the third try. Not bothering to get up, he examined the pen fiercely. The question of the pen's behaviour was suddenly the most important thing in the world. He held it at arms' length, above him, so that it was a silhouette against the ceiling lamp. In his head, the pulse ran and ran. It wasn't a big deal. What the fuck had happened? It wasn't a big—

He grunted. The cap had been on the wrong end. JD had a belated realization about just how drunk he was. He pulled the cap off and put it back where it belonged, on the other end. He twirled the pen experimentally once, just to see if it still worked, if he still had it. He got through three and a half full revolutions before the pen slipped out of his hand and he was asleep on the carpet.

He'd fallen asleep a couple of times with a lit cigarette the previous year and that was the first warning he'd had about his drinking getting out of hand. He could go for months without a drink, but when he got on the train, it was usually to the bitter end. All that remained, the final act to the weekend, was to determine whether the ride was done for the night or whether he'd wake up and decide he had a few more stations to blaze through.

He jerked awake two minutes later, his breathing erratic. He had the usual moment of supreme disorientation. Where the fuck was he and how long had it been? Sometimes he lost minutes, other times hours. He looked around. It had been minutes. His eye fell on the pen on the carpet. The pen, with the cap on the right end this time. And the rest of the weekend came crawling back to him, wearing its shit-eating grin. Yes. Sure. Ah.

It was another closed loop in front of him. If you want the motherfucker to spin right, have the cap on the right end.

JD blinked.

He sat up slowly and crossed his legs. He felt himself waking with a rush, the buzz from the alcohol beaten back by something much more substantial. It was like an orgasm and a splash of ice water all at once.

JD grabbed the pen, jumped up and crossed to his desk. The pieces were still arranged there. His eyes swept through the system, but he wasn't really looking at the desk any more. He'd seen through it, once, and now he couldn't see it any other way. He took a piece of paper and wrote:

'A'. And then, below it: 'B'. He looked at it for a moment. Below it, he wrote:

'We own A. We own B.'

He smiled, his eyes still on the paper.

'That's right. We own everything,' he said. 'We are the Lizard King.'

He capped the pen, tossed it to the back of the desk, picked up the glass of whisky and drained it in a long swallow.

'Cheers.' His eyes shone. He nodded. 'Cheers.'

~

The second legendary meeting between the three men took place at the old warehouse at eight-thirty the next evening. The boxes of drinking glasses under the tables had long been replaced by boxes of mobile phones. It was the 28 June, the day they turned the corner.

JD was the last to arrive. Mike had been at the warehouse for much of the day. He normally clocked a couple of hours in the morning and then went off to lunch. The system was so streamlined that he could head home after lunch on most days and nap. He would head back to the warehouse around three in the afternoon and sort out his follow-ups.

Aziz got in from a long day at work. The constant shift between directing a growing scam and helping the rich get richer at his day job was beginning to grate on him. He knew now how it worked. People got rich on apathy—that was the fertilizer that fuelled fortunes. The people who got rich did things that other people didn't want to do. In twenty years' time the world was going to be about the rich and the poor; there would be nobody in the middle. He intended to be on the right side when it happened.

JD let himself into the warehouse at eight-thirty-one, munching on a sausage roll. He went straight to the pantry and bustled about. He found cups and milk and then tossed aside their regular teabags and reached for the Twinings that Aziz had instituted.

JD plonked the cups on the table and sat down.

'Anyone got a cigarette?' he asked. Aziz slid across his packet of Marlboro Lights.

'Pussy fags, A,' JD muttered, lighting the cigarette nonetheless. 'It's the taste at the end of them, mate, lights. They're...' he struggled for the right word. 'Unpalatable,' he finished. 'Like smoking a sponge. That's been dipped in nicotine.' He clamped the cigarette in the corner of his mouth, eyes half-lidded against the smoke, and reached out for a piece of paper.

'We made a mistake up top,' he said. His eyes flicked from
Mike to Aziz. 'Or at least I did,' he amended after a pause.
He quickly drew a set of three boxes, one below the other.

'Call them 'A', 'B' and 'C',' he said, inking in the names
beside each of the boxes, running them in order—A to C.
'This is a part of the chain that we're part of, right? Now,
think of 'A' as the importer here. They're the ones—legit
and non-legit—who bring the stock in from the EU. Okay?'

Aziz and Mike nodded.

'So 'B' and 'C' become obvious, right? Same as any retail
chain. Importer, goes to vendors, and then they in turn sell
to the smaller retailers.'

JD drew on the cigarette and then stubbed it out. He
looked at the diagram carefully. He nodded.

'The mistake I made was thinking that we were a
'B' company.'

Mike suddenly sat back in his chair, and the tension
disappeared from his face. He looked up at the ceiling and
exhaled, shaking his head.

'Motherfucker,' he said softly.

Aziz felt the familiar mixture of confusion and irritation.
In a room with these two, it was a regular occurrence. It made
him feel like an outsider, like he missed the joke every time.

'I don't understand,' he said. JD nodded and began to
speak faster now.

'If we're the 'B' company, which is what we've been
behaving as, then it's impossible for us to isolate ourselves. It's
impossible, because we're smack in the middle of the chain.

The vendors you sell to will trip you up eventually, not the government. Because we touch so many people. But think of us as 'A'. All you do is put another company in the middle, at level 'B'. Level 'B' buys every single fucking phone from us, and it sells to whoever wants the phone—everybody—selling *and declaring* everything. It's completely legitimate. 'B' are good boys. But every three months, when reclaim time shows up, the company they bought phones from, paying VAT, the 'A' company, has disappeared. You can't doubt 'B', because every other transaction they've made is completely above board, and on paper. All the way down the three months. They get their reclaims and carry on. But, *this time*, there's no issue with word getting around because—'

'Because we own 'B' as well,' finished Mike.

This game had what the first system lacked, that elusive little knot that was going to allow them to disappear. The Cleartone scenario would never arise here, it couldn't. Not if they *were* Cleartone in the first place. 'B' would declare everything. They would simply be unfortunate enough to be buying from a crooked importer. 'B' would get a good-boy lecture from Excise—be more careful about who you deal with—and they would, of course, deal with someone else for the next quarter. Except—and what do you know!—that those guys would be crooked too.

'We'd probably have to kill the 'B' company and set up another one every six months,' said JD. 'Otherwise they'd throw up all kinds of wrong signals, an honest company with a hundred percent record of buying from crooked importers.' He shrugged. 'Apart from that…'

Apart from that, this one would stick. This one was infinite.

Aziz looked up and JD grinned at him.

'You can only close a loop if you're either at the beginning of the chain, or at the end of it. That's it. That's what we missed.'

Aziz shook his head.

'I should've seen it,' he said. It was a basic tax dodge. You posed as your own consumer and you could drive figures both ways. You're not making a profit because of the cost of raw materials, but you're buying your raw materials from a company that you owned. Aziz hadn't thought it possible to pull that scam in a system as open as the one they'd been struggling with. He had thought that there were too many people involved, too many possible snags. Except JD had taken exactly those things and used it for camouflage.

Aziz sighed and nodded.

'I guess that puts the Dubai trip on the back-burner for a bit.'

Both Mike and JD stopped. Aziz looked at both of them, amused and exasperated at the same time.

'Where the fuck else do you think we're going to turn all of this white? Glasgow?'

There was a second of silence. JD mouthed 'Glasgow' and Mike shook his head, and then all three of them were laughing. The sound rose out of the office, into the pink glow of the dying evening, and it was the sound of a promise.

JD sat up in his chair. The eyes were still laughing, but the tone was soft and serious.

'Right,' he said. 'Who wants to be a millionaire?'

~

JD told Aziz about the men he wanted to front the 'B' company in hushed tones in one of the Private Gaming rooms at the Palm Casino in Mayfair. The criterion for these two men, according to JD, was simply that they had shown up at the right time.

Aziz had gotten JD and Mike Palm Beach memberships the moment they had cleared the first loop of the first system. And it was here that Aziz realized for the first time how necessary Mike was. Because Aziz, beyond a point, simply couldn't understand JD.

Aziz had become a member at the Palm a year ago. He had no urge to gamble. Half his clients moved through the Palm during any given week. The *real* meetings took place here, between games of blackjack and poker, somewhere around the third single malt.

From the first set of flutters at the roulette table, Aziz began to see the paradox that controlled JD. In spite of his talent and his imagination for margins and loopholes, JD was a degenerate gambler at heart. He believed in ritual, he believed in cycles and signs. And he believed that the game would claim them in the end. The house would win. It ran through the core of who JD was. And this knowledge was what allowed him his reckless abandon— the genius that he brought to the game. Because there was nothing to lose.

'I really don't see how you stumble into a couple of stray Rastas and decide—'

'You've got to trust me, A. Nine months down the line from your pitch and you still don't know what I am? No.' JD was smiling. 'You knew, and you know. I'm still that guy. But the money's going to turn in about two weeks and we're a month away from being legitimate millionaires, so it's sending all sorts of twitchy signals to your brain. Don't trust it.'

He was dead serious, but he was also gentle. They were in an extraordinary situation, he and the man across the table from him, learning the plot as they went along. There was no natural learning curve here.

'Now that that's settled,' JD said, 'I think I may have—*may have*—figured out another way to sweeten the game. Shall I tell you about it?'

Aziz had looked at him, half amused, and nodded.

~

'It's simple,' said JD. The casino continued to churn around them. 'I'm gonna go on a naming binge here, bear with me. French Communications—Dijon Phones, right? Sells to our 'A' company.'

'Atlas?' said Aziz.

'Atlas Trading,' JD agreed. 'Dijon has the stock sent into our freight company in London. The stock is under the name of the importer—Atlas—who will allocate it to the next company and so on. The importer buys at 100 without VAT and offers it to the 'B' company—our Jamaican boys— at ninety-five plus VAT. They in turn add their fifty pence and offer it to *us*—a third, new company further down the chain—at ninety-six plus VAT.'

Aziz stilled and grinned. Here it was, the next tweak.

JD nodded.

'You like that? Myself, I love it. We market the product, get top dollar and decide how much we want to keep with us as profit. One, two, three pounds. Send the rest down the chain. So…' JD made a lazy gesture with his hands.

Aziz complied.

'So on a hundred-pound phone, we have at the importer ninety-five, plus seventeen-and-a-half per cent VAT. Total of a hundred and eleven, minus our cost of a hundred. That's GBP eleven pound sixty. At five thousand pieces, that's approximately fifty-eight thousand pounds a day.' Aziz paused and showed his teeth. 'What we're talking about here is a systematic induced inflation. We're driving the entire chain. By being the entire chain.'

'We be 'A'. We be 'B'. We be 'C',' said JD with satisfaction.

'Fifty-eight thousand pounds a day, huh?' asked Aziz.

'Rolling,' concluded JD. 'Every day.'

Aziz let the twist run through his head. Four in the morning, surfing single malt, still locked in. God, he could get used to this.

'I can't be the director in this company,' he said after a while. 'Not when I'm running the Freight Forwarder. Split it. I'll run the logistics chain, and you guys set up the buffer company chain.' He smiled. 'It's time to see what you guys look like in suits.'

~

They had the luxury of being able to argue about the name. The 'C' company meant permanence. Discovering the knot between the 'A' and 'B' companies had allowed JD to understand the *actual* VAT scam. The profits came from the volumes. And seeing that, in turn, had allowed JD to shift the axis to a point further down the chain, a space they hadn't occupied yet. They needed to show up as a big, flashy operation at the 'C' level.

'This one never folds, right?' asked JD. The three of them were having the conversation as they walked, looking for some place that would serve them something to eat. It was late. It was always late. Aziz couldn't show at meetings until almost ten on most evenings. And they'd instituted a blanket ban on donner kebab joints. They were looking for a Turkish guy selling burgers.

'It can't,' said Aziz. 'Works both ways. The 'C' company shows the 'B' company as being legitimate. Therefore, we're above board on this one. There's some mutual back-scratching going on here.'

'Two months on average per 'A' company,' said Mike. 'Because that's the obvious evil. Six months on every 'B' company, because otherwise it's just unbelievable, them getting fucked at every turn. But this one's permanent in the display window.'

They found themselves on a bench, clutching styrofoam containers, passing two cans of Coke between themselves. JD sat on the backrest, his feet on the bench. Aziz was listening to him, while Mike stood in front of them, watching both.

'Call it the Principle,' said JD. Mike raised an eyebrow.

'P-L-E. Princi*ple*. Not fucking principal.'

'Why?' asked Aziz.

'In programming terms, this is unique. Instead of the program running the system—in this case, 'declare the VAT'—our little system is running the program. We engage, we *pay*, when we want. But our system is set up so that it all looks picture-perfect.' He chucked his container into the bin next to the bench. 'Don't call us. You don't need to. Instead, *we'll* call you.' He looked from Mike to Aziz and then back to Mike again. 'In programming terms, that's the Hollywood Principle. "Don't call us, we'll call you." This, though…' he thought about it. 'This is the Heston Principle.'

'Huh.' Mike mused over it. 'If it's a system, why don't we just call it the Heston System.'

JD stared at him. 'You cunt.'

Aziz cracked up and Mike snickered through the side of his mouth.

'Besides, Principle's what U2 call their management company,' JD offered.

'I thought you hated U2,' said Mike after a pause.

'I do. But look at how rich they are.'

~

JD was right about the fronts. Alistair and Kenneth *were* the best possible men for the job. Brian was too valuable to tie down. He was their Swiss army knife, constructing deals, driving the van, and he could beat the payments out of vendors if the occasion arose. He'd been cashing in more and more sick days at work and making runs through Europe for them. If they had to tie Brian down, it had to be on something far more valuable.

There was big money in the 'B' company. Because the chain went all the way down to the retailers that their 'C' level company sold to, it opened up Nokia's entire range of phones to the Principle, not just the Communicators. That would bring in between eleven and fifteen per cent profit per unit, depending on cost price. For the first time since they had rolled the VAT game, they became volume racketeers.

Alistair and Kenneth. Second-generation Jamaicans and, as JD knew, a right fucking godsend when all the signs had been loaded just right at Maidstone. And now the fold. They appeared at necessary times.

All along the line, right from a moment of madness in a room that they still didn't know about, to the last three steps on an aerobridge in Heathrow, years into the future, circumstances colluded. Circumstances colluded like they do three times a century. Things just… *happened*.

JD wasn't surprised at how quickly Alistair and Kenneth bought the pitch over three more pub visits. He was fascinated, though, at how many people would jump at the chance to make a living off the books. He knew how it worked in the Indian community, how ambivalent his dad and his dad's friends were about 'business activities' that weren't strictly legit. If you were making money, it was okay. If you were making money off the government, it was better. You couldn't get rich clean in India, his dad had once told him. You had to take what you could. And somewhere along the way, the moral compass of a generation—his grandfather's, he thought—had simply made the adjustment. When they came to England, they brought the same hunger with them.

And now he saw it all around him. It wasn't a skin thing, a colour thing, although he had believed it was for the longest time, and had been ashamed of it. But he saw it in Alistair and Kenneth, and the larger quarter they represented. JD had feigned shock when they told him about their extracurricular activities running a small piracy racket.

'What, no weed?' he had asked.

Kenneth had fallen about laughing.

'You little racist!' he said. Then, after a pause, he added, 'But sure, man, I could hook you up with someone. We've all got someone we know.'

JD thought that that might've been it, that single statement. All of them had someone they knew. Because all of them needed alternate routes. To get rich, or to get high, or to get the right watch on a tight budget. You did it when you wanted the phone line fixed and when you needed gold because the eldest daughter in the family was getting married.

'Who else are you going to go to?' asked Aziz when JD told him about it. 'The banks? We got no banks. Not really.'

It *wasn't* just an immigrant thing. It was a class thing, pure and simple. This was the cycle that swung around every ten years when people were either rich enough or poor enough to worry about where the real dissatisfaction was coming from. And it became the centre, the diseased heart of the country. Because that was where they wrote the rules, and people chased their tails based on the rules. They'd slink back home, exhausted, unsuccessful, while the bigger wheels just turned and turned, and a world that was never theirs moved further and further away.

You could wave a flag, picket no. 10, burn your fucking bra, riot in Brixton, Notting Hill and Chapeltown, and write some ridiculously good tunes, but that beat would never change. It was as old as Time. The tiny gap between need and want, between desire and a hard kick to the head. Mind that fuckin' gap.

You turned the only way you could. You turned to your own people. The network where someone just knew a guy, and you could get your job done.

Motherfucker, JD had thought. This is a fucking revolution.

~

Toward the end of July, Val found herself looking at a series of unconnected dots on the VAT graph. Beating the VAT trap wasn't a new scam. Customs had known about the chink in the system since 1992, the abolition of barriers to internal trade. Every three or four years, a new group of cowboys would appear on the scene. Val had yet to see a VAT fraud stand the test of time. The money always blew up too quick, and sheer size made identification easy. She was looking at a series of defaults at the importer level. Customs and Excise would normally shut down between ten and twelve companies a month—importers who simply tried to market goods and disappear before the quarter was up. Val knew that her department was probably missing a greater number of defaulters in the grey market, but that was impossible to police. Instead, she extracted vengeance when she saw corporate fraud. Grey market losses were part of the waste in an economy this size.

The reports had no pattern to them. They were files detailing closures and suspensions, nothing out of the ordinary. The only thing that intrigued Val was that the dates matched so closely. It was as if all of the busts had been of companies that were part of a wave without being aware of it.

For a second, her forehead creased. This would be the likely entry-point, if she'd ever decided to design a VAT fraud. Here, lost inside a constant tide of information that ebbed and flowed across six months.

But if it *was* a constructed spike, then it would have to obey certain rules.

Val spent the next three hours creating a graph of the last six months. The vertical axis was time, the horizontal axis was the number of defaults. The distribution should have been random. Instead, she had six spikes, rising from left to right, the signs of positive correlation. Defaults on dates that were, almost unconsciously, close together. By the end of the day, Val knew that she had a scam on her hands.

And, clearly, some kind of genius and audacity had gone into the fine details of the structure, because it hadn't been stopped yet.

Val began to explore context. There had been a slew of applications for VAT numbers, and companies with existing VAT numbers had been changing hands with increasing frequency. She saw a rising number of trading companies that had opened bank accounts in the last three months, and she pulled bank records going back a further three. Definitely a ripple, and definitely gathering momentum. In the last two weeks there had been a series of discrepancies on the VAT reclaim. The dynamic between the vendors and the people they were buying from was interesting. Given the surge of new importers, the number of reclaims should have been much higher. But there was good, careful distribution here. Something had started in January, which meant that she had discovered it at the end of a six-month cycle, two steals in.

What surprised Val was that this could have gone undetected for another six months. Her job was to wield a rubber stamp after a cursory scan. She'd had time, and she'd been playing around with numbers. And she had seen a collection of reports ordinarily never viewed against each other.

She had spotted a fraud that the system would have let slip by unnoticed if not for her own idiosyncrasy. *That* worried her.

Val listed her recommendations, sent the file on its way and asked to be alerted about any defaults under investigation that involved visits from VAT officers. She asked for regular checks on banking and paperwork, the two things that scammers usually got wrong. And she made an appointment to update Wexler.

Val wanted to nip this in the bud before anyone had any delusions of grandeur—before things got really ugly.

~

Three days after the second meeting, JD went to see Sudeep Sen, Sumit's brother. JD hadn't seen Sudeep since Christmas, and that had been a quick visit. VAT had consumed him since then—JD was the first to forget his pilgrimages. It surprised him more than it surprised the others. He knew how Aziz viewed his obligations to his family. Aziz didn't even think of them as obligations. Mike's time for Billy was non-negotiable. Sunday mornings, like church. And Palace home games during the season, if he could. JD had been driven nuts by the number of cancelled Calais runs because there was a Palace home game.

It left him; the lone gunner.

JD struggled, as always, with doing something just because it was *supposed* to be done. That reluctance made him a great scam-runner and a problematic relative.

His mother, normally a genius at minding her own business, had swung by his room one afternoon.

'Pam,' said JD as he waved her in. His mother's name was Paramjeet. Everyone called her Bobby. It's a Punjabi thing, he'd once told Mike. Six-foot-two Sikh with tits you could break rocks on and everyone calls him 'Tiny'. JD was the

only one who called his mother 'Pam'. He started calling her
that after he heard his father use the name, one night during
dinner, a very long time ago, when his parents been younger
and much happier. His father had been a bit drunk, back in
the days when he used to get good drunk, and his mother
had managed a couple of glasses of wine as well, which was
very rare for her. JD had never heard his father call her 'Pam',
before or since.

'Pam' became one of his names for her. Three names in
the three languages that JD had grown up speaking. Language
colour-coded his childhood. Punjabi was either the most
tender or the most savage, Hindi was the social tongue, even
at home, and English was either affection, or a serious but
rational discussion. English was man-to-man.

His mom went to Punjabi straightaway and he knew he
was in for a bollocking.

'Go and see the Sens, Jai. I've been telling you for months.'

'Come on, Mom. It's not like I'm sitting around
doing nothing.'

'And what are you doing?' Pam paused. 'Right now?'

She had a good point. He'd been sleeping off the victory
of the second meeting. Except that wasn't quite true. JD
couldn't see it. But this game wasn't done. The loop had
another loop inside it. He was looking at a doorway to
something, under a gentle rain of cell phones.

He'd been dreaming.

Pam shook her head. 'When you realize what this means,
all of this, you'll be much older.'

JD had heard this lecture before. But he didn't roll his

eyes. His mother looked like a little girl trying to express a fundamentally big idea that she understood but couldn't articulate. Then she said something she'd never said to him before.

'People remember.' She was almost talking to herself. 'People remember when you visit at births. And deaths. You may not know it then, they may not know it then, but they remember later and they are grateful.'

'Mom? What the hell are you talking about?'

'Go and see the Sens, Jai. They're three streets away.' With that, she was gone.

JD stood up, reached for his jacket and then sat down again. In his fit of celebration over the past two nights, he'd drunk the cough syrup he'd been stashing for Sudeep. He sent out a text and sat back. He'd have to defer until tomorrow.

Sudeep Sen was one of his favourite people in the whole world. The Sens were extended family. There was a time when he'd have picked their company on most nights. And Sudeep told good stories, great stories.

Sudeep was a big man, but soft. He had no edges or angles. He was tall, very tall for a Bengali— around six three—but he looked like a very skinny boy who had just ballooned. He had a squat face that could have been sensual but instead made him look like a perpetually surprised toad. He was ugly in a charming way, because you spent no time on the face and the mind got to you almost immediately. He wore thick glasses and had a habit at looking over the top of the frames when he was in conversation. He was the smartest person JD had ever met.

Sudeep Sen was the greater enigma around their neighbourhood—the anti-Aziz. He was the mystery that plagued subcontinent folk, the question for which there was no answer. He had done brilliantly at school, was a thoughtful, responsible elder son in a family of academics and had studied engineering on a scholarship. Then, at the age of twenty-two, he simply turned his back on the world. He refused to continue his education, or get a job, or talk to anyone who tried to ask him what the problem was.

The community came looking for reasons, like flies to an exploded carcass. Some supposed it was a girl, and a broken heart. Others thought it might be because he was gay. JD had never asked; they could have all been true, along with what JD believed had actually happened. For a family that was normally both forthright and remarkably accepting, it was a subject that had been buried very deep, possibly never to be examined. The Sens never spoke of their son's withdrawal from the world. They behaved as if it had never happened. Soon, it was just one of the things in the closet at the end of the passage.

~

Of the things that JD had heard, the one he supposed was the closest to the truth was the simple fact that Sudeep had had a nervous breakdown after graduating. It didn't surprise him. He knew how hard people drove their kids, especially if they were gifted. Your mind was the pass out of jail. And if a kid was unlucky enough to be good at school, it became a community project, a share in the reflected glory, a vindication of their collective sacrifices. JD knew only a few kids who had been as smart as he had been; smart enough to disguise their ability. Then again, none of those wankers had had to grow up with his dad, so he felt that he was due that particular break.

Sudeep simply snapped. JD had also heard that there was some drug use involved. That would explain the Sens' denial as well. Blowing up an exam was okay; you could deal with that. But when it got to nervous breakdowns and the drug use, the average Indian family was far more likely to lose its mind. Bengalis were like Catholics. Guilt was their primary industry.

The Sens did something that JD never forgave them for. They sent him away to India for a couple of years. The reasons were never discussed, and JD never knew whether it was to spark an appreciation of what Sudeep had in England, or whether it was punishment—banished to a distant outpost, dreaming of red double-decker buses and telephone booths. And fucking Marmite. When Sudeep returned, he was a changed man. The accent was gone, and so was the blinding confidence. The world was no longer his for the taking. He was a shambling parody of himself, fat and sloppy. His mind was as sharp as ever, but he didn't give a fuck any more. He told his parents that he had no interest in getting a job, no interest in being 'productive'. You could hear the arguments three houses away, night after night, for weeks on end. Until Sumit had surprised everyone by siding with his elder brother and telling his parents that he would be responsible for his brother, he would pay his way and could they, finally, please leave him the fuck alone?

JD had a single memory of that time. He remembered that it had been after Sudeep had returned from India, and Sumit had made it to university. JD had been closer to Sudeep than Sumit growing up, but Sumit and he had become friends in the two years that Sudeep had been away. Occasionally, they spent time together and startled each other with their growing stocks of filthy stories. And JD had become a star in his own right. He talked too much, but he directed his relentless barrage of shite in all directions. JD never held back in front of assorted parents. He was also one of the few people who weren't embarrassed about not going to uni. He and Mike rolled with some style. They didn't advertise what they were doing. But a lot of the kids around Heston knew.

It was like they were an underground band, two years before they hit the big time. They were a whisper that would begin to build.

The visit had to do with a computer, JD recalled. For a while, he'd been the neighbourhood priest, called on to consecrate computers after they'd been bought. A lot of people wouldn't turn their machines on for the first time unless he was around. Aziz would've turned it into a resource. JD did it with as much patience as he could muster, but that was it. People wanted purchases turned into certificates— they were doing the right things with their money, they were doing the right things for their kids.

JD always found the gestures empty, mindless. The sham

always exhausted him. It also terrified him in a distant way. He didn't know why until that night at the Sens'.

They'd been sitting in Sumit's room, the room he still shared with his brother. The house was too small and very welcoming. The Sens tried to bring Calcutta with them, twenty years ago. But the house had never been meant for four adults. Sudeep should have moved out by now, into a small apartment in the city, a man on the rise, looking for a bride, for the perfect combination of doe-eyed virginity, the songs of Rabindranth Tagore and terrific breasts. Mr and Mrs Sen had been planning to move out for years, into a smaller place, in a better neighbourhood. Except, as Sudeep was fond of pointing out to JD, things had taken a screaming turn to the left a few minutes before interval.

The house was Deep-Freeze Migrant. JD knew it well. Some of Sumit's clothes still lived in suitcases—they'd never outfitted the house with enough wardrobes for four adults. That had never been the focus. Instead, getting the kids a foothold. Everything else was secondary. That always made JD sad, when it wasn't pissing him off. He simply didn't get it. There were ways to live. And a shadow-existence so that your kids could grow up damaged in their own ways, obligated by guilt, didn't seem to be the brightest idea. People saved bottles of perfumes for years.

This shite was fool's gold.

Sumit and he had been sitting behind the desk in Sumit's room, neck-deep in wiring. JD carried a utility tool in those days—a bastardized Swiss knife with a series of screw heads. He could disembowel computers in seconds. He once wondered about why he never went into the computer business, white or grey. After a while, he was surprised to discover that he liked computers too much. He didn't know what to make of that.

They were arguing about RAM and hard disk sizes. JD had opened up the cabinet to show Sumit where he could install a second fan. Stores always tried to sell customers a new cabinet for the CPU when they were just trying to get the machines to work a little bit faster. There was always room for more RAM, in JD's humble opinion.

They heard the other door on the first floor, the door to the room next door, smash open. JD heard the knob go through the wall. There was the sound of furniture being shoved across the carpeting, and then a dull, flat, thump.

Someone screamed. It was the closest thing JD ever heard to a howl. The scream was inarticulate, not even a word, just the smashed and raw ends of something that might have been a human voice. It sounded like an animal had been gut-shot and was standing there, intestines slipping through its grasp, slithering onto the carpet, pooling like a scar.

JD's first reaction was to raise the knife. Even before he got to his feet. That was when he noticed that Sumit was gone— he'd left while JD was still processing the sound he'd heard.

There was a dull snap from the landing outside the door. And another. And another. Like something was trying to build up to a rhythm. Like something was struggling inside a closet, trying to force its way out.

His paralysis broke and JD moved quick. He was out of the door in two steps and he pivoted to his right, his right hand gripping the door frame, because he sensed that that was where the sound was coming from. He was lucky he turned, and he was luckier still that he was holding on to something. Otherwise he would have gone home with broken teeth that night.

The bookcase-cum-cabinet that had stood between the two bedroom doors for as long as JD could remember lay sprawled across the landing. If JD hadn't slowed to pivot, he would have run straight into the cabinet, tripped over it, and with his momentum, he would have gone face-first into the back of the cabinet.

For a long time, JD wished he had. He wished he'd gone straight into solid wood, broken some teeth and blacked out.

The knife almost slipped from his hand. JD caught it out of reflex, without looking down. He couldn't look away from the scene in front of him.

Sudeep was on the ground, propped up against the wall, where the cabinet so recently stood. His glasses had been knocked off his face, but he looked up steadily at his father. His face was expressionless. Without the glasses, he looked naked, like he'd been stripped.

Mr Sen stood in front of his eldest son. He sobbed silently, tears rolling down his face. With his right hand, he raised his belt, and smacked his son across the face with it.

Snap.

With his left hand, he was holding off his other son. Sumit was crying so hard that he couldn't stand up straight. His arms moved like he was drowning, up, above, insistent, fading. He looked like a child asking to be picked up, *please*, because he wasn't just tired, *please*, but because he was afraid, because they had all been reduced to a scene from a bad film, because they had fallen into a nightmare and no one would wake up, *please*. His father was holding him off and holding him up at the same time.

Snap.

Sudeep's head turned. JD could swear that he heard the tendons creak. Sudeep looked at him. A cut was beginning to open up above his left eye. His face was beginning to swell up—welts ran across it like he'd been branded—but he was fucking unrecognizable.

The whole scene was fucking unrecognizable.

Snap.

JD saw Mrs Sen, framed through the bedroom door. She was sitting on the floor, slumped against the bed, weeping, staring at her hands. She looked like she'd received bad news over the telephone, not like a fight from a ghetto had broken out in front of her eyes.

Snap.

Sudeep nodded to JD. It was a gesture of recognition, of solidarity. It was the acknowledgement of a man who had engineered his own death. Then he turned to face his father again.

Snap.

The look forced JD back to life. He pocketed the knife and stepped over the cabinet. Mr Sen, a man who had once taught JD fractions, didn't see him. His right arm cocked back again and JD caught the hand easily. He locked the wrist and gently pushed the older man back towards the wall. JD sensed Sumit drop away. He got both arms around old man. He increased his pressure on Mr Sen's right wrist and felt the belt fall to the ground. It whispered down the side of his jeans. It was whispering shit he just didn't understand—something fundamental had been knocked out of his view of the world and he just didn't know what it was. Mr Sen's hand groped for the belt twice, and realized that it wasn't there any more. His arm reached out and JD was afraid for a moment that the older man was going to try and hit him. Instead, he grabbed JD in a panicky hug. For a minute, JD fought his revulsion. His first thought was to push Mr Sen away and put a fist through his face. Then he remembered that, a long time ago, Mr Sen and he would go hunting for Tintin animated films in video stores during the holidays. He hugged the old man back and Mr Sen collapsed against him, crying harder.

'It's okay, Uncle,' said JD, mostly because he didn't have anything else to say. He later realized that it was the only time anyone said anything.

A doctor, a friend of the family's, swung by later. No hospital visits, no police complaints. That was just the way it worked. Sons against fathers. Wives against husbands. Family cats against the kids. The house was still. People nursed their grief privately, in corners. Something had died, all right.

JD left as soon as he could. He left Sudeep muttering thickly in his sleep, his face still looking like someone had run over it, systematically, with a truck. The doctor had sedated damn near everyone. He would've sedated Sumit too, but someone in the house needed to be conscious. He even offered JD a shot. JD shrugged it away. He had an appointment with a bottle of booze and his headphones. The evening had punched a hole through the middle of him and he needed to fill it. Otherwise, that gap gibbered madly. This was it, the heart of their lives, the immigrant dream. The world was made up of broken people, snapped in half under the strain they thought was the prize at the end of the rainbow. No one was fucking exempt. They were, all of them, JD included, puppets in someone else's show. That was inescapable. Some fucking accountant would catch up with them, toting a bill for damages to be inflicted. And it would never change. They were the wrong colour, the wrong species. There would always be someone richer. And there'd always be someone poorer, who they'd snap in turn. He'd been handed advance notice. No one was going to claim him. He was going to ride this fucker as long and as hard as he could, and he was going to do it alone.

The game, the big game, was cheap magic. Street corner hardsell. A pimp who offered dental insurance as a benefit.

JD wanted no part of it.

~

That had been four years ago. Since then, an uneasy truce had held. Sudeep didn't talk to his parents. He spent most of his time in his room, emerging only for meals or to go and watch the occasional film. No one ever spoke of what had happened. JD tried to never think about it, because that was a place where his rational view of the world fell apart. It made him feel like he was Jimmy Tipnis.

The Sens' house had become a different planet; cold, arid, everyone drifting along, suspended in their own private hell. But he'd made a promise to his mother, so JD went.

He made his quick hello downstairs. Mrs Sen was welcoming and distant. She nodded him up to the first floor and went back to reading a thick Bengali magazine. JD ran up the stairs and knocked on the door.

'One sec.'

JD looked to the left of the door, at the bookcase that had been propped up again. As usual, it was crammed full of books, ranging from cheap thrillers to manuals on mechanical engineering and everything in between. One of the glass doors of the display cabinet had broken, and had been pieced together with packing tape. JD could only guess that it had happened that night. The packing tape obscured the photos that had been carefully organized at one time. It showed a family trying to embrace their life in England. And photos of both boys accepting certificates in school. The packing tape made the light on the photos look muddy, like someone had applied a sepia filter to a glass case of memories.

The door opened. Sudeep's face was utterly blank. He saw who it was and grinned.

'Ah,' he said. His voice was soft and thick, like he hadn't spoken to anyone in days. 'The werewolf of London.'

JD grinned back and ran his hand through his hair. He shrugged. There was a reason he'd been putting off this visit. He was suddenly very close to tears. It was Sudeep who'd given JD rock 'n' roll. When they'd been kids in school, they listened to what everyone else was listening to. Sudeep had once heard JD get into a deep philosophical debate with someone about 'Ice Ice Baby' and had showed up two days later carrying a Queen compilation.

Sometimes, when he was very drunk, JD was convinced that Sudeep should have been his father. He'd been that much of an influence, every step of the way.

'Come in,' said Sudeep.

JD waited until Sudeep had closed the door. He pulled out the two bottles of cough syrup in his jacket and handed them to Sudeep. He always did this first. It saved Sudeep the embarrassment of having to ask the bullshit schoolboy question. 'Are you, um, carrying, any, you know…'

Sudeep smiled. He pushed up his spectacles and held the bottles up near his chest, like he was examining a fine wine. He nodded.

'Codeine,' said JD. He felt shy, almost ashamed.

Sudeep smiled and nodded again.

'Give me a minute. Then let's go for a walk.'

'Sure.'

For some reason, Sudeep would never drink the cough syrup that JD supplied in front of anyone. He always took the bottle to the bathroom. And they always took a walk after, because he had to get rid of the bottle.

As JD stood there, waiting, he wondered why he felt the way he did this morning. He looked around the room. He wondered what it would be to be reduced to this, trapped in a dingy little room out of choice, dependent on a brother and on cough syrup delivery. He'd gotten a taste of this in his room a little while ago, trying to close the loop. He didn't know what would have happened if the game hadn't revealed itself to him the way it did.

He supposed that it wasn't really worth thinking about.

Sudeep let himself back in the room. His eyes were teary, like he'd been coughing hard. JD knew from experience that the sheen would settle into a glaze in about ten minutes. It took an expert to notice that glaze; if you were careful, you could stay on cough syrup for a very long time without anyone having the slightest idea. Sudeep had once called it the most cost-effective vice he'd ever come across.

They went walking. JD always felt like he'd come to visit a well-meaning uncle after a long time. He'd spend the first part of the conversation bringing Sudeep up to speed. Up until a few months ago, Aziz and Sudeep had been the only people outside his work circle of Sumit and Mike who were aware of exactly what JD was up to.

Now he was down to one. A glazed-over, better dressed version of Dink. For a second, JD thought about the money riding on the game, and about Cleartone. He wondered about whether he should be telling Sudeep any of this at all.

JD savagely slammed the door shut on that thought. He began to talk faster, brighter, painting the picture in fluorescent strokes. But he ran out of conversation soon enough and they fell into the kind of silence that he was afraid of. In the old days, Sudeep would have asked him a dozen probing questions. Maybe he would have marvelled at the game. There would be a conversation about gardening tips and cooking and the political situation around the world. Sudeep used to build conversations like jazz. A single note heard, interpreted and returned. There was never an agenda; the process was the point.

Instead, they sat on a low stone wall at the end of the street. After a while, Sudeep asked if they could share a cigarette. JD lit a cigarette for Sudeep and gave it to him. He'd begun to wet the butt the last few times JD had come to see him. Sudeep was the one who'd taught JD that wetting the butt was the worst kind of smoking etiquette.

He'd never thought of himself as sentimental, but he felt like he was at a wake.

'One day soon, Jai, in, I don't know, ten or twenty years, a gang of people will pull someone from behind the wheel of a Ferrari and set them on fire.' Sudeep was looking down at his cigarette as it burned, watching the smoke twirl and twitch, like a distress signal. His accent was somewhere between India and Aziz, but it made him sound older and wiser, truer somehow. JD smiled. Signs of life. That was a good thing.

'And when they set the Ferrari driver on fire, they will pause for a minute in the middle of that frenzy and realize that it's just the first action that's difficult. You just need to crack the dam. Then they will torch the first Gucci store they see.' Sudeep turned to look at JD. He nodded and smiled. He pulled on the cigarette and let the smoke curl out of his nostrils as he spoke.

'People don't trust the government. People don't trust the banks. People don't trust the police. People don't trust the judges. They don't trust big business. They don't know it yet. They feel it. But they don't know it. It's coming, though.' Sudeep gestured once to the sky, a lazy, circular arc, looking like an impossibly weather-beaten professional madman. 'Blood on the moon. The actual dance. Real fucking democracy.'

JD didn't know what to make of it. Sudeep tossed his cigarette to the ground and looked at JD again.

'The world runs on pussy.'

'What?' JD looked at Sudeep. He was genuinely puzzled. Sudeep had once smacked him across the mouth because he'd called a girl a bitch. He'd been something like seven. Then Sudeep had told him that if he ever heard him talk badly about or to girls, he'd beat the living shit out of him.

The look and the tone of JD's voice were lost on Sudeep. He looked bored, disinterested, like JD should have seized on his visions of a middle-class apocalypse and treated them like a prophecy.

'Pussy,' he repeated. 'Whatever, you know. Desire. Want. Lust. Those things.' He looked at JD and smiled. JD thought that he had never seen anyone look so sad, ever.

'You never escape, you know. Whatever you do. They simply mark the place in the sky you reach, before you crash back down.' Sudeep leant forward and wiggled his foot about. The shoelace had come undone. He bent forward, trying to reach for his foot. He couldn't. He shook his head and crossed his leg, bringing the right foot onto the left knee. He still couldn't get his fingers to the laces. He'd begun to wheeze from the effort. He was about to stand up and try propping his foot on the wall they were sitting on when JD spoke up.

'Sudeepda, let me.' JD couldn't remember the last time he'd called Sudeep 'da', older brother.

'No, no—'

JD ignored him. He went down onto one knee, effortless in comparison to Sudeep and tied the shoelace firmly. He stood up.

'Thanks. It's the weight, you know…' Sudeep trailed off.

'It's okay,' said JD. 'Really.'

But Sudeep wouldn't look him in the eye. JD stood there, helpless. He didn't know what he could do. He didn't know what he should say. He didn't know what would offend Sudeep. Finally, he ran out of options.

'Do you want to head home?'

'Yes. Yes.' Sudeep nodded. He struggled to his feet. JD noticed for the first time how much weight he'd put on. He'd always been a big guy. When he got back from India, he was fat. But this was something else. Sudeep was obese. He still wouldn't look JD in the eye. He turned and began to walk towards the house. JD followed, a little way back, mostly unsure of what to think.

Sudeep got to his house about and turned and faced JD. He planted his feet across the tiny path that cut through their garden. JD's mom and Mrs Sen had spent years transplanting cacti in that garden. JD read the stance perfectly. This was it for this visit. There was no going back upstairs.

Sudeep gestured with his hands and smiled weakly.

'I'm sorry, man.'

'It's okay,' said JD. He meant it too.

'It's just, after all of this, you know, you want to be able to tie your shoelaces yourself.'

'It's okay. Really.'

Sudeep nodded. He wasn't done.

'It's good, this thing, this mobile phone thing. It's very good. You're going to make a lot of money.'

'I—'

'Let me finish.' Sudeep paused. His eyes narrowed and, for the first time that morning, really looked at JD. For a moment, he was the man he was always meant to be, not the fat thirty-four-year-old washout who lived with his parents. JD felt like he was being fucking X-rayed.

'You're the one everyone worries about. Mike's got his feet on the ground and Aziz is a bastard, lying snake, and no one in their right mind should trust him.'

'What—'

'It's a job, Jai. Stop calling it a game. It's a job. Treat it like that and you'll be fine.'

JD took a deep breath. This is why he'd been putting off this fucking visit. And this is why he preferred being on his own. Everything apart, this strange morning apart, everyone in the fucking world had an opinion and a half about how he should conduct his business.

'Listen, man,' JD was starting to get angry and he didn't care enough to hide it, 'I'm tired of all the fucking university geniuses telling me what I can and can't do.' He paused, trying to stop himself before he said stuff he'd regret. 'Get off my back. I don't get on yours.'

Sudeep nodded.

'Okay,' he said. 'Okay.' He appeared to think something over and then he made a decision.

'Stay close to your own people.' Sudeep grinned. 'Of

course, that means you'll have to figure out who your people *are*.'

JD'd had about enough of this ominous Children of the Corn number.

'You look after yourself. I'll see you.'

'You know, I don't think you will.' Sudeep's voice was soft. 'You're about to get very busy. It's going to be a while. Good luck.'

JD would have hugged him. Ordinarily. But this was no ordinary morning. He held out his hand. Sudeep looked at it. Then he shrugged and shook it. JD turned and began to walk. His head was churning and he wanted to return to VAT as soon as possible. The real world, it seemed, was a very strange place.

'Jai.'

JD stopped and turned. He waited. He was pretty sure he deserved an apology. Instead, Sudeep looked down at his hand. Then he looked up with a shit-eating grin that JD was familiar with but couldn't place.

'If you're, you know, busy, then... how?'

'Huh?'

'I mean, if I don't see you for a while, then, uh, you know...'

'No, I don't know.' JD was actually curious. 'Help me out.'

The shit-eating grin returned. JD recognized it for what it was a split second before Sudeep spoke. He'd seen it a million times, towards the end of most weekends.

'Cough syrup?' he asked.

JD looked at Sudeep for a few seconds. There was nothing in his face.

'I'll text you the number,' he said. 'Tell him you got the number from me.' He didn't wait for Sudeep's response.

Two hundred quid apart, he might have spent the morning with Dink.

And that was the real tragedy, because that was the last time he saw Sudeep.

2.3

The Heston Principle went live in the first week of August. They applied for a monthly VAT licence, and by the time the application was approved, they were installed in a new, larger warehouse in Heston. They were all exhausted after more than a month working overtime to set up channels and vendors and transport, populating both levels 'B' and 'C'. Kenneth and Alistair—Fraser-Powell Trading—had been in the market since 4 July, opening the day after the Wimbledon final. They worked slowly, reaching out to all parts of the vast network of vendors that Mike had collected, establishing their credentials, declaring everything and maintaining impeccable records. They were still buying from Aziz's contacts in Italy and France, biding their time until the switchover.

By then, three of them were aware of the steadily rising group of competitors.

How'd they get their start in contraband, all those years ago? JD heard from Mike, and Mike had heard the muttering in the streets. Back then, they haunted the local chippy and the minicab stands, like their fathers haunted their locals and their grocers. Everyone was looking for a tip. About the stock market, about horses, about football teams, and about how to get rich quick.

Breaking the law was incidental. These boys wanted in, and they didn't have the time or the money or the plain drive to haul themselves through university and set the course of their lives. They simply reached out and grabbed what they wanted.

The mutters had began in January. Suddenly Hamilton and Dewan weren't dealing in booze and fags any more, now they were buying mobile phones. And selling them. And they were starting companies like they were setting up card games. This was the new play. And once you'd followed three months of it, through the rising tide of chatter in pubs and on street corners, and once every damned theory had been exhausted, it wasn't too difficult to understand *what* they were doing. The question was did the numbers make sense?

As soon as they killed the first company and disappeared before the reclaim, other companies sprouted from nowhere like a bad rash.

Brother, the numbers couldn't be ignored.

The Principle could've moved by the third week of July, but they stayed out of the market long enough for the crunch to hit. The smart competitors anticipated Excise much like the Principle had done. They ducked, peddling phones to vendors who got dodgier and dodgier, but keeping themselves—and the money—in the game. The rest of them never saw it coming. Four months after they had booked the profit from charging VAT and not remitting it, a bunch of import boys suddenly found that the vendors simply wouldn't buy from them any more. A lot of them were still on the phones arguing with their vendors when VAT officers knocked on their doors with questions and invoices.

The Principle waited two weeks beyond, while the dust settled and the demand for mobile phones went through the roof. When they finally entered the fray, the importer controlled by the Principle was the high-volume player that was the answer to everyone's prayers. The stage was set for a burn, pure and simple.

In the first week of August, Fraser-Powell Trading, hoping for a less erratic inflow of phones, switched over to Atlas Trading as their primary importers. JD answered the first phone call himself for the sheer pleasure of sticking it to the dogs.

He opened with three thousand Nokia Communicators that had been sitting in the chain since April. He dropped the five pounds, tagged the VAT onto it, and then sent his child out into the world.

He pulled in a hundred and twenty thousand pounds of profit. Thirty-six hours later, the Heston Principle, run by a gentleman by the name of Mike Hamilton, bought the entire stock from Fraser-Powell Trading. While he sat on the phones at level 'C', waiting to see how much profit he could bank by selling the Communicators legally, JD took his cost price and turned it into nine thousand Nokia 6210s. This time, because it was a cheaper phone, he pulled in only ninety-nine thousand pounds of pure profit. Only.

Twenty-four hours later, the Heston Principle bought the entire stock of 6210s, adding much needed variety to their portfolio of available phones. JD had spent half an hour pissing himself laughing. The figures did it.

In three days he'd made two hundred and nineteen thousand pounds of pure profit that the government would never see. Alistair and Kenneth had pocketed twelve thousand pounds themselves. And JD had twelve thousand phones that he could sell at any moment. The hell of it was, all of the two hundred thousand odd was profit, if he wished it to be. Or he could just pour it back into the system and then really watch it go.

What a fucking conundrum, he thought. Get rich now? Or get even richer three weeks from now?

Or then again, why not do both?

~

Two days after the second system launched, JD dragged Mike and Aziz, and a handful of others—Alistair and Kenneth, and Sumit and Brian—to a newish club called Crysis. JD had already been once. Aziz had received the original invitation, some sort of client–promoter–potential–partner nexus and he'd fobbed it off to JD. Aziz was normally very good at attending the increasing number of openings and premieres he was invited to, but clubs really weren't his scene.

JD went. He discovered Moet Chandon. He alternated between the champagne and Jaeger-bombs and danced his ass off. It was the first night out he'd had in a very long time that didn't end in a fight or leave him feeling vaguely unsatisfied. Mike and he were years past thirty-pound vodka drinks causing outrage. But JD had always gone into the better clubs feeling some sort of pressure to spend his money, just to prove that he *could*. The opening was different, though. He was relaxed and he had fun. He made out with a girl for a bit and wasn't too disappointed when he went home alone. He knew he'd be back. He liked the place.

So he dragged the boys over. Mike and Aziz went in with some trepidation. They'd known JD the longest. When JD went in expecting fun and it didn't materialize like he expected, he tried to cause it all on his own. The result was like being in a car that was about to crash—you could *see* the evening go off the rails. And then it was a crap-shoot: coppers, fights, stolen road signs, vomit, weed runs at four in the morning, bicycle-jacking and maybe some tears. Any combination of those elements was possible.

They got in early. The place wasn't too loud, at least at the beginning. JD bounced across to the bar to get to the first round.

'Hi.'

'Mr Dewan.' The bartender grinned at JD like he was a long-lost brother. Aziz was standing behind JD and he rolled his eyes.

'Lemme guess.' The bartender held up his hand. He looked like he was about to read JD's mind and he *knew* that he looked ridiculous. So he just milked it for what it was worth. He stared at the table in the corner that the boys had blocked for the evening.

'Three bottles of Moet. To start with.' The bartender

said it like it was a diagnosis. His tone implied that he simply would *not* put up with an argument.

'And—' It was the first thing JD had tried to say. The bartender interrupted him.

'The Jaeger-bombs are on their way...' He pointed to two trays that were being ferried to their table. The bartender turned to JD and extended his hand. He and JD shared a complicated Ben Hur handshake. JD pointed at the bartender and wagged his finger, as if he was admonishing him. He dropped his credit card on the counter and they began to walk back to their table.

'Very fucking eighties, Jai,' said Aziz. 'Where the fuck's Tom Cruise?'

JD stopped. He turned to face Aziz. He looked genuinely pissed off.

'Who the fuck's the guy behind the bar then?' he asked.

They both burst out laughing.

They had a surprisingly good time that evening. Sumit and the Jamaicans hit it off immediately. They spent the whole evening trying to top each other with stories of the ridiculous shit that the people they knew got up to. Within ten minutes, they'd agreed on the format. Each story had to begin with 'Oh yeah? Well, I have a friend...'

The highlight, as far as most of them were concerned, was Sumit's story of a 'friend', a technician who had to pee into a bottle of mineral water during a community theatre performance of *Macbeth*.

By the time ten o'clock rolled around, Mike had been on

the dance floor for over an hour, killing it. Brian spent most of the evening at the bar, impressing girls with an inexhaustible range of magic tricks. The coins, however, always seemed to reappear in places that were a little less innocent than behind the ear. Sumit and the Jamicans kept at it, rolling joints and going 'Oh yeah?'

And half the people who walked in through the club seemed to know Aziz. He drifted from table to table, like he owned the place. He nursed a drink for a long time and let the parties occur around him. He was still switched on, he was still at work in a sense, and he knew it.

JD was standing at the bar, playing Brian's wingman when he heard a voice he recognized.

'Oh, hello.'

JD turned. Pamela stood there, wearing a purple dress that ended six inches below her waist. She was wearing heels and she towered over JD. Her legs were spectacular. He was lucky that he was smashed. Otherwise he would've done something stupid, like spill his drink or try and come up with something clever.

He realized that he could stand there, watching her for hours.

'How are you?' She slid closer to him. Somehow, she managed to whisper the next question, even though there were in a club that could rival an Anthrax concert for volume.

'How's your mom?'

She waited to see how he'd react. She looked amused, like she always did. JD didn't know whether he wanted to break her nose or whether he wanted to pull her into the Gents and go down on her for hours. He looked her up and down once. He paused at her thighs. He made sure that she saw him look. He looked up at her.

'She's fine.' JD waited for a second. He thought about it. The thighs won. The dress won. The need to wipe that look of amusement off her face won. 'Can I get you a drink?'

'What are you drinking?'

'Moet,' said JD. He held out his flute.

Pamela made a small moue of distaste. She was closer to him, JD realized. She still smelt like he remembered. He found himself responding to that scent, like this was an animal exchange.

'Weell…' She sighed. Her breath was warm in his ear. 'Moet's not my thing.' She made it sound like there was no way that it could be *anyone's* thing. 'I like pink. But…' Pamela began to turn away.

The Moet tipped JD over the edge. He went from wanting to sleep with her to needing to fuck her. He wanted power over the expression on her face. He wanted to be the reason she finally lost control.

'Oi!'

The bartender turned to him with a grin on his face.

'Can I get some pink champagne instead of this shit?' The question was bright, charming and aggressive.

The expression on the bartender's face flickered for a split second. He looked at JD, he looked at Pamela, and then pulled on a smile like a mask.

'Sure.' He looked at Pamela.

'Crystal Rose, please.'

'Let's get some bottles,' said JD.

'Sure.'

Aziz watched Pamela swiftly steer JD away from the table he'd started the evening at. There were four other people at the table, three of them women, all of them dressed to the nines. It was a good-looking table. Aziz had to hand that to them. They looked like they belonged, not like they were on the prowl. Every outfit and every handbag was designer. Aziz thought about whether he should break it up now. A bottle of Crystal Rose cost six times the amount of a bottle of Moet. Aziz didn't mind the cost, but what were you spending it on? And then he decided that JD needed to ride this one out. You couldn't buy an education like this. Let 'im go at it. If his little romance got out of hand, Mike or he could always step in.

Aziz leaned on the bar and waved the bartender over.

'Chris.' Aziz pulled out his wallet. He put a fifty-pound note on the counter. And he handed the bartender his credit card. 'Don't mind my friend. He's... happy.' Aziz grinned. 'Keep them greased.'

'Cheers, Mr Basrai. And don't worry. She'll keep him on the wheel as long as he'll go. He's her hamster tonight.'

Aziz paused. His grin got wider. He pulled out another fifty-pound note and put it on the counter. But he didn't take his hand off the note.

'Tell me, then.' He was absurdly happy. This was a goldmine. 'Tell me everything.'

'She makes a percentage of every bottle of Crystal we pop at her table.' Chris was grinning as well.

Aziz laughed out loud. He turned to look at the table.

JD had gotten going. Everyone else at the table was in splits. Except for Pamela. She looked slightly bored. Aziz shook his head.

'Sure. The Channel doesn't pay for itself.' He looked at the table one last time and turned back to Chris. 'Well, it might, the next few months.'

They both laughed. Aziz took his hand off the note. He drained his glass.

'Can I get a Scotch, please?'

'With pleasure, Mr Basrai. This one's on the house.'

~

Pamela led JD onto the dance floor much later that night. He'd lost track of time in the club. There had been more than three bottles of Crystal. JD didn't know how many. He and Pamela had nipped out a small door at the back at some point. JD was happy just following her through the crush of people. They were close, back to front, and they pushed against each other as they made their way to the back. Pamela knew a guy and she *loved* coke. JD paid for it, without question, because this was his party. He was the happy asshole and everyone loved him.

When they danced, finally, when they made it to the dangling promise tagged on to the end of the evening, JD remembered all of it, wrecked or not. There wasn't anything romantic about it. But she was good. He watched her move for a long time. She led him, she ran the show. Through smoke, through strobes that reduced them to a succession of frozen images. There was sweat, and spit, and eye contact with an inch between their faces. She moved against him, moved so slow, she let him stand there as she moved her ass against him but wouldn't let him put his arms around her. The beat went through him like a jackhammer. He was on unlimited adrenaline.

It was maybe three when they were done. JD'd had an erection for about four hours. He felt like he was thirteen again, hoping to get laid for the first time. He could barely stay upright, but he had no choice but to follow Pamela as she pulled him into the Gents. That beat had driven everything else of his head. He didn't know when the other boys had left. He didn't know where his credit card was. He didn't care.

Pamela whirled JD around so that he was up against the wall. She leaned in, looked at JD for a second, and suddenly dropped to her knees. She pushed up his T-shirt and swirled her tongue around his bellybutton. JD jerked back—it was unexpected, but her hands were behind him now, slipping under his boxers, digging into his ass and she slid one hand lower and squeezed, pushing him back towards her. She tracked down his stomach with the tip of her tongue, leaving a glistening trail. JD moaned. His hand dropped down past her head and undid his belt buckle. His hand found her head. She shook it off and stood up again. She laughed.

'Not so fast. You've got to earn it.'

Pamela licked the side of his face and ran her tongue over his earlobe. She breathed into his ear and started to slowly lick it. Her right hand slipped into JD's boxers. She cupped him gently and then squeezed. JD ran his tongue up and down her long neck and then they were kissing, hard, sucking, pulling, biting. Her hand moved up and down and JD was almost instantly ready, his back arched, with a grimace on his face. She'd been leading him on for hours. It was over in seconds.

They slid down the wall, both of them breathing in gasps. Pamela pulled away. She looked at JD. She extracted her hand. She wiped most of the sticky mess on JD's shirt. She looked amused. She stood up. JD tried to follow but she pushed him back down gently.

'Hush. Go home.' She smiled. 'See you around, soldier.'

JD laughed, sitting on the floor of the loo. He ran his hands through his hair.

'Can I get your number?' he asked.

'That's really up to you,' she said. And then she was gone.

~

On 1 September, Aziz put in his papers at Lexington Brothers. JD stood up and applauded when Aziz broke the news.

'It's a marriage now, A,' he said. 'And you've just thrown away the birth control pills.'

Aziz was out of the blocks almost as quick as the Principle themselves. Within those thirty days, Aziz had branched out into his own law practice. He was the third most sought-after lawyer in the country when it came to a certain section of society, and he carried it like a shield. He also invested in a small Indian restaurant, a real estate firm, a garment import–export business, and he began to inject large volumes of cash into the Freight Forwarder to conduct legitimate business that had nothing to do with the Principle. JD and Mike, on the other hand, took a step back as the money started to pour in, and then attempted to dropkick the pure fucking exhilaration of it into the world. The shit hit the fan—enough for the crash meeting that *really* started the merry-go-round—when JD bought his mother a house.

~

As far as Aziz was concerned, they still needed to stay low. Flash clothes were fine. New phones and large televisions he could live with. Insane amounts of clubbing and better booze, like the expedition to Crysis, were inevitable. And Aziz hadn't been able to stop the cars. Mike bought himself an E39 M5 and JD settled on a Range Rover turbo diesel the size of a small house. He wanted, he confessed to Aziz, to drive *through* traffic.

But, for the most part, the Principle managed to conceal from the world at large that, as of somewhere around 15 September, the three of them were worth over a million pounds each. Aziz spread his share across the web he was constructing around himself. For JD and Mike however, the Calais chapter of their lives hadn't even been a year ago and they didn't quite feel like millionaires. They'd been chasing that magic word for as long as they could remember and now that it actually applied to them, no one even knew it. To *be* a millionaire, people had to reflect it back at you. Otherwise, where was the fuckoff value? They'd come out of nowhere to make their first mill at twenty-six and yet, as far as the world was concerned, they hadn't come from anywhere or done anything. They had not arrived.

~

JD gave the house to his mother with his usual kamikaze flamboyance. He'd been a stranger at home for nine months. He went there to sleep maybe four nights a week, otherwise he'd call his mother around ten to tell her he'd crash at Mike's or at the office. He had been living like a travelling salesman, peddling VAT, and he had loved it.

His parents didn't know what to make of it. There was a quality of detachment that was alien. JD looked through questions. His gaze was fixed outside the walls of the house. It was adult, and cold, and unconsciously cruel.

While this strange, older JD wasn't around the house much himself, his presence could be felt in the things he left behind. The television got bigger, and JD subscribed to the most expensive satellite package available so that his dad wouldn't have to go to Mike's house if there was a test match on in India. He lavished gifts on his mom—bags and shoes, a new oven, a dishwasher. Things that were completely out of place in the little house. The gifts had a quality of penance. They were things that were *supposed* to be there, because someone on the telly said so.

The idea had always been there, he realized. It just gradually revealed itself to him as he walked home at night with a grimace on his face. It was the thing he knew best, and the thing that he loathed the most: Heston. It was the smell that got to him as he walked, worse than ever. You just couldn't wash it away. It was dirty and mean, and ever so small. He studied his surroundings like an outsider, like he was looking at an ant farm. He saw kids grouped around the fronts of burnt-out houses, passing beer and weed back and forth, like he had done a million years ago. He looked at clusters of empty cough syrup bottles and thought of Sudeep Sen, the prophet of Hounslow. He heard laughter and arguments and dogs in the distance. Somewhere, someone was always fighting.

And it was only then that JD realized that he was looking at a car crash. Heston was a pile-up. People didn't know that this *was* it, the trip was over. They wore a desperate air of entitlement on their sleeves. Someone owed them the life they saw on telly. They were to be given it, as if being born in England was the only qualification you ever needed. It was just easier to stand around and make it someone else's fault.

They'd arrived, though. This was the promised land. What they needed to do was place one foot in front of the other and start walking.

This place was quicksand. No one wanted to believe it.

The more he thought about it, the more he needed to get his parents away.

~

He put them in the Rover on a Saturday afternoon and drove them out to Kingston on Thames. From Heston, it was like driving into a movie. The air was better, the streets were clean, and the houses had large gardens. They stopped at one of them, a neat two-storey place done in white. It was like every other house on the street. You knew at first glance that the neighbours would leave you alone, but that they were a phone call away. It was warm and ideal, open to blue skies in a way that Heston could never be, unless they tore the whole damned suburb down and started from scratch.

The three of them stepped out into a welcoming quiet. JD could hear birds chirping and leaves rustling in the breeze.

JD's parents were under the impression that he was buying this house for himself, perhaps to share with Mike. They were slightly awed, because it clearly wasn't cheap, and their son had evidently come a long way over the past year. They knew he was riding the mobile phone boom, and that some part of it was off the books, a little under the table in the way that every business conducted itself, claiming advantages wherever it could. It was impressive, all the same.

JD's dad, like all dads post-retirement, kept his eye on the figures around the world. He estimated that he was looking at a minimum investment of two hundred and fifty thousand pounds. And then his Indian-ness asserted itself, cutting through the awe. If his son was fool enough to want to move out, he would make sure that the house was worth every penny, that it was Value for Money. So for the next hour and a half, JD's parents put the house through its paces, poking and pushing, testing every doorknob and faucet, and the heating and the geysers, in each one of the four bathrooms. They checked the views, and the kitchen and both the gardens. The house passed muster. It was, they had to concede, a lovely house in every way and would be a great place to live in.

JD waited for the judgment. He knew how important it was for both of them to like the house, and for them to make that choice without knowing that the papers had already been signed two weeks ago. He waited for the approval to come from both of them, although he knew that for it to work, it had to be his mum. She needed to see it as a blank canvas that would take her vision. She was already trying to draw up a list of the things he needed to do to the garden, the things he *should* do. After all the time spent away from them over the months, it was a joy to be immersed in that murmur again, to hear the controlled excitement in her voice. He waited for the pause that inevitably came when they had exhausted their fund of advice.

They looked at him expectantly, wanting to hear what his plans were.

JD dropped the entire set of keys—every door, the two-car garage and the small shed in the back—into a cup and slid it across the counter to his mother. She wrinkled her eyes at the cup, then looked at JD.

'It's yours, Mom. This—' He waved his hands, trying to encompass a space that was six times bigger than anything she had ever lived in. 'This is yours. It's for you.'

There was silence. His mother shook her head. She reverted to Punjabi almost immediately, like she always did when she was stressed.

'I don't understand.'

JD grinned at her.

'Yeah, you do. You just don't want to. This is your new house.'

'And I bet it's also two times more expensive to live here then Heston, too,' his dad cut in. His father hated surprises, and he hated it even more when JD trumped him. 'You don't even have a proper job. You've only been bumming with Mike, trying scheme after scheme. And now this?'

JD held up his hand and kept watching his mom. It wasn't meant as a slight, but he'd never done that to his father before. He was still looking at his mom. This was the closest he was ever going to get to a business card.

'Mom?'

She said nothing, just held her hand to her mouth and looked at his father. So JD looked at him, too.

'I'll pay the difference, Dad. I've been offering to pay the household expenses for years. Except that you won't let me, because you're such a stubborn old fool.'

His mother gasped, but JD was grinning, and his dad watched him for another moment. A smile began to spread across his face. It was one of the things that JD loved about him, the major reason that they were still real friends despite all the bad blood through the years. He shook his head ruefully and grinned back at JD.

'A stubborn old fool,' he mused. 'It would explain why you're such a fool yourself.'

JD turned back to his mother. She was looking at the keys as if they were some exotic, possibly toxic flower. They scared her, because they were so unexpected, and because they would always stand for money her son had wasted trying to please her. JD slid off the stool and walked over to her. He took her hand in his hand.

'Come on, Mom. The only question is whether you like the house.' He waited, but she was still quiet.

'And I think you do. Don't you?' She nodded silently. Then, she let loose the final defence, the impenetrable logic of an Indian mother that no one would ever win against.

'But everything we know is in Heston, Jai. All the markets, and all my friends, and all your father's friends. This is a new neighbourhood after knowing and building everything for thirty years.'

JD reached out and held her cheek, and then tilted her head up so that she looked at him.

'I'll buy you a car, Mom. And a bloody driver, okay? Live there, sleep here. Or any way you like. Keep the old house. But take this one too, okay? As a gift. For twenty-six years of having to put up with me.' He was grinning as he said it, but his mother burst into tears. After a moment, she nodded.

'Thank you,' she whispered. 'Thank you, it's very lovely, thank—'

'Hush,' said JD. 'You're welcome. Thank *you*.'

He hugged her tight, and she hugged him back. Then his father thumped him on the back hard enough to drive all the air out, and his mother was laughing, slapping him lightly because he had pulled a surprise that had worked.

JD remembered the moment for a long time. He hadn't finished school, he was difficult to live with, and he had drifted from scheme to scheme. Angry, often incoherent, he had always felt chained down, that life was long, hard, a series of bewildering limitations. But he had bought his mother a house that she loved.

A fucking revolution.

~

When Aziz called Mike, asking for a meeting about the house, Mike kindly asked him to fuck off.

'You're out of your mind,' he told him. 'I know why you're worried, but you're out of line. The answer—' he cut across Aziz's interjection, raising his voice slightly. 'The answer is no. Seriously, fuck off. You were in line when you told him off about Cleartone. Not here.'

Aziz and JD met in Aziz's car on a Tuesday evening. JD was mildly surprised that Aziz turned up with a chauffeur. It was bad practice. Most of his work happened in the car, on the phone. Why introduce another set of ears? The car itself was a new addition as well. There'd been the Golf and then the BMW and now there was this Jag. Of course, thought JD, if you were a hotshot lawyer, you were *expected* to drive something that looked like it should be left in a glass case.

And JD was expected to get excited about buying his mother a fucking dishwasher.

Aziz saw it in the set of JD's jaw. JD knew why he was here, and it could very well become a breaking point. Isolation, the distance Aziz so craved, didn't cancel out the fact that he needed JD and Mike. This was a partnership because they could do things that he would never be able to. Mike had handled Cleartone for them. And Brian was theirs, as were Alistair and Kenneth. A large part of the Principle's momentum came from the weight Mike and JD carried, and they could pull that weight for someone else if he pushed them too far.

The driver pulled into an open stretch and parked the car. Then, without a word, he got out. JD nodded. Aziz turned back. JD continued to stare out of the windshield for a moment. Then he looked at Aziz.

'What's the deal, A? I can't buy my mom a fucking house?'

It was Aziz's turn to look out of the window. It was a legitimate concern. How long was he going to keep a group of men like this away from the money they'd scammed?

'Will you listen to me? Without bullshit?' he asked. He was still looking out of the window.

'Sure.'

'Okay.' Aziz turned back to look at JD. 'Gimme a month. Keep your head down, just for a month. And then the world's your fucking oyster. You do what you want with your money. But give me a month. And keep your head down.'

JD digested it. He nodded his head, once. It was a sharp—it sealed the deal. Then he smiled.

'Dubai?'

'Dubai,' Aziz agreed. 'It's time to turn it white.'

~

The damned house was actually kamikaze. For the first time in a long time, JD misjudged the situation completely. There was too much side on the cue-ball after potting the easy red in the side pocket. Break gone, frame gone.

JD thought the house would buy him distance. He knew he'd caused awe. He thought he'd achieved escape velocity.

His mom saw it differently.

In the middle of shopping for the new house, snowed in under wallpaper choices and new linen, his mother collared him one afternoon in the old house in Heston. JD had rarely seen Pam like this. She was caught between the guilt of excess and the thrill of newly found money muscle. JD was buying everything in Egyptian cotton; he was walking around stores they'd only ever peeked at from the pavement and tossing his credit card around. He understood this confusion of delight and horror that his mom felt because he felt it too.

There was a difference between having money and being rich.

Pam had mentioned something about shopping for his house and his family, hint, nudge, wink, and he'd brushed it aside like he'd done every time marriage had been mentioned since he'd turned twenty-three.

But his mom came to see him one afternoon, just as he was trying to figure out how to smoke a joint without having to sneak out. For all his wonder about the zoo at the Sens', it never once occurred to him that he was a twenty-six-year-old millionaire who was camped out in a tiny room in his parents' house. He just wanted to get high and he wanted to think about the game.

'Jai.' His mom sat on his bed. She dried her hands on her apron and sniffed at them once. She hated the smell of detergent on her palms. JD had never seen anyone wash their hands as much as his mom.

'Pam,' he said. JD couldn't remember a time when he'd been in this good a mood, consistently.

His mom sat there for a while, looking at the carpet. There was more white in her hair than ever before—she'd started greying when he'd been a kid. JD had been telling Pam for years that she ought to colour her hair completely white, get her Indira Gandhi look on. She looked small. And she looked worried. JD thought it was residual guilt about the house.

'I've spoken to Mrs Walia,' she said in English. Then she looked up at him. 'About finding a girl for you.'

JD sat in silence for a minute. He wasn't aware of it, but his forehead creased, a sign that he was getting angry. This wedding thing had been a running joke for three years. But his mom had opened the circle, she'd brought in outsiders, she'd commissioned the pimps.

Arranged marriages worried him deeply. He thought they never worked, not really. He hated how the whole deal functioned, how a network of acquaintances and friends would draw a deep breath, make their conclusions and start spitting out names of eligible young women. He hated how the process treated the girls—he'd seen it happen to people he'd grown up around. They were paraded around like show ponies. She can sing, you know, someone would fucking simper while everyone sat around trying to debate *just* how good the tea was.

He wanted to get laid, a lot, by honeys who could become

fragments of the dreams he'd had growing up, at the snap of a finger. He wanted the thrill of the chase, he wanted flesh, and the soft salty tang of sweat. He wanted to be blown, handled, spat on, cursed at. He wanted heads thudding against tiles and the floor and headboards in hotel rooms across the world. He didn't have that with Pamela. He knew that. He was just having fun trying to find out if they'd ever get there. He was just paying for a different kind of poison.

Mostly, he just wanted to be left the fuck alone. On a lot of days, he was happy not seeing Aziz and Mike. He was on the verge of something. He felt that this game might be endless.

He thought that he'd just stepped off the path, he'd avoided the trap. And now he saw a roadblock that he thought he'd avoided completely.

'I'm not doing it,' he said. His voice was flat.

'Jai—'

'No!' JD hadn't meant to yell. But the pedal got floored anyway. His voice began to rise halfway through the word, surprising him. His own vehemence surprised him.

The silence rolled back from the house, like the echo from a big gun. JD looked at his mom and immediately regretted yelling.

The thing about being Punjabi, he thought, was that the little things were just that little bit different. His mom had that glint in her eyes but they weren't going to tear up. Oh, no. His mom's face got still. It hardened. Then she grinned, the original grin that JD had inherited. She looked like she was going to crack him open right there, rip out his heart and tap dance on it. For fun.

'You want to get into a yelling match?' It was a challenge.

'No, Mom.'

'You remember that when I want, your father is scared of me?'

'Yes, Mom.'

She glared at him for a further few seconds. She sighed. She went back to looking worried.

'What do we do?'

'About what?'

'About this!' JD saw the well-loved mixture of exasperation and love. 'This isn't normal.'

JD looked at her calmly. They had come to the heart of the matter much sooner than he'd anticipated. He leant forward in his chair. His eyes never left his mother's face.

'What else about this is normal?' It was the closest the two of them ever came to talking about the secret they all avoided, like an open well in the backyard. Where *all* of this was coming from. The house, the telly, Dad's Mercedes, the new sheets, JD's good mood. Their feet automatically carried them away from that corner; it had become a habit.

'What do I say to people, Jai?'

'Tell them the same thing. This is not normal.' JD sat back. He grinned. 'Tell them that I'm making up the rules as I'm going along.'

Pam wasn't convinced. She sat there, in glum silence. She shook her head.

'You don't know people, Jai. How they talk.'

'So what, Mom?' JD's voice was gentle. 'This *isn't* normal, Mom. I need you to believe this. They'll be talking about this for years to come. Look at me.' Pam complied. She was really trying to process it, thought JD. 'This isn't some middle-class dream. No one won the lottery and went back to their normal lives with a little bit of extra money, okay? I don't care about the people outside this house, I never have. But you need to understand this, please. When I was little, and Dad would do that dance about being a doctor, an engineer, a manager, you were always the one who pulled me aside and said that you'd be okay if I was a sweeper as long as I did it well, and it was what I wanted to do. Right?' JD slid off the chair. He sat on the carpet, cross-legged, in front of his mother. He put a hand on her knee and peered up at her.

'Right?'

His mother nodded.

'So what's different, now?'

'The money, Jai.' She grimaced. 'They'll just ask and ask and then...' She shook her head vigorously. She patted his hand.

'They'll never see you the same way, Jai.'

JD grinned and shrugged. His mother nodded as if she agreed with him.

'They'll never look at us the same way also.'

And there it was. The actual argument. How far did the effects of trail-blazing extend?

Pam knew she had him. She hadn't come up here to manipulate him. But the truth was ever better than beating around emotion and tears. So she'd been brought up. However, she wasn't averse to the occasional low-blow.

'Also, people will slowly start saying you're a gay.' It was delivered as a bored observation.

'Christ, Mom. I told you to stop watching *Eastenders*. Watch those Indian things. Much better. And it's 'gay'. Not 'a' gay.'

'Beta, will you at least meet these girls? That's all. I promise. No pressure. Don't have to marry them. Just meet them?' She looked down at him, and she looked absolutely miserable. JD rubbed his eyes with the heels of his palms, hard. He was clueless about this stuff. He ran his hands through his hair. Then he thought: what would Mike do? What would Aziz do?

The answer was easy enough.

'I'll do it,' he said. His mom grinned and kissed the top of his head. As she got up, he said, 'I don't want the family bullshit. If you want me to meet them, I'm doing it as a date. Me and the girl. Coffee. Dinner. Something.' He looked at his mom. 'I won't drink. Okay?'

Pam nodded and began to leave the room. She was grinning like a fool.

'And don't make them all Punjabis, Mom,' JD called after her. He heard her sigh as she went down the stairs.

'Okay, fine,' she called out over her shoulder. 'I don't know why you make such a fuss, but fine. Learn from Aziz. He didn't have any conditions.'

JD was barely listening to her. He was caught in a momentary, vivid daydream. He'd never believed in love the way they sold it in the movies. But he wondered about what it would be like to meet someone through this process, as fucked up as it was. Suppose there was someone, a law student, maybe. They could talk about the things that were important to them, and have the chance to show each other why those things were important. It happened over the space of a few seconds, these unconnected, interconnected images of long, dark hair, a first-ever Arsenal game in person, arguments about music, being able to just take off to Bali for a holiday because they felt like and finding each other in bed, bringing each other along, learning the other's bodies. The dream lasted seconds, but it was powerful. It woke some small, unknown hunger in JD. And then he realized what his mom had said.

JD burst out of his door.

'You what?'

Pam paused at the foot of the stairs.

'What?'

'What about Aziz?'

Pam began to grin.

'You mean you didn't know?'

~

When they met next, JD sprang his knowledge on Aziz like an accusation. Aziz was nonchalant. Since the house, they were careful around each other.

'Yeah. It's been on the cards for a few months.'

'You got engaged?' JD didn't know whether to punch him or throw him through a door. In the end, he settled for a hug.

'No, not yet.' Aziz disentangled himself from JD's clutches. 'After we get back from Dubai. My grandmother—'

'Oh, yeah. Sure.' JD slowed down a little. He'd been

carrying on like one of them had just scored a goal in a big game. 'Why didn't you say anything, though?'

Aziz shrugged. 'We were waiting for everything to fall into place.' He looked at JD and frowned. 'I would've told you, you know. I was going to tell both of you in Dubai.'

Somehow, JD wasn't quite sure of that.

~

The Principle killed Atlas Trading on 26 September, nine days before the quarter ended for Fraser-Powell Trading. They had two companies ready, ghosts that just needed to be brought to life. Brian himself was going to run the second, new, importer. The second 'B' company, as had been the case with Alistair and Kenneth, was already in the game.

But, for the next two weeks, they simply waited. The Principle wanted to be sure that the dodge worked. The VAT game had caught on. Alistair and Kenneth reported two other companies that were running the same scam, survivors of the first game. Momentum had begun to gather.

The Principle were marking time, five months after they had rolled the dice.

~

Some time in the last three months, eight million pounds had exited the system. Val could see how all the trails disappeared into the dirty haze of the reclaim structure. But eight million pounds was nothing in the context of where Excise operated. Eight million out of fifty billion didn't merit much official consideration.

For Val, though, that particular Monday morning was a turning point. The scam jumped off the page. The carry-over impressed her, sounding a faint but disturbing alarm. April through to July, and now through to the end of September, and they were still here— whoever they were. They were small, *negligible*, and they refused to go away, like grit in an oyster.

And that was what Val was afraid of. Eight million, she knew, had just been the price of the ticket, a test of the system. If they made it past this reclaim, Excise was in for the show. They would go from slowly bleeding the system to jamming a syringe in its artery. Regardless of the number of arrests and further loopholes, they were going to see the number scream like a rocket. Out there, someone had just realized a life's dream.

The little group that had thought this up—whether in conjunction or independently, Val didn't know—had exhibited the rarest of traits in tax scams: patience. What Val appreciated here was that someone had taken the time to set this up very correctly. The simple fact that it had only been eight million pounds was proof in itself.

Val recommended banking. And paperwork. It was all she had, and it was number fourteen on the board on the first day. Within three days, it had been forgotten by everyone else in the department, and the VAT problem became Val's pet hobby. The question she carried on the tube, and on the walk home, all the way up to her door, was haunting in its simplicity. How was she to discover the root of this, the spark that had ignited this scam, when the perpetrators were always hidden to her?

She didn't know who they were, which was fair enough, but she didn't know what they were doing—and that was the hell of it. Small-time VAT scams were starting up all over the place, and dying natural deaths. Yet hidden from all of them, even from the people they arrested, was a small group of men who were making themselves disappear, every single time. How did they do it? And where had they started?

~

Kenneth told the story.

'Them boys came,' he said. The dogs, sniffing down a trail that had gone mysteriously cold at Fraser-Powell.

'Where did we buy our *phones* from? Well, you know, from here and there, but mostly from a company called Atlas Trading, guv. What's the problem?''

The two Jamaicans had sat there, impassive, slightly— properly—curious, behind a wall of paperwork, concentrating very hard not to break.

'I nearly pissed myself laughing,' said Kenneth. 'It was like being back in school where two of the teachers heard there's a dirty magazine stuffed in someone's desk, but they're not sure *where*. They didn't know, Jai. I swear to you. I mean, they suspect, that's why they were there, but there wasn't a damn thing those boys could do about it.'

'That's sounds about right,' JD said. 'There must be three hundred trails they're running down.'

'Trying to, anyway,' Mike put in.

'They were guessing,' Alistair said. And if a copper's guessing, you *know* he don't know.'

'Did they say anything about Atlas Trading?' Mike asked.

'The man says, "But this Atlas Trading—there's no one there."' Kenneth put his palms up and looked side to side in a don't-ask-me gesture. 'He tells us the office is shut down and no forwarding address. Do we know anything? So I tell him, "Well, they *did* say that they were having some trouble with the stock coming through, so we shifted to someone else."' .

Alistair chuckled and lifted his G&T. 'They explained it all nice and slow as you please, so that we might understand. New scam, this VAT thing. You never know if you're buying from a crooked dealer or not.'

'Yeah, but knew we exactly the shits we were dealing with,' Kenneth laughed.

The paperwork had held, spectacularly. The Principle— Atlas Trading in this context— hadn't put a foot wrong. The dogs came, they drank coffee and looked at books, asked questions and left. The drill was worn down, or the answers had been the same everywhere they'd shown up.

'They even gave us the lost lads' speech before they took off,' Kenneth said. 'It's a serious offence. Don't try anything funny, and call us if you see anything funny. And stay away from crooked importers—make sure you know who you're dealing with.'

'Imagine our embarrassment.'

'And we meant it too!' Tears were streaming down Kenneth's face. 'We were shifting to another dealer *immediately*.'

The knot held. It was time to *really* go to work.

Two importers, two chains. The Principle threw caution out of the window this time, and moved four million pounds in the next month.

~

Aziz had met Rishi Tiwari three years ago. The first meeting occurred in a way that Aziz was now accustomed to. He got a phone call from someone else, introducing Rishi, explaining that he had a problem. Aziz set it up for the next day. Rishi was clearly both nervous and embarrassed. He came into the meeting in denial and sagging under the usual guilt—it wasn't his fault, he was just doing what he saw everyone else around him doing. A public display of vulnerability to strangers, for the subcontinent folk, was tantamount to getting caught masturbating.

Rishi ran one of the endless dodgy bureaus de change in East London. Aziz knew that a good number of the exchange bureaus were money laundering fronts dealing in piddle—six months worth of savings wired home through a holding company in a tax-free haven, with a neat charge up front. Rishi had been hauled over the coals for criminally stupid accounting that could hardly be anything *but* laundering.

Aziz straightened the matter out in weeks. They pleaded misunderstanding of rules as a result of the cultural gap and language trouble. The case collapsed because jurisdictions across non-EU nations were always problematic—Dubai and Hong Kong were the principle destinations before the holding company forwarded the money to where it was meant to go—and because you could turn Immigration Control on its head by painting the victim vulnerable enough. Aziz filed it away for later use, refused payment and sent Rishi on his way. Within a year and a half, he had access to half the money launderers in the East End.

In the last week of September, the Principle started shutting down the current accounts in which they had parked the pure profit they'd taken from the importers by beating the VAT reclaims and started wiring the money to Dubai. The Principle used a series of covers—investment firms, venture capitalists and dotcoms. The amounts were never larger than eight or nine hundred thousand pounds since anything above that was asking for extra scrutiny.

The Dubai counterpart in this game, one of the laundering fronts that Aziz had befriended, would request that the payments be sent to Hong Kong or Dubai. From here, the money would be filtered twice or thrice through a range of companies. It always showed up on paper as investments arriving and profits sent out—or loans simply given or repaid—on phantom transactions that never existed. In the end, the money went into a Special Purpose Vehicle company owned by Jai Singh Dewan, Mike Hamilton and Aziz Basrai. The SPV's whole purpose was that it could make loans and investments worldwide, and the money it sent out looked like it was from trading profits locally in Dubai, or loans from financial institutions.

When the Principle needed cash in London, the Dubai counterpart would receive money from the SPV and send it to their London branch. The cash would then drip-feed into the system. On the books, the feed was a distribution to over twenty people on the street—importers, 'B' level merchants, retail-level companies around the Heston Principle. The Principle's name never showed up anywhere, insulating them from the laundering trail completely.

All that remained was for them to get to Dubai and sign the papers that would bring the SPV to life. Otherwise, the chain was up and running.

~

The Principle were done signing contracts in three hours on the first day. The rest of the trip was a tutorial in money and fucking—the holiday that Mike and JD had dreamed about since they'd started making a living.

Up until this week, the two of them had been able to track the progress of their personal wealth through ATM receipts. They'd always worked hard for their money, and they'd thought they knew where to spend it. Until they got to Dubai. They were virgins here. It wasn't just better food in first class when they had flown over, it was the fact that the stewardess knew their names. It was the speed with which they got off the plane and sailed past immigration, past the nervous Indians and Pakis. It was the BMW Sevens for each of them, waiting at the airport.

Aziz let the other two run wild for the first two days before he began to point them in the right direction. He let them drink Absolut to their heart's content and then pointed them toward Grey Goose, then Stoli, and then Chopin. If you were going to blow up your cash, you might as well do it right. The same applied to the girls they were picking up. Two nights of pulls at the Plaza disco later, Aziz—who had been passing through Dubai on a regular basis for two years— decided that he needed to brief them about the hooker hierarchy in Dubai beyond the usual mix of air-hostesses, tourists, expats, and the rest of the compliant meat at the club every night.

'The Russians are the most abundant.' Aziz nodded towards two girls gliding around the buffet counter. School was in session at the hotel café during what should have been breakfast had they been keeping track. Mike looked again. You had to really look, but they were made up immaculately. The clothes were casual, but expensive, and the jeans were like second skin.

'It's the Plaza. So there's a standard. Out at the cheaper clubs, they get a bit dire. There are girls there who look like transvestites after a three-day bender at six in the evening.'

Mike was halfway through a medium-rare porterhouse and sipping a Coke, though Aziz could smell the alcohol through his pores. JD's lips squirmed and danced over his teeth as he worked his scotch, and Aziz thought he could actually *see* the vapour coming off him. But JD's eyes were still sharp and it was a holiday, after all.

The penalties for getting caught with even a little cocaine in Dubai weren't worth the risk, even to JD, but there was no problem in scoring a legit prescription for Ephedrine. When he crushed the pills up it gave him the same ritual he got from

coke, even if the high wasn't quite the same. But, again, it
was never about the high itself. It was ritual.

'The Russians overran the Dubai prostitution racket a lot
like they did the underworld back home,' Aziz waved JD's
smoke away from the poached egg he was waiting to pierce
with a corner of toast. 'I got the godamned anthropology
from the man I used to work for. The Ethiopians are
interesting, but fairly rare now. The Ugandans, well, they're
downright nasty, but they fuck like freight trains.'

'Don't fancy fucking a freight train,' JD laughed around
a mouthful.

Aziz ignored him. 'The Moroccans are the most valued,
which is why you'll never see them.'

'Never say never,' JD said. 'I can bloody well try a
Moroccan girl if I like. It's a free market. Fuck's the point of
being a capitalist?'

'And don't let the bastards tell you any different.' Mike had
been egging JD on the entire trip. 'Why shouldn't JD have a
Moroccan if he likes? Nothing wrong with him.'

Aziz looked at them indulgently, like he was trying to
educate two cousins from the country. 'They're the ones
reserved for the Sheikhs, and they pretty much disappear
from the airport. Off the plane and into the Bentley.'

'Fucking Arabs,' Mike shook his head.

'Right?' JD snubbed out his cigarette. 'It's the fucking
Doxy all over again.'

Aziz's ears pricked up. He had an idea what they were
referring to, but here he had something really useful to teach
them. 'The Filipinas, though,' he said. 'They're the real prize.

They commanded the market for years until the Russians showed up. And they're not as easily available. But...' Aziz dipped an end of toast through the surface of his yolk. 'If you can find yourselves the *right* Filipina, you are going to remember it for a long, long time.'

'Don't trust him,' Mike told JD. Both his partners stared at him. 'The man's been pulling white girls for two days. He doesn't want your competition there.'

~

It was around three the next morning when JD met his Filipina, and the next thing he knew it was dawn. He imagined she was one of Aziz's fabled Moroccan girls because in that light, so strange and muted through the gauzy curtains, and her face so close, she could be anyone. And so could he.

He watched her enormous dark eyes gazing down at him, her small palms flat on his chest as she writhed. She was breathing through her mouth and her eyes kept getting bigger, her face kept changing, growing, seeming to come closer and closer though he could never tell if it was really coming towards him or not.

He saw something there in the dark between them, in the animal rhythm, the loops inside loops—the endlessness.

But it did end. Everything did.

A hard sound came out of his throat. She held still above him for another few seconds, biting her lip. Then she said, '*Fuck!*' and hopped off him.

JD heard her footsteps pad into the heavier darkness and the shower turn on.

She came back wrapped in a hotel robe, smoking one of her own cigarettes, and curled up in the chair beside the bed, balancing an ashtray on the arm.

'I was almost there,' she said. Smoke drifted on the pale light. JD felt like he was in a waking dream.

'I'm sorry.' JD rolled onto his elbows and reached for his packet of cigarettes on the nightstand, lighting up. There was a glass of Chivas and recently melted ice beside the cigarettes—he reached for that, too.

'It's not your fault.'

'Well, you don't know me,' JD tried. 'Maybe if it was someone you really liked.'

'You're all right.' She smiled at him. 'It just goes on and on, you know?'

JD stared at her. He felt a strange exhilaration, shot through with fear. He was on a ledge, he always had been, and it was a long, long way down. Only, he didn't know where else to be. He had never known.

'Endless,' he said. It was little more than a whisper.

'What?'

He finished the Scotch, poured himself another and sat up in the bed, the sheets pooled around his waist. The girl gestured for the glass with her chin. He passed it to her.

'This bloke grew up down the street from me,' he said. 'Jimmy Tipnis. His dad was Indian and his mum was English. Typical product of England.'

The girl tilted her head to one side and her brow furrowed. JD knew he was about to become Story-Telling John, but it wasn't as if he'd hired her off the street for thirty quid. They'd partied together for hours, done a respectable amount of drugs together. There had to be some basis for friendship in there. And besides, she'd started it.

'So Jimmy, he grew up thoroughly ordinary. You know, successful in little ways, completely unspectacular, but a regular, decent guy. He did okay in school, but he didn't go to University because his family couldn't really afford it so he went to work for his dad in their dry-cleaning business.'

The girl nodded. She passed the Scotch back to JD. He sipped.

'The shop did all right, especially during the festive months and towards the end of the year when you get all the Indian weddings. Jimmy was still poking about, trying to find ways to move up in the world, make something happen. He was trying to get to university, trying to get his father to expand the business. They'd even signed the lease on a small shop closer to Southall. It made sense, you know, to cash in on a specialized knowledge of how to wash sarees when people pulled them out of suitcases every year.'

He paused, watching her. Light was beginning to creep into the room. The world was forcing its way into this story and JD already felt like he was short of time. He saw that the girl's face was freshly scrubbed of last night's make-up. She looked older now, but prettier, more natural. More like a person. He would have to do another line very soon or that would bother him more than he was ready for just yet.

'Yes?' she said.

JD meant to take a sip of the Scotch, but gulped a mouthful and nearly choked on it. His eyes watered.

'So Jimmy was bright, he had ideas, he didn't drink too much, he watched normal porn, and the lad even had a steady girlfriend.' His pulse had quickened. He felt the familiar signs. Like he was being wound up for launch. JD drained the glass at once, trying to fucking feel *that* already. 'So then, then—without an explanation, not even a fucking note or any apparent reasons, Jimmy Tipnis upped and killed himself at twenty-five.'

The girl shifted in the chair and said nothing. JD felt the crash coming, at the back of his throat. The girl must've sensed something, because she caught his eye and tapped her nostril. He turned back to the nightstand and fetched the kit.

A minute later, though it felt much longer to JD, he was on his elbows again, telling the girl, 'And it became, like, the great mystery of my life. Why did Jimmy Tipnis kill himself? Everyone had a theory, of course. Racism, weird cults, homosexuality.'

Ice cubes tinkled in his drink as he spoke and some Chivas escaped the glass. The girl held out her hand and JD passed it to her.

'I had my own theory,' JD said, smoothing his hand over the Scotch stain under his chin. 'We were never really close or anything, but our fathers had been friends for years. I mean, I knew him. We didn't have to be the best of friends, I knew this guy, you know?'

The girl nodded over the rim of the glass. Now JD badly wanted a cigarette, but he didn't want to turn back to the nightstand. He didn't want to move. He knew it. Here, now, in this room with this girl and the fleeing dark, he got it.

'Jimmy Tipnis killed himself because he was afraid of every other choice. The choices weren't terrifying, but they all meant something different from the norm. He was afraid of doing anything except just exactly what was expected of him. To any other kid around him, it looked like he was right the fuck where he was supposed to be. But everything he really had to look forward to was hard work and bullshit and surrender.'

The girl took her own packet of cigarettes from a pocket in the robe, put two in her mouth and lit them both, never taking her great, dark eyes off JD. She handed him a smoke and the glass of Scotch.

He thanked her, then took a drag and a sip.

'Jimmy Tipnis killed himself,' he said, 'because he was afraid. He was afraid of the boring, of every day, of his own fucking face in the mirror. And that's what happens if you listen to your parents long enough. Or anybody else, for that matter. Fuck that.'

The girl sniffled and rubbed her nose, smiling, and held her hand out for the glass. Then she said, 'You're telling me?'

~

The next afternoon, JD stumbled around Dubai Mall with a list. He felt foolish, and more than a bit ashamed. He clutched his mobile phone like a Bible. He was completely at sea, amongst sizes and colours. He thought it would be a quick visit, but it stretched into a three-and-a-half-hour expedition. He stalled Mike and Aziz as long as he could, but finally gave up his location.

The two of them showed in ten minutes, in regulation tourist wear. Shorts, white shirts, dark glasses. They walked into the store and found their friend dressed in black, saddled with shopping bags like he was a modern art installation depicting the idea of a Christmas tree.

'What the hell's going on?' asked Aziz.

'You look like you just robbed a funeral,' observed Mike.

'I. Yeah.' JD looked from one to the other. 'I really don't want to discuss it.'

'Yeah, but we do.'

They found a coffee shop and sat down. Mike and Aziz dispossessed JD of his shopping and his mobile like they were pickpockets let loose on a Swiss tourist.

'Jesus.' Mike continued to pull clothes out of bags. 'Fuck.'

Aziz, meanwhile, was scrolling through JD's phone.

'Channel, Prada, Cavalli, Armani, Versace, Choo.' He paused. 'This cannot be an actual text message. Please tell me this isn't an actual text message. This reads like an ad for a distress sale in fucking Cosmo.' Aziz snapped his fingers at JD. 'Jai?'

'Yeah, I— '

'*Bally*? You bought Pamela a Bally? It's not even on the fucking list...' Aziz's voice trailed off. He was scrolling through the phone again.

'No, I bought that for her.'

'She gives you a shopping list from hell, that you comply with, and *then* you buy her a ten-thousand-pound handbag?'

JD was blushing. It was the only time either Mike or Aziz had seen him blush.

'I felt bad about last night.'

Aziz held his head in his hands. It was Mike's turn to pick up the interrogation baton.

'Is she your girlfriend?'

'No.' Even JD seemed to realize how bad it sounded. 'Not yet.'

'I hope she's worth it,' Aziz muttered. His head was still in his hands and he couldn't stop shaking it.

Mike burst out laughing. He laughed loud enough for people to look at them. Aziz looked up, curious. Mike got himself under control but it took him a while. He shook his head, indicated that there was something he wanted to say, and burst out laughing again.

'Sorry,' he said finally. He drank some coffee. He looked at Aziz. 'This is going to slightly confronting for you.' He turned his attention to JD. 'Begging your pardon, my friend. Up top. Really.' Mike was biting his lip, trying to stop himself from laughing again.

'Have you slept with her yet?'

Aziz's head shot up. He looked thunderstruck.

JD cleared his throat.

'I, um, refuse to answer that question.'

Aziz groaned. He grabbed his head with his hands, as if he was in pain. Mike just sat there with a huge grin on his face.

'You're fucking unbelievable.'

'Jai.' Aziz was looking at him very seriously. 'Look. It's gone on enough, okay? There's women like this walking around London. You're like Cleartone to them. You're the easiest play walking.'

JD said nothing.

'You're going to be spending a lot of money on this bird. And then she'll start talking to you about a whole bunch of cousins she has, and can you hook them up? All of 'em will be guys, and she'll hug them much too tight and for much too long. Oh, good lord—'

Aziz went back to grabbing his head. He'd seen JD fidget as he spoke.

'She's already started, hasn't she?'

JD didn't answer the question. They sat in silence for a while. Aziz looked like he had the world's worst headache. Mike couldn't get the smirk off his face. JD looked absolutely miserable.

'Look,' he said. 'I'm not saying that you guys are wrong. I'm just saying that I'm enjoying the ride and I'm okay with what's going on. That's all.' He looked around the table once. He was going to be defiant about this. And the other two knew that there wasn't much they could do.

'Fuck it,' said Aziz. 'Just make sure you don't stay on too long.'

~

When the Principle brought Dubai to a close, Mike was downstairs clubbing like an animal. JD and Aziz spent the last evening in Aziz's suite. They sat in the living room, drinking single malt at a sedate pace, looking at the glittering city below them. Aziz had rigged the DVD player, and it played endless jazz.

JD stirred. Time seemed unimportant here. This felt like the single moment of calm in a chaotic, powerful dream.

'What's on your plate when you head back?' he asked.

'The engagement?' Aziz frowned slightly. No one had mentioned the impending engagement since they'd landed in Dubai. It seemed impolite to do so.

'Nah.'

'I'm going outward, and I'm going deeper.' Aziz paused, sipped whisky. 'Before I'm done, they're going to need to dynamite me out of London. And if and when they do, I'll take away eight hundred million pounds.'

Even a year ago, the figure would have startled JD. Not any more. He understood the grease that moved that wheel.

'I'm going to go back and I'm going to spread the word in certain circles. I'm going to put some subcontinent kids through University.'

JD frowned. 'You're going to give them loans?'

Aziz shook his head. 'They can pay me back if they want—at zero interest. If they want. And if they're able. But the...' He searched for the right word. 'The *grant* isn't contingent on repayment. They just need to be deserving, in the right kinds of ways.'

JD was silent for a moment, trying to get his head around it.

'What're you trying to do? Create an army for yourself?'

Laughing, Aziz said, 'Nah, mate. I don't have those pretensions.'

'Then what, A? What's with the Robin Hood gig?'

Aziz nodded. The Robin Hood mention pleased him. He

concentrated very hard, Miles rolling on in the background, endlessly. Aziz leaned forward in his chair.

'Have you heard the word *havala?*'

JD started to shake his head and stopped. It was familiar in a way that he couldn't place.

'About five years ago, they almost brought the government in India down with havala.'

'Huh?' It was involuntary on JD's part. This, he hadn't been expecting.

Aziz shrugged—it wasn't important, it was an example.

'It's-money-laundering system. But it's really a system of favours, okay? You trade favours. Legal, illegal, it doesn't matter. But you need patience. They don't have that in the West. Sometimes you have to wait ten, twenty years. And it's not always about profit. But it *is* about favours. And everybody remembers.'

There was a long silence as Aziz lit a cigarette. JD remembered it as a haunted moment because it was one of the very few times that he saw right into the motor that drove Aziz.

'It's two things, JD. I'm rich, and I'm going to get much richer. You could view it as chance. You *could*,' he repeated because JD was shaking his head. 'I don't believe that's the case. I saw, I *see* opportunities. They're there to be taken. And I take them. So then it's my duty to spread it around. That's what I believe, that's what I was brought up to believe, and that is why we—as a colour—survive wherever in the world we go.'

He stared into JD's eyes.

'And that makes me essential.'

The penny dropped for JD. Aziz stood at the centre of hundreds of thousands of conflicting currents. He walked with opportunity, every step he took. He had done it because he recognized that community was the only advantage he possessed in a strange country that was so very different from his own.

'Dalal is a dirty word where we come from, Jai. It means broker. But people take it to mean bhadwa—a pimp. But dalals turn the world. Even gods have dalals. Priests are pimping God, teachers are pimping their philosophies. I'm a dalal, Jai. I deal in favours. Some I take, and some I give. And I do it well. That is all.'

JD saw the sense in it, and the mad ambition. He'd never be able to do it himself, but he respected it. He respected it because it was a weapon, an even greater one than money, and he respected it because he could see Aziz make it work. Plus, it was fucking crazy. Things like that always had his approval.

He laughed a short, sharp, barking laugh. 'You're scary, mate. If you ever invent a religion, we're all fucked.'

Aziz grinned back. He picked up his glass and raised it to JD. 'You're pretty scary yourself, Jai. You're a storm-front, the eye of the fucking madness. I've never seen anything like it.'

JD raised his glass in return. The compliment meant the world to him, coming from one of the two men who had all of his respect.

'Cheers, bruv.' Aziz smiled at him and, for just one moment, they had rolled back a decade. JD would remember it vividly. It would become the clearest memory he had, that moment from that week in Dubai. After that, things became too jagged, too much of the final charge of the light brigade.

They drank.

'Where did it come from, A?' asked JD.

JD never knew what prompted the question. Much later, he would think about circumstance seriously, about the right time and the right place, and about the statistical improbability of poker hands. Straight Flush. Spades. Six-hundred-and-fifty-thousand-to-one.

And they had no fucking idea.

The question threw Aziz completely. He looked like someone had smacked him across the face. JD had an absurd urge to apologize. He opened his mouth but Aziz shook his head.

'It's... I—' Aziz looked at the floor. JD had never seen him like this.

'I'll tell you what. Zero moments—'where'd it come from?'—are a bit like... making sausages.' He smiled. Better this time, almost natural. 'And that's something—'

'—that every good Muslim kid knows a lot about,' finished JD. It was an old joke. 'You okay?'

'Sure,' nodded Aziz. 'It was... unexpected. The question. But it was what I was thinking about. Because of chance. Because it came from chance.' Aziz paused again. JD was reminded of their conversation on a park bench ten months ago. Aziz wasn't struggling with what to say so much as *how* to say it. He looked at JD. He waited until something satisfied him. Perhaps it was simply the fact the he would have to tell someone, ultimately.

'I nearly blew the Master's exam. I don't know how I got through it. I don't remember it. I don't remember it at all.'

JD began to ask a question and stopped himself. He didn't know which question to ask. The assumption that Aziz had always been the near-perfect student was like a law of nature. This was like the first time that you discovered that your dad could be wrong.

And... he didn't *remember*?

Aziz looked at him like he'd heard the question.

'It's not a metaphor.'

'Booze?'

'Some,' said Aziz. 'Other things. Mostly terror.'

No drama, nothing but fact. That, thought JD, was perhaps the scariest thing.

'Three weeks in deep space. Lived on panic. Like fuel.' Aziz stopped and sighed. JD had never seen anyone look so old, so tired—he was even worse than Mike had looked when they thought they were going to lose it on the Calais run.

'You know what happens, right?'

Jimmy Tipnis, JD thought.

'I fell asleep one night,' Aziz told him. 'Thought I'd pick up the slack the next morning. I'd been thinking it for months. I woke up forty-five minutes later and I knew, I just knew, that if I waited even a second longer, it would be too late. I picked up the first book I saw. Tax Law. Read. Made tea. Read. And I don't know if it was because I was coming out of the longest fucking blackout I'd ever had, or what. But I read seventeen-and-a-half per cent, made tea thinking seventeen-and-a-half per cent, got back to seventeen-and-a-half per cent. And then I just *saw*. Saw a scam, drew a flowchart, checked it out.'

Aziz stopped, fumbling for a cigarette.

'Burnt it after—the flowchart. Year-and-a-half ago. Dream fucking scam. Your Ultimate Game, Jai. The Holy Grail. And here we are. Millionaires, all.'

JD frowned. Aziz laughed, the most natural sound he'd made in the past few minutes.

'I'm running with the most rabid pack of motherfuckers I've ever met.' He grinned. 'It's a compliment.' Aziz felt the filter go hot and soft as he dragged on his cigarette. 'Okay,' he said. His voice was soft. 'Okay. Just to pass the time.'

JD simply waited, there, outlined by the window, looking at Aziz.

'I didn't know how to do it, you know. All I knew was that the profit in this scenario—the one that came to me late at night—was predicated on demand and supply. If you could control demand and supply, then all you had to do was run the loop over and over again. And the money would fall into place.'

Aziz's hands were turning the trick with the lighter, over and over. He stopped and looked at JD.

'I'm telling you that this thing is perfect. It's the best thing that anyone's ever come up with. And I'll tell you why. Within what you did with buying *our* stock from level 'B' *ourselves* is the Pandora's Box. If you apply that to the whole process, then it's a landslide, Jai. It's a fucking natural disaster.'

JD shook his head. The conversation was suddenly moving too fast. Aziz leaned forward. The lighter kept snapping open and then clicking shut.

'In this game, Jai, where's the profit coming from?'

'The—' began JD and stopped abruptly, clamping down so hard on the second word that he accidentally bit his tongue. Something crystalline, geometric—a structure that he could sense very clearly, was forming in his head.

'What would people say, Jai? People who are not me and you? Where's the profit?'

'The phones,' JD whispered. He felt like he had seen a great, complex truth for the very first time.

'But people like you or me, Jai. What do we know? Where does the profit come from?'

'The VAT.' Tears stood in JD's eyes.

Aziz snapped the lighter open again and struck the flint. JD saw the flame catch, but he didn't really see it.

'What I'm asking, JD, is what happens if we close the loop all the way? What if we populate the level beyond "C" as well? What happens if we complete the process you've invented? We *keep* buying. All the way. We buy from "C", and then we buy from that level, call it "D", and then, fuck it, we set up something in France that buys from "D".' Aziz paused. Smiled. 'Want to complete it for me?'

JD had to clear his throat. He felt like Aziz must have when JD had figured out the closed loop process. The clarity of seeing a permutation so fundamentally simple that it changed the face of the planet. Systematic induced inflation, Aziz had called it. And it *was* a natural disaster. All he had to do was take them back to the beginning.

'If we buy in France,' he said, 'then we can just send the same phones back again, through the forwarder.'

Aziz nodded. '*That's* money from air,' he said. 'That's the game. That's...' Aziz raised his eyebrows, urging JD to finish the thought.

JD looked at him, wiping his eyes. 'Perfect,' he said. 'It's the perfect game.'

There was silence. Aziz looked down at the lighter and realized that the flame had settled into a column of orange. He snapped it shut. His head was roaring. The iteration of the game had been turning in his head for weeks but it was only now that he'd spoken it out loud for the first time that he could fully believe in it. Aziz had seen the possibilities the moment JD closed the loop. Now it was real. And he was in charge again.

'You asked what was on my plate? I was going to tell the two of you when we got back. And then we were going to spend the next two months setting up this—this ghost industry—and then just bleed the Exchequer dry. That's the plate. Heaped fucking full.'

JD looked up and Aziz flinched. JD's eyes held a blank, anonymous ferocity. For a moment, there was a stranger in the room. Then JD blinked, and he was JD again. He looked shaken and very unsure of himself.

'Can I—' he began, but stopped himself. There was something here, something monumental. It was there in Aziz's word *ghost*, and in the Hollywood Principle. The *system runs the programme*. It talked to him. It danced for him, whirling in and out of reach.

The Ultimate Game. The Perfect Game.

The once in a lifetime shot. The money machine.

He had asked Aziz at exactly the right time, and Aziz had used the right words, and then it had somehow all fallen together, in the right way, at this very moment. He was hesitant, because he had no idea what he meant to say. He thought he might have something. He thought he might have—

'Something that controls the tide,' he mumbled.

'Pardon?' Aziz looked concerned.

JD shook his head. 'Sorry. It's just, something like this, it *would* be like controlling the tide, wouldn't it? Because it would be like controlling the economy.'

Aziz tilted his head back, as if judging the distance between himself and a gorgeous car that might go out of control. Eyeing JD down the bridge of his nose, he said, 'Have you got *another* idea?'

JD held up his hand, just like he had held up his hand in front of his father.

'A glimmer. It's probably nothing. But I need some time. Could I get a little time?'

Aziz nodded, slowly. 'Mate, you take all the time in the world. It's your company as much as it's mine.'

When you saw something, you couldn't unsee it. When you began an action, it was irrevocable, whether you completed the action or not. Knowledge was a permanent scar. And knowledge made a whore out of you. Because your trigger never changed. You could control your reactions to anything, but you could never control your impulses.

Aziz hadn't lived with the loop for three months, trying to find a way in. When you learned to see the loop, *everything* was an extension of the loop. And JD saw it. But did they have the balls for it? It boiled down to the same question as ever.

Did he believe?

~

JD had his sunglasses on, the window shade down, and his reading light off when the flight took off for London and the air-hostess brought him and Mike their first Bloody Marys. They were sore, they were satisfied, and they wanted more. There was no end in sight.

Turning to Mike, JD watched him above the rims of his shades for a moment. Then he said, 'Did I ever tell you about Jimmy Tipnis?'

'Sure,' Mike said. 'Bloke offed himself.'

'Well,' JD began, 'there's more.'

For a long while after, JD would wonder from time to time if the goddess in his room had been real, if he'd really told her those things before he ever thought to tell them to his best friend. He wondered if he would even know her if he ever saw her again.

And he wasn't at all sure that he wanted to find out.

2.4

JD was the only one who stopped at duty-free. He was the only one with anyone to shop for. When he emerged, Aziz was gone. Mike peeled off into London on the way in from the airport. They needed more offices, and they needed to staff them. They were building an economy.

JD was alone the rest of the way back to Heston, and he would be alone for the better part of the next month. He was dreaming again.

But before the train rolled out of that station, they had the small matter of an engagement.

~

Mike brought Billy along to the engagement. JD had blurted out the idea when Aziz handed them their invitations a few days after they returned from Dubai.

'Bring the kid,' said JD airily. 'Be good for him. See a Bollywood wedding.'

Mike had done his research after JD had told him about Aziz's engagement. He'd marvelled at how they'd been blindsided by a development that had clearly been months in the making. It was none of his business. But he liked to know. Mike was with JD's dad on this; he didn't like surprises.

He knew enough to know that it wasn't likely to be Bollywood in any way. The card he was holding was proof of that. But JD had gone ahead and put Aziz on the spot when Mike wasn't even sure that he and JD deserved an invite to this gig.

'No—'

'No, it's fine,' said Aziz. 'Please do. That would be good. Would you like me to invite your sister as well?'

Mike grinned and shook his head. If his guess was right, Cathy wouldn't want to be part of this. This engagement was likely to be intimidating. JD clearly had no idea of what he was talking about.

But he would take Billy along. It *would* be good for him.

Mike didn't like kids. He found them noisy and needy. On the whole, the concept of family left him cold. But he and Billy had become friends naturally and easily. He'd never had to pretend to be a father figure, or a role model. He liked that Cathy had let the kid be. Billy was a grave child. He was shy and fiercely bright. He had a strange sense of humour—very dry. He liked to find out how things worked. And he gradually found out that Uncle Mike would usually let him find out how things worked if he behaved himself, and if he asked politely and if it wasn't too dangerous.

Mike had started putting money away for Billy three years ago. The kid didn't know. And neither did Greg, his father. Mike had only mentioned it to Cathy once. He just put away a small percentage of every bit of money he made. He didn't care about too many people but he thought that his nephew was a good enough kid to have the ability to decide what he wanted to do with his life.

And he thought that it might be interesting for Billy to attend an engagement that, in many ways, was a small, understated, but important event in the London calendar.

In spite of what JD thought.

~

Although it was a Saturday evening, they went old-school. Mike and Billy drove across to JD's. They got in the Rover and drove across to JD's parents. They piled in and set off for the heart of town. The destination was a place that Mike hadn't even heard of. It was an exclusive Indian restaurant called 'Durbar'. They didn't advertise, they weren't in the rankings, they didn't make the *Observer* lists. They were just a very expensive Indian restaurant in the heart of London that ran solely on word of mouth. They had a set menu and they were booked through to the third week of January, two-and-a-half months away.

JD continued to ply Billy with unwanted advice.

'It's all about your steps, see? Now, you're not Asian, obviously—'

'Obviously,' muttered Billy.

'—you watch your mouth young man, obviously, so you're unlikely to be abreast with the latest developments in the steps department, see? They come up with new steps all the time. All sorts of sh—ay—stuff. Screwing on light bulbs, crushing out cigarettes, swivel them hips and get atop a train even. They must've died when that thing went through the tunnel.' JD looked back at Billy, perched in the centre of the rear seat. There was an instant chorus:

'JD—'

'You damn fool—'

'Keep your eye—'

'Just drive, would you?'

JD let it all slide past him.

'You just bring the confidence, young man. You gotta *look* like you know what you're doing. That's all.' JD nodded at Billy calmly and went back to driving.

Mike spoke up from next to Billy. He'd given up the front seat to JD's dad, even though he was about half a foot taller. JD's dad tried to fight it, but Mike knew enough to know that they had to roll into this place with Mr Dewan in the front seat.

'Her dad's the head of neurosurgery at the National Hospital for Neurology.'

'Eh?' JD glanced at Mike quickly.

'It's one of the biggest hospital and research things in the world.'

'It's also part of the University College trust,' put in JD's dad.

'What does that mean?'

JD's dad shrugged. 'He's probably going to be on the board, within the year,' he said.

JD looked at Mike. He was completely lost.

'He's a big man, JD.' Mike grinned. 'Probably no dancing today.'

JD groaned. 'It's an *orthodox* gig. Probably no discreet room in the corner either, huh?'

Mike shook his head.

'Damn it.' JD looked back at Billy balefully. 'What do we do with you, you midget?'

The same question, thought Mike, applied to JD.

~

'Durbar' was beautiful. Mike had expected nothing less, and yet he was still struck by what money *could* buy. The entire restaurant had been taken over for the function—both the main dining room and the garden. To JD's relief, the arrangements were better than a discreet room in the corner. Two bar counters, with top-notch booze. It wasn't limited range, Mike noted. There was no house whisky. You could order what you pleased.

The whole place shimmered. The effect was that of little pockets of light, bottled, poured wherever required. Mike saw dozens of candles, setting off the white and gold décor. About as many Chinese lanterns seemed to float in the air; different sizes, all of them dialled down so that the place looked like it was lit by a hundred setting suns. The restaurant glowed from within. It wasn't intimidating, as he'd feared. Instead, it seemed to lift you to its standard.

As they walked in, Mrs Dewan leading the way and Mr Dewan leading a slightly overwhelmed Billy, JD hung

back and tapped Mike's arm. Mike slowed, checked that Billy
wasn't looking around for him, that he seemed comfortable
enough with Mr Dewan, and then stopped. He turned
to JD. For the first time, he noticed that JD's eyes were
slightly bloodshot.

Mike made a face at JD. He tilted his head to one side,
looked at JD for a moment, sighed and shook his head.

'I smoked one in the afternoon,' JD said. 'Because I
thought they'd be pouring bhangra through the speakers.
Shoot me.' He reached up and fiddled with his tie. Both of
them were wearing new suits. Afterthought or no, they'd
made damned sure that they looked like Aziz Basrai's friends.
They weren't business associates here.

'Why d'you know so much about her dad?' asked JD.
'Why d'you know so much about this engagement?'

'I wanted to know, when you told me.' Mike looked at
JD carefully. Bloodshot eyes aside, he was sharp, all the way.
'Also, I got a little worried.'

JD turned his head and looked into the restaurant,
through to the end of the driveway they were standing in.
Aziz's parents had met his own at the door, and were being
introduced to Billy. As he watched, he saw his dad look around
for Mike and him. Aziz's mother raised her hand. She waved
and then beckoned them over. JD raised his arm in return.
He looked at Mike again.

'He's gone very public, hasn't he?'

'Mate, this thing is a social event. Seriously.' They'd begun
to walk, slowly. 'I wish him the best, I really do. But we've

got to keep the Forwarder separate. Because, any monkey business, and he's going to be in some papers.'

'We're going to be in the papers ourselves pretty soon,' said JD absently.

'Huh?'

JD briefly turned the grin on. He thumped Mike on the shoulder once.

'You'll find out soon enough. But eyes and ears. This is a working lunch.'

~

It didn't turn into the covert fact-finding mission that JD had hoped for. It was still a surreal evening because all the pieces didn't quite gel for Mike. It all made sense, yes. But that didn't mean that everything fit.

The evening started going downhill the moment they walked in. JD had barely made his jibe about a working lunch when he was accosted by Pamela.

'What?' she demanded. 'You thought I wouldn't know?'

'I—'

'When were you going to tell me? Why am I not your date?'

Mike let them drift away as they argued. Well, as Pamela hissed and JD stuttered. He'd seen Pamela on and off for the last little while. She seemed to have become attached to JD, without anyone having any control over it. Like a medical condition. Like a case of the clap. Except that she was also an unending pain in the ass.

If he wasn't sleeping with her, then there was absolutely

no reason for JD to be within twenty miles of her. Mike could cheerfully drop her off the side of a very tall building.

Mike was about to start looking for Aziz when he saw JD's mom—Mrs Dewan—making her way across to her son and the attractive young harpy he seemed to be arguing with. Mike watched her walk and began to grin. This thing was going to go off like a fireworks show. JD probably deserved it, given that he'd let his vampire hang around for as long as he had already.

And then he remembered that Mrs.D had activated Mrs Walia. She was looking to get her son married. Actually. Honest to God.

He was looking at a lit fuse heading towards a pile of gunpowder. Even JD didn't deserve this. Mike whirled around, trying to locate Billy. The kid was dutifully standing next to Mr Dewan. Mike waved his hands above his head, knowing that behaviour of this kind was probably frowned upon at this restaurant. They might toss him. He didn't care. Billy spotted him after a few seconds. The kid smiled in relief, raised his hand in return and took one step towards Mike. He stopped. He looked alarmed. Mike waved even more frantically. Then he made a big pantomime 'Stop' gesture, followed by 'Stay there, I'll come and get you.'

Fuck, thought Mike. The kid looks like this is his worst nightmare. He grinned. 'Sorry', he mouthed. He held up two fingers. 'Stay, I'll be there in two minutes.' He used the thumb and the index finger of his right hand to push the corners of his mouth up. 'Smile', the gesture said. 'Relax'.

The kid nodded.

Mike turned and started walking immediately. He nearly walked into a server with a tray. He swerved and kept going. His speed was just short of a run. He was going to be late, he could tell. He could see Mrs Dewan tap JD on the elbow. Both JD and Pamela turned to face her. He was going to be twenty-odd seconds late. Mike was still eight feet away when he could hear the end of the introductions.

'—Pamela?'

'Malhotra, Aunty.'

'And you are…?'

Mrs Dewan directed the question towards JD, but she left it open. JD and Pamela answered the question at the same time.

'Just a friend—'

'—his girlfriend actually—'

There was a second of absolute silence.

Mrs Dewan managed one word 'You—' before Mike got there.

'Hey, Pam. Hey, Mrs D.' Mike had no idea that he could sound this breezy. 'Jai, I'm very sorry, man. But I need to borrow your mom. Billy's a bit, you know…' Mike's right hand was on Mrs Dewan's left arm and he squeezed it firmly. The older woman didn't miss a beat.

'What happened to Billy? Come on, come on.' With that she turned and started to walk.

JD flashed Mike a look of genuine gratitude even as Pamela began to turn towards him with murder in her eyes. Mike didn't wait. He was out of earshot in a flash. He fell into step next to Mrs Dewan.

'Tell me, Mike.' Her tone was dry, almost brittle. But the eyes danced.

Mike thought about how much he enjoyed her company. 'Yes, ma'am,' he said.

'Should I be worried?'

'Where that woman is concerned, we should all be worried.' He looked at Mrs Dewan briefly. 'But he's not going to marry her.'

Mrs Dewan nodded, once, to show that she understood. And then she dropped the subject.

'I'm sorry, mate,' Mike said to Billy. 'I needed to go help Uncle JD out.'

'What happened?'

'He's having a few problems.' They both watched JD drain a whisky as he continued to get a bollocking from Pamela. She seemed livid. JD was doing his best to not meet her eye. And Pamela kept trying to look him in the eye. The two of them were engaged in a dance of sorts, a continuous shuffle as Pamela orbited planet JD.

Satellite of love, thought Mike and had to stifle a snort.

'What sort of problem?'

'Hmmm?' Mike looked down at Billy and grinned. 'Let's just say that he's taken a mis-step.'

'Is something wrong with his confidence?'

Mike was delighted.

'You know, I think, finally, something may be. It just may be.'

～

Aziz's fiancée was a staggeringly beautiful young woman. Her name was Tasleem Malik and she could have been a model. Or a film star. Instead, she was wrapping up her Master's in Clinical Psychology. Mike warmed to her straightaway because of the time she took to put Billy at ease. He'd been okay at the start, but he began to clam up about ten minutes into the party. Mike couldn't blame him. He felt a little bit like that himself. There were clearly a lot of important people here. The atmosphere was just slightly different, slightly electric. He and JD contributed to the charged air. Mike knew that much. But it affected him, all the same, because he hadn't been prepared for it. He could tell that JD was going through the same thing. He'd turned up that charm. Everyone next to him was his new best friend. When JD got into that mood, he was almost impossible to resist.

There were more white people than Mike had anticipated. Some of them were Aziz's clients. And some of them were friends or patients of Dr Malik. But the white people didn't clump together—which was interesting. People here largely knew each other. Mike felt a sense of increased focus when it came to him and JD. People were curious. And that tied into what he was feeling.

What had Aziz gotten himself into?

The match made perfect sense. Tasleem and Aziz were handpicked, confident, successful. And beautiful. It made sense. This was like minor royals being matched. They clearly liked each other. They clearly got along.

Except that some part of Aziz's income was coming from highly unusual sources. And when a family like the Maliks was involved, that wasn't as easy to, uh, square, should the VAT scam ever come out. Mike had been introduced to Dr Malik. He was a quietly impressive man, polite and soft-spoken. It was just that Mike and he were interrupted eight times in the two minutes that they spoke. Mike recognized some of the faces. There were a couple of MPs. And a pretty famous actor. This was not an engagement, nor a development, to be taken lightly.

For a moment, he felt a sense of panic so strong that it was almost a premonition. All of this, their individual kinks, this need to be a shadow, to be rich, to be famous, to belong, and to put off football, three months at a time, was just smoke. For a moment, Mike spoke JD's language. It would all be blown away, one day, because the winds would decide to randomly change direction.

Then he shrugged, located Billy and made ready as both of them were introduced to Tasleem.

Mike folded his hands in a namaste, properly, because he was a stranger meeting a lady for the first time. This stuff was second nature by now. He was pleased to see that Billy was following his lead. Tasleem laughed. She was delighted. Then she extended her hand.

'Congratulations,' said Mike, shaking her hand. 'I'm sorry. I didn't know about whether or not a gift was appropriate.'

'That's quite all right, thank you,' Tasleem replied. 'It's not a tradition. Actually,' she said, turning towards Aziz 'neither is an engagement, but we're trapped between two worlds and trying to make the best of it. But that's quite all right.' She paused. 'And who is the young man?'

'Billy,' muttered Billy. He was looking at his shoes.

Tasleem grinned at Mike in a very likeable sort of way. She held out her hand and wiggled her fingers under Billy's nose. The boy looked up at her.

'I'm tired. I've been grinning at people for the last half hour. I'm also thirsty. I'm looking for a drink and some company.' In spite of the exquisite outfit, she deftly hunkered down, so that she was at Billy's eye level. In heels, it was some feat. She didn't talk down to the kid, Mike noted. She just looked at him for a bit.

'What say?'

Billy shuffled his feet for a bit. Then he realized that the lady wasn't going anywhere.

'Sure,' he said.

'Come on, then.' Tasleem grabbed Billy's hand and they began to head towards the closest bar counter, stopping ever so often to say hello to people along the way. Tasleem made it a point to introduce Billy to every single person they met.

Mike watched them for a bit. The panic was gone. It was what it was. He was proud of the kid. And he worried about what would become of Billy in a couple of years, when he hit the age of nine and the outside world vacuumed him away. Uncle Mike wouldn't be cool then. Maybe Aunt Tasleem would remain cool for a bit longer.

Mike turned to Aziz, who'd been watching his fiancée and Billy cross the lawn. For a second, Aziz looked the most content that Mike had ever seen him. He looked alive, but not eager, like he'd been carved from stone and was still the most vital thing on the lawn.

'Congratulations, man.' They shook hands. 'She's beautiful and she seems very lovely. You're a lucky man.'

'Thanks. Thank you.'

Mike saw JD drift towards them, looking in the same direction as Aziz. He caught Mike's gaze and shook his head once, just slightly. He had a look on his face that Mike had seen before. It normally surfaced when JD fought with his dad. He used to look like that as a kid, Mike thought, after people refused to pay after he'd hustled them at snooker.

It was what Tasleem had said. Caught between two worlds. Because JD was a street poet. A magician who turned sleaze into gold. And he'd be prowling the border between two worlds, like a sentry on duty, like a bastard Customs officer, until he broke down the walls or the walls broke him.

Either way, Mike decided, he was rooting for JD. Because something about this evening didn't feel right. Aziz would get caught out or he'd manage to sell the lie. Either way.

'How'd you guys meet?' asked Mike. He'd been silent for too long. And he wanted to break through the babble in his head.

'Our families, Mike.' Aziz sighed.

Maybe he's not completely sold on this, thought Mike. Maybe.

Someone yelled for Aziz. He waved back and turned to Mike.

'I've got—'

'Yeah. 'course.'

'Enjoy yourselves.'

Mike watched Aziz go. The reluctant Crown Prince, called

into action. Mike shook his head. It was unlike him to be this vindictive. It was like he'd smoked the joint instead of JD. As he thought about it, JD popped up next to him.

'Legal Jesus,' he said, looking at Aziz talking to Dr Malik.

Mike laughed. JD turned to him and grinned.

'You reckon Ted's going to struggle with the food?'

'Yes. Yes, I do.'

'Right,' JD nodded. 'Let's take off and get some burgers. Enough of this high society shit.'

Mike clapped him on the shoulder, hard. 'Come on, Mansell—,' he grinned.

'—back to hell for the likes of us,' finished JD.

~

Val went to see Wexler in the first week of November. The photocopies on her desk had replaced the crossword she normally had in her bag. She looked at them during lunch, and when she drank her tea, and in the afternoons when her 'In' tray had been cleared. She had been seeing signs of increased velocity. The banks had pulled themselves in tighter, but Excise were where they had been a month ago—making smalltime VAT busts of the usual idiots who were trying to ride the end of the wave. Val looked at the figures from the last quarter and she looked at the numbers in front of her and she was pretty sure that by the time Excise got to December, they would be looking at twenty million pounds, over the course of the last nine months, which had simply disappeared.

The secret was out. The smell of blood was in the air. And the scam-runners would come like a swarm.

Val spent days at her desk trying to run the numbers through every pattern she knew. The information wasn't in front of her, that much was obvious, but she was certain that if she ran over the numbers again and again, she would begin to understand *where* she needed to look for information. She refused to look at numbers on her screen because she couldn't look at enough documents side-by-side, so the printouts she insisted on were strewn across every available surface. Queen Canute, the office called her, sinking slowly under a tide of paper.

Val worked on the VAT scam the way she had worked on everything else. It started at eight-thirty, and stopped at five. But she spoke to Ken about it when they were sitting in bed that night sharing a cigarette, the first time in fifteen years that she'd brought her work home with her. The scam had slipped through her defences somehow, and it intrigued her because she couldn't find a single way into the matrix this lot had built around themselves.

In the end, during those first three months, she came up with two things. The first was a statistical improbability, but was the one hunch that felt right to her, the one that made sense instinctively. The second was the earliest sign of what they were dealing with—the size of the problem.

Val stopped all work one Tuesday afternoon and requested account closures going back three months. She had specific parameters: Current Accounts opened and closed within the last three months, and amounts upward of five hundred thousand pounds. She hoped to spot a quick journey of a large amount of money that came in and stayed, or came in and disappeared. It had to go somewhere.

But there were simply too many entries. Current Accounts opened and closed by the dozens at every major *branch* on a daily basis, and a countrywide search jammed the servers for a while. The query showed nothing. Val was surprisingly pleased. These boys—or girls—running the scam had discipline. In a strange way, she approved. The ethic was good, smart.

The second hunch, though, really underlined the stakes for Val. What were they doing, these boys, that hid them so well? If she stepped back far enough, the answer was obvious. And it made a startling amount of sense. Val paused and drew a diagram. And *then* realized the full ramifications of what she thought the loophole was. The realization made her sit back in her chair, looking out of the window with fierce concentration. It was clever, very clever. And also—at most—undetectable. She couldn't task-force this. No one could. But, she supposed, she owed it to Wexler. He ought to know what she was thinking. She sighed, picked up the phone, and called him.

Wexler was short and balding. Had he been taller, he would have been scrawny. He moved quickly, with the trim fussiness of small men. Wexler respected Val greatly, although they didn't get along, and Val felt much the same way. He was a very capable man, but he was hard-headed and often took only the bits of advice that made sense to him. As a consequence, his results were often fragmented——good in parts, awkward in the rest.

'It's only a theory. I don't have any proof,' Val began. Wexler nodded, one hand clasping a suspender, and the other resting lightly on his desk.

Val's hands were in her lap, her gaze fixed on them. She was trying to find the right way to express what their problem might be.

'I've been running the numbers in my free time. You know, the mobile phone spurt that we noticed last month. I've been cross-checking them with as much data as we've been able to pull. The problem is that it's such a small ripple that most departments have already forgotten about it.'

Wexler nodded a question at her.

'Eight million. Quarter ending September,' Val said. 'And I think it'll go to twenty by December.'

Wexler smiled. To his credit, it wasn't condescending. It was a smile that said he understood that there was a tic that bothered Val substantially, but it was a tic that was so small their attempts to mine for its genesis were pointless.

Val shrugged. This wasn't a crusade or her life's work. It was a question of the job she was paid to do, her craft, and of protocol. The same things she was observing on the other side of the fence.

'It's only a theory.' She waited. 'Twenty mill by the end of December.'

Wexler was quiet for a long time. Val could see the institutionalized response forming. She jumped back in before it finished, perhaps only to test her theories in front of an audience.

'It's the escalation I'm worried about. Not the figures. They'll be past us a year-and-a-half before we know it's happened. And I don't know what it is about this lot—but it's there. Two reclaims. They've beaten two reclaims. And there's only one real way in which they've done that. And *that's* the worrying factor. That's where the problem is.'

Wexler offered nothing.

'The only way that the people running this scam have been able to hide this from us is if the people that they're dealing with, the people who are buying the phones from them, are part of the scam too.'

Wexler's eyes snapped to her. He was startled.

'What I mean is, they're dealing with someone who they *know* is running a fraud. I think the transaction occurs with that full knowledge. Which would mean that it's probably at the importer level.' Val paused. 'Of course, that leads us to the main problem.'

She let it rest there. Seniority came when you filled in the gaps yourself. Wexler ran his hand across the top of his head.

'We can't check that, Val.' She nodded. 'Because if they're working with prior knowledge, then it means that everything they show—every piece of information—every single bit of paperwork, is going to be above board.'

Val nodded again, waiting for the inevitable conclusion.

'It means that it could be every vendor in the country. I mean, it makes all of them suspects.' Wexler paused and

Val knew it was only now that his mind was approaching the sheer size of the thing.

'I can't stop people from opening up new companies,' he said. 'I just—I can't do that. I can't stop people from opening up new companies…' He paused again, mentally choking on the irony. 'Not when we're missing twenty million pounds.'

Here it comes, thought Val. They had come to this parting of the ways in every war-meeting they'd ever had in the last two years. Wexler would want to find the money. If they did, then it warranted action. They could only move down the reactionary path because that was what they were coded to do. Val wanted to find the method. For that they needed time, and they needed resources. And no one committed resources on the *possibility* of twenty million pounds.

Wexler sighed. 'I'll grant you the danger, Val. But if there's no proof of the money, then I can't commit to anything.'

He looked at her. The meeting was done. They were exactly where they had begun.

Which left, thought Val, the actual conclusion unsaid. The VAT reclaim structure existed to enable free market entrepreneurship. The same system was now being used— with the full knowledge of the Excise department—to shield a massive tax fraud.

And there wasn't a damned thing they could do about it.

~

Completing the chain—buying and selling mobile phones all the way down the line, into France and back again—was all Aziz could think about when they got back to work. But

JD sensed a problem with Aziz's system. Aziz didn't want to hear it. He was starting to get fed up with how much time it took to set up each iteration of the game. He knew it, and the other two knew it. Aziz was beginning to realize that, regardless of his lecture to JD about patience, he was losing his own and it could cost him his edge.

As a concession to JD, Aziz didn't set up the whole chain, choosing instead to run three potential loops with three very small-volume companies. And by the end of the third run, he'd begun to see what JD had been on edge about.

Beyond a point, running that same set of mobiles became a huge problem because they *were* the same set of mobiles. Meanwhile, the manufacturers were introducing new models every two weeks. Because the whole point was to get people to buy a new mobile phone every six months by releasing smaller ones, shinier ones, ones with better cameras.

Stitching the ends of chain together would allow the Principle to recycle phones for a while, but it was three weeks at most, and then they were left with having to dump phones that just weren't cool any more. After that, they'd have to splurge on a new set of stock, dealing in massive volumes to make up for lost time.

It didn't make sense. The design had been clear, the idea itself was a legitimate. But, like the fold, the real world application needed a tweak. And before he could sit down and consider what that tweak might be, JD had pulled him aside.

'Wait,' he said. 'That was a good speech you gave me about being patient once. I don't have any speeches for you, A. Just wait.' JD looked Aziz, trapped between the security of knowledge, and the vulnerability of not having seen through the game all the way. Yet.

Aziz opened his mouth to speak.

'Wait,' JD said again.

Aziz shut his mouth, set aside the chain, and waited.

～

The third legendary meeting of the Heston Principle—in reality, the first meeting of the Principle as a legitimate, functioning company—occurred on a Wednesday, 6 December, 2000, just two weeks shy of a year from the first meeting on a park bench in Heston. They were at the warehouse again. This time, it was a matter of tradition.

That was the night they opened the door and let the outside world back in. JD remembered it because from that moment on, time changed. On the back of the meeting, the next two years were to become nothing more than a shadow sliding up the side of a building in minutes. They went from dealing in seconds to moving blocks of time. *Everything* changed.

～

The Principle were scheduled for eight in the evening. The table was loaded with booze and cigarettes and two ashtrays. JD showed up at seven-thirty, carrying a whiteboard still wrapped in plastic. Mike looked at him and raised an eyebrow. JD ignored him and found a spot on the safe where he could prop the board up against the wall. He stripped it and then fished out a marker from his jacket. He pulled off the cap with his teeth and then paused for a moment. Then he leant forward and wrote 'WELL, THAT'S LIKE HYPNOTIZING CHICKENS' in neat letters. He looked at it in a satisfied way and then added 'I'm worth a million in prizes' under it in his more usual scrawl. He turned to Mike and grinned.

'Iggy Pop. It's important that we're channeling the right spirits.'

Mike looked at him bleakly. 'Lemme guess. It's a charm, right?'

'Why fuck with me, Mike? Really. Whatever works for people, okay? Stuff makes people happy and you don't necessarily have to understand it. You support Palace, right, and do I ever say a word?' JD held up his hand against Mike's objection. 'It's okay. I forgive you. After all, we got Wright. So *that's* all right.'

Mike shook his head. JD was in one of his Pied Piper moods. All you could do was strap in and hang on. The ride was liable to be unpredictable. 'Forgive,' he muttered under his breath and let it be.

Aziz arrived on the dot of eight, underlining the atmosphere. The world was wound two times too tight tonight. There was no small talk, just greetings and then silence. JD felt the bright glare of attention from the two people who knew him best. It was time. He smashed the cigarette out in the ashtray and looked at both men. A comma of smoke hung in the air and lazily curled away. JD breathed out once, sharp and short. He lit another cigarette. Then he grinned the sunshine grin.

'Okay, gentlemen. This is the second lecture in the series. Welcome to loop mechanics. Listen.'

He sat back and exhaled smoke. His eyes shone. Outside the rain fell softly. The silence was immense. JD could hear the other two breathing, the tiny squeaks as they settled into their chairs. He sat back himself, crossing his legs at the ankles, stretching out under the table. He began to talk, quickly, calm and emotionless.

'We started with something really simple. Bring a phone into this country, charge VAT and disappear before we had to remit *that* VAT to the Exchequer. What we didn't realize up top was the fact that if we did, we were ultimately going to get caught—because the fold would keep showing up. From there, two things happened. We hid the fold, by becoming a larger part of the chain. And when we did that, Aziz saw the *whole* chain. We could start a fucking merry-go-round by being, at every step, the *next* purchaser. It's endless. We're now going to be able to bring the same phone through the country over and over again.' JD paused. 'But we still haven't seen it all the way through. That's not the whole game yet.'

Mike felt like he'd walked into a conversation too late and he had to try and figure it out as he went along. Aziz lit a cigarette. His eyes were half closed, head tilted up to the ceiling. JD was as serious as Mike had ever seen him. He looked young, and very pale. He's getting hot, thought Mike. JD cracked a beer from the eight pack of Foster's in front of him and drank half of it in one swallow. Aziz stirred lightly, stretching his legs out under the table. It felt to Mike like they'd just finished a hand of poker. His concentration remained rock-solid, unwavering. He didn't stir or stretch.

'We own the closed loop,' JD said. 'All the way. From the EU into the UK and out into the EU again. We own the Freight Forwarder. We own *everything*. But we still don't know how important that is.'

The atmosphere in the room changed slightly, as if one of them had left the table and opened up a window. The air got keen. JD looked at Mike.

'Where's the money coming from, Mike? In the eleven pounds that we're making in this little scenario, what's the physical process that allows us to buy and sell and make the profit?'

Mike thought about it for a minute. The answer was so fucking simple that he couldn't believe that JD had asked him the question in the first place. So he thought about it again, trying to see if he had missed anything. No. It was fucking simple.

'Demand and supply,' he said. 'We exist to bring the phone in. And someone buys it from us, at whatever price. Without that there's no trade and no profit. There's nothing.'

'Right,' said JD softly. 'But if you could control demand *and* supply, you can spin the system, right? You could run it, balloon it out, drive it exactly the way you wanted to. Suddenly, everything changes. Right?'

'How the fuck—' began Mike and stopped. He didn't understand it. But the current of possibility raised the flesh on the back of his neck. It was JD's next question that really threw him.

'What do you know about Trojans?'

When he thought about it, even years later, Mike would always return to that one point in the conversation. Because the whole thing had been a mind game from the start. As good as the second system had been, as profitable, it was nothing in the face of what JD dreamt up.

The Principle stacked the deck, at the very beginning, in a dirty little warehouse in Heston, and JD palmed all the aces. A year would pass before the dogs realized that the game was fixed to begin with.

JD had done it because it was the only thing he *could* do. More than any of them, for JD it had been the statement of his life—of his genius and his anger and his raw lust. Even then, it had the charm of a magic trick. Because they'd pulled an insane sleight of hand at the very beginning. It happened because JD had made two calls at the first meeting.

Fucking Trojans, Mike would think to himself. The boy was out of his fucking mind. All the same, Mike was very glad that JD was on his side.

It had been that kind of ride.

~

'Huh?'

JD had made one of his seamless edits, jumping ahead eight moves in the conversation, dialling in from another continent.

'Trojans?' asked Mike.

'Trojans,' replied JD.

'Trojans,' mused Mike. 'Oh, bloody hell. Trojans.' He sighed and turned to JD. 'Like the horse?'

'Like the horse.'

'Like the people who got had by the horse and the dirty Greeks crawled out of the damned thing and killed the lot of them as they slept after getting trashed, or blown, or laid, because they thought that the damned war was over and the fucking Greeks had left them the aforementioned horse?' asked Mike. He wanted to be clear about this.

'Like the people who got had by the horse,' began JD 'so that the dirty Greeks… well. Yes. Yes, those Trojans.'

Aziz watched it back and forth with avid interest. It was like being at a tennis match.

'Like the condom, JD? Like the record label that gave us reggae in this country? Like fucking skinheads? Like the fucking car? Because I'm a little bit lost here. We're doing some sort of an epic trek through history—you know, the fucking Odyssey and racism in this country, all the while driving a bad British car, listening to the Wailers and walking around stark fucking naked in some American condoms. It's very Monty Python, JD. I fucking applaud you.'

JD grinned. Mike crossed his arms and shook his head. JD drained the first can and then reached out and cracked his second beer. But he didn't sip it. He looked at the slight whiff of vapour that was gone almost as soon as it had appeared. Then he looked at Mike.

'Trojans. As in computers.'

Mike thought about it. His knowledge of computers was fairly limited. He'd been sceptical when the buzz around computers had erupted when he was in school and everyone was trying to get their hands on a Sinclair. It was huge craze because you could play 'Operation Wolf' at home. There was even a gun that came with the unit, if you bought the fully loaded package. The game came on a fucking cassette tape. That was the cutting edge when they were in school. All of them had lined up to play it. But there were a precious few others who were mucking about with BASIC, trying to write little programs that drew graphs for them or whatever. JD had been one of those kids, always trying to get the machine to do things, subscribing to magazines to get new codes. Mike didn't understand the fascination then, he didn't understand it now, and he'd been startled by the way computers had flooded their lives in the past decade. Computers made him feel old and out of place, like he was his mother's age, unsure of what to do with a mouse in his hand, knowing vaguely that it pointed to things.

Mike shook his head. 'They're like… viruses.' He faltered on the last word. He had no map here. Besides, he wasn't too sure what a virus was.

JD waved it away. He wasn't interested in specifics.

'You're sort of right. In that, a Trojan is something that actively does bad things to your system.' There was a faint flicker of interest from Aziz. 'It's malware. It does… shite,' said JD. 'I'm not interested in a lesson, but you need to understand this. Fundamentally. For a virus to work, *you*— the user—need to do something, okay? Actively. You need to run a program. And then it starts to work. A Trojan, on the other hand, is something that tells you it's one thing-,but it's actually something else. So, when it's working, there's something entirely different going on in the background.' JD paused and looked at the other two men.

'Typically,' he continued, 'most Trojans are configured to introduce a back door into the system. You're running something—a game, a screensaver, whatever—while your system is communicating with the creator of the Trojan and running an entirely different set of commands. It's basic, boys. We're not running software, but you need to understand this.'

'So it's a front?' ventured Mike.

JD nodded. 'Essentially, yes. But this is where the difference lies. A front is a façade, it's a mask. A Trojan is something that tells the system that something entirely different is going on. It's—' He put up his hand as he saw Mike begin to ask a question and continued. 'Malicious. A Trojan is a vicious bastard. And a Trojan's job is to lead you down a different path. A path that's completely removed from what's going on.'

Mike shook his head. 'I don't get it, JD.'

JD got up from the table and crossed over to the board. He drew their current model of operation on the board in a series of quick strokes.

'Look at this,' he said, pointing at the diagram on the whiteboard. 'In this game, everything revolves us buying and selling and hiding the mobile that we haven't paid VAT on, although we've charged it. Why can't we declare it? Why can't we sell to people other than ourselves?'

'Because it's illegal.' said Aziz clearing his throat. 'Because the man who buys it from us will have to show it in his books. Which is why we're dealing with the Jamaican boys, and with Brian's boys. They know it's illegal, and they're covering for us.'

JD nodded and walked back to the table. He looked at the second beer, but he still didn't sip it.

'What does this system turn on? What's the thing that holds us back, even though we're piling up cash by the bar? The one thing that makes us careful, still? The one fucking limiter that you can't get around? Whatever way you look at it, the one thing that haunts you, late at night, when you're counting the money?'

'The reclai—' Mike stopped. Aziz was holding up his hand, looking at JD through narrowed eyes. He thought about it for a moment.

'The phone. The mobile. The mobile itself. The...' Aziz hesitated. 'The *thing*.'

The smile on JD's face died slowly, as if someone had dialled down a dimmer. The other two had to make the leap—here, *now*.

'What happens if you take the mobile out of the game?' he asked very quietly.

There was a moment of absolute silence. Then Aziz sat back in his chair.

'Oh my God,' he breathed. He sounded like the air had been knocked clean out of him. 'Oh my God.'

Mike looked at the board, trying to see it. He looked at JD and shook his head. Aziz slumped in his chair, staring at the table, his mouth moving. Mike felt like a stranger in the room who had stumbled onto something intensely personal and complicated.

JD watched Mike with bright interest. He snapped his fingers once, changing the scene in some subtle, fundamental way.

'Don't think about the mobile, Mike. What happens if *there is no mobile*? What happens if you run the entire system with ghost stock?'

~

This time the silence was longer, dragging out for over a minute. Or maybe it was three. Something in Mike's mind popped. It was the thought of the ghost stock. Once introduced, it refused to let go. Never, in all his years, never in the stories he had heard, and the myths that he and JD had tracked down, had something so simple been so fucking profound.

JD was proposing that the major part of the game would be run with no stock at all. That it was, once you got past the window dressing, essentially a magic trick. To the outside world, it would appear as if they were doing one thing, when in essence, they were doing something entirely different. Mike didn't know the details yet, but this was a fucking revolution.

Fucking Trojans. Jesus, thought Mike. *This* is a eureka moment. Bloody hell.

JD drank the second beer in two long swallows. His

throat hurt and he was exhausted. He sat down at the table, lit another cigarette, and looked at Aziz.

'There's another diagram,' he said, 'but I'll get to it in a moment. This whole thing turns on one detail. We have to control the *stock* not the demand. If we can control the stock, we control everything. Demand. Supply. The works. The play just passes *through* this country. Here—'

JD got up and crossed over to the whiteboard. He rubbed out the first diagram and drew a new, more complex one.

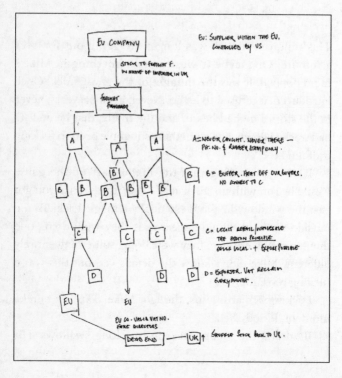

He turned to the other two. 'There's still one huge problem, but we'll get to that in a minute. Because that's going to become the opportunity. Otherwise, this is the breakdown,' JD began. 'We have to be the Freight Forwarders. We're the ones that bring the stock into the game in the first place. That's the knot.' He paused. 'You filter twice. The first set of companies is all us. Call them "A"— there's a blast from the past. The stock comes to us from the Freight Forwarder. Okay…' he paused again.

The central idea had been the main one. As Aziz had explained in Dubai, it was possible to create and populate all of the chain. It was possible because they controlled the Freight Forwarder. But JD had understood *what* the Forwarder could do. The only way JD would get the system to turn for him was if he could get into it. And the only way to get into it—at a level where you could exercise almost complete control—was at the beginning. The very beginning of the chain, not just in England. And from there had grown the second idea. That the stock was not only interchangeable, but that it was inherently expendable—as long as they maintained the correct protocol. The rest was packaging.

JD pulled on the cigarette. 'Okay. We'll talk about this in real world terms. Say we go back to using the Nokia Communicator we ran in August.'

He began to ink in the numbers through the flowchart quickly, talking as he did. Apart from the faint squeak on the whiteboard, and the sound of JD's voice, the room was utterly silent.

'The Forwarder dumps at the "A" companies, they're

the importers. They're in at three hundred. No VAT because they're buying from the EU. They, in turn, sell to the "B" companies at two ninety-five, plus VAT. These are the buffer companies. They're us, all of them. That's how we control the price ceiling, and the demand. From "B" we mix with the actual river for the first time. "C" is the retailers, selling locally and exporting as well. *Some* of them are ours—like the Principle. Some of them are completely legit, just like the Principle or any big electronics operation. And some are ours, simply to drive demand.

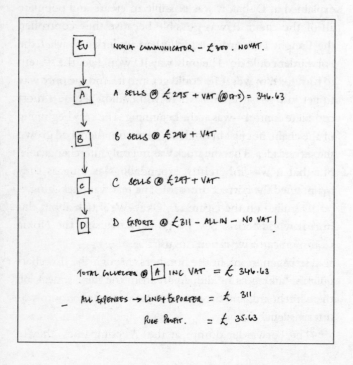

EU	NOKIA COMMUNICATOR – £300. NO VAT.
A	A SELLS @ £295 + VAT (@17·5) = 346.63
B	B SELLS @ £296 + VAT
C	C SELLS @ £297 + VAT
D	D EXPORTS @ £311 – ALL IN – NO VAT !

TOTAL COLLECTED @ ⬚A INC VAT = £ 346.63

ALL EXPENSES → LINE + EXPORTER = £ 311

RULE PROFIT. = £ 35.63

You name it, they're in there. Wait—' he said, cutting off Aziz before he could interrupt. 'I know what your objection is. There's a fix for it. It's in the system. But let me finish. "C" buys at two hundred and ninety-six plus VAT. Locally, we sell at two ninety-seven plus VAT. And either from "C" or from "D", you put in a requisition from the EU again. You're exporting. So you sell at a mark-up, say three hundred and eleven. You're going into France at three hundred and eleven, because there's no VAT involved there. And someone there pulls the stock one step further. And there,' he said, turning back to Mike and Aziz, 'it disappears. Because we're the fucking company in the EU too.'

For the first time that evening, Mike made the jump before Aziz. He saw where JD was going before JD said it.

JD looked at Aziz. 'You're wondering about letting it get to the retailers. The legitimate ones. This is what I'm telling you: that's not the game at all. The game is to get it *away from them* before they open it. The game is the demand. So the box never gets opened. That's the game.'

Aziz looked at JD open-mouthed. Mike's head was spinning with a rush of blood he couldn't control. It was the volume of information. And it was what the information implied.

'If you time it right, you can run the same phone through the system ten, fifteen, twenty times. Sure. You don't worry about the fucking model that you need to sell, do you? And if you get it right... if you get it right—' said JD slowly, savouring it all the way. 'If you get it right, you can run an empty box through the system. All the way. Over and over again. It's the perfect machine. It's a merry-go-round.'

JD turned back to the board.

'We collect three hundred and forty-six pounds and sixty-three pence at "A". We buy it back in the EU at three hundred and eleven. Everything else, the system pays for, the pounds we're dropping at each stop. That means the pure profit is thirty-five pounds and sixty-three pence.'

JD looked at the other two. 'Thirty-three pounds fifty-approximately—of pure profit, per phone. That's thirty-three pounds fifty for a phone that doesn't exist. Thirty-three pounds fifty out of thin air.'

He shrugged. 'After that, it's whatever you want to do. A thousand phones, two thousand. After that, it's how much you want to run.'

JD grinned.

'After that, it's how rich you want to be.'

~

There was a sense of release in the room after JD had finished his preliminary explanation of the model. Mike and Aziz poured themselves their first drinks, trying to attack it from all angles, looking for ways to break it down, or to make it better. JD drank his third beer. He nursed the can, no longer charging through it. He lit another cigarette but mostly let it burn. Now that he'd said what he said, he grew distracted.

He'd shown them something beautiful, almost perfect, and now he felt cheap. Because it still wasn't good enough.

As brilliant as he had been tonight, he still needed someone to tell him that. Couldn't own it otherwise. He hated these moments, when he felt that hole in his ego so keenly that he knew he'd essentially been built around it, and that nothing he did would ever fill it up enough.

Aziz watched the other two carefully, from a great distance. Belatedly, he'd realized the consequence of what he had done—the consequence of that first meeting, almost a year ago. The realization was bitter. He couldn't change it, but that never stopped the mind from considering what might have been. And the bitterness was his to have.

He saw that Mike and JD could move mountains. He saw the brilliance of JD's system and he saw that the groundwork they were laying down at this very moment would serve as the perfect stage. Nothing needed to change. They were perhaps two months away, but they had finally understood the scale of the scam.

Except it was a three-way game. They were equal partners, but there were two of them. Aziz did not wish to cheat them, they were great lads, but he had wanted more than anything to control the game. Now he saw that it would never happen. And he understood that the essential differences between him and them were irreconcilable. They would never be on the same page.

He didn't even know if he'd meant to pull JD into the game when he went to Nikhil Chadda's engagement. He'd been thinking about it. But he hadn't made up his mind. Until he ran into his oldest friend. Like everything else in the last year, things had just happened.

Aziz held up his hand and asked the one question he had left.

'Jai. The one big problem. The one that could be the opportunity. What is it?'

JD nodded. 'It's very simple. If it's only us running through the loop at this volume, we're going to stick out by a mile.'

Aziz frowned. 'What do we do, then?'

JD grinned the dazzling grin for the last time that evening. It was, in many ways, the one thing that he'd been waiting for. The final icing on the cake, the *real* knot, the final lunatic genius 'fuck you' that was going to blow the dogs out of the water.

'This one's yours, A,' he murmured.

Aziz watched him, impassive.

'It's the dream scenario, Aziz,' said JD. 'It's your idea. I'm a scammer, a margin-runner. For me, the Perfect Game's about the money coming through. With you, it was always the question of *where* it was coming from. All the way back. Oxford. And the pitch.' He paused for a long drink of water. The room was very still, witnessing an encore that topped the evening's entertainment.

'Why do we have to run through the loop alone, A?' JD asked.

Mike turned to look at Aziz. He saw gooseflesh beginning to form on Aziz's arms, still resting lightly on the table. Mike knew he was looking at one more monumental sidestep, perhaps the greatest one that evening. Only Aziz's breathing gave him away. It was harsh, anticipating a blow. JD leaned forward.

'Where's the money coming from, Aziz?'

The answer took Aziz a minute. He swallowed hard and said, 'The VAT.'

JD let it sink in, the full ramifications of what he was suggesting. He asked the final question, one for the ages.

'What's the opportunity?'

Aziz looked at him. He shook his head once and smiled. He shook his head again. He couldn't believe it. He couldn't believe the size of the country they had crossed in a single step.

'We tell other people,' he said.

2.5

Between the ages of eight and twelve, Aziz possessed a small rectangular mirror that he'd brought from Pakistan to England. It had been one of his sacred objects. The mirror had intricate designs all around the border, delicately etched. His grandmother had gifted it to Aziz after his grandfather had passed away. She told him that he had become a man, and it became one of his most treasured possessions.

The mirror had shattered on the flight to England when he was ten. Aziz didn't allow himself to think about the trip too often. He'd had to conduct all the conversations because his mother had been terrified and bewildered, and he remembered how his confidence in his achievements at school was obliterated when he couldn't understand a single person at the airport. They hadn't known how to pack, which is why the mirror had shattered in the first place. Clothes were in cellophane covers, creases all perfect. They had packed as many spices as they could lay their hands on. Later that night, Aziz's father had sat in their one-bedroom flat, laughing while pots and pans emerged from the four suitcases they had carried between the two of them, along with thirty dollars that they had cobbled together and stuffed into Aziz's socks. They had migrated like refugees.

Aziz remembered watching his father laugh and hating him, this man who had become a stranger in the two years since they'd seen him. As they pulled their things from the suitcases, Aziz had understood the mistakes they had made, the waste of space and the lack of thought. But his father's laughter quietly underlined how raw he and his mother were, how unprepared, how brown. It was a size thing. His father could laugh at the two of them because he was bigger, because he was the man, because he was the money.

Aziz never forgot. He kept the broken mirror for the next two years to remind him of the taste of being diminished, of being the second man.

He also remembered the mirror because it had bewitched him. When he stared into it on grey Sunday afternoons, locked in his room, it showed his face in a hundred pieces, dozens of incomplete, jagged reflections of himself that would leave him hypnotized. He imagined that he was looking into the broken surface of still water, trapped in time.

He got the feeling, gazing into so many possible versions of himself, that the gleaming shards could begin to move and meld into each other at any instant. This was how parts became one. How things snaked together.

And in the weeks before the Great Game began, the shattered shaving glass was the only way he could visualize the chaos of how the world around him reached out for the third system, the web that grew from the three of them.

The rest of them couldn't see even that much.

~

The Principle were looking at anywhere between twelve and fifteen companies that needed to be incorporated and staffed. They needed a minimum of five exporters, beyond level 'C', in order to be able to control demand and divert stock back to the EU. They needed to populate all of level 'A', the import companies that would take over from the Freight Forwarder. The second system hadn't prepared them for this. Compared to what they were about to do, that was for kids.

With at least three people working each 'office' they were looking at hiring forty-five people. Each of them had to be briefed and then drilled to within an inch of their lives. Like the drivers on the Calais runs, they had a simple story, mostly true, that they never varied from. Beyond this, they had to learn the system, the clockwork precision with which orders needed to arrive and then depart, an exquisite set of dominoes falling in a forty-two minute blitz through London.

The Principle were looking at a detailed, and very careful, recruitment process. And JD would never interview the candidates this time around. Mike painted smaller pictures and he talked in a straight line, whereas JD went off on stream-of-consciousness tours through the world at large, finishing coolly with, 'So, you'll do it?' when no question had been asked.

Instead, JD had to find a way to track transactions across twelve different companies at different stages in the process, nailing every penny in place and finding a path for the stream. The task suited him well, having neither Mike's patience, nor Aziz's EU contacts.

Aziz was left with the most intricate part of the equation. He had to consolidate their Freight Forwarder, and he had to find them their exit point in Europe, the conclusion to the paper trail where the 'phones' would be pulled out. Somewhere in Luxembourg, or France, or Belgium, so that they could disappear and then be recycled to the top of the chain. The carousel had to pass behind a black curtain at some point, for a brief moment, and then re-enter view like nothing had changed. And the paper trail from the EU company needed to vanish into thin air.

JD had brought Aziz to the edge of a roaring wall of possibilities and simply pointed. It was all he could have done. The ghost was Aziz's, and Aziz's alone and he finally grasped the heart of the VAT burn over the course of three hours, back and forth, on the motorway to Bristol.

~

By then, Aziz needed updates from his office just to know which day it was. After a while, it had all become one city, one trip.

Places like Bristol had assumed some significance. Any student town had a huge turnover of mobile phones. The Principle had silently been populating similar places over the past three months, even before JD had dreamt up the third system.

Aziz needed a quick, nominal conversation with their West Country transport, but it had to be face-to-face. Their attention to detail was the only thing that was going to carry them through the game when it rolled. And Aziz welcomed the drive. His three phones would be off and, for the first time in weeks, he would have silence. Driving always put him right.

The Principle would have to run two parallel chains, he thought. The first was, obviously, the phones, or something masquerading as the phones. This was the chain that the money moved down. They paid a commission to the Freight Forwarder, and one pound at the 'A' company. The 'A' company—the importer—was a ghost company, no office space or staff. The 'company' existed in phone calls, orders from different parts of the chain. The 'B' company, on the other hand, was live. They were all versions of Alistair's and Kenneth's outfit, the legitimate vendors, picking up a profit of a pound. Not only were these companies real— staffed, valid, *physically* present—they were clean. One step further down from the 'B' would be the 'C' company. This is where the Principle, or variations thereof, operated. And it was here that they were within touching distance of the export companies.

Aziz had known for a while now that the third system was their coming out party. They were at the export-end for the first time. If you were exporting, you were up for a monthly review, and that was the one where the friendly officers handing out pamphlets on the dangers of dodgy importers *didn't* turn up. Instead, you got the mean dogs. The Principle needed watertight paperwork. You had to stand eye-to-eye with Customs as they grilled you for hours on every transaction. And *then* they signed your reclaim slip. Therefore, the three of them had to be controlling that part of the chain.

They were going to bring the phones in, or at least the idea of the phones, and then they were going to *start* the pitch at the 'C' level. Even if it wasn't the Principle, even if it was a legitimate electronics vendor, the same rules applied.

'Call him Adrian Smith, right,' Aziz muttered to himself.

Adrian dials in. He's not one of your guys. But he's aware that there's a pile of money to be made in the mobile phone boom. At level 'C', Alistair and Kenneth, Jamaica Phone Traders, sell him a phone that's two hundred and thirty-five pounds, a phone that's completely legit because the VAT has been paid on it. Ten minutes later, there's a phone call from a legitimate company in Germany that's offering two hundred and six pounds for the same order of phones that has just come in through Adrian's door. The deal means Adrian gets his investment back straight away, along with a profit of six pounds to boot. The thirty-five odd pounds will make their way back to Adrian via a reclaim, courtesy the Exchequer. It's a win-win for Adrian; he'd be a fool not to bite.

Meanwhile, the chain pulls the phones from Germany to Luxembourg—this time, to a ghost company that's essentially an empty warehouse.

Pause. Three days. Or five, maybe. And then the same carton of phones begins another trek across the Continent, coming back to the Freight Forwarder.

And again, and again.

The Principle didn't *have* to be the purchasers at 'C' level. Even if they sold to a legitimate vendor, the end result was the same. The Great Game was the perfect model for reverse engineering. You could sit down over coffee and cigars on a Sunday evening and say to the guy on your left, 'I think we ought to do twenty-two mill this month.' Then you just figured the number of imaginary phones you needed to run, and you went.

You could go as many times as you needed.

If you looked at the game in terms of the VAT burn, and *the VAT burn alone*, the structure changed entirely.

If. If you were looking at a five mill VAT burn then you were looking at a turnover of thirty mill. VAT on thirty mill was five million two hundred and fifty thousand quid. For thirty mill, you were therefore looking at a hundred and fifty thousand phones, or something that simply pretended to be a phone. That part didn't matter any more.

Aziz looked down at the cup of coffee that had been cooling at the table. He was thirty minutes ahead of schedule. He'd pulled over on Park Street and walked into the Boston Tea Party. He needed to put the results of the drive down on a napkin. The hippie in dreads behind the counter had grinned at him and etched a marijuana leaf on the cappuccino with the last of the foam. It was a neat trick.

And it was perhaps the best example of what the Principle were about to do. What a lot of people wouldn't understand was that all they were doing was simply taking the foam off the top, every single time. The drink remained unchanged. That was the magic trick— the profits came from the volumes in a process that was dressed to look absolutely legitimate.

If you could set up two chains with the entire loop running twice then you could run the calculation that Aziz had just done in the car at an average of ten times a month.

Thirty-seven-and-a-half million pounds. A month.

They were currently at two.

Aziz clenched his jaw. There was a high, keening sound in his ears, and he felt light-headed. *This* was coming from the fucking sky. Forty mill, a month.

While he could, while he was still calm enough, he began to think about what he needed to do.

The system had been split clean down the middle. They needed paperwork that made it look like they were pushing phones. On the other hand, they were pushing through boxes of junk mobiles, empty cartons, the same phones, all of it, at crazy volumes, supported by the paperwork they were generating, because they had a VAT target to meet.

The paperwork had to be tight. They had to stay on top of it.

There was time for one more thought before the rush of blood to his head drowned out everything else.

The ferry receipts across the Channel, and on the train that ran in the Eurotunnel, were always on the basis of weight. No one bothered to open up the vans, they simply weighed the van and signed over.

Which meant that the Principle could run this set-up with a load of junk mobile phones. Which, in turn, meant that he was shortly going to have to enter the scrap business.

~

Excise got back to work on the 2nd, bleary-eyed and hung over. On the third floor, they witnessed another silent accident. Fifteen million gone from the VAT reclaim structure. And they could still write it off as bad accounting. Fifteen million was nothing in the face of the fifty-billion-pound train. Val knew it was just a matter of time now.

During that first week of January, Val broke one of her oldest rituals. The week back from a substantial break—and in a government job where you were tracking money, anything above three days was substantial—was critical. It was where you caught up. It normally took Val three days, if the break was up to two weeks long, and she could make back the time that she had lost. Because the same process took the rest of the office between a week and ten days, she could treat that little window in the same way that she used the twenty extra minutes she had every morning because she was in by eight-thirty.

This time, Val did nothing for three days. She didn't look at her notes, or at the vast mountains of paperwork that were now strewn through the office. She didn't send out memos, or ask for files. She sat at her desk drinking tea and playing Freecell and Solitaire. In a day, her right index finger began to hurt because she wasn't accustomed to using the mouse so much.

Fifteen million pounds had exited the system in the last quarter, almost doubling the amount in three months straight.

And Excise hadn't a clue. Beyond? No one gave a rat's arse. It was annoying. And worse, it brought with it the dull foreboding of being the solitary midwife to an imminent mess.

Val had seen the numbers from October. They were three million over her estimate. But she could damn near bet that they were, very soon, going to witness an epic escalation. And she had come back from the holidays wondering where she wanted to direct her energy.

Where was the fracture line? Twice the group or groups behind the scam had run this model. The paperwork clearly held. And, if her hunch about the knot being at the importer–retailer junction was right, the loyalties, or at least the loyalties born of profit, clearly held too. That brought her back to banking, and wherever she turned, all signs pointed in the same direction.

Val felt an uneasy kinship with the men on the other side of the fence. Though she hated to admit it, they had her respect. Because they had gone about this in exactly the same she would have, if the mood had ever taken her. The money was neatly organized, it didn't draw attention to itself. There was regimental control to the scam—it breathed logic, and an intimate knowledge of how the system worked.

But the banking. The banking worked in her favour because that was the only time these men had to link with the outside world. Everything else was isolated, under lock and key. Except for the banks. The banks, then, were the slight advantage she had. Because there were people she could reach. And perhaps squeeze.

So what could she do to shake up her boys? Because that was about the only move she could make at this point. What could she do to throw them off-balance?

Her boys. In a strange way, it was almost personal. If she didn't claim possession, no one else would.

Val spent the first three days back from Christmas trying to get inside their heads. She watched the cards on the screen and let her mind wander. She tried to imagine ways for her boys to buy safety in an environment where every step they took was illegal. In case things went wrong, where was their protection coming from? What were the possible points of leverage?

Val dismissed the idea that they had a man inside the department off the bat. There was simply no percentage in it. Her boys had done too well so far to run the risk of trying to buy someone from Customs. Customs wasn't even close yet, and an approach would be more of a clue than anything else they had done.

The first whiff arrived on Thursday. She had been thinking about casinos because, over the three days that she had been considering her next move, gambling was the one analogy that kept occurring to her. Val was sure that she was looking at an elaborate card scam. It wasn't just about the skill. Her boys had been—the word, if she remembered it correctly, was—colluding. The surest way to buy an unfair advantage in a casino was a crooked dealer. Most dealers, on casino orders, were crooked dealers. This was especially true of Blackjack, where dealers second-carded to make their own hands better. But if you could find and win a crooked deal—

Val paused.

She ran it against the checklist of her experience. She didn't think the query would throw up any genuine wrong-doing. But if she had her boys pegged right, if she was giving them the respect that she thought they deserved, then this was going to be a slightly nasty surprise.

Val could think of two specific instances, both in Switzerland, and both during the height of the Cold War, where this hunch had paid off. Circumstances were different here. All this would buy her was time. Time, and perhaps one damned move in the open that she could wave in Wexler's face. But the scramble was well worth the pain. The pain was the whole point.

She paged Craig Daley. By the time he knocked on Val's door three minutes later, her monitor was switched off, and she was already tearing through the first of the files that had been lying ignored in her 'In' tray for the last three days. Val looked up.

'Craig.' She had to clear her throat. She hadn't spoken to anyone since the morning. 'I want you to drop whatever you're doing, okay? Everything. Whatever it is. I don't care. I'm authorizing it.'

Craig frowned and nodded.

'Send out the word, and follow it through hard. I want the file in by Monday if possible please.'

'Sure, Val.'

'Hit the high-street banks, and then all the merchant banks, loosely, that have any accounts with reclaims from the VAT remittances. It doesn't have to be exact, but try and stay in the general area. The top twenty, say. I want attendance records for the last six months. Down to the damned janitors—everyone.'

Craig gaped at her silently. Val let him process the request for about ten seconds. She nodded.

'Yes. You heard me. Attendance records.' Her politeness held for a further three seconds. 'Go, damn it!' She stopped him at the door.

'Craig.' He turned to look at her, slightly wary and still puzzled. 'Don't be discreet about it. Make it loud. Make it a demand. Make sure it's heard.'

~

Aziz had it by five o'clock on Friday afternoon, roughly twenty-six hours after the request had gone out. And he knew, without the slightest doubt, that he was looking at the first of the dogs stirring.

Sumit had left three messages asking for him to call, the last two within fifteen minutes of each other. Since they were expanding the chain to fifty people, and nothing important could be said on the phone until JD figured out a security protocol, Aziz had Paul pull over at a telephone booth. He called Sumit on the office landline and set up a meeting. With the meeting set, Aziz forgot about it. He was moving through London like a knife, tidying up anything he could anticipate. Within the week, once the finances were in place, he was scheduled to travel for a large part of the next month and a half.

Paul dropped him off three streets away from Leicester Square and peeled off to meet him on the other side. Aziz flipped the sunglasses onto his forehead and stood on the pavement for a moment, in the cold, letting London catch up with him. He let out a single breath, drawing it out at long as he could, so that his heart began to pump harder. In a moment, his clarity sharpened. Every time he paused, he had discovered over the past few weeks, his body would start to run down. He lit a cigarette, shrugged on his overcoat, and started to walk. He was switched on and ready.

Sumit was waiting with two cups of coffee. He looked as tired as Aziz felt, and he lacked the command to disguise it. They had been killing themselves over the new system. They had taught themselves to never think about the size of what they were doing, but they couldn't stop it from catching up with them physically.

Sumit, on closer inspection, looked like shite. He had lost weight and his eyes were set deep in their sockets.

'Thanks,' Aziz muttered. He hadn't asked for coffee but it seemed like a good idea at the moment.

They walked on Charing Cross Road in silence for a while. Around them, tourists and Londoners swarmed about, happy and without a clue—the place, as always, was humming. We should do a lot more meetings here, thought Aziz. You can't buy cover like this. He turned to Sumit and nodded.

'I don't know what to make of it,' Sumit admitted. 'But I had four separate phone calls today, and I thought you should know.'

Aziz sipped his coffee. Sumit didn't wait for him to comment.

'No one knows what to make of it, or what the hell is going on. But Excise showed up at the banks this morning, kicking down a lot of doors and asking for attendance records from the last six months. Everyone—managers down to janitors. And they've made it priority one, they want everything in by the beginning of next week.'

Aziz held the coffee in his mouth for a second, then swallowed carefully. He nodded—he knew the implications well enough.

Attendance records were the most immediate sign of a banking scam. If a teller or a manager, particularly, *didn't* take the leave available to them for a period of three months, then you knew that they were running something. You based the assumption on the simple truth that no one in their right mind was going to share a scam, especially in something as contained as a bank. Therefore, the easiest way to read it was to find the manager or the teller who refused to take leave that was due to them.

'I don't think the tellers will be a problem,' Sumit began, 'but—'

'The managers,' Aziz put in grimly. 'We pushed ours pretty hard four times in the last year or so.'

'We spread it around, though,' Sumit argued, mostly trying to convince himself. 'Pressure across the board, random distribution—like always.'

'And I'm sure we'll feel all the better for it in when we're in our fucking cells.'

'But, Aziz… fuck!'

'Look, mate, the simple fact is that we can't control the managers. If any one of them decided to pop into work on a day they were supposed to be off because they felt better about overseeing a dodgy transaction in person, we've got no way of knowing.'

Aziz pulled out another cigarette and looked Sumit up and down as they moved.

'And it's no help to walk around looking like shite, Sen. You've got panic all over your face and it wasn't such a great face to begin with. Seriously, man, sort yourself out. It's not the best time to start acting Indian.'

Aziz slowed, and then stopped entirely. Sumit looked genuinely hurt for a second, on top of the panic. And then his professional face slid across his features. Aziz knew that face. It was how Sumit looked when he dealt with white people who made him feel brown. Aziz couldn't remember the last time he'd lashed out at someone like that, just to make them feel bad about something they couldn't control. Aziz hadn't meant to say anything about Sumit's face. But the kid was infecting his nerves and he couldn't have that.

He thought about apologizing. He held his breath, trying to concentrate on the problem.

'Let's just both get ourselves sorted out,' he said. 'Let's just think for a moment.'

He frowned as he tried to tail back through each of those major junctures, trying to see if there was anything that stood out. The Principle had activated the managers when they'd opened, over a year ago. Nothing extraordinary, just supervision. The managers had been alerted when both the first and the second system had gone through the first of their quarterly reviews. Again, the Principle just asked for a little extra care, keeping their eyes open for anything from Customs and Excise. Only the current process had Aziz worried. The cover was good, but their present status was the most vulnerable one. The fifteen bank accounts that had to go online—*now*—for the third system, the ghost run. The Principle weren't criminals, but they were soliciting latitude from the managers, asking for a little consideration in the face of stricter banking laws.

Aziz looked at the pavement beneath his feet. This was a design call and it needed to be an intelligent bet. Sumit shifted on his feet, looking off into the distance.

'They've just asked for attendance records? No strictures, no changes?'

Sumit shook his head. 'Not so far. Just the same guidelines they set out last quarter. Just attendance records. No changes.'

Aziz nodded. 'Okay.' He was putting the pieces together carefully, hoping they would hold together for the next two months.

'One: Nothing on the phone to you any more. Nothing.

If any manager wants to talk, set it up face-to-face, and put a protocol in place. No texts, okay? Nothing.'

Sumit nodded.

'Two: If the records go through Monday or Tuesday, then it's the rest of next week to process it, and then about three or four days into the week beyond it *if* Excise finds something they want to do anything about. That's almost two weeks, counting weekends. If they're only pulling attendance, and there's been no other strictures, then anything we do in that time will show up a month later. I want those accounts. I don't care if we don't have the people in place. You do it. Get Brian. Get the Jamaicans. Anybody, okay? Get me those accounts.' Aziz paused. 'And if we want the accounts—'.

'We need Jai and Mike to get us the money,' finished Sumit.

'Three.' Aziz looked at the pavement again. The light was fading fast. 'Turn up the recruitment. Hard. There's no time. We need boys. We need bodies.' Aziz looked up at Sumit. 'What does Mike call them again?'

Sumit smiled the ghost of a smile. 'Soldiers.'

'Right.' He made a twirling gesture with his right hand. Get 'em in, it said. Get them through the door.

'I need the paperwork, Sumit. We've just jumped the gun.'

Sumit sighed. 'Five,' he mumbled.

'Five,' Aziz agreed. They looked at each other for a moment. Aziz cleared his throat. 'Take the foot off the pedal, Sen. Slow it down this quarter. We don't need the money. Wait until we have the full chain. Slow it down. Two mill a month, both companies together. Okay?'

Sumit nodded once more, then he turned and began to walk away. The crowd swallowed him in seconds.

Which, thought Aziz, left the bigger problem six months down the road. He had anticipated it, because he had an idea of the volumes the Principle were going to be generating, but someone up in the Excise office had signalled intent. Someone had shown their hand.

Excise was going to shut down banking. They would do it six, nine months down the line, but they were going to do it. Suddenly anyone wanting to deal in mobiles wasn't going to get a bank account. Aziz could see it as clear as day. He didn't know why he was sure as he was, but intuition had been in every aspect of this thing since day one.

He knew what he was going to do. He had just received an advance warning. He would refine the system even further. Once they moved into electronic transfers, they were going to fuck the Exchequer raw. He just needed to find time to get to the Caribbean.

Aziz turned and looked about him once. He had a powerful sensation of being apart from the people around him, utterly and completely removed. The feeling flooded through his veins like ice-water.

The face-off was coming.

He breathed out once, grabbed his phone, and dialled Paul as he began to walk.

~

Most of the thirty-eight soldiers they'd picked up over the next two months were, frankly, a bit Championship. Because that was how JD wanted it. Despite his knack for windy circumlocution, the Principle had ended up putting JD in charge of recruitment when he had pointed out the distinct advantage of bringing in a certain type of boy that, until he explained it, would have seemed like the worst idea in the world.

They were already behind schedule when the reports from the first round of meetings between their boys and the mainstream business community began to trickle back to them around 10 January. Bank managers were calling Sumit and yelling at him to send them men who at least had some pretensions. JD had spent half an hour giggling when Sumit recounted what had happened when their army of former plumbers and contractors gone around to bank interviews and meetings for VAT numbers over the last three days. Regardless of how well they knew the system, these were clearly men who had been wielding wrenches until last week.

'How come you've decided to go into the mobile phone business?' was the standard opener.

It was met with a pause. And then the pause got longer. Clearly the relays on the new entrepreneur weren't the greatest.

'Um,' the soldier would offer. It was at this point that the person conducting the interview got interested. He would put the pen down, or turn away from the terminal in front of him, and really *look* at the person across the desk from him. The soldier's brow would furrow. This was beyond anything he'd been expecting.

'I have some mates...' he would offer slowly. The

interviewer would nod and pick up the pen, or turn back
to the terminal, not knowing that the dagger was to follow.

'They, um, think I should get in. That's what they told
me.' Another pause. And then, confident for the first time,
he would add. 'Basically, because I'm a bruv.' The soldier
would then nod enthusiastically. 'There you go, guv. I'm in
business because I'm a bruv.'

The absurdity of it was glorious, especially to JD. It was
like sending a bunch of apes to a Mensa interview. They'd
been sprinting through process, but they had forgotten the
window dressing. There needed to be some sort of barely
plausible reasons for the mass plumbing exodus. They needed
a story, a cover, something.

Five days into the recruitment process, Mike and JD
started compartmentalizing the jobs on the basis of the
talent they needed: a handful of smart boys, people who
had to control bigger parts of the chain, and a larger army
of foot-soldiers who, above all, were interested primarily in
the money. This was an important distinction. The new boys
needed to hold their own in bank meetings, and to handle
the occasional raid. They couldn't be too thick, but they also
couldn't be clever enough to understand the implications of
what they were doing. If they picked up someone that clever,
they were asking for trouble. There were enough Indians,
Pakistanis, and East Europeans who were happy to man an
'A' company for two-and-half months and then simply skip
the country with fifty or sixty thousand pounds. That was
enough for them, enough for a nice life back home.

And, of course, it made it very easy for a 'B' company to

shrug their shoulders when eventual defaults got traced back. The guy skipped the *country*, guv. How was we to know?

'It's like goddamned immigration services,' Mike told JD.

'You made a brown boy work for the BNP, you remember that,' JD shot back. The two months went mostly like this, the two of them tossing stupid one-liners back and forth on the phone while they traced their own paths. Mike did most of the legwork, while JD pointed him in the right directions. He found guys in pubs, and at his local chippy. He swept the local minicab ranks every two days, finding the hungry ones with a little spark, the guys biding their time until the right break came along. And his reputation throughout Heston was such that everyone knew what they were getting into. Competent or not, no one fucked with Mike Hamilton.

The rest of the boys were the more permanent rotation building the 'B' and 'C' companies, every six months or so. They were happy enough making up to five thousand pounds a day, more than most of them made in a year.

The majority of their cast was made up of Indians, Pakistanis and Bangladeshis. JD weighed it down with the great truth of the subcontinental community. Here, being a bruv was the entry card, and everyone knew it. Most of the soldiers they picked up had passports—it was impossible to open a bank account without one, and it was as close to a prerequisite that the Principle could afford.

JD perused the passports himself as they did their own interviews. He had six people who had been to Dubai in the recent past, undoubtedly on family business. They went to the top of the list immediately. Here was the legitimate reason: I went to Dubai, and someone, someone in the family, pointed out the opportunity and said they'd fund it. So here I am. Second-best were people who had been back home in the recent past. Fewer numbers there, only three, but much the same story. As for the remainder of his cast, JD made the decision, in part, because Pamela continued to hound him about a job for her 'cousin'. And the rest simply picked up the chant. I know someone, the guy who lives next to me, or my cousin, or my sister's boyfriend, who told me about this and said he'd cover for me to get in. In other words, *because* I'm a bruv. But then, brown people ran in bruv packs—they were notorious all over the world because of ties they brought with them. They were the Chinese before the Chinese had become the Chinese.

By the end of it, they literally had to shut the doors on the growing queues at their offices, and JD was fighting to get some white boys meetings. Brian found them some, along with Alistair and Kenneth, who also gave them their token two black men. If they had ever lined up, they would have looked like they were bloody UB40. It was to become their identity over the next two years, in spite of Mike and Brian. They were the Indian mob, they were the Pakis on the rise.

But, man, the amount of units they shipped.

~

The third week of February was to become the defining moment of their lives. For Aziz, it was a war, and he fought it on war-footing, like a mongrel general who would change the face of Europe forever.

Mike worked London relentlessly. His was a season of meetings in small cafés, and side streets. It was the season of bank managers and bulk laptop deals and warehouses that he leased. It was a season of grey London, mining deeper and deeper underground, finding routes and angles and soldiers. He lowered his head in December and only came up for air toward the middle of February as the show opened.

But it was JD who saw it the clearest, as they might have anticipated. Of the three piggies, as he put it, he was the one who stayed home, hunched in Heston, tracking everything. There was no descent into the blur that Aziz and Mike worked through. Instead, he had a series of vivid, brilliant mental snapshots of every step of the journey, and every fascinating detour. He traced the journey, from the first step on a park bench in Heston over a year ago, until they were no longer on the ground.

JD hadn't expected it, and neither had the other two, but by the time February rolled around, he had become the soul of the Principle, the place where they got it right and the place where it all went wrong.

PART THREE
THE JIMMY TIPNIS

'I've seen the future, brother:
it is murder'
—*The Future*, Leonard Cohen

'I'll sit and spin for a little while
If it's the end of days
I'm goin' out in style
Too much, too young, too fast'
—*Too much, too young, too fast*, Airbourne

'Well, I got one foot on the platform
The other foot on the train
I'm goin' back to New Orleans
To wear that ball and chain.'
—*House of the Rising Sun*, The Animals

3.1

21 February 2001.

Jai Singh Dewan stepped onto the curb across the corner from the old warehouse in Heston. Over the past month and a half, the old warehouse had become JD's office. And for the next three hours, it was Mission Control.

The first consignment of ghost stock—junk mobiles—had come in six days ago and had been sitting at the Freight Forwarder, waiting for a sign from the 'A' company.

Aziz was at the Freight Forwarder, Atomic Sell Fone Logistics, controlling the release notes for this first round.

Mike was in an office complex in London. He was sitting on the transport, waiting to bring the stock in, and waiting to take it away.

And JD was now standing on the pavement outside the warehouse. For this moment, he was nailed to the spot. His assumptions about control, he realized, had been one of the biggest illusions he'd ever let himself fall for.

'Every day a fucking lesson,' he whispered to himself. He drew a long, shuddering breath. His skin wanted to crawl off him and walk away. Chills were coming in waves, every three minutes or so, like a fever.

Thirty minutes from now, their feet would leave the ground and then they'd just have to see how they landed.

JD turned abruptly. There were reasons why he had stepped out of the warehouse. He needed chewing gum. He was also out of cigarettes.

JD had gone through a pack in two-and-a-half hours this morning. He'd stubbed most of the cigarettes out after only three drags, or he'd let them lie in the ashtray forgotten. It wasn't a question of whether or not he could remember if anything like this had ever happened to him—it hadn't. Instead, he was trying to ride it out, while his fucking memory, his relentless recall, pressed in from all sides.

JD checked his watch. Three minutes past eleven. He didn't have much time.

~

The attendance check on the banks had been the wake-up call. The Principle were confident, even secure, that the scan wouldn't show anything. But it had shattered the vacuum.

No matter how careful they were, how secretive, they were mobilizing what amounted to an army. They had been a ten-man operation expanding to fifty. The signs were easy enough to read. If the Principle were going to reverse engineer profits from level 'C', building everything around how much VAT they wanted to burn, then it was just as possible to reverse engineer their *intentions* from what they were constructing.

That sense of urgency lent itself to a desperate, suicidal creativity as they set up the ghost system.

There were two design calls and one considered, executive, decision. The three things that would became their signature. And sow the seeds for the biggest party blow-off any of them had ever seen.

The Jimmy Tipnis had its roots in those three moves, in January 2001.

~

The Principle moved JD to the head of the board on the two things that had become their top priorities—the security protocol, and the recruitment process. The security had been his to begin with, and the recruitment became his when he figured out the Army of Bruvs.

Until Cleartone, JD found the idea of security on the phone a bit of a joke. Back then, he had thought that Aziz was being paranoid. But then their numbers grew. And grew and grew.

What worried JD was how *open* they were, how much of the third system was in public view. Up until now, the dirty three minutes that mattered most occurred in the middle of the night, away from other eyes. Now, everything they did had to look right; the boxes had to go to vendors, and had to come back, inside business hours. This system worked, in essence, on the fact that *nothing* was hidden.

There was no point being naïve. The Principle would be under the scanner inside of two months. When people of a certain kind started making real money—money that spoke even if you were trying to keep it quiet—other people were going to listen in.

In the end JD went with the simplest thing that he could come up with. He'd thought about satellite phones, and scramblers that they could attach to their landlines, and about a secure BBS online. But all of that was clunky, it took space, it depended on your access to a computer and the internet. Besides, they were going to leave trails no matter what they did.

So JD JD-ed it. If trails were inevitable, then you littered the way with so many trails that whoever wanted to track them would never be able to tell one from another.

JD made sure that all six of the central game-runners— the Principle, plus Brian, Sumit and JD's assistant Jaswinder Kapur—picked up a third cell phone, beyond the work and home numbers that they all already carried. This was a 'basher,' the street term for a use-and-throw phone with prepaid minutes.

They were on a two-week rotation pattern. Every second Friday, JD would pick up a new SIM card and a new phone from a random location. Just switching SIM cards wasn't enough. A phone registered all the SIM cards that had been used on it with the parent network. Once he had a new number for the third mobile, JD would text that number to Mike's *current* third mobile. Mike would save the number, and *only then* would head out and buy his new phone and

SIM card. Then he'd card Aziz's old number with both his and JD's new numbers. Again, only when Aziz received the two numbers would he head out and buy his own new phone and SIM. And then card the number to JD. And JD would complete the circle as he'd opened it, carding Aziz's new number to Mike. It was tedious but it was necessary.

Once the information had journeyed through the inner circle, the numbers went out to the other three men.

The guys that needed to talk to JD had JD's number, never Mike and Aziz's. Never the whole chain. Only the three of them held the complete pieces to the puzzle, and only when they put the pieces together would the system turn its tricks. They were delegating, yes, but they were also unlinking themselves so that the original members of the Principle were isolated.

It wasn't a high-tech method, but it made complete access, or any sort of comprehensive penetration, almost impossible. JD was willing to allow the world to listen in, if the world could even find the number. The three members of the Principle didn't know where the numbers were coming from.

And if one of them *didn't* buy, or access, or forward their new number, for whatever reason, the train would simply stop moving. It reduced their individual importance in the system to its most fundamental. For the deal, any deal, to go through, they needed to talk to each other. If they didn't, no burn today.

~

JD paused for a moment before he let himself back into the warehouse. His hand trembled when he tried to punch in the access code. He looked at his hand like it was a specimen in a laboratory, like it belonged to someone else. Every game came to this, every time, every single time.

He was fucking petrified. He needed to fix this *now*.

He breathed in once.

The cold overwhelmed him from the inside out. The closer he got—every time since the first time, all the way back when he was seventeen—the colder he got. His senses intensified; shapes, sounds, and even the flavour of the wind growing crisp and precise.

The burn was here.

JD pushed open the door. He took long, quick strides through the loading bay and up the stairs, but it still seemed to take forever to reach the office.

Jassi, pale and quiet, started as JD burst in. His hands jerked away from the laptop in front of him and one of his three mobile phones went skidding across the desk. JD caught it automatically. He looked at the phone and then at Jassi. Panic had been spreading on the streets since the morning. They were in the middle of the machine now, in the middle of the first raid.

'Calm down.'

Jassi nodded. He made a choking sound as he swallowed, trying to respond.

'Just stay with me. I'm here.'

Jassi nodded again. He almost sagged with relief. JD ignored him. He settled in his chair, in front of his own laptop.

Three mobiles waited for him, alongside the four landlines.

'Don't guess it. Don't think,' he said. 'Look at me. That's all you need to do.'

'Sure, boss.'

JD tossed chewing gum onto the table. He popped four pieces of spearmint from the pack. He slid two pieces across to Jassi. Once Jassi had picked them up, JD began to work his gum. He looked at his watch. Ten minutes past eleven.

'Come on.'

~

The Principle had been in the game for ten days now. For that first run, they had only looped through the companies that the Principle controlled, all the way from top to bottom. The big advantage was that they could afford to be sloppy the first time out. Even if the companies didn't know that they were buying from other companies controlled by the same three men, any one of the six game runners could tackle complaints about paperwork or stock being late. Hold on, lads. And then, on the third mobile to one of the other five, asking about what the fuck had gone wrong down the chain.

Even then, the first run had been hairy. Aziz nearly had an aneurysm, and Mike had gone around the offices, tossing furniture left and right, and slapping a few people. When the French importers called the company at level 'C', the receptionist that came standard with the serviced office accommodation put them through to the office. But, in the said office, the damned phone simply kept ringing, on and on, on endless call-wait. The French guys were unable to get through because the genius at 'C' was on the phone himself, trying to place a bet with William Hill. And when the importers had tried to raise the other guy at the office, George, his mobile had been dead because he'd forgotten to charge it the night before.

So right away the guys in France started losing it. It took a fifteen-minute frenzy of calls to impose order and, before it was done, one of the higher-ups in France broke protocol by calling Aziz on the wrong mobile phone because he couldn't get through to the third one. Compartmentalization was a double-edged sword. The Principle were isolated, sure. But compartmentalization also meant that France had no idea they were buying from the Principle themselves, and that there was no need to panic.

The fuck-up had been as much of a blessing as they could hope for. The design held, the transport worked—eventually—even if the execution had been messy. They had gone through once, with scratches, but they were still alive.

The boxes of phones now waiting at the Freight Forwarders in Hounslow had re-entered the UK for the second time in ten days. Technically, the Principle had already crossed over the line: they were now illegal. But they hadn't infiltrated the outside world, hadn't sent the stock to vendors they didn't control.

Until this morning.

In the end, their timing couldn't have been better. When the phones had re-entered the country on 15 February, Mike had simply shut them down. He didn't know what he was waiting for, but caution seemed like the right play. In the elaborate patchwork of calculation and intuition that they had assembled, it was a question of feeling for the right tear that they could slip through.

They waited for four days. The tension stretched them thin. It was cold fucking turkey after running so hard setting things up for two months straight. But it was a matter of instinct and Mike was allowed this one suspended moment in the air. They waited with him, jaws clenched, the phones alive and ticking like bombs.

And then, on Monday morning, the 19th, a pig fell over somewhere in Essex. By that evening, fear was stalking the streets. More importantly, fear was stalking boardrooms. Mad Cow was here.

JD woke up the next day with an idea. All he wanted was confirmation. Mike and he brought every newspaper they could lay their hands on as they made their way to the warehouse. There, they watched TV endlessly, switching between news channels. Once he was done with the newspapers, JD went online to see what he could dig up.

As they edged towards eleven-thirty that morning, the outbreak of Mad Cow disease was the only story in Britain and the wisp of an idea in JD's head evolved into a fully formed, solid shape. There was just one more thing. He went third mobile to third mobile with Sumit to check it out.

What JD wanted was the rumour in the corridors. Sumit raised Aziz, and then went through four sources and called back in fifteen minutes. It wasn't official yet, but the EU was going to announce a worldwide ban on British meat, animal products and livestock.

JD hung up and turned to Mike, his heart pounding in his ears. He cleared his throat.

'Go tomorrow,' he said thickly. 'Go. It's the mother of all distractions. Go. It'll be like knifing someone in the ribs on a crowded street. We'll be gone, in the tube, and off at Tower Hill, the knife in the river, before anyone has a fucking clue.' He paused.

'Go,' he repeated. The word was toneless, implacable, and as close to a direct command as possible when he was talking to Mike.

Mike watched his face. The two of them had charged through the years together, and it was only right that it was just the two of them at this moment, in the last gasp before they broke loose. He looked like a man biding his time before he crossed the road. It was really that simple. It was a quiet moment, a practical moment. *Intent* was born in silence. All it took for a machine to start up was the flick of a switch, and you didn't need anything beyond silence to make that happen. You simply had to recognize the moment.

Mike cocked his head to one side, the ghost of a grin changing his face.

'Right.'

And so they rode into the country on the back of a dying pig.

~

'Set up the con-call.' JD had waited as long as he was going to. It was eleven-twenty-two. He would never again make the mistake of pushing the play, but he was going to open up the channels. This day was like no other, in all sorts of ways. The launch was one thing. The *way* the Principle were having to launch was another.

Because of the chaos during the first run, they'd had to split resources. Aziz had the Forwarder, Mike had the transport and JD had the accounts. In that set-up, Jassi was JD's number one. But his role had been designed to run at the Forwarder's, along with another of the new kids—Rich Howes. Running junk stock meant that all the Principle had to do was book a series of orders. The pitch started with Alistair and Kenneth shopping the stock—for this run the dummy mobiles were being marketed as Communicators. Because the stock lived at the Forwarder's, every stop on the chain passed through the Forwarder's. Whoever bought the pitch would communicate this to Alistair and Kenneth. This, in turn, would be communicated to the Forwarder, who would then ask for the documentation from the new company.

And that, in turn, would set up the rest of the chain.

Just for this first run, because JD could under no circumstances work at the Freight Forwarder, the booking process had been shifted to his office. Once they had it up and running, it would shift to the Forwarder's, leaving JD to simply track the money.

Jassi dialled the number and pushed the speaker phone button. He laid the phone on the table between himself and JD. The panic had vanished and JD approved.

'Hello?' Rich sounded sharp as well.

'It's JD.' There was a moment of silence. 'And Jassi,' JD added as an afterthought.

'Are we going?'

'Not yet. Just stay on the line. It's going to be an hour or so.'

'Sure.'

JD settled back into the chair. He tried to get his head clear, tried to ignore the numbers trying to crowd in from everywhere. His fingertips rested lightly on the edge of the desk. Only the hairs at the back of his neck refused to stay with the program. A minute passed.

'Rich?'

'Yes?' Rich's voice was sharper still, cranked up another half a notch. Patience, thought JD. What a bitch. And yet, everything turned on it. On the simple act of being able to wait.

'This is just to confirm, again, that only the phone calls this morning are being routed to this office. Everything else, including all the faxes, and all invoicing, remain yours.'

'Yes.'

No jokes. No posturing. No 'roger' or 'copy'. They had whittled everything down to the bone-dry essentials, waiting to start the fire.

The landline next to Jassi rang. He ignored it, looking at JD, waiting for the very first order. JD was staring at his hands. He let the phone ring twice, pleased that there hadn't been a peep out of Rich on the mobile lying on the table. If there had been, JD would've kicked the living shit out of him later that evening. He nodded.

There was no hesitation from Jassi. He punched the speakerphone button on the landline.

'Atomic Sell Phone Logistics.'

'This is Kenneth Powell. Reggaetone Trading.'

'That's right. Good morning, Kenneth. This is Jaswinder.' He was clear and confident. JD nodded once, to show him that he was doing fine.

'Hi. Okay. You're housing six thousand Communicators for me. Correct?'

Jassi tapped at the laptop in front of him. It wasn't necessary—for this first run, all of them had the numbers by heart. But it was what he was *supposed* to do. And this system was a habit lived, a manufacturing process. Every step the same, over and over again.

'Six thousand. That is correct.'

'Okay. Please allocate them to Metro B Limited.'

JD stirred slightly. The first outside company. Jassi, on the other hand, didn't miss a beat. He was an actor here, mouthing the lines he had been given. It wasn't his script.

'Sure thing, Kenneth. You're aware of the procedure?'

Kenneth laughed. 'Yes, of course.'

'Please send me a fax on your letterhead to the—'

'—same effect,' finished Kenneth, still chuckling. 'You guys are like seatbelt announcements on planes, man.' He paused. 'It's coming.' He hung up.

Jassi didn't pause to check with JD. He hit the speakerphone button lightly to disconnect the call and began to type rapidly. He had barely gotten through half the entry when Rich's voice came through the other speakerphone.

'Fax coming through.' He paused. JD heard the chair swivel in the office in Hounslow. Rich's voice, when he spoke again, was both softer and slightly muffled. His back was to the phone and he was craning his neck in an attempt to read the incoming fax.

'Reggaetone Trading.' Another pause, this time longer. 'Six thousand Communicators.' The final pause. 'Metro B Limited.'

Jassi didn't even look up. The moment the order had been confirmed, he resumed typing. The first fax was the first domino. This was likely to heat up really quick and he needed to stay on top of it. He didn't see JD clench his jaw, for the space of a second, as the first order came through.

They were in.

JD's mobile beeped once. As per protocol, this was Aziz's message to him, confirming the first order. JD read the message twice, slowly, letting the fact, the physical fucking reality of it, settle in his mind. He gave it the moment it deserved and then nodded. He deleted the message—texts were apt to clog the memory at this rate, and this stuff was never meant to remain anyway. The message was simply to signal the one thing that mattered most.

The carousel had begun to spin.

~

Three minutes later, Metro B Limited checked in.

Six thousand Communicators? Housed at the Forwarder?

Yes, said Jassi. Reggaetone Trading had already sent the

fax through. Would Metro B Limited now please send the Forwarder their paperwork stating that the payment had been made to Reggaetone?

Coming.

A minute-and-a-half later, Rich chimed in from the still-open landline. The fax had come through.

Jassi looked at JD, who nodded back. This was it. The first plant. According to the schedule, the exporter would call inside of six minutes. The bait would be swallowed easily, thought JD. He'd pulled up the file on Metro B Limited on his laptop, part of the database that the Principle had been gathering for over a year. He had this morning's details by heart. But, much like Jassi, this is what he was supposed to do. Check the detail.

Metro B were a mid-level distributor. Not heavy numbers, but a good, thorough track record going back at least three years. They would, they should, jump. But, just for this first time, JD's nerves refused to settle. Anticipation and fear. Because this one was the comic book stuffed into their pants while they sauntered out of the store, whistling.

This one was the rite of passage. Here, they became men.

Meanwhile, they waited.

~

The Principle were running junk mobiles because it fulfilled the three criteria that blew the door off the hinges. They had ten mill to play with, ten mill that had come into the system from outside. The junk mobiles ensured that the ten mill went the farthest, because the phones could be recycled endlessly. They kept up on the hottest models, and the mobiles in the warehouse could become exactly the model you needed it to be. And the junk allowed the Principle to run at a wild pace. Multiple deals like the ones planned for this morning became possible because there was no waiting on their stock of junk mobiles. They could go as quickly as they needed to, as many times as they needed to.

Economic Viagra, thought JD.

The Principle were still playing dodge with the IMEI number. The International Mobile Equipment Identity number was unique to each handset; Customs hadn't made IMEI checks mandatory yet but that would come. Originally, the IMEI number was meant to identify the phone in case of theft. But, because it was unique ID, over the years it had been appropriated as a fail-safe device to point out and insulate phones against rip-offs from China and the Far East. And, logic followed, it had become an indispensable tracking device in the realm of corporate fraud, and now its uses extended to warzones and terrorist outfits. The final application of a manufacturing code as a purely reactionary checking tool made sense to JD. He'd met enough liberals who moaned about how their every move could be tracked online, and that was true. But if you didn't want the government to know about the porn you were surfing for, there were ways around it.

JD had more than an amateur's knowledge of public-key cryptography and supported it wholeheartedly. Recent developments in onion networking and file-sharing were going to become critical over the next few years. JD thought that, ultimately, people like him were going to change over to anonymous internet banking—using digital money—for *all* their financial transactions. Just him and Dubai, and a laptop.

There was already word that it was going to be possible to *generate* IMEI numbers. The breakdown was simple. The IMEI comprised the Type Allocation Code from the British Approvals Board for Telecom. The rest of the code came from the manufacturers themselves, and was easy to penetrate. It was the crooked bank manager principle again, the exchange of small favours round the back of the building. The hard part was getting the check digit from the Luhn algorithm at the end of the IMEI that was never transmitted. But it was something that a kid with a computer could do.

They weren't in the IMEI shit yet. IMEI checks would be the last recourse for Customs because it was so bloody complex to check batches of phones. But the check *would* come. And the Principle would have to find a response. Otherwise they'd have to go back to shovelling real mobiles instead of junk stock and JD, for one, was much more interested in being a businessman these days.

~

The phone rang. Six-and-a-half minutes, on cue.

'Atomic Sell Fone. Jaswinder here.'

It was the same guy from Metro B Limited who had called eight minutes ago.

'Hi. This is Max from Metro B.'

'Yes?'

'I have some action on the six thousand Communicators that you're holding for me.'

'Yes, please?' Jassi was very, very good, thought JD. He sounded slightly bored, another guy just making a living somewhere in Hounslow. Even the entries, the soft, continuous clatter as he fed the first acts of the scam into the computer, were just the gentle sounds of an office running, nothing out of the ordinary.

'The requisition is for all six thousand Communicators,' Max continued. 'Release to Trans-global Trading.' Max sounded slightly dazed. Shipping his entire set of mobiles within minutes of making the original purchase was, for him, a windfall. And the VAT, of course, would eventually make its way back to him.

'Just to confirm. All six thousand Communicators, yes?'

'Yes, please.'

'Thank you, Max. Please send me a fax on your letterhead confirming the same along with the price, and also fax me your release note.'

'Will do. Faxing straight away.'

The Principle had breached the outside world good and proper. Alistair and Kenneth had dangled the bait in front of Metro B Limited. And Metro B had just shipped the entire stock to the bait that Trans-global, a company that the Principle controlled, had dangled in turn.

They completed the play seven minutes later. Channel Trading, one of the three French import companies that

Aziz controlled, pulled the phones across the border at three hundred and fifteen pounds per.

Every piece of documentation—including the exporter's invoice, purchase order, payment proof—had been received via fax. All that remained was the CMR document from the receiving company stating that it had, indeed, received the phones. And since they controlled the French company, getting the document when the vans left later that day wasn't going to be difficult.

They had completed the first circuit. Infiltrating the outside world, and pulling the stock back in by controlling the demand. But the morning wasn't done yet. The Principle had one more test to get through. And this one would determine whether or not they could go crazy.

JD let the dust settle, let the boys recover from the first run, giving them room to breathe, waited until he had moved through the seconds, until a minute stretched all the way past four that afternoon. Then the moment came. It trembled in his hands. He squeezed every last millisecond out of it.

He looked up.

'Ready?'

Jassi nodded.

JD picked up his phone and began to type out a message with blinding speed. Once the message was complete, he sent it out immediately and began to scroll through pages on the laptop in front of him. He was looking for an exporter to plant—that was the real test. If they passed it, they were going to blow up the country.

The ASF Logistics phone next to Jassi rang while JD was still reading, trying to pick between two exporters.

'Hell—' began Jassi.

'It's Kenneth.' The laughing voice from earlier that morning had been put away somewhere. 'Ready, Jai?'

'Go,' said JD, looking at Jassi. He nodded once.

'Okay. Six thousand Communicators. Shipping to the Heston Principle.' Kenneth paused. 'Fax coming.'

JD waited until he heard Rich's voice over the speakerphone.

'Reggaetone phones. Six thousand Communicators to the Heston Principle.' As soon as he heard it, JD dialled the number that he'd been looking at on his laptop.

'Hello? Dynamic Cellular?'

Jassi couldn't hear the other end of the conversation; this call was off JD's personal mobile, not on speaker. But he watched JD nonetheless. JD sat in the chair, elbow on the desk, like he'd been carved from stone. He was looking straight through Jassi.

'Hiya. My name's JD. I got your number off the Almanac. Who am I speaking to, please?'

A squawk from the other end.

'Alan.' JD paused. He grinned. 'Right, Alan. I'm sitting on six thousand Nokia Communicators. Possible to ship to you. We're looking at three hundred and two, plus VAT. How does that sound?'

JD listened. And then laughed.

'Nah, mate. That's right. It's three-oh-two if you pick up all of them. Getting to the end of the month, y'know?' JD cradled the phone between his shoulder and his neck and began to type. 'You know you're getting a good enough deal. That's a great price for a Communicator.' A pause. 'Uh-huh. We're with ASF Logistics. Works out of Hounslow.' He looked at Jassi and shrugged, indicating towards the corner of the office. 'Just a sec—here's the number...'

The printer in the corner began to whir, startling Jassi slightly. He swivelled around and got up, managing to get to the printer just as it spat out a single page. Jassi scanned through it quickly while JD began to wrap up the conversation. He was looking at a release note, a concise table drawn up on a Word document, along with three lines of text. Reference number 7684, confirming six thousand Communicators to Dynamic Cellular, ending with a request to 'please contact me if you need any other information' and the single line that stated that the data enclosed was confidential. Jassi walked across to JD and got his signature—as one of the partners in the Heston Principle—on the bottom of the page. Jassi fed it into the fax machine and dialled the ASF fax number before JD hung up. The release note was already halfway through.

'Rich,' murmured JD.

'It's through,' came the prompt reply. 'Heston Principle. Acquired from Reggaetone. Dumping all six thousand units to Dynamic Cellular. Waiting for their fax.'

JD didn't look up. He stuttered through the first twelve entries in his phonebook, looking for Channel Trading in France. All the boys, especially the six central game-runners, saved work numbers with numeric prefixes before names. Local 'B' companies were '1'. 'C' companies were '2'. Export was '3'. The EU companies were '4'. On a run like this, the practice saved valuable seconds. JD dialled the number and had the phone to his ear before Jassi sat down again.

'Dynamic Cellular. Plant it,' he said. And hung up. He lit a cigarette, blew out a jet of smoke and looked at Jassi.

'What d'you reckon?'

Jassi knew what was expected of him. This too had been drilled into him.

'We're getting through. Even—'

'—if it kills me,' finished JD, nodding. He pulled on the cigarette, crushed it out and leant back in his chair. He felt nothing; there was no longer any sense of anticipation. He had frozen it out. All that remained was for the pieces to fall into place, as he had willed them to.

The phone rang four-and-a-half minutes later and Jassi put them onto speaker phone straight away.

'ASF Logistics?'

'Yes?'

'This is Alan from Dynamic Cellular…' Alan finished the sentence as if it was a question.

'Yes. Go ahead, Alan.'

'You're holding—'

'—six thousand Communicators.'

'That's right. Can you please arrange for a release to Channel Trading at three hundred and fifteen pounds per? All the stock?' Alan could barely contain his joy. He'd clocked a crazy profit on a deal that went down seven minutes ago. And all the VAT, thought JD, was eventually going to make its way back to him. Fucking win-win. All the way around.

'Sure. Just send me a fax with the particulars, please.'

Jassi hung up the phone. For the only time that morning, he didn't start typing immediately. He simply looked at JD, his heart hammering. He'd seen the play, every inch of it. And he still couldn't believe it, couldn't believe the epic balls of it, and the fundamental genius that drove it.

JD nodded.

'That's it,' he said. 'Every time out. That's all we have to do.' He nodded again. He reached for his cigarettes and grinned the sunshine grin. It was an invitation.

'Again?' He considered it. 'Oh well. Why the fuck not?'

As Jassi began to dial, JD lit another cigarette, turned to the laptop, and began to make the first of a million entries.

~

JD knew that the spreadsheets, which so carefully tracked the flow of the money, were the most damning piece of evidence in front of the right pair of eyes. The spreadsheets were the only one of his rules that he had broken when the third system went live. He had sworn to himself that he would never commit anything to paper. But he was dealing with fifteen companies here. And that wasn't counting all the other companies that they were dealing with, the ones that the Principle didn't control. A spreadsheet was the only way even he was going to remember where and how the money went out, and how it came in. There was simply no other way. Not at the volumes they were working at.

And regardless of a lifetime spent with nothing but contempt for the dogs, JD wasn't going to delude himself

that the right pair of eyes didn't exist. Of course they did.
The game ensured that. It was the one thing that Aziz would
never understand, not until it bit it him in the arse, and
then it would be too late. The same rules applied to games
everywhere. Whether it was the Calais runs, or bloody Nick
Leeson, or drug-runs out of Myanmar. Catastrophic failures
were written into the game from the word 'go'. They were
one and the same thing. Somewhere, something would
evolve and they would either change games, or they'd turn
and run. Or they'd get caught. The third possibility was never
to be thought of. That was the jinx.

Otherwise it was simply a question of how long you could
ride it. Of how much money you could pull out of the air.

The spreadsheets covered the entirety of the cycle.
The cycle was determined by the target. Then, two sets
of printouts. Unlike every other piece of (legitimate)
documentation, the printouts would never be left in an office
and neither would this particular laptop. The office was only
for the paperwork generated during the games, the invoices
and the ferry receipts, and acknowledgement slips, always
categorized by date, and always ready for checks. As for the
printouts, the evidence of the *actual* march of money, the trail
of the burn, one set was to remain with Aziz, and stashed
wherever he saw fit; the other was with JD, as was the laptop.
He had his place—behind a pile of cartons in the attic at his
mother's new house. Once the month was done, once the
cycle was complete and the targets met, and the money was
present and accounted for, the spreadsheets were deleted
and then run through a program that made data recovery

impossible. Then they would each burn the printout and confirm it via SMS.

But nestled in the pocket of JD's overcoat was a small hard disk, portable, USB-powered and shockproof. This was a decision that he had taken himself, much like other decisions taken in the creation of the third model because they had been so scattered. Mike had worked recruitment—even beyond JD's intervention—and logistics all by himself. And Aziz had held the burn close to his chest. The less they knew about the complete system, the less the people under them would know. Their complexity made them the great shadow in the sky. It made them part myth.

In his own little space, JD had woken up one morning with the need for something he could point at. He couldn't quite explain it. Perhaps it was an insurance policy, although he trusted the other two with his life. Perhaps it was nothing more than the desire to have an element of control, of possession, over a game that had largely come out of his head. The rest of it had been easy. Mike had the street. Aziz had boardrooms. JD had a collection of misfits and outcasts. The hard disk itself was easy to find, and also easy enough to chuck out a car window should he ever need to. It was the encryption program that had taken some finding. He didn't want something that you could buy off the shelf. He wanted something harder, lesser known, difficult to crack and light enough to run quick.

At the end of every cycle, just before the bonfire of the printouts and the deletion of the files, JD would encrypt the spreadsheets and copy them into a drive that resembled an average, personal use, storage device. There was some music, old e-mails, and porn. And at the end of every month, he would back up *that* drive and stick the back-up in a safe deposit box somewhere.

Perhaps the decision was simply a testament to the game.

Or perhaps it was the sense of paranoia that had infected him since their meeting with the Russians.

~

The Principle had known that they would have to go to the Russians within a week of the third meeting. Over the past year, they had made between twelve and fourteen million pounds, but as soon as they started to put together the third system, all of it began to flow out faster than it had come in. They were haemorrhaging money, at least in the short term. The previous two systems had some distinct advantages that JD badly missed. First, when the game was smaller, so was the cost of getting in. The three of them had started with a hundred grand. Here, they had poured millions into the system, ranging from the obvious to the absurd. They had to pay salaries, and rent office space, and they also had to buy some of the soldiers' clothes. It was impossible to be taken seriously if you turned up for meetings in torn jeans and skateboarding shoes.

They needed an injection of capital that would spark the deals. There was no way around it. When they got to the finishing line, they'd be skint. They were hoping the profits would balance out the payments on interest. It was a question of *when*, not if.

The Russians ran the parallel credit system through most of Europe now. The Principle waited until half past January, when they were as close as to being ready as was possible. They were losing money every week, in tens of thousands of pounds, because everyone was sitting around, waiting.

Mike and JD had one name: Federov. He was an old contact from the booze runs, and over the course of the last five years they had run three orders for him personally. This was the one place where they *didn't* need a credit check. Still, it took thirty-six hours for the meeting to be confirmed, after they had sent out the request.

Mike made the call on Wednesday, 17 January, 2001. The channel was Gary Block, and all they told him was that they were looking for a loan. Gary didn't want the details and they didn't offer them. They had no direct access to Federov. Even when they had run three orders for him, the calls had come from him, always off a different number. The Russians were in another league, the Principle had to keep reminding themselves. Once you had put in the request for the first meeting, you were allowed no further communication. If the Russians called back, you were in. If they didn't, you went elsewhere.

They were confident they'd get the meeting. Beyond that, it was down to the same old bullshit. How much of a capitalist was the guy sitting across from you? The Russians didn't need the VAT burn. They had the drugs. That was the real money. And the Russians had the loan business to turn the powder money white. It was, at root, as elegant as the Principle's third model. The two halves of the business meshed like a combination lock. In this world, you became what you needed to be.

Aziz decided to sit this one out the second the other two brought up their Russian. On the surface, it made sense. He didn't know Federov at all and the engagement had pushed him into a different stratum of society. He needed to be careful. But, for all of Mike and JD's stories about outrunning tails off the M25, Aziz was much more of a survivor than they'd ever be. He had no qualms about being the unseen face. *If* the shite hit the fan, then anonymity bought him a day. However far down the line that day was, if it came, then that single day would be worth his life.

At eight in the morning on the 19th, Mike and JD met their contact just off Soho Square. They changed cars twice, heading farther and farther away from central London. At the second change, they were both frisked, and their mobiles examined. JD braced himself, waiting for a struggle over his mobiles. He didn't care if he was going to meet the Pope. This was a business transaction, and no one took away his phones without prior notice. It wouldn't be good for any of them.

Their phones were handed back to them. Into the third car, onto the M1. When their escorts finally decided that they weren't being followed, they turned into the first Services.

Their car arrowed into a parking spot. A man got out of the front passenger side and motioned for them to get out as well. As they did, another car pulled in from the off ramp. This one was pay dirt, a black BMW Seven. JD hadn't even seen the driver of their own car get out, but as soon as the BMW slid into the space next to them, both their escorts were out and holding doors open, the front and rear passenger seats, on opposite sides. JD shrugged and got in next to the driver, and Mike walked around the car to get into the back. The whole thing took about thirty seconds. They had been split up cleanly, unable to look at each other easily. The driver gave JD a single cold glance, as if he was memorizing a crime scene before the event. Then he faced forward and began to drive.

From behind him, JD heard a voice that he would've recognized anywhere, even though he had only met the man three times.

'Do you still have your mobiles?' The voice was surprisingly soft. There was laughter underneath the question—there was always the possibility of laughter under that voice. The accent was flawlessly neutral.

'Yeah,' said JD tersely. He was slightly off-balance. The relentlessness threw him. There was no option with these guys, no thank you, please, no small talk. Mike and he had been cattle driven into chutes.

'Yes,' the voice behind him sighed. 'They're not happy about it either.'

JD frowned. He turned to see Federov grinning at him.

'I'm not going to lie to you and say it's the *first* time,' said Federov. 'But it's not very common. How are you, Jai?' he asked, leaning forward and offering JD his hand. His pronunciation of his name, thought JD, was bang-on. He had the upturned vowel at the end just right, not making the mistake of calling him 'Jay' like almost everyone else did.

JD twisted around and shook Federov's hand. He was

thinner than when JD had met him last, and he was paler, if that was possible. The eyes had faded toward translucence, as if he was physically becoming harder to spot. But his grip was as strong as ever. And his face wore an expression of dry amusement that JD remembered well. It was the *only* expression that JD remembered.

'You're well?' asked Federov.

'I'm all right. Yourself?'

'Not too bad.' Federov paused for a moment. 'Still terrorizing the virgins of Heston?' This was an old joke. It was also a reminder that he had done his homework over the past day-and-a-half.

JD tossed out the standard response—'There *are* no virgins in Heston,'—but his eyes flickered towards Mike for a split second as he did. It was Mike who had taught JD how to mine conversations this way, to understand the stops and turns, to hear the actual questions being asked.

Mike was quiet, listening, half-turned toward Federov, less than himself as he slouched in his overcoat. His hands rested on his lap. He committed nothing. He would wait until the end of the world, if that's what it took. JD understood, perhaps for the first time, that what the world didn't realize was that Mike was his trump card.

And then they were in the meeting.

'Who am I talking to?' asked Federov.

JD nodded to Mike and turned away. This time, he eyed the driver for a moment, then turned and looked out of the window. They were barrelling down the M1. He hoped it went quickly. He had no desire to end up in Birmingham.

Behind him, he heard the snap of a cigarette case. Federov, he remembered, smoked small cigarillos. He had once told JD that they were the only substitute he had found for Russian cigarettes. JD had smoked a few of those down the years and they had made him weep. They were that fucking strong.

'Mike? JD?' The question was a quiet murmur as he offered the case around. They both answered in the negative. There was a click and a snap as the cigarillo was lit. In a moment JD smelt a sharp, bitter tang, almost like dark chocolate, as the smoke drifted past him.

'You need a loan.' It wasn't a question. Mike must've nodded, because JD didn't hear him say anything.

'I'll have to cap it at ten million, Mike. There is no way I can justify an amount greater than that to the—' Federov paused for an instant, then finished the sentence with a smile. '—to the *two* of you. You're going to be considered booze runners for a while yet.'

The Russian hesitated again before adding, 'Even though it is a very good scam. Very good, indeed.'

JD shut his eyes for a second and shook his head slightly. He felt the remnants of his boyhood being squeezed out, inch by inch, by the situation which he had created. In the back, Mike surprised him.

'Thank you,' said Mike evenly. He looked up from his hands and smiled. 'I don't have an option, do I?'

'No, you don't,' agreed Federov.

Mike nodded and looked at Federov. In the front, JD felt his heart speed up.

'Here are the rules,' Federov said. JD heard the slight

rustle as he switched the cigarillo to the corner of his mouth and began to tick off the list on the fingers of one hand. JD memorized it as Federov spoke. That, even more than the first real march of the phones, was where things began for him.

'I'm assuming it's field money?' Mike nodded. 'And the question is, is it legit? Is it a corporate set-up?'

Mike nodded again.

'You'll need to show it on the books, in the contracts.' Federov paused again. 'Interest at five per cent. Monthly. This is how the contract is to be structured. Put it down as a twelve-per cent loan from Alex Holding Company—I'll send you the sort codes in a week. Forty-eight per cent is to me—again, I'll give you the details—in cash. Four per cent a month. Interest payable every month. In cash.'

Federov looked at Mike very carefully for a full minute. Mike waited, because he was certain that Federov wasn't done. Not in the important ways at least.

'Two more things, Mike. This is very important. Because violation of these two terms means you've broken our deal. One, because this is a corporate set-up in a public arena, there must be no way that the money is traced back to us. None whatsoever. This is your guarantee in exchange for *our* guarantee. Am I clear?'

Mike nodded a third time.

'The second is the interest payments. The interest needs to come to me on schedule. Every month, like clockwork. Otherwise...' He let the word hang in the air, inviting Mike to fill in the blank.

Mike finished it as the ritual demanded. 'Otherwise the

entire amount comes to you inside three days. If we can't do that, you'll kill us.'

JD caught his breath. It hadn't occurred to him. It certainly hadn't occurred to him that it would be said out loud. And if he had thought someone would come right out and say it, he never would have thought it would be Mike. But now that it was in the air between them, it made sense. Mike hadn't come here to fuck around.

'Very good, Mike.' Federov's voice was still soft, still polite. 'If you default, then the entire amount comes to me within three days. Otherwise, yes, we will kill you. If the money is traced back to us, we will kill you.'

Federov let the window down an inch, tossed the cigarillo, and shut the window again. Turning back to Mike, he continued, 'But please think about what you said, Mike. What you said was, "You'll kill us." Think about who we would consider included in that "us".'

'It's only JD and me borrowing the money.'

'It's a big enterprise you're starting, is what I'm pointing out. A lot of people to keep in line. A single weak link, as they say.'

Federov sat back in his seat, watching Mike.

The condition wasn't a threat, or even a warning. The condition was the closest thing to advice that Federov was ever going to give them. He wanted no illusions about this. If they signed the contract, the penalty was not negotiable. And he underlined it with his silence.

Mike looked Federov in the eye.

'Done.'

Federov nodded. JD's speeding pulse made him dizzy. They had pawned their lives as collateral, on the strength of a crazy scheme that he had dreamt up. Federov reached out and tapped the driver on the shoulder.

'Misha,' he said. The name seemed to be a command. The driver immediately began to slice through to the left, looking for a place to turn around.

Smiling around a new cigarillo, Federov asked Mike one more question.

'So where do you want it?'

~

By a quarter to one in the afternoon, Jassi—working without prompts from JD—had set up three loops of the circuit in addition to the first two that morning. He had run down the same path that JD had laid out, planting another 'C' level distributor, and another exporter in addition to one all-Principle-owned-company chain. JD had run it like he was crash-testing a new car. Every possible option, on the first day. He had run the first plant himself, then he had seen Mike and Jassi run the second one without any coaching.

And only now, with every deal done, through a perfect storm of faxes, would the first of the vans begin the rollout. The vans would be loaded with four shrink-wrapped pallets of five hundred secondhand phones each. Every van carried two sets of paperwork in case they were stopped at the EU border. One showing that they were coming, and the other to show that they were going. The drivers, a merry crew handpicked and bulldozed by Brian and Mike, knew which set of papers to show, depending on the questions they were asked. If they weren't stopped, they were delivering phones. If they *were* stopped, they were setting off to argue about wrongly delivered stock. And once they'd cleared the check, each van would pull over for a smoke-break and put away the second set of junk-stock papers. The final sign-off was always to Mike, who would shred the paperwork that hadn't been stamped.

Jassi waited until the final fax had gone through, until their mobiles began to receive messages that the first of the vans had begun to move. He closed his laptop and waited in silence. He rubbed his eyes once, hard. Light turned to black under the pressure of his hands, and then a red so deep that it was purple. Still, he wasn't satisfied. JD knew he wouldn't be. He'd just seen a miracle for the first time in his adult life, and shit like that always took some getting used to.

'That was the burn?' he finally asked.

JD grinned and nodded.

Jassi looked down at the closed laptop. He was still working out what he wanted to ask and looking at JD was unsettling. He, along with Aziz, was where the madness had begun. And that madness had infected both of them. When the game ran, they were difficult to look at, to be around. That complex, layered pressure was halfway between pain and ecstasy and while Jassi understood that, he couldn't quite explain the relish with which they operated. This was more than a job, more than a scam. They were hedging their egos. On the whole, Jassi preferred Mike's company.

But he still needed to write the morning up in his head.

'The junk stock means…' he hesitated.

JD watched him carefully. He relented. The kid had done well. And he needed to understand.

'Spit it out,' he said gently. 'If you say it out loud, you'll start to believe it.'

'The junk stock means that the phones don't matter. When we started, I thought it meant that we were simply running a system where the junk stock *acted* like the real phones. That we'd treat them exactly like we would actual stock. That we'd send out vans for every order and try and take them back once they got to the vendor. Instead…' Jassi laughed out loud. 'Instead they're like fucking chips. They're like futures in the stock market.' His eyes shone as he made the final leap. 'The junk stock allows you to kick-start the machine. Only, there's nothing in it. It's… it's a fucking ghost!' He was laughing by the time he finished.

JD only smiled.

This is what Aziz had done. This is where he had brought them.

The whole deal had turned on its head. Until this morning, regardless of the nature of the scam, the Principle had been mobile phone merchants. They were now burn merchants.

The ten mill had been divided between two exporters that the Principle controlled— five mill each. Reclaims came back to the exporters forty-five days after the shipment. So their two exporters would have to work alternate months. But the game had shifted completely. The Heston Principle, and the two chains they controlled, and the momentum they had generated, had already drawn commitments of a further thirty million from other, legitimate, exporters. Because the fucking profits were that good.

A forty-million-pound VAT collective. Which meant:

Exports of a million phones a month. Quoted at an average of two hundred and fifty quid, each. A projected turnover of two hundred and fifty million.

As legitimate merchants, the Heston Principle were making a ten per cent pure profit on the turnover of every single deal. Earning them twenty-five million in the first month.

This was the trick. The reclaims weren't the profits. The reclaims simply allowed the system to turn over, again and again. The profit came from the *volumes*. That was where the fortress cracked. The volumes.

It was a theoretical infinite. The same set of 'phones' were going through England thirty-three times. Making them money each time.

The trick here wasn't the product. It was the *process*. Over and over.

JD watched Jassi leave, heading for the Forwarder's and his first debrief. He allowed himself the luxury of swivelling the chair away from the desk so that he could stretch out his legs. There was work to be done, but it could wait. He was at peace, nervous energy at rest. There was no victory march, no ringing chorus. The Principle were now parts of a wave, they were the components of industry.

JD wanted to let it sink in, the one-time charm of it, the thrill of watching the trick work for the first time. That was all he would get. That was all he ever got. He wondered idly whether it was the same for the other two, whether victories were as hollow, every time out. He doubted it. They didn't seem to share his obsession with blowing the world up in the first place.

After a minute, he picked up his mobile and sent a message to Jassi, telling him to ensure that they would be ready to go within a day. The Principle would still have to control the burn—the payments had to clear all around. Regardless, the month was packed. They needed to be ready.

JD leaned over the laptop and began to make the entry, but before he did, he looked out over the office one more time. For a moment, tears threatened. It was immaculate. He tasted contentment, and it was the sensation of an endless fall with no fear of what waited after.

He breathed out a long, shaky sigh and started to type.

After that, things happened very quickly.

Val actually had time to set out a list of the resources that she would need. It put her in a good mood, like taking time and care over a Christmas shopping list. She was an old-time shopper. She liked to browse. She liked to see what the fourth row on the left all the way to the back just might have in store for her.

There was some rumbling down the corridors for the last two weeks before the end of the quarter and then the earth shifted under their feet. This wasn't a shiver, it was a *shove*; the kind of collision that spawns new continents.

First quarter of the calendar year, 2001. Last quarter of the financial year, 2000–01.

As of 31 March, one hundred and twenty million pounds had disappeared. Gone. *In one quarter*.

For the first time in years, Val closed the door to her office when the news began to filter through. Confused voices carried down the corridor throughout the day as if her coworkers were lost in a maze. Val didn't mind the chatter so much, it was the shell-shocked expressions that bothered her. She had work to do. She began to pull files again, over and over, her right index finger tracking for her like it had done since she was a child. She kept her ears open on her tea breaks or on the way to the printer. It was enough.

The information was moving in a swarm. A hundred million *still* wasn't a big enough blip to conclusively put a halt to anything. Excise were, however, looking at a six hundred per cent jump in three months flat, and that was enough to make anyone sit up and notice. But even now, when the problem was right in their faces, every resource that the Government could enlist was being thrown at Mad Cow Disease. A huge part of the economy was in tatters. In the current climate, all the Exchequer could do was to glare at the VAT problem and hope that no one else noticed any time soon.

Excise hadn't known that her boys were there to begin with. That was the real nail, and that was the cause of the panic. Excise only knew about the one-hundred-and-twenty-million pound-shaped hole in the door because of an inter-departmental memo that Val had sent to Wexler. Desmond Cook from Customs, an old friend of Val's, had scrawled a note to her on a post-it and stuck it on the plastic cover of a folder that was on its way to her for a routine stamp.

There's a lot of mobile phones this quarter—more than Xmas avg. Checks out? Your end?—Des

Val read the note and frowned slightly. This was an unexpected development, from a direction she hadn't considered. She had been watching the reclaims, looking for companies that were shutting down regularly, defaulting just before quarters rolled by. The *product* itself wasn't of interest to her. She was looking for a tax fraud.

She had weighed the table down with files from the past three months and, working quickly through the afternoon, had done the backwards calculation on the amount of reclaims that needed to be paid out for the volume of phones that had made the declared trek through the country.

Simple math on a simple calculation that almost no one ever made. Why would anyone? They had been trained to look for the dodge once the product had been sold. That the product *itself* might be the dodge went against everything they had been taught.

Her boys were recycling product. They had made the jump into a system proper. And this was a wildfire. It smelt of ambition and defiance. It was an invitation to a fist-fight.

Val thought of the resignation lying in her drawer. She sensed that for Excise to have the smallest hope of gaining any ground, this would have to be a grim slog through the mud. It would proceed inch by inch, deal by deal and bank account by bank account. She simply didn't know if she still had it in her.

In the end she stayed because it was a Wednesday. It was that basic. She wanted to give it two more days and, on the back of that, a further week. That was as far ahead as she could think.

Val raised Des on the phone and confirmed that the figures, in fact, *didn't* check out, and that she was afraid that he had stumbled onto something quite a bit larger. She gently bullied him into sending her an official memo. When it came, she pushed it through to Wexler with a folder cross-referencing her own findings.

And as all hell broke loose, she sat back and composed her shopping list.

~

Aziz got home just before five in the afternoon. He parked the car in the basement, pushed a button on his watch and sat there for a while in the darkness. He stared out of the windshield, hypnotized, not really looking at anything. He was alone. No one needed anything. He didn't have to make decisions. He didn't have to gamble. He didn't have to put on the superhero cape and fix things.

The alarm went off five minutes later and Aziz stirred. The basement had become an addiction. He'd lost thirty minutes in the basement one day. He hadn't fallen asleep. He simply drifted for a long time. Since then, he set an alarm. He knew that he needed those five minutes.

Aziz tossed the keys to the concierge.

'How are you, Mr Basrai?'

'All right, Toby. You?'

'Not bad, Mr Basrai, not bad at all.'

Toby had fallen into step like a bodyguard. He was two feet ahead of Aziz, but matched his pace exactly. He hit the elevator button. The doors opened with a soft hiss. Toby leant in to punch the floor.

'Second, please.'

'Ah. Off to see senior Mrs Basrai.' Aziz owned three apartments in the building.

'Only every day, Toby.'

Toby grinned good-naturedly. Aziz hooked his jacket on his index finger, slung it over his shoulder and nodded. He turned and waited for the doors to close. As they did, he remembered what he wanted to say to Toby.

'I'm expecting a visitor in a while, Toby. Ms Tasleem Malik. Would you—'

'No problem at all, sir.'

~

Aziz rang the doorbell to the second-floor apartment, although he had the keys. He'd bought his parents the other apartment on the floor and he lived two floors above them. Within a year, he reckoned, he'd buy the building.

The door opened. The nurse had her attentive, professional face on. She smiled when she saw who it was.

'Mr Basrai.'

'Hi, Meera.'

He'd spent a great deal of money finding a top-notch nurse who spoke Urdu, Punjabi and Hindi. They were rare. He'd finally tapped into a service provider who looked after Bollywood actors and wealthy subcontinent people after they elected to have certain kinds of surgery in England, away from the public glare in their own countries. But this girl, in her late twenties, insisted on speaking to Aziz in English. And she wouldn't address him as 'Aziz'.

'How is she?'

Meera tilted her head slightly. She was a very fine nurse. She was also an interpreter, and a forecaster.

'Foggy. Foggy today,' she said. 'It's the same, the same dip from last week.'

'Okay.' Aziz tossed his jacket onto the sofa. The apartment was beautiful, but stark. It looked like a hotel room. Every wall had a handrail bolted on. Aziz began to walk towards the first bedroom. He stopped and turned to look at Meera.

'Do you want to step out for a while? I'm here for an hour, at least. I'll take care of whatever needs to be done.'

'Well, she was finishing her tea…'

'I'll take care of it.' Aziz smiled. It was tired but genuine.

Meera nodded. 'I'll run down to the ATM. And I'll make us some tea when I get back.'

'That'd be great. Three cups? My fiancée's coming by in a bit. She said she'd like to meet…' Aziz shrugged, indicating the corridor.

'Oh. I'll pick up some cake then. And she should change.' Meera paused. 'She'd want to be in a better salwar.' She looked worried, and that pleased Aziz. He'd chosen well.

'Why don't you tell me which one? I'll pull it out and iron it while you're downstairs and then you can change her when you're back.'

'Excellent. Thank you.'

Aziz watched her go. He ran his hair through his hair once and stood there, in the corridor. He was suddenly nervous. It happened every time. That's why he always asked Meera to leave. It made sense—it was a nice gesture. Meera spent all day cooped up in this apartment. She did a good job. She deserved the opportunity to head downstairs and clear her head for twenty minutes.

But Aziz also didn't want her to see him like this. For those ten seconds as he hovered in the corridor, before he crossed into the bedroom, he was always close to tears. He never knew what to expect. He thought of it like waiting in front of a firing squad, except that they were looking to cause bodily harm. They wanted him maimed, but alive.

Enough, he thought. Not in the least because the woman in there would have smacked him, hard, if she'd ever heard the run of his thoughts. He walked into the bedroom.

His grandmother sat in her wheelchair. She sat, framed by the window, like a figure in a painting. It looked like the instant before the light took her.

Might as well title it 'Anticipation', thought Aziz. The glare from the window made it impossible to see the medical equipment—the drips, the monitors, the trays, the bedpans, the syringes. Just an old woman, sitting in the sun. For a moment, just for a moment, it was possible to ignore the smell of medication.

Aziz walked around the bed. She heard him approach. She turned around to look at him for a moment. Her gaze drifted back to the window. Aziz slowed as he got close. She had developed a tendency to get spooked of late, and then only Meera was able to soothe her back to some sort of normalcy.

Aziz hated that word.

He sat down on the carpet, with his back to the window. He leant against the wall. His grandmother had lost a lot of weight. Her clothes hung off her tiny frame. She looked like she'd drifted down, off a cloud. Her skin was still beautiful, fair, smooth. When he was young, Aziz always thought that she'd been made from marble. She'd certainly run the house like it.

Aziz had never met anyone else who made as much sense as his grandmother. People might have been smarter. They might have had more ability. But for brute practical mindedness, his grandmother was the gold standard. She'd been tough, but she'd been fair. They'd been friends from day one. She loved him and he loved her. She snuck him treats. She backed him when he fought with his parents. She soothed him after he had nightmares, when he sat up bolt upright late at night, terrified by dreams of missing children and dreams of hiding under the sofa as a bad man came calling. She taught him rummy on hot, dusty afternoons when no one else would entertain a mind that wanted more, more, more.

Her eyes were still as he remembered them. Clear, like glass, dimmed with age. Her eyes were a pale amber, the remnants of a brown that had faded over decades.

Ever since she'd arrived in England, her eyes were clearer every time Aziz looked into them. She was uncoupling, whether she was aware of it or not.

'Hi, daadi. Hi, Nusrat Daadi.' Aziz spoke softly, in an unconscious imitation of the tone she'd used on him, a million years ago, putting the baby to sleep.

Something flickered in those eyes. She looked down at Aziz. She smiled. It was radiant in the light of the setting sun.

Then the grin slipped into a pout. Her eyes were clear

again. Aziz could swear that they were just fractionally lighter, those eyes.

His grandmother held out a fluorescent yellow sippy cup that held her tea. She waved it at him. She grinned again.

'Gah,' she said.

~

Aziz talked to her while he worked. He cleaned her face. He washed her hands and then moisturized them for her. Her hands were the only thing she'd been vain about, before the Alzheimer's. He lifted her off the wheelchair. She felt like a child in his arms, a small child grown impossibly old and sad. She clung to Aziz when he lifted her up, suddenly afraid. He soothed her by saying 'hush' in her ear, softly, repeating it until he felt her relax. He was careful to pronounce the word like he'd heard it growing up, more like 'huh'. Shushing sounds made her wet herself. She was wearing adult diapers, and Meera changed them quickly and efficiently when the need arose, but he wanted to spare her the indignity. The fact that she wouldn't know was the greatest indignity of all.

He put her down on the bed. He cleaned out her wheelchair, getting biscuit crumbs and some grains of rice from lunch. He cleared out the little pocket to the right, where she tried to secret away cream biscuits. He disinfected it, carefully, using the mildest cleaner he'd been able to find. Strong disinfectants made her sneeze. Then he found talcum powder and a small bottle of cologne and made the wheelchair smell like home in Karachi and not some medical necessity.

Aziz talked through it all. He told her about the game, about where they were, about what he was thinking, about where he thought they'd all be a year from now. He talked to her about Tasleem and his parents, about JD and Mike's nephew, and about the weather and where he'd eaten lunch. He barely knew what he was saying. He just filled the silence with the sound of his voice.

He found a washed and starched salwar and ironed it expertly. His grandmother had taught him how to iron when he was a kid. And also to sew. And cook. He talked to her as he ironed. He sang to her in a tuneless baritone, but with a grin on his face

In his heart of hearts, this was penance. He was serving time. Every afternoon, if he could, he pulled his shift because he believed that this was his fault. He'd had only one dream growing up, after he'd moved to England. He was going to bring his grandmother over. He was going to reconstitute his family. He would build from scratch the place in his memory where he had been able to move, to live, without carrying the weight of the world on his shoulders. There had been a time when he was just as happy climbing a tree in the garden, and being taught that if he rolled a mango just right, he could tear off the skin at the tip and drink the pulp down.

She'd been the greatest of his charms—the day he left Karachi, his luck had turned. The flavour of his world changed. He'd taken on *that* responsibility—he became the boy who became whatever the room needed him to be.

He'd done it for his mom. Then his father. And by then, it had become a habit.

It had just taken too long. Too long to get to a place where he ignored the well-intentioned advice and bought an apartment and sponsored a visa and sent a flight ticket across.

Two people came across on that flight. His grandmother, Nusrat Daadi. And the clear-eyed, slack-jawed goblin that lived in her head and took control, hour by bloody hour.

She still had clear days. Good days. He treasured those days. He sat there, her hands clasped in his, feeding off her warmth, trying to make the old stories as vivid as possible, trying to banish her inner idiot as far as he could.

But he'd waited too fucking long.

Tasleem's visit had been her idea. They'd had dinner once. And they'd caught a film together. They'd avoided questions like 'tell me about your family'. They were starting to get to know one another. And it seemed right to take it slow. They both felt that they'd stumbled into something that might be rare. It went beyond attraction. They were both solitary people, painfully smart, successful like they'd been bred for it. And they'd found a place where they could be silent for long stretches of time.

They were perfect strangers.

Aziz had called Tasleem to ask how she was. She asked if he wanted a cup of coffee over the weekend.

'I'm travelling, sorry.' He was scheduled to fly to the Caribbean. But he was surprised at how restless the statement made him feel, like he'd let her down.

'Shame.'

Aziz loved to hear her speak. Soft, but hard-edged, almost mechanically perfect enunciation. She took her time over her words. And she wouldn't speak unless she had something to contribute to whichever conversation they were in. It was a rare gift.

'How about today?' she asked.

'I'll be at my grandmother's,' he said. 'Which is the same place I'm at. You could come by, say hello. And then we could get an early dinner.'

He'd been hoping she'd say no. Although it would be good to see her. Tasleem left him soothed, less heavy.

'Sure,' she said.

And now here she was. They'd exchanged small talk over tea—how her day had been, what she was looking forward to over the weekend. Aziz waited until she was done.

'Come say hello.'

He pushed open the bedroom door, stood aside and waited. Tasleem stood beside him for a moment. She looked at him and then moved towards the bed. Aziz lent against the doorframe, shirt sleeves rolled up, tie loose, waiting. His head was tilted to one side, like he was about to watch a distant acquaintance take a difficult, but necessary, test.

Tasleem sat down on the bed, next to Nusrat Daadi. Tasleem looked at the old woman for a while, very still, as if she were fragile, like a half remembered dream. In a minute, she looked like she'd been sitting at that bedside for years.

Nusrat Daadi turned to Tasleem. She'd been lying there, looking out of the window. Aziz couldn't remember her ever looking in any other direction for any length of time when she was in this room. Her eyes were luminous. She looked at Tasleem. She looked through Tasleem. She reached out with her left hand and touched Tasleem's check. She smiled. Her eyes crinkled and a tear rolled down her cheek and disappeared, like it had never been there. She dropped her arm back to the bed and turned to look out of the window again.

Very gently, Tasleem picked up daadi's arm and cradled it in her lap. She began to stroke the inside of the forearm, lightly, using her fingertips and nails, but barely touching her skin at all. It was hypnotic to look at, a steady rhythm, like a whisper, it's okay, sleep, it's okay, rest now.

Aziz saw the arm relax, the fingers curling up like a little girl's, secure in the knowledge that a grown-up was close by. He saw the eyes close once, flutter open, anxiously trying to locate the window, and then close again as his grandmother fell asleep.

Tasleem waited another minute to make sure that the old woman was fast asleep. She slid the arm back onto the bed. She looked at Daadi for a bit, then reached out and tucked a wisp of hair behind daadi's ear. She sniffed her hand once— the hand she'd used to stroke the old woman—and sat there, with the hand covering her nose and her mouth. She ran the back of the same hand across her eyes, once, and then stood up. She walked back to the door. She looked at Aziz intently, searching his face for something. They stood like that for a while, very close together. Her eyes swept across his face one last time and she looked down at her hands. Then she stood up on tiptoe and kissed Aziz's cheek, surprising him a little. She turned back to look at the old woman.

'You don't need to tell me about your past. If you don't want to.' She turned back to him and smiled.

'The past stops the day before we get married. Now,' she tapped Aziz on the shoulder, 'do you want to head out, or order in?'

Aziz rubbed his face.

'Out,' he said with a smile.

～

By the end of March, the Principle alone had cleared sixty million pounds. Sixty million pounds in six weeks of being in the game proper. By April, the whole world was scrambling to get on board the VAT boom. Two interest payments had gone through to the Russians, and JD had already created a dedicated bank account operating out of Dubai that dealt only with the repayment of their loan. He signed for it himself, because he didn't want any of the soldiers to know. Beyond that, they were setting off on raids twice a week like kids let loose in a toy shop.

Aziz and JD sat up one fine drunken night with the mobile phone Almanac. Every genuine exporter, large, small or ugly, was in front of them, with contact details, descriptions and locations. They set up a bizarre social calendar, tailoring the pitches so that the exporters would bite.

Aziz estimated that about half the exporters—the ones who dealt in the big money—were fairly certain that the phones were simply passing through their warehouses between two stops run by the same group of people. It didn't matter to the exporters, because the paperwork was like clockwork, and their returns were assured. That they might have been shipping the *same* set of *junk* phones over and over again was the hidden knot at the top of the game, and it was the one thing that the Principle were rabid about keeping an absolute secret.

By the end of April, the Principle were burning about thirty mill a month. That equated to about a hundred and eighty mill in turnover. At a base minimum, if they dealt only in the top-end models, that was approximately six hundred thousand phones.

That was a lot of fucking phones.

~

Mike paused for a moment in front of the Palm Casino. The valet had whisked his car away but Mike decided to wait and finish his cigarette. He had a meeting at a half past eleven on a Friday night, in a casino, and he was fifteen minutes ahead of schedule. JD was on a tear in there somewhere. Aziz had messaged a little while ago that JD had been at the blackjack table for over an hour, pounding the odds.

Meanwhile, Mike was standing out on the street, trying to get a handle on the last six weeks. Of the three of them, he'd always had the least ambition. It had made him the most rational part of the Heston Principle. For Aziz, the VAT game had been a mission in leverage, the spoils leading him to even bigger things. And JD simply had to keep running, needed new traps to beat every three weeks. Otherwise he'd start messing with the mechanism in his head, creating traps for himself.

For a second, Mike wondered if whether the Calais contraband game had been a better fit for JD and himself. Things had been less... *complicated*. VAT, on the other hand, was all about complication. If you complicated the trail enough, you were making ten million pounds a month for yourself.

The fucking percentages just danced there.

Mike tossed away his cigarette, nodded to the man at the door and strolled into the casino, looking for his partners.

~

Mike waded through the gentle hum that pulsed around the gaming tables. He felt like he'd been dropped into the heart of a big machine. Which was true. Part of the crowd that *actually* governed the Western world could be found passing through the Palm on most weeks. Money attracted money. Here the rich could let their guard down.

Mike spotted Aziz almost as soon as he entered the room. He was in the middle of a meeting, Mike didn't know who with. Aziz nodded briefly and Mike nodded back. He had no urge to find out what the conversation was about, though he suspected that it was why he was here. In the meantime, he sauntered across to the bar. He had barely ordered his pint when JD popped up at his elbow.

'You on a table?'

JD shook his head.

'I'm done. It occurs to me that the odds may slightly favour the house.'

'D'you win or lose?'

'What's the difference?' JD grinned. That meant he had been on a tear at the blackjack table, counting down like a beast until he'd gotten ahead of himself and started playing double or nothing, negating the skill that had carried him for an hour or so. That was pretty much the pattern every time JD gambled.

They parked themselves at the bar, the quietest spot in the room. In Casino terms, this was early evening. Runs were just beginning. Most of the activity at the bar was confined to picking up orders to deliver to the tables. They drank for a while in silence, watching the room.

'What's he up to?' Mike finally asked, nodding in Aziz's direction. 'What's with getting all the information on the game accounts and lining them up? I know he's going electronic. But what's he *doing*?'

JD made an expansive gesture with his hands.

'I got a theory,' he conceded.

'Fuck off. No, really?' Mike sipped his beer. 'You have a theory. Wonders will never cease.'

'I'm telling you, Mike. You think *I've* got a God complex? Aziz makes me look like an amateur.'

'You might as well tell me already. Waiting's the worst part with you.'

JD laughed. 'Okay. All right. Just remember that these are all guesses. I'm pretty sure they're right, but they're guesses.'

Mike nodded. Without much conscious thought, he

later realized, he ended up watching Aziz for much of JD's explanation.

'Tell me about fearless leader,' said JD.

'What do you want to know?'

'What's been out of the ordinary? In the recent past?'

Mike shifted his attention to JD and then to the pint glass on the counter in front of him. He smiled. Half past eleven on a Friday evening, all of them worth fifteen million pounds each. Aziz, as both Mike and JD knew, was worth three or four million pounds more. They didn't know how many things Aziz had his fingers in. Aside from his law firm, the Freight Forwarder and the VAT game, there were restaurants, production deals, real estate, three internet businesses, and fuck knew what else.

And it still wasn't enough. For all three of them. Here they were, building games within the game. Mike gave the question his full attention. He filtered through the obvious extras and found the answer that JD was looking for.

'The trips to the Caribbean?'

JD nodded. Aziz had been making bi-monthly trips to the Caribbean since January. Schedules didn't matter. Aziz found the time to make those trips.

'I'll bet you five quid that he's touching down on the tarmac at Georgetown,' said JD. 'Cayman Islands. It might be my fault he hasn't told us. After the sing-along around the whiteboard none of us will bring anything to the table unless we've come up with the whole fucking play. It's—sorry.' JD sighed and shook his head. 'It's not important.'

'Right,' he began again. 'Cayman Islands equals off-shore

banking. It's a question of form and function: banking in the Cayman Islands is tax-exempt. Therefore they've got a ton of top-quality service providers. That means that Aziz is looking to transfer to electronic banking. And *that* means that a transaction that takes us three days here—payments to clear, to receive—takes *minutes* in an electronic system. It means that we could do four deals *a day*.'

'Jesus.'

'It's like throwing jet fuel into the burn. But that's not the good bit. It's not even the better bit. That's what's scary.' JD sipped his drink and shook his head. 'This is the better bit. The Cayman Islands are amongst the rare category of top-class off-shore financial centres that aren't subject to EU laws. Including full and complete non-disclosure of any details. Obviously, this includes identity. Which means that if we shift all our accounts off-shore then we just fucking disappear off the map. We're the ghost in the machine.'

Mike digested it for a moment. 'And that's just the better bit?' he asked.

JD nodded.

'What he's trying to do, I think… what he's trying to do is find someone who'll open a bank. He's trying to find someone who'll launch a bank.'

'What the fuck?'

Mike looked at Aziz and back to JD and saw that JD was watching their partner, too. There was awe in his eyes.

'Think about it, Mike. If we had a platform, electronic, out of jurisdiction, that was solely dedicated to the VAT burn, what the hell are you going to do? That's…' JD slapped the countertop. 'That's as close to Mach III as we'll ever get.'

'That's what the meeting back there is for?'

JD nodded again. 'I think he's got a name, a face. That's why we're allowed to stay up past our bedtime,' he said, sipping his Scotch. 'And I'll bet you another five quid. If the lessons from the last year stay true, then everyone we deal with is going to jump onto this bank. It means VAT is just going to go fucking nuts. A bloody bank is going to turn this into Beatlemania.'

Mike knew that JD was right. Money was doing strange things to them. Everything had begun to have a blank cheque quality to it. The more money they had, the more do-overs they had, like they were in a videogame with an endless supply of bonus lives.

They had new, odd habits and odder rituals. Mike knew that JD had developed a more lasting relationship with cocaine than he had before. That, in itself, didn't worry Mike. Mike stopped worrying after JD's ketamine phase, and he gave up completely when JD had—just the once, admittedly—smoked a cigarette dipped in aftershave lotion. JD saw green for about two hours. Not *tinged* green, he saw *in* green. Mike knew JD's chemical appetite—if it was on the market, or even if it was just a rumour, he'd be at the head of the queue.

But he didn't much understand the method. JD used cocaine as a launch, and then he drank himself under the table. That seemed contrary to Mike, given what he knew about uppers and depressants. Why the hell would you spike yourself and then spend the evening dropping the spike methodically? Why not follow either one to its logical conclusion?

And why, when you had a memory for the ages, would you try and lay your hands on anything that would allow you to fuck with it?

It was the Everest theory, that's why. You did it—whatever *it* was—because you could, because it was there. Those were the same reasons why Mike suddenly had two accounts at William Hill, and he was betting more in a week than he had in most months over a year ago. He now had the money to put his football knowledge to the test. He understood it, he read it, he breathed it. And he put it on the line every weekend, on every game. He spent Saturdays and Sundays holed up in his living room, surrounded by two televisions, picture-in-picture, while a third one droned in the kitchen.

Mike grinned suddenly. If he'd seen anyone else doing that when he was growing up, it would have taken him less than a second to understand that the guy was out of his fucking mind. However, if you were worth twenty-five million pounds, it was simply eccentric.

What a world.

And what about Aziz?

No bad-boy quirk there. No reputation for idiosyncrasies. He'd found money instead. And he was growing more distant than ever as he tried to stack it up wherever he could find it. For Mike and JD, the money had been the end. For Aziz it was a means—a ticket. But, Mike wondered, to where? And what would Aziz do when he got there?

In the distance, Mike saw Aziz stand up and begin to shake hands with the four men he'd been talking to. As the men left, Aziz picked up a manila envelope from the table and began to cross the room towards the bar.

'Bingo,' said JD softly. He tossed back the last of his drink in one swallow. That was three down for the night and he was ready for business. Mike simply pushed the rest of his pint away. The two of them swivelled on their stools as Aziz approached.

Aziz held out the envelope towards JD.

'We're going to the Cayman Islands next week. Three days at least. Tell the boys. They need to hold the burn, and they need to be ready to go when we're back.'

JD turned to Mike. Mike sighed, reached into his wallet, pulled out a fiver and passed it across.

~

By April, the mobile phone racket had become a national pastime. It didn't matter if you were a top electronics retailer or a janitor down at the local NHS hospital—even seventy-five pence was going to get you in at some level, just so that you could feel the momentum ruffle your hair. The rush made policing impossible. Every day was an ever-growing, ever-changing knot of leads. Each trail needed a finger, and it needed time.

Val had Wexler's attention now. The paperwork had blown up in his face and all they could do was fight for information, try to make up ground. Val got her meeting with him on a Friday afternoon. Excise would be in limbo for the next seven weeks, until the general elections on 7 June. The government was never going to tackle anything this big so close to an election, especially on the back of Mad Cow.

Wexler looked on, wary, as Val let herself into his office. Her preparations, as always, were immaculate. She dealt only in facts, reminding herself not to make this personal. She had been going into meetings for close to two decades with increasing belligerence, but there was no time for that now. They had two problems. The first were her boys. The second was how they'd get the ministers to see the first one.

As she sat across the desk from Wexler and opened her file, she looked up and was struck by how ragged the man looked. He had the aura of a cornered dog about him.

'It's a bit like looking at an epidemic,' she said after a pause. 'Isolation is what we'd like—that's the obvious thing. We'd like to be able to pause things and examine each case, but…'

Wexler frowned. Val waited.

'But there's a lot of them,' he finished. 'Cases.'

Val nodded. If she'd been in another mood, on another day, this would have been the moment to rub his nose in it. But she owed Wexler a little more than that.

'Response, if we're honest, and if we're actually qualifying it, would move along two streams. They both arise from the central problem, but they're the two things that we need to follow at the same time. If we're—' It was a tough phrase, but it had to be said. 'If we're to have any hope.'

Wexler rubbed his eyes, looked at Val for a moment, then nodded for her to continue.

'We have to contain it. That means precautions. Tighten paperwork, launch a few raids. It doesn't matter if they don't amount to anything. It's nothing more than bashing the pipes a bit, letting some noise ride up the whole house. At the very least, it'll scare the nervous ones. And it'll make the others a little more careful.'

There was no response from Wexler. Val had hoped that by now his eyes would have started the route over the room, signalling that he was at least really listening.

'The other is isolation,' she went on. 'It's the only way we're going to be able to examine *anything*. Let me sweat the banks, Peter. And let me start shutting them down if there's so much of a whisper of anything out of the ordinary. Any defaults and we'll start crashing those accounts.' She paused, then added, 'It won't be enough. They'll find another way. But it'll give us a narrower field to look at. And for once—for once we'll be doing the damned driving.'

With that, she was done talking. There was nothing left to say.

Wexler rubbed his eyes again. His eyes were always bloodshot afterwards, making him look slightly manic. He dropped his hands and folded them on his desk.

Val knew that this was the pass. They would part ways here. Her request would require a major departmental commitment, a huge shift in direction and resource allocation, just weeks from an election. That Wexler managed to run the department with any sort of autonomy was a testament to his political skill. One of the reasons Val respected Wexler was because she didn't have to deal with undersecretaries and ministers and the new-age mantra of the Labour government. Under Mrs. Thatcher, they would have been blowing up dustbins by now. But globalization had made the world soft, more accommodating, leaving the door open for thieves, mostly because the pockets of power, the industries and the consortiums, *wanted* the door left open.

Now it was Wexler's call. Val gave him a minute and then began to gather up her papers. There was no sense of disappointment. She had come into the meeting knowing that the best she could do was equip Wexler with the range of options that were open to him. There would be other recommendations and, most of all, there would be unseen pressure from up above. Then Wexler nodded his head briskly, as if he was shaking off the last twenty minutes and looked at her.

'The election's on 7 June,' he said. 'I can't commit resources.'

Val started to say that she knew, and that she was in no way judging him, but before she could, Wexler surprised her.

'I can give you four people.' He paused, calculating. 'Make it six. I can give you six people.'

Val was too stunned to reply.

'I'll authorize it. Reports to me. Alone.' Wexler was picking up pace now, more confident in the action of delegating. 'It's totally above board, but keep it a small circle. At least until the election's done, or until they've sorted out the Mad Cow mess.'

'And the banks?' Val asked.

That was the big commitment. And that would open up the circle inside of two days. That was where Wexler would have to test his own weight against the machinery of the State.

Wexler smiled, for the first time in days.

'Sweat them, Val. Sweat them and we'll square it the best we can.'

He held her eye for a moment and then nodded. By the time Val let herself out of the office, Wexler was already moving through the pile at his desk, head down.

~

'Hi, Pam.'

'Jai?'

'Mom? You get a boyfriend? Who the hell else calls you Pam?'

'Jai.' Pam paused. 'You didn't meet her?'

JD *had* met her. He was looking at her walk away as he talked to his mother. Namrata, her name had been. She had an excellent ass. She'd also been really nice. Smart, funny, frank.

Their cup of coffee was done in an hour. He'd felt like her brother. He didn't mean that in a good way.

'And?'

His mother's question brought him back to Earth.

'Nah, Mom. Not her.'

He sounded so unconvinced that he was sure that she

was going to cotton on to it *this* time and really lay into him. He pulled away from the phone slightly, in preparation for a blast of Punjabi.

'Okay, beta.' There was a pause. She sounded about as sincere as he did. Fine pair we are, he thought. Master criminal and his mother. Sounding like two tired phone operators auditioning for a soap opera. And trying very hard to not land parts.

It had been coming, though. They both knew it.

'Okay,' she repeated. 'How are you?'

'I'm okay, Mom. Getting by. We're looking to fly out tomorrow.'

It was why he'd called. He had no one else to call. He felt a need to call her and tell her that he was scheduled to travel. In case something happened. In case the plane crashed. In case the Russians came calling because an interest payment didn't go through.

He found himself thinking of that morning outside the Chaddas'. He'd spent a moment alone, outside, in the garden, before he saw Dink, thinking about how his parents and their friends could manufacture magic, how they could conjure the idea of home out of thin air.

How they had each other.

He wasn't frantic about getting married. He liked his life too much. But the string of arranged dates that his mother had set him up on had showed him another world. It had shown him another way of looking at the world.

JD met around eighteen women. He thought it was that many. He couldn't be sure. The count might have been sixteen, or twenty-four. This was the marriage burn. It was difficult to keep track.

He'd gone through a graded curve. The *kind* of woman changed through the process. After he'd agreed to his mother's request, the pimp-aunts had lined up the first batch of six very quick. JD remembered that bunch of harpies well. Each of them was attractive, made up to the nines, wealthy, connected and had turned marriage into their life's mission. JD felt like he'd been plonked into a feature-length advertising film. The whole thing—and he'd been able to appreciate it for what it was because he really didn't give a fuck, he wasn't actually serious about getting married—was a marketing campaign in the guise of something else.

Every single one of them had been a lesser version of Pamela. He didn't mean that as a compliment either. She was still around, although much less central to his life. They'd both come to consider each other longstanding addictions. They'd still get in touch on the odd weekend, if they were bored, just to see if they could the other to crack.

JD knew that she was probably sleeping with her 'cousin', Sukhdev. That kid had peddled for a bit before he came to work for the Principle. And because JD had got Sukhdev the job, it had changed the relationship between him and Pamela. And theirs *was* a relationship. They'd been trying to fuck each other over for a very long time. She was still digging for gold. He was trying to get into her pants as much as he could. There was comfort there.

She'd probably throw a shitstorm if she found out that he was screening women, apparently to marry them. But he didn't care. The other women, once he'd firmly rebuffed the first lot, came in dribs and drabs and were, on the whole, much, much more interesting. These girls had some sort of radar, JD discovered, just like some people could tell gay people straight away, and how other people knew, instinctively, which car they could jack on a particular street. They knew, almost instantly, that JD wasn't a serious suitor. Most of them were in the same situation—they'd showed at the coffee shop, or the restaurant, because their parents had asked them to. A couple of them were secretly engaged. One of them had been married.

JD was complicit because he was a passenger in this game. And he became father confessor. He felt like some long-lost brother to the lot of them. And not in a good way.

He suspected that his mother knew. She knew that he was just showing up for attendance, so that she could return to her circles and tell people that she was doing all she could. But JD also thought that his mother knew that he kept saying that the women simply weren't his type to get them off the hook. They weren't friends. He never saw a single one of them again. But he wasn't going to let on that they were engaged, or married, or didn't want to get married. In that, they'd formed a club. They were protecting their parents from themselves.

But he still liked to prowl the perimeter, looking at a world that he'd never access. Like his date this morning.

Namrata. Bahal. Corporate lawyer.

She'd walked in, clocked him in three minutes, told him that she wasn't really looking to get married. So they chatted about coffee. And work. Over the course of the hour, they'd talked about children and the choice of schools, and what money actually meant in the world today. They'd touched on music, and politics, and food. They'd argued and laughed. By the end of it, they could've been friends.

It reminded JD of the life he'd left behind. And he quite enjoyed it.

He was glad that his mom had banned divorcees. Otherwise, this thing might have actually borne results.

'Where are you going?'

'Cayman Islands. The Caribbean.' He stopped himself. 'The West Indies.'

'Holiday or work?'

JD laughed.

'They're the same thing, Mom. You stay well. I love you.'

~

The Principle flew out to the Cayman Islands on 12 April, a day before Good Friday. The long Easter weekend was no good for the burn. The EU was taking off to Prague and cheap alcohol. The Principle went in the other direction.

The manila envelope Aziz had produced at the Palm Casino contained a photograph and an A4 sheet of paper. The photograph was blown up to regulation headshot and, as far as casting went, their man was both unexpected and a cliché.

'Guy looks like Tim Roth,' said JD, peering at the photograph. It was true. If Tim Roth had been playing a shifty European banker, with a nasal accent, and at least one nasty habit. All this without having met him.

'He's Pumpkin,' decided JD. 'That makes Aziz Honey-Bunny. And that's fuckin' apt.'

'What if he's Mr Orange?' Mike observed. 'Who's that make Aziz? Or he could be that ponce in Rob Roy.'

'Piss off, right? They both got killed.'

'Well, I didn't see Pumpkin winning any fucking prizes himself.'

Tim Roth was John Vangels. Vangels was an ex-oil tycoon who had played out his welcome in the Middle East by 1998, after he'd burnt his bridges in Russia, where he'd made his first fortune. That was the sum of the information the Principle had access to. The rest was a collection of rumours and recommendations, shadows that befitted a man who'd operated like smoke his entire career.

That, and the fact that Vangels liked pretty girls and Tattinger—and was currently parked in Bermuda on a super yacht.

~

The Principle moved with the speed and style that Aziz had been working towards his entire life. They flew business, with four exceptionally attractive women in tow. The girls weren't hookers, although sex was part of the transaction if you paid enough. They were— loosely put—extremely high-class escorts. Their jobs were to make a social situation work first, and then the bedroom. Two of them were models,

one a struggling actress, and the fourth a trainee chef. Aziz
had used women from this particular contact for a couple of
years now. Occasionally, he needed someone to accompany
him to a party, someone he could flaunt, and someone he'd
set up to leave with a client who just happened to be at
the same party. At other times, he simply set up a string of
clients with the right kind of women for the desired London
experience. These girls were desirable as hell, surprisingly
good conversationalists, and they could fuck the socks off
black footballers. Two at a time, if needed.

And they knew how to be discreet. If they blabbed, even
to their friends, they'd be out of a job before they could blink.
There were enough sexy women walking the streets who
would kill for a chance to make this kind of money. Aziz
had once seen an Indian businessman drop a hundred and
twenty-five thousand pounds on a week with a girl. She was
now on a daily soap, well on her way to becoming a celebrity.

The seven of them checked into a hotel for the night. Aziz
and one of the young women didn't manage to make it down
to an early dinner. JD and Mike, on the other hand, turned
a rum-tasting session in the dining room into something
approaching a rave inside of half an hour. Between the two
of them, they bought every table at the restaurant a minimum
of two of the finest bottles of rum available. They emptied
the entire stock of Neisson Rhum, prompting the staff to go
running out before the stores shut at ten. JD wandered from
table to table, clutching a bottle of Pyrat XO, urging people
to 'get their Jamaican on'. It might have been offensive, but
he was a good drunk. They commandeered the band, then

the waiters and most of the diners. By the time they'd ended service, most of the restaurant was on the dance floor.

They assembled at six in the morning, JD still clutching a bottle of rum, and occasionally chasing it down with beer to keep himself going. They transferred to a luxury yacht that they'd leased for the week, a three-storey, ninety-five-metre behemoth called *Salome*. While the girls checked into their rooms and JD lounged about in the pool, Aziz prowled the foredeck. Aziz had hoped for a hundred-metre yacht, but they'd had so little time to set this play up. He was relatively confident that they'd done enough to open the transaction. At this stage, that was all he was looking for.

Aziz found himself leaning on the railing, staring at the water as it rushed past him. He felt like a conductor, just before the audience filed in. And yet, even with the pitch so close, part of him thought about Tasleem. He'd taken the girl upstairs last night without a second thought. This was like breathing for the Principle. Sex was part of the burn.

But he'd woken up this morning feeling unclean. It wasn't guilt—he knew himself too well for that. He never needed to bring this up. With Tasleem, or with anyone else. He and the boys were bound together, in every imaginable way, from their childhoods to Daniel Terry's nose.

He'd let himself down, though. He dropped under some standard that he'd set himself. If he had to try and explain it, thought Aziz, he'd say that he wasn't worried about disappointing his fiancée. It was that she'd understand. That she'd see him and accept him for being a lesser man.

I'm done with the pulls, thought Aziz. He grinned

ruefully. He felt like he'd crossed a threshold this morning. This is what it was like to be an adult, then. If so, he welcomed it.

By a quarter past eight, the Principle were parked next to Vangel's yacht—*Armaan*. Rumour had it that it was named after Vangel's friend in school. Aziz repeated the name to himself, 'Armaan.' Probably Persian. In Urdu, although 'wish' or 'longing' were acceptable, 'wistfulness' was the more appropriate translation.

Too fucking right, thought Aziz. If we get this off the ground, then we're the flood. We take everything.

Armaan, though it was only ten metres longer than their yacht, dwarfed it by some degree. Four tiers, and a helipad. The signs were promising.

By half past eight, the first of the Tattinger had been popped and the girls were clustered over the foredeck, sunbathing in bikinis that amounted to nothing more than bits of coloured string. The men had disappeared, and the crew, as promised, were invisible. The sun slowly continued to rise from a horizon that shimmered almost beneath the eye-line. Here the world left you alone, until the sun climbed higher and set fire to the sea at noon. Then, it would be time to fish.

At nine, JD flicked the sound system on and turned up The Clash as loud as they would go. London Calling.

Before the song was over, they saw signs of life aboard *Armaan*. Two uniformed men, in succession, emerged from the bridge and looked at the yacht parked next to them. The thing about money, thought Aziz, the thing about docking in Bermuda, was that if you were plonked next to a near-hundred-metre yacht that was playing loud punk music, you couldn't quite yell 'Oi! Fuck off!' There was protocol.

Vangels emerged four minutes later. He was in a bathrobe, belted, wearing sunglasses. He looks like a heroin addict, thought Aziz. The man was practically emaciated. He had the air of an aging, forgotten rock star. He clasped the rail that went around the main deck and watched the girls for a while. Another uniformed man delivered coffee on a silver tray. Vangels sipped it, and then pushed his sunglasses up. He looked bemused, an older witness to the unnecessary vigour of youth.

Mike made his entry, dressed in shorts and shades and nothing else. He stopped to snap a bikini on one of the girls. She dissolved into a fit a giggles. Mike made his way to the bow. He looked rough, there was no way around it. He looked like a man who didn't fuck around. He paused at the bow and stared out. He pulled out the champagne bottle from the bucket, enjoying the tinkling of the ice in the morning sun, and poured himself a drink. He turned and nodded to Vangels. Vangels returned the nod, still bemused. Mike grinned.

'Did we wake you up?' Mike's voice was low, but it carried across the gap between the yachts.

Vangels shrugged. Neither here nor there, the gesture said. It was oddly endearing.

'Jai!' Mike let his voice travel up the three tiers this time. 'Jai! Turn it down, you idiot!'

The last two words floated away into a much more

welcoming quiet. Vangels smiled, reciprocating the politeness from the tough guy. Mike pushed his sunglasses up.

'Breakfast?'

~

Vangels was low-key, urbane and very far from a fool. While Aziz hadn't expected him to immediately grab a tit and go to work for them, he was surprised at how much of a neighbourly visit the first hour had been.

Vangels had been polite and charming, but that was the extent of it. He revealed nothing about himself, and he asked no penetrating questions of the three men. He simply asked where they were from, their answer prompting vague reminiscences of the time he had spent in England as a young man, when the world had been far more innocent, as he put it. He chatted up the girls as an old flirt does, asking them what they did, complimenting them, offering them their chairs as they sat down to breakfast.

It was coming to eleven when Aziz found himself sitting on the foredeck with him, alone. The girls were in their rooms, sleeping off the previous night. Vangels clearly caught the drift, because he chatted to one of the girls in particular over breakfast and she had promised to go over to his yacht that afternoon. Mike and JD were at the bar, Mike having taken over JD's rum-drinking duties while JD smoked a series of impossibly strong joints.

The picture was complete, and they were some kind of image, thought Aziz. Vangels knew. And Aziz knew that

Vangels knew because the older man had wandered away on his mobile for five minutes after breakfast. A man who'd been dodging governments that long, and who parked in Bermuda for months on end, would know in one phone call who the three men were. As he should, as he was supposed to.

Vangels settled into a deckchair and accepted the cigar that Aziz offered him.

'So. Two English boys and a Pakistani lawyer? And you're partners?' he asked finally.

'We are,' said Aziz with a smile. 'You could have simply asked.'

Vangels shrugged. 'I did,' he grinned. 'At my age, one doesn't like surprises.'

Aziz nodded, his smile growing. He pulled out his phone and tapped out a number.

'I'm sorry to show up unannounced then,' he said. As Vangels began to speak, Aziz shook his head. He locked eyes with Vangels. At the bar, JD stifled a snort.

Someone answered the phone.

'Sir.' Aziz said. 'He's here. In front of me.' Aziz listened again. Then, without a word, he held out the phone to Vangels. The other man looked at the phone, and then looked back at Aziz. Vangels took the phone gingerly, as if he were running down a list of people who might be on the other end, and he wasn't happy to hear from any of them.

'Yes?' There was a momentary expression of puzzlement. It was replaced with disbelief, and Vangels burst out laughing.

'Shah? Are you—?' He laughed again, but he was listening carefully. 'Hmmm. So you? No? Oh.' Vangels looked at Aziz.

On his face was a look of flat calculation that JD recognized well. 'Very well.' Vangels hung up and looked at the phone for a few seconds. He handed the phone back to Aziz and settled back into the deckchair, pulling on the cigar.

'What do you have in mind?'

At the bar, JD turned to Mike.

'Everybody be cool,' he murmured. 'This is a robbery.'

Mike turned to JD and sipped his rum. 'You don't remember how that scene ends, do you?'

~

For the first time since the launch of the first system, time slowed without the Principle actively controlling it. The creation of a banking system was out of the Principle's hands. A new bank was a sizeable investment, and it needed to comply with the laws of the Cayman Islands. It had to be up to a certain standard.

As soon as they had flown back from Bermuda, Aziz started the process of prepping all their accounts—every single company through the entire chain—for the final transfer into the offices of the First Caribbean Traders' Bank. The Principle hadn't moved yet, they were still within the limits of the Bank of England. The transfer was a massive paperwork operation, mostly because the accounts were scattered across countries, in dozens of shapes and sizes.

In a weird way, the closures had become a stock-taking exercise. JD responded with his usual malice, taking the opportunity to re-examine his averages—the companies that had been good to them, and the companies that they could bitch-slap. That May, they cached their targets. Vangels and Aziz had been circling each other ever since Bermuda. The wait nearly drove Aziz out of his mind. He knew full well that Vangels was having the Principle checked out as thoroughly as possible. It was going to cost two-and-a-half thousand pounds to open up every new account at FCTB, and for *every transaction* FCTB would take one per cent of the amount transferred. Vangels would make money at every single stage of the journey. If electronic services were going to allow them four deals a day, then that was about twenty-four transactions a day for the bank from one single company. Vangels had already set up shop in London, with a single representative who would start to map the accounts as the Principle wanted.

Aziz knew that Vangels would eventually open up the banking platform to anyone who played the VAT game. There was just too much money. Then Customs would get interested, even though the Cayman Islands were out of EU jurisdiction. The Principle had to get to the platform first, just like the burn. Aziz pushed as hard as he could as they inched towards the formation of the First Caribbean Traders' Bank, knowing all along that Vangels was stalling to build a database of potential customers he could offer the same service to.

Mike, meanwhile, couldn't have picked the Cayman Islands out on a map three months ago. Now, as he took his time strolling to the warehouse in the afternoon sun, he understood the particular joys of offshore accounts, and of electronic banking, and how Nigerian dictators got rich on interest as opposed to stealing the principle.

And it was a good thing, too. Whispers were beginning to float up to them. The Principle knew before anyone else because they had their bank managers, but it was a question of hours this time around, not days. By the time May had rolled around, the paperwork demands for new accounts had become seriously difficult. Bank managers were having to account for *everything*, every word spoken in a branch over the course of a day. The checks, JD said, were as if they were applying to adopt kids instead of trying to get some business done.

Account closures would follow. If there was a company with as much as an asterisk next to its name, and even one transaction was slightly dodgy, they'd get shut down.

Then Excise would target the reclaims for specific companies, and then spread it to transactions, and then entire groups that ran together. And, ultimately, they would pull banking privileges. If anyone wanted to open a company that had anything to do with mobiles, they were going to land on their arses on the pavement outside.

The game had turned again. Someone, somewhere, had understood that the burn was the central element. The dogs were in the game, prowling the perimeter.

Mike was so engrossed with the idea that he passed by something truly extraordinary and kept walking. But colour followed him as he moved—a red so exquisite, so shimmery that it wouldn't be left behind. His mind drew the shape of the thing behind his eyes, the lines, lines flowing with the joy that other people got from symphonies.

He stopped but didn't turn around at first. There was still

that vague chance that the image in his head was some kind of a mirage or momentary hallucination. Because it could not be there. It *had* to not be there.

He turned slowly, heart pounding. It was there, lines and colour, shining in the sun. For a moment, Mike couldn't breathe. He sat down on the pavement and, hands jittering, he lit a cigarette. Then he called JD.

He had to call *somebody*.

~

JD got moving as soon as he hung up the phone. He was up to his eyes in spreadsheets, but Mike sounded bad, his voice was choked and shaky. He was three blocks down the road and JD covered the distance at a pace just short of running.

He turned the corner and slowed. Mike was sitting on the pavement ,smoking. JD was halfway to him when he saw what Mike was looking at. And as he completed the distance, he made the connections himself. He joined Mike on the kerb and stared. Then he held his hand out for a cigarette and lit up.

'*Fuck,*' JD sighed.

'Yep.'

'Ferrari?'

'Testarossa. 512 TR.'

JD watched the bloodred machine through the smoke he exhaled. 'Ah, well. I don't suppose they're particularly rare?'

'They made two thousand two hundred and eighty of them.'

JD nodded. 'Well... so long as it's not in mint condition or anything.'

'The cunt may as well have parked a fucking giraffe on this street.'

The lines spoke. There was no doubt about intent here. This thing was built to go at only one speed: Crazy. It looked, thought JD, like it had been designed by someone in a constant state of ecstatic horniness. It made his mouth water.

'Fifty?' he asked.

'Thereabouts,' Mike agreed. 'Hell of a bargain.'

A Ferrari in Heston was a magnet. That's why it had been bought. A red Ferrari in Heston? That was rock star territory.

JD considered the implications. This is how the world saw him, saw them. Someone who *worked* for them had bought himself a Ferrari. This was beyond anything they had imagined. JD envisioned the trail through September, and then beyond. Ten mill a month. Like a pay-cheque, like a backwards EMI. In a year, even if Mike and he didn't burrow it away in investments like Aziz was doing, they would both be worth a hundred and twenty million pounds. Each.

That was private jet territory. That was Amex Black territory.

This was the moment they'd dreamt about all their lives, but it had taken them a month-and-a-half after the gates had been unlocked to actually realize that the trip was done—they'd arrived.

The Ferrari was parked in front of a minging house owned by one of their soldiers.

JD drew on the cigarette and flicked it into the street.

'What—*who*—did he used to be?'

Mike's answer came back without a pause. 'That's Joe Tarr.' He grinned. 'Used ter be a plumber.'

Almost a dozen soliloquies suggested themselves to JD immediately. So much for Heston being a dying dump. So much for getting a degree. Look Ma, no hands. On the wheel of my Ferrari.

Used ter be a plumber.

JD snorted and shook his head. Mike looked at him and smiled.

'I bought a secondhand Range Rover,' said JD. 'And I bought my dad a Merc. Only...' He gestured wildly at the thing. 'To have *this*.'

'We got a bit Jewish, eh?' asked Mike.

'I blame Aziz. This is what you get when you tell people not to spend their own money. It's like telling Catholic girls to never fuck. They overcompensate.'

'They go fucking crazy.'

JD and Mike looked like two twelve-year-old boys gawking at a sports car, waiting for the incredibly exotic owner to emerge so that they could pester him with questions. How fast did she go, mate? Zero-to-sixty in four-point-nine, as far as Mike could recall. Maybe a shade slower. After all, this *was* secondhand.

'Think about it,' said JD. 'Six weeks. That means—he's 'A' company right?' Mike nodded. 'That means that he's put away eight hundred thousand phones. At a pound per. Even if he's splitting it, and we're absorbing costs. He's still made three hundred thousand pounds.'

They sat in the sun for a while longer, looking at the TR. Mike lit another cigarette and shared it with JD.

'And all I'm worried about is presenting Pumpkin with the correct data on the accounts.'

'Come on,' Mike said, getting to his feet. 'Let's go in and slap some sense into him.'

'I'll say. It's going to be a fiscal tutorial for the ages. Buy a *house*, you fucking moron, that you can park that car in front of.' JD shook his head. 'I'm beginning to sound like my mother.'

They waited in front of the car for a moment longer.

'Let's do it,' said JD as they began to walk toward Joe Tarr's house. 'And I'm telling you right now that as soon as we're done, I'm going to buy some Arsenal shares. But before that, I'm going to buy you a cup of coffee. Or, I'll just buy you the damned coffee shop.' JD paused to kick a tyre. 'Because it clearly doesn't matter.' He grinned at Mike. 'Viva the revolution, bruv.'

'That's what my fucking plumber told me.'

~

Joe Tarr's lesson aside, the Principle never stood a chance of keeping so much money contained. After a while, they didn't even try. They were twenty-something millionaires. For them not to live it just didn't make sense. What were tens of millions of dollars for in the fucking first place? Within a month they were making footballers look like amateurs. They made Oasis look like amateurs. They were young, obviously local, obviously working class, and they were suddenly setting spending records behind every velvet rope in London. They were some sort of venture capitalists, was the best the newspapers could make out. They had burst out of nowhere and the press couldn't get enough of them. The name eventually made it out to the sub-editors scrambling to uncover anything about the three men who sometimes moved in a group of thirty hard boys, burning through the city like a comet. They drew football skanks and groupies and hungry Page-3 blondes looking for publicity. They started pulling from all parts of society—TV stars, actresses, topless models, girl bands... they were the rough lads who had made good, and they went through the posh part of town like a raiding party.

They were the Heston Principle.

~

They moved to Chelsea, Millionaires' Row, all three of them.

Almost immediately after the Joe Tarr excursion. JD decided that Mike needed a Ferrari. After all, he was running the plumber who was running the TR. It was only fair. The boys hadn't yet completely embraced the fact that, with their bank accounts, a phone call would normally put wheels into motion. So they rolled along to HR Owen in South Kensington. They argued about the comparative merits of the Modena versus the Maranello. Except that most of the argument, good-natured as it was, occurred at the door of the showroom as JD smoked cigarette after cigarette. In about ten minutes, they'd drawn a crowd, turning the decision about a two-hundred-and-fifty-thousand sports car into a public debate. Finally, JD had had enough.

'Fuck it,' he said, turning to Raphael, the man who'd been showing them the cars. 'We'll buy both of them.'

There was a collective gasp that JD enjoyed very much. It kind of rendered a debate useless if both options were actually viable. He turned away and eyed the horizon moodily.

'Mike.'

'Yeah?'

'We still have the Joe Tarr problem, don't we?'

'Where you park the car, you mean?'

'Not Heston.' JD turned to look at Mike. 'I'm getting *that* dust off my feet.' His gaze transferred from Mike to Raphael, who was filling out forms furiously.

'Raph?'

'Yes, Mr Dewan.'

'Here's a question. If you were buying one of these cars, where would you park it?'

Raph simply stared at JD. Mike joined JD and grinned at Raph. Even he had been infected by the afternoon's mindless good cheer. It took some getting used to, the fact that you could behave like *this*.

'Come on, son. Don't be shy about it.'

'Well,' Raph gestured weakly. 'Here. Somewhere here, I suppose.'

'Chelsea. Right,' said JD. 'You're our tour guide.' And with that, he picked up the keys of the test-drive car, turned and walked out of the store. Mike grinned at Raphael, mouthed 'come on', picked up the other set of keys and exited the showroom. Raph closed his mouth, shook his head and ran out to join them.

The two Ferraris raced each other to the other side of the borough, joined by a Jaguar. JD had dialled Aziz imperiously while driving, asking about real estate agents in Chelsea. Aziz's natural curiosity was too much, and he joined the sports-car stream.

They invested exactly that one afternoon in the house hunt. Aziz found himself representing the *idea* of estate agents, even though three of them showed up within forty-five minutes and accompanied them during that whistle-stop tour through the most expensive real estate in the country. Aziz had found a house for Tasleem and himself, although he hadn't moved in yet. And it *was* a house, gated, with a small driveway, self-contained, set back from the road.

'You got a garden, bruv,' said JD, as they stood around the property. Aziz had shown them the place as soon as he could, trying to get them to think about their decisions. The three realtors stood in the driveway, on their phones, like they were the secret service, or wedding coordinators, running up lists of potential apartments, getting people from the office to run across to this travelling circus with brochures and laptops with presentations and photos. JD had shaken their hands, nodded and said 'We're buying, boys. Now dance.' Outside, Raph and Paul tried to park the three cars like they were a valet service that moved with the Principle. They would continue to do so for the rest of the afternoon.

'I want somewhere where a whole wall is a TV, though. I want a study. I want to sound-proof the whole thing. And Mike wants a swimming pool.'

They turned around and off they went again, two Ferraris and the Jag, with the estate agents following.

Eventually, although it was only later that afternoon, Mike went to Knightsbridge, into an apartment complex that came with a valet service. More importantly, he had a twenty-metre heated swimming pool, and both driving and putting ranges in the basement. The movie theatre, the concierge promised, would be open in less than three months.

JD got increasingly morose through the afternoon, and he responded by getting hectic. He was tipping doormen and bell boys, and Raph and the estate agents. He swore that he was going to buy a house that afternoon, that he wasn't going home until he knew he could move out of that hell-hole. Mike read it as an oncoming bender. Later, he would wish that he hadn't.

By six that evening, both Aziz and Mike were chivvying JD along, as he had chivvied them earlier that day. The sports-car circus continued to roll, accompanied by the agents who had already made one sale, but were now along for the ride. JD insisted that he was going to find what he wanted in SW3.

The full gang walked into a four-and-a-half-thousand -square-foot apartment near dusk. This was the penultimate stop for the day. JD stood at the door for a while. Two apartments per floor, and both occupied corners. A long hall stretched to a wall of glass. The high ceiling made the

apartment seem like a box open to the sky. There were doors
on either side. Down the righthand side JD knew, without
looking, each of those rooms would have similar windows
as the apartment turned the corner and ran along the side
of the building.

'Open the doors, please,' he murmured. The agents did.

The last of the day poured in through the right, a series
of shafts, all the way down to the wall of glass on fire. JD
crouched by the door and lit a cigarette, watching the smoke
as it coiled its way through a maze of light. Shadow. Light.
Shadow. Light. They might have been standing in a cathedral.
There was silence here, unhurried. Mike watched JD from
one side. Aziz was going through the rooms, one by one, like
JD's dad had done, testing every door, every faucet.

Fuck knew how much he'd have to spend to furnish
it. The place was as empty as a cell. And JD was glad. He
wouldn't have fallen in love with it had it been cluttered.
The symmetry pleased him; it was a plane that trapped light.

He turned to the agent who had brought them to
the apartment.

'Do it.'

'It's four million, two hundred thousand.'

JD waved it away.

'Do it. And see if you can get the other apartment on this
floor.' He turned to Mike and Aziz and grinned.

'Well, boys. I found my cage. Let's get a drink.'

~

This was the roll-call:

Nobu, George Club, The Ivy, Royal China, Gordon Ramsey at Claridge's, Stringfellows, Tramps, Annabelle's. Flashbulbs marked their attendance. Stories about their spending records were getting out. People were talking, people didn't know who they were, and people were interested.

It was the weekends in the Presidential Suite at the Dorchester, Park Lane, ten thousand pounds a night, snorting cocaine off the girls they had hired, picked up, invited. Like Poison, JD declared. The music was shite, but they had a condom-vending machine on the tour bus.

It was the consecutive nights at Casinos across Europe, dropping hundreds of thousands of pounds on a whim.

But they hadn't had their defining moment yet, thought Mike. He'd been a passenger on the ride thus far—he could out-drink most of the boys, but waking up in anonymous hotel rooms next to anonymous women wasn't quite *him*. He liked the girls, and he got more of them than the other two, but desperate clubbing left him cold. The rampage they were on wasn't about having a good time. Instead, like most of JD's savant decisions, this was a performance. Look at us. We're better than you.

Eventually, Mike decided that if that was what JD really wanted, then he'd give it to him in a dose big enough to choke on. Something that could not be topped. Something that might just leave his friend feeling they'd done enough for once.

They'd have a party.

But how did you throw the party of a lifetime for a multimillionaire super-geek? Especially one who was out every night, ticking off a list of hotspots to hit before the seventh drink? Mike knew it turned on history. Because that, above everything else, was what JD measured himself against. And as soon as he had that, he knew what he wanted to do. Really, it was the only sensible choice.

~

He dialled the Doxy, a distant conversation from Calais playing through his mind.

'Hi. I'm looking to book the VVIP room for a Saturday night—29 June. It's for a friend's birthday.'

The manager politely declined. The room was already booked, all the way to the end of September.

Mike frowned as he hung up. And then he smiled. Taking no for an answer had been for other people the last few months. There was *always* a fucking way.

He thought about calling Sumit, and then decided to visit Aziz at his office. The pretence of Aziz being the Principle's ghost member had gone out the window around the third time they'd been in the papers coming out of clubs together. Besides, Mike just found it amusing to pop by.

Aziz shook his head when Mike told him the idea. He rubbed his eyes when Mike added the one hitch. It *had* to be the Doxy. Because that's where they needed to put the Arabs in their place.

'God. Of all the possible ambitions.' Aziz sighed and picked up his phone. He dialled. The phone must've rung once before it was answered.

'Phil? Hi… Well, thanks, very well… Sure. Hold on a second. There's someone here who needs to talk to you.' Aziz held out the phone to Mike. Mike looked a question at him. 'It's my concierge.' Mike took the phone.

'Hello?'

'Hi. This is Phil at American Express Centurion. What can I do for you?'

'I'm looking to book the VVIP room at the Doxy on the 29th. They say they're booked through to the end of September.'

'Hmmm. This'll take a few minutes, sir.'

'Sure—' Mike began. Aziz held out his hand out, asking for the phone back. 'Hang on.'

'Phil? No that's fine. I understand. All I'm saying to you is that about thirty men and about twice as many extremely attractive women will aim to break some sort of long-standing spending record at the Doxy. Is that enough?'

There was a brief answer and Aziz hung up.

They talked business for a few minutes. Since April, they'd updated themselves on FCTB as often as they could. It was a side venture that had begun to throw an ever-increasing shadow across their lives. Mostly, they worried about Vangels going public too soon about his specialized services. Heat of that nature, they could live without.

By the time the phone rang, Mike had almost forgotten that he'd activated the Amex Black Concierge Service. The phone call itself was proof that its reputation was richly deserved.

Aziz listened for a minute. He put his hand over the mouthpiece and looked at Mike.

'The room's done. It's ours. Phil says that there's a fair chance that the owner, who he just spoke to, will tip off the paps. Press a problem?'

'At a birthday party?' Mike grinned. 'For Jai Singh Dewan? When he's going to be in one of those moods? Mate, bring 'em on. I feel sorry for them already.'

~

The day of the party, the Principle read in the papers that the management at the Doxy had bounced an offshoot—admittedly distant—of the Royal Family and their Eton set to the Red Room in order to accommodate JD's birthday party. There was a crowd of reporters at the door when the Principle showed in a convoy of Bentleys and Porsches led by the Hummer that had been Aziz's birthday gift to JD. By the time the Principle got down to action inside the Doxy, and word began to trickle back through the grapevine, the pavement was a knot of reporters jostling for space.

Every table started with a bottle of Crystal, arriving at the table with a sparkler going off. By the time the servers had completed the first round of orders, all directions led to the VVIP room. In about forty minutes, the Principle and their boys had taken over the club. They were dancing at every table, buying everyone a drink, boys disappearing with girls every four-and-a-half minutes. Mike even started sending bottles of Crystal out to the paps on the street with orders not to let them go dry. By the time they emerged, the paps loved them. Granted, the paps would love anyone who got them drunk, but the boys were also one hell of a story. Even if no one quite knew what that story was.

The Principle had dropped forty-eight thousand pounds on champagne alone. The bill had been sixty-three thousand pounds. They had paid with a single credit card.

And this wasn't the first time, the murmur went. This was the third time that month.

Aziz was still okay, smiling as they emerged into the artificial daylight of a hundred rapid flashes. Mike was simmering from the fight he'd almost gotten into when someone had tried to stop JD from taking over the DJ booth on the regular dance floor. Mike had been edgy from the start of the evening. They'd made sure to exclude Pamela from the guest list but she'd found a way to show up regardless. She came with Sukhdev in tow, further complicating the situation. They couldn't just toss a soldier. But the longer they stayed, and the more they danced, the angrier JD got and the more he wanted the music changed. Now JD was trashed and Mike was keeping him on his feet with an arm firmly around his shoulders as they made their way to the cars.

'Just wanted some fucking rock and roll,' JD mumbled.

'I know.'

'What is it with all that fucking techno rubbish? It's only my fucking birthday, you know.'

Behind the buzzing wall of light, the paps were shouting

the usual questions. Who the hell were they? Where did the bloody money come from? One got through to JD and he tugged on Mike's T-shirt to get him to stop.

JD steadied himself against Mike's shoulder, turned to face the cameras full-on and raised his palm to the lights. There was silence. He grinned.

'We are the revolution,' he said slowly. The enunciation was perfect, no slurring, but his lips squirmed over his teeth. Mike gently nudged JD's back with his thumb. 'We are the walrus.'

He grinned again.

'I'll tell you what,' he said after a pause. 'I'll tell you it, what it is.' He thought about it, his lips beginning to twitch over his teeth again. Mike took hold of his arm, thinking he might go down, but JD straightened himself up and leaned away from him.

'The hippies wanted peace and love,' he said gravely. 'We wanted Ferraris, blondes and football teams.' There was scattered laughter, a smattering of applause, and JD added. 'But right now we could do with some bloody burgers as well. And after that I think I'll have my nurse here carry me back to me mum's.'

JD flashed the peace sign as Mike reached around his shoulders and gathered him off. Aziz stood by the side, smiling like an elder brother.

'That went surprisingly well,' Mike said, loading JD into the back of the Hummer. He shut the door behind him and told the driver they'd hired for the night to go.

'I'm fucked up, Mike,' JD said as they started to move.

'Really? I could hardly tell. Let's get some food and you can sleep it off.'

JD suddenly grabbed the front of Mike's shirt again, this time with both hands, and pulled him close. No trace of his trademark grin remained on JD's face. His eyes were a manic blur. Mike could smell the sweat on his face.

'I mean I'm fucked up, Mike. Seriously.'

Mike watched JD carefully. He took hold of JD's wrists slowly and got him to let go of his shirt. 'Just calm down, Jai. Relax.'

'When have I ever been calm? Name once. When's it going to happen? I'm fucked up, Mike.'

Tears shone along rims of his bleary eyes.

'You're just worn out, okay?' Mike told him. 'We just had a pure and total success, mate. The fucking blow-out to end all blow-outs.'

JD started to laugh, his shoulders shaking, as the tears ran down his face.

'But it doesn't end anything! Don't you get it yet? Nothing ever ends. Where does it all go, Mike? Where does anything ever go?'

Before Mike could say anything, JD's crying turned into a coughing jag. He doubled over, away from Mike, and sent his share of their storied evening all over the floor of his brand new car.

JD's performance outside the Doxy made the headlines on four of the London tabloids the next day. It went on the file as the definitive portrait of the Heston Principle.

The scene inside the Hummer never made the papers.

3.3

Customs hit the mobile phone boom like a ton of bricks, starting mid-June. Aziz wasn't surprised. Labour was back in power. Files had simply been waiting, and now they surged forward. It was taking frustratingly long to set up FCTB. At the rate they were going, it looked like they wouldn't be able to make the final jump to electronic banking until August, but the Principle had committed to the process. They had invested time and money, and they no longer had the luxury of being able to walk away, to examine other options at their leisure. With the permanence of their success, the Principle were slowly rooting themselves.

The mobile phone market was a seething mess and it was completely understandable. For the guys who didn't have the Principle's kind of money, the first fold was the ticket into the system. That was the one where you could walk in with three hundred phones and start to generate the capital that would allow you to enter the Great Game.

The Principle watched with some awe as Customs came out of the woodwork, pissed at having been held at bay for over three months.

The penalties were unexpectedly savage. Until June, if you showed up for your reclaims and the company that you had bought from had gone missing, you were okay—the defaulters were the bad guys. Now, association was enough. You didn't get your reclaims. You were shown the door and your account was shut down. And by then, you couldn't get an account anywhere else. The banks were beginning to hand out thirty-day notices like they were pamphlets.

The new scammers reacted to the crackdown just as the Principle had expected them too. They shit themselves looking for alternate banking, never realizing that trying to solicit bank accounts only made them more visible. They went from grey-market to white hot, fucking ultraviolet, in a matter of days—the easiest targets walking the streets. Customs crushed the small-timers in two weeks, most of them good, hard-working boys who had seen the prize from the VAT game on the front pages of the tabloids, and in the whispers about the three men who had ridden the bullet out of Heston.

Customs smoked out the legitimate vendors and then went after the defaulters. They were moving like a stampede.

~

The Principle read the signs from a long way away. In the third week of June, 2001, Aziz began to prepare for a raid. It was only a matter of time. The Principle weren't running the fold-model, but they were players in the bigger fraud. They knew it. Customs knew it. But arrests swung on proof.

The Principle pulled themselves in. The word went out: No cutting corners, every inch of the paperwork had to be word-perfect, and the soldiers needed be on the watch. Those of them in the know needed to behave like everything was utterly legit, down to the last keypad. They brought genuine goods back in, switching from junk mobiles to Nokia, with a smattering of Samsungs. And they tightened the presentation at the main warehouse, the Freight Forwarder's.

The Forwarder was Aziz's crown jewel. The warehouse could hold up to five hundred thousand units of stock at a time, all of it protected by high-tech, high security, incongruous in the back-alley network of cargo routes behind Heathrow. Inside, the mobiles lived in a cage as the insurance required. The Principle spent money on it because they were selling the illusion. Aziz had a trained staff manning it, down to the two secretaries, and both Rich and Jassi on a rotation, but on 26 June, he shifted out of his chambers and started to work out of the warehouse of ASF Logistics in anticipation of the raid. He wanted to be there when Customs and Excise hit. He wanted to see what he was up against.

~

Val had a single, fierce burst of joy on the Monday after she and her team of six had sent forty-three accounts packing. They knew the panic that they had caused. They also knew that the herd was on the move, trying to find other banks, and that by this time next week they would have put an even hundred companies out of business.

Still, they weren't satisfied. They knew that they were only skimming the surface. It was 19 June, and they were examining—as much as possible—the effects of their actions on the reclaim structure. Her team had caused a significant jag in the graph. Part of it, Val knew, had to do with people realizing that Customs suddenly had teeth. However, because they had drawn blood, there were already calls for more. Nothing begat success like success.

The seven of them were looking at a moving graph. Val had found that Craig actually had some gifts after all. He'd managed to find a way to factor the information they received every day and reduce it to points that could be plotted. They were pulling figures from eighteen different sources a day and it took something to be able to reduce them to Xs and Ys. It meant that they were looking at something that moved, like a stock market graph. They had been plotting the graph for five weeks and, through a process of elimination, they had worked the default/claim axis. And their little stunt had split the fraud.

The real action, though, was concentrated around the companies associated with third-party payments. Hundreds of little companies littered the path, but they circled around a handful of nodes. Val was sure that the little companies were all essentially paper companies. These offices might have a cubicle and a printer, but they existed to lay the trail. They were there to clear the passage for the value to run through, like bodyguards for hire.

The invoices came into the node from the paper companies. And the money was sent out of the system at the request of the paper companies. It was a neat loop, enclosed, and out of reach. *If* the paperwork was in order. And that was worth checking on. If her team caught them out, that was fantastic. If not, then they were at least keeping the scam-runners on their toes.

Here Val's team allowed themselves a little guesswork.

Craig and Mary saw four companies. The other four—Nigel, Colin, Gareth and Nicola—saw three companies. Val saw six. Two of them were really very good. They had sunk so low that they were almost impossible to see. The clue wasn't in the cash, it wasn't even in the third party payments, it was simply in the volume of phones. Val knew that the six companies she was looking at were dealing in an unholy amount of phones. Even in comparison with something like Carphone Warehouse, these boys were shipping at a rate that they couldn't possibly explain.

At the top of everyone's list was Atomic Sell Fone Logistics, the Freight Forwarder that supplied a company called the Heston Principle—which was reclaiming between thirty and forty-five million pounds a month. They had shown up the earliest, and they had grown at a steady, geometric rate.

~

Advantages didn't come cheap. Val ran the third party payment theory past the heads of all the corresponding departments. She also dispatched Craig to the phones for a day-and-a-half, chasing Nokia. The departments responded—

yes, the concentration was at the third party nodes. The bias was so heavy it glowed red. Nokia responded too; the volumes were out of sync with their *worldwide* production.

Word came back to Val from every source she'd bounced the theory off. Just like every other time, every past trail that slowly grew warm. Once you saw the path, it changed the way you looked at the landscape.

Her team had started pulling double duty. The first part of the job had been the tracking, and it was becoming obvious that the second part would be to shut the VAT scam down themselves. *Everything* was now coming their way—leads, recommendations, great bleeding requests. They had pulled favours and worked themselves to the bone while the people around them hadn't even known there *was* a problem. And now, suddenly, they had been anointed the parents. It was their baby because no one else would have it.

What were the spot-checks? What were the policy changes? What was the strategy now? What was the combat on the ground?

It was the Treasury. It was the Chancellor of the Exchequer. It was the ministers who had suddenly been reminded of their duties and their constituencies.

It was politics. Val had no taste for politics, so she handed that end to Wexler, who was only to happy to play that game. All the sudden action seemed to give him a renewed sense of vigour, and it had come from a monumental decision that he had taken under his own steam, at his own risk. And he was good at whatever it was one did with chancellors and ministers.

Customs lined up the third party nodes for visits. They stamped phones post-inspection, making recycling more difficult. The started the legislation making IMEI numbers mandatory, even on export deals. They couldn't spot-check IMEI numbers, so Customs had to settle for external certification of the viability of the IMEI numbers across entire shipments. Val knew that she would never get the one policy shift that she wanted the most—the ability to physically check each van as it came in from the Continent. That would just stop the money train completely. Instead, she worked towards locking down banking for the mobile phone business. Another three months of living with four or five hundred million pound drains, and she would have that clearance too.

Val worked from what she liked to think of as the reverse angle, testament to how much she had come to respect her boys. She looked at the restrictions not in terms of the law itself, but as the hurdles she would hate the most if she was trying to break the law. And each time she pushed a policy change through, she got her team of six to check how difficult it was going to be to get around it.

Her boys *would* get around it. Val had no doubt about that. Their paperwork would be great, they had probably begun shifting to overseas banks, and they were as hard at work as Customs in trying to find ways to generate IMEI numbers. But with each move, either side, they were moving into smaller territory. Much like that game where teams of two tried to dance on folded pieces of newspaper. You kept folding the pieces of paper until the teams around the room were struggling to stand on a tiny scrap. That was where they were headed, she and her boys. To a very intimate dance.

~

The point of no return for Val arrived at half past seven in the morning, ten days after the third party payment model had become her department's primary focus.

Halfway through her second cup of tea, *The Guardian* done, she paused. She had brought the cup up to sip, but it stayed where it was, a foot off the table. She had just flipped over *The Sun* and the cover story suddenly had all her attention. What caught her eye was the photograph. Three young men were exiting a club at the front of a happy mob.

The three men in the photograph looked like a single entity. They were facing the camera, but all three of them were looking in three different directions, like an album cover for The Who. They were frozen in transit, one white man and two Asians. The one farthest left was easily the most polished—you could tell from the way he dressed, and the way that he allowed himself to be photographed. The other two were so out of place that they belonged entirely. They were a couple of originals, thought Val. The three of them held the stage equally.

Val saw the name. 'The Heston Principle'. She saw the quote, the one that had made the headlines. About wanting Ferraris, blondes and football teams.

Val knew she was as close to being sure as she was ever going to get. The paperwork, the files, the trails that you dug up, only took you so far. It always came to a point where the factors fell together in ways that were undeniable. Or you just had to close your eyes and take the leap.

Val went to see Wexler the next day. She never quite knew what it was that made her finally certain, and whether the photo in the newspaper had anything to do with it.

Wexler had the minister. He had the Exchequer. He was bathed in the warm glow of success that is very rare in the Administrative Services. Nothing is ever pandemic, yet Val had delivered him something that *was* pandemic in this context. The small runners were being gunned down. And he had everyone's ear on the restrictions, and on policy.

Val wanted raids. She got raids.

~

Even Aziz was impressed by the scale of the operation. It was a proper raid, not three asshole PCs turning up and waving bits of paper around. Customs sent out *three hundred* officials, all at once. They spread them over six companies, and through the chain that each company had set up. Customs clearly had a strong idea of how the scam was being run because they concentrated on the Freight Forwarders.

Aziz saw the officials from the window on the first floor. He simply watched and waited for a full minute, trying to mine the situation for as much as he could at first contact. There was not much to do, except message the top of the chain that they were about to get raided. The rest of the contingencies, including the spreadsheets, had been taken care of weeks ago. Aziz saw the cars. Two, then three, and then four. He saw the men striding out, with purpose, beginning to seal themselves in as they entered the office. They superseded security—no one was to be called, no one was to be informed, no one was to leave or enter until they were done.

You had to hand it to Customs and Excise. They were moving in at two in the afternoon on Friday, 6 July. And no one could move until after they had torn the place up and satisfied themselves that there was nothing to be found. That could take two days, if they wanted. *That* you didn't expect, not civil servants willing to give up their weekends.

Aziz smiled and picked up the third mobile. He typed out 'The Church is here… will call when I can.'

As he was about to hit 'Send' the phone beeped. He hit the disconnect button, leaving the text in the editor, and opened the new message. It was from JD. He saw 'The Church' at the top of JD's message and immediately exited it.

His fingers flying across the keypad, he went back to the editor and sent his first message to both JD and Mike, and then to Jassi, Rich and Brian. Whether they'd all be able to read the message or not was pretty much a coin toss. They might be in a warehouse right now, switching off their phones as he was about to do. Or they might be sitting at home, drinking beer, about to have the buzz killed by the crash message. On the whole, Aziz preferred being here. If he was on the outside, with no way to keep his eye on things, even at this level, from his office, he'd lose his mind.

As long as his message got through to one person,

everything would stop. That, he was sure of. That was the one big failsafe built into the phone protocol. A signal from any one of the founding fathers, and the deceleration was absolute.

Aziz cleared the text and then switched the phone off. He wasn't worried about receiving calls and messages, it was the *number* of them that he worried about. Not in front of the dogs. Then they'd know that they'd caused panic and that he was one of the people that panic got reported to.

He chucked the phone into a drawer, carelessly, hoping it would look like it had been chucked in there without much thought. Then he got his game-face on.

Aziz had found that negotiations worked better for him, especially in situations where jurisdiction was slightly unclear, if he went on the attack right from the start. Offence added to the confusion. The raid and the seal this afternoon, for example, was utterly legit. What no one was ever sure about was how far the warrants extended. That was always murky, and it could always be challenged, and Customs lived in mortal fear that some of the information they gathered would be thrown out of court on a technicality. And then, of course, they were in danger of getting the entire case tossed.

Aziz waited for the light knock on the office door. These skits always began politely. He picked up his phone. He didn't dial.

'Yes?' Aziz waited in the chair. To rise would be to show eagerness.

The door opened and the first of six men, as far as he could count, began to troop in. They'd tried their best, but the suits weren't very good. In most company, that wouldn't matter but here, Aziz was going to make them feel it.

'Fuck you.' It was his standard opening.

'Sir—' began the lead Customs official.

'Fuck you,' repeated Aziz tonelessly. He was almost smiling, but not quite. He held the phone out as if the officer should take it. 'My lawyer. Your arse. And a whole lot of pain. For everyone involved.'

'Sir—' the official began again and Aziz cut him off, again. He pushed it up another notch. Outrage, in certain circles, was truly a precision art. You couldn't go too far, but you always went as far as you could go, and as early as possible. Just like the VAT burn. You had to establish demography.

'I know. You have a warrant. You have all the warrants. And you're walking in here on a Friday afternoon and none of my people can go home for the weekend.' He locked eyes with the lead official. 'You have a warrant. What you don't have is consideration. And I *will* make you sorry that you weren't considerate. You have warrants. I will have injunctions. And if you've done your homework, you'll know who the fuck I am. And by the time I'm done with you and your department—what *is* your name?'

'Craig Daley.' Diffident and respectful, low-key in ways that were both good and bad. There was no fear in this particular party, Aziz noted. And that made it more interesting. It demanded care. Aziz nodded.

'Craig. Mr Daley.' He paused. 'By the time I'm done with you and your department, you'll wish that it had never crossed your mind to come calling here. Not only will you not

find anything, in return you'll find yourself so badly strapped
to your desk in about a week that you'll need a court order
in order to take a piss.' Aziz paused again.

'I'm assuming that you don't speak either Hindi or Urdu?'

'No.'

'Good,' said Aziz, and it was the most conversational tone
he had assumed during the encounter. 'Because if you did,
we'd be talking about your mother.'

That one got through. Daley stiffened slightly. There
was no attempt at a retort, but the room got keen. The raid,
Aziz had decided the second Customs had come through his
door, was personal.

But before anyone had a chance to send the situation
towards any of the directions that were now possible, a voice
from the door stilled all of them.

'That's not very nice, Mr Basrai. And why would we
assume that you're hiding something.'

Aziz swivelled in his chair. He was looking at a short,
bright-eyed woman in her mid-fifties. She was the head of
cavalry charge, then. But she was looking at him levelly, as
if there was nothing at stake and they both knew it. She
looked amused.

Aziz sighed loudly. He'd done well. And there was nothing
for her to find anyway, since they'd cleared everything almost
two weeks ago. But of the things he could not or would not
do, trash-talking around an elderly woman was very close
to the top of the list.

'Look at me, ma'am,' he said. 'Every time a Customs
official sneezes in my direction, I freeze. You get used to

it after a while. After all, that's why everyone came here in the first place a generation ago.' Aziz left the last statement open, wanting to see if she was going to rise to the bait, but guessing that he was out of tricks for the moment.

The lady simply shrugged. It didn't concern her. Historical imperatives weren't her problem. She simply needed the next few hours of his time.

'There's a lot of money in the mobile phone business suddenly. And we're British. So naturally we're wondering about how we've suddenly become so successful.' She smiled. 'We were wondering if you could help us in any way.' Her own bait, in return. Aziz refused it.

'We'll be done as quickly as we can,' she said. 'I don't think that any of us have any desire to eat into the weekend any more than you do.'

Aziz came around the desk and crossed to her. He paused for a moment and then extended his hand. She shook it with a sharp business-like tug.

'Would you like some tea?'

'Yes, please.'

Aziz walked back to his desk and picked up the phone to have his secretary bring the tea. Before he dialled, he cradled the receiver against his shoulder and looked up at the lady.

'May I have your name please?'

'Valerie. Valerie Stewart. Customs.'

~

Customs made short work of the raid. They were done in seven hours and at about half past nine Aziz sent the last of his staff home. There was nothing to find, so there wasn't even a sense of an anticlimax. The Customs officials left after taking photocopies of all the paperwork. They stamped a random selection of the phone stock in the warehouse. The Principle were sitting on about fifty thousand units. Aziz watched the process impassively. The stamping had absolutely no pattern to it. And that was the point. If the Principle wanted to filter the stamped stock, then it would be a hell of a job, fifteen hours in the cage, trying to find the unstamped boxes, never quite sure whether they'd gotten all of them.

The raid had been calm and well-organized. Customs asked for no favours, there was no pressure, and the staff mostly kept to themselves. Only three people in the warehouse knew the score. Most of the staff were simply stock-boys or stock-girls, sitting around, twiddling their thumbs.

It was okay. It was gone. Everything was good.

But the urge to get the banking out of the country was now physical. The lack of any sense of anticlimax from the Customs team got Aziz thinking. It was because Customs hadn't *expected* to find anything. There was no scent of a chase. The check had been grim, thorough and plodding. It was a command that needed to be executed, one more trail struck off the list. And because they hadn't been expecting to find anything, Customs would be back.

Aziz sat in the front seat of the Jag, the ignition off, thinking. The silence in the car seemed to magnify the silence in the parking lot. This was one of the few situations where he was at a disadvantage. Despite the range of his ambition, he hadn't grown up staring down raids and bluffing the dogs. For the other two, there was a learned rhythm to this. For him, although he had held up well, even under the questioning, it left him uneasy.

There was awful clarity for a brief minute. Aziz saw the flaw in the design of the game for the first time, and it was a flaw that was entirely obvious. Regardless of the size the Principle had imagined, this thing had been the reverse of imagination. You didn't believe it until you lived it. And none of them had ever considered every possible ramification— they had nothing to compare it to. Slogging it out with Customs was going to become a life, a process, lived. Days into weeks into months and down through the years. Like the burn, the Principle were locked into it until they let go.

Aziz suddenly understood what Customs had seen. It wasn't a question of one raid. The Principle were equipped to handle that, and Customs knew it. But the cover would break down when the pattern became raid-upon-raid, week after week, along with minor checks that came back again and again. They had gone out too fast and too hard, and there was no real way back down.

Under a sustained barrage, something would crack.

For a second, he thought about what he had to lose. He was no longer the student who'd jerked out of bed one night, drenched with sweat, in a T-shirt he'd had for eight years, and opened up a volume of tax law.

His world was softer now. He'd opened up. Revenge had been put aside. He was no longer the metronome he'd once been—a relentless, impersonal intelligence that simply outlasted everything and everyone else.

He stood to lose more than VAT. And he needed to be sure, because there were now things in his life that he could not risk. He didn't name her, not even in his head; for fear that the universe was listening in.

There were three questions:

Would it be them? Was the break something the entire chain could handle? And did he tell the other two?

In rational light, the percentages held. They could take the hit. That much he was sure of.

Aziz took a deep breath and held it as long as he could. His forehead was furrowed in concentration. This was a hell of a call. And the call was his because Mike and JD hadn't been here.

He fought instinct with intellect. He measured intuition against technique. And, ultimately, he was the polar opposite of JD. It held. Systems held. His belief in himself held. Aziz blew out the breath and forced himself to relax. He shook his head, dismissing any lingering doubts. Then he started to switch on his phones, waiting to hear how the others had held up.

As JD could have predicted, he was looking in the wrong places. Aziz still believed that whatever the threat was, it would come from outside their system.

~

There were arrests all over the shop. Soldiers got busted at every stage in the chain. When the dust settled, the Principle were short of nine men. Twenty per cent of their workforce was either behind bars, or trying to negotiate terms.

And *still* the knot held.

None of the arrests had anything to do with VAT. Instead, boys were getting picked up for unholy amounts of cocaine stashed in office desks. The cops found some highly illegal pornography. But the majority of the arrests were on the basis of the soldiers' money, amounts up to fifty thousand pounds in cash, simply lying around. Because the game accounting was so good, it meant only one thing—the soldiers were trying to evade income tax.

Mike and JD made appropriately glum faces while they were in the crash meeting. When Sumit left, they locked the door and erupted into some sort of war dance.

'We should really thank her, you know,' said Mike.

'What?'

'Well, she made a man out of you, crash-tested the system and took out the guy I've been trying to toss for months.'

The bust of possession of cocaine involved Sukhdev. He'd been snorting at work, *with* Pamela. It was JD's dream come true.

Pamela had called JD. Her one allotted call. And then her family had called JD incessantly. JD did something he'd never done before. He sicced Aziz on them.

Aziz sorted it out in one afternoon. He went to see Pamela's family with a briefcase. He laid out, in the plainest possible terms, who he was and what he could do. He went to the meeting with references for the best possible lawyer in this context; someone he'd already spoken to. He'd already arranged for the bail amount.

And then Aziz leaned forward and explained that if JD ever heard from Pamela again, he would do everything in his power to systematically destroy her family. Even if JD were to dial her number while he was drunk, she was to disconnect the call. If they ran into each other in public, she was to find the nearest exit. If JD was the victim of a hit-and-run and she was the only person for miles around, she was to turn and head in the other direction and Aziz would make it okay.

It wasn't a complicated negotiation.

The fallout from the raid should have been ugly. Instead, the truth was beautiful. The system was untouchable. The Principle could now, conclusively, survive as idiot soldiers as long as they played the game correctly. As long as they were careful about the dummy mobiles, the junk stock—and the substitution of stock was something that only a handful of people ever knew about—the Principle were home and dry.

All of them believed it. And the false alarms, the arrests that had nothing to do with VAT, gave Aziz just the excuse he needed to forget his fear. He never told anyone about his impressions immediately after the raid because he didn't think it mattered.

The *system* held.

And he forgot what JD had believed in all along. That failure was written into the system the same way that its genius was. Two sides of the same coin.

~

By Monday morning, they were drinking coffee and telling jokes and hiring new soldiers but they couldn't decide when to start another run through the loop. Enough companies had cleared the raid for them to go back to business immediately, but they were waiting for signals from their network to tell them everything had checked out okay. And they wanted to make sure that the burn itself, the much larger process that they had sparked, maintained its equilibrium. Customs had hit the six biggest players all at once. They had pulled nothing, but everyone just sat still.

By Friday, JD had had enough of sitting on his arse. Five working days after Customs had swarmed their offices around Heathrow, he woke up in the morning with a clear head and got on the phone swearing.

'You're a lot of nancyboy pussies,' he announced. 'What the fuck are we waiting for?'

'Yeah?' Mike replied. 'What the fuck have *you* been waiting for?'

'Good point,' JD said, the old gleam in his eyes.

'We're criminals, boys. Let's do some criming.'

And they went back to work.

~

This was another pattern Val knew: initial success, and then a great, black nothing. She had to keep reminding herself and her team that it was to be expected. Hundreds of millions of pounds didn't move by accident. The first set of raids had shaken off the amateurs for a while. They were now in middle-game. Her department had made themselves visible. Nothing had happened. Val hadn't expected anything to happen. But now they could develop strategies according to the next set of moves her boys made.

Val was certain that they were going to move that banking off-shore, possibly make it electronic. Every week she was making it more and more difficult for the scammers to obtain bank accounts here, or to operate them with any degree of ease. She would never get her hands near the off-shore accounts. She could only check the paperwork that marked the entry and exit of the money. And if, only if, she had proof, would the accounts be accessible to her.

So where did it leave them?

The department had to irritate the hell out of them. Small checks, smaller raids, one office at a time. They would be little dogs nipping at their heels. And Val had seen and heard about the talent that these six major players were using. The majority of them were idiots.

There was already one encounter that had become legendary in the office. The man who'd been running the company that served as the feeder valve between the importers and retailers was so badly out of his league that he'd clearly been played. That one conversation would become Craig's great party trick for years to come.

Craig and another official found their way to a six-by-six cubicle housed in a serviced office accommodation complex. They were met by the dead-eyed certainty of a man who'd been smoking a great deal of marijuana a short while ago.

'What's up, guv? What can I do for you?'

The other official asked to look at his paperwork while Craig chatted with the man, a Mr. Geoff Arald.

'How did you get into the mobile phone business?' asked Craig. Before Geoff had a chance to answer, the second official chimed in without looking up from the paperwork.

'You used to be a taxi driver?'

Geoff stopped himself, digested the second question and nodded sagely.

'I 'eard two blokes in the cab. Bankers, they was. Mobiles, they said. To themselves,' he added hastily. 'Mobiles. Some survey in the paper. The next boom in the tex space were going to be everyone and their uncle wanting a second phone.' He looked at Craig uncertainly. 'And I thought, Why not, Geoff? If everyone's buying, then...' Geoff made a gesture with his hands, indicating that he had simply gotten lucky.

'Your turnover's been fifty million over the past three months,' said the second official.

Geoff simply shrugged—in a very likeable way, decided Craig—and stuck out his chin. It was as if Don Corleone had been a weed-addled idiot, thought Craig.

'What can I say?' Geoff asked. 'I got good friends. God likes me.'

'That's fifty thousand pounds, Geoff,' said Craig gently.

'Too right,' said the second official. 'How in the hell?'

Geoff hadn't taken the hint in Craig's tone.

'The internet, guv,' Geoff said seriously. 'It's not just for porn, as most people think. There's buyers and sellers. I just kept looking.'

'How many suppliers do you have?' asked the second official.

'Just one. Spirit Phones.' It was unbelievable, thought Craig. He has no idea what this story *actually* sounds like.

'What's the name of the director at Spirit?' The questions were getting quicker. Craig kept the friendly look on his face.

'Erm.' Geoff held up his hand and began to cast around the table. After a minute, he emerged with a filthy business card. 'Allen,' he said brightly.

'How many times have you met him?'

'Oh, never.'

Craig had to stop himself from shaking his head.

'He's a busy man, he is.'

'So a guy called... Allen?' Geoff nodded. 'Allen, who you've never met, calls you up and offers you millions of pounds worth of phones? On credit? And you think that's normal?'

'It's my creditability, guv. You can ask anyone.'

The second official's head snapped up. There was a moment of absolute silence as he tried to work out whether he'd just been punned, or whether Geoff was... well, Geoff.

'How do you price your phones?' asked Craig.

'Just add a pound. Not too greedy. Everybody wants phones.'

Everybody *did* want phones, thought Val when she heard the story. They wanted phones so much that her boys were selling thrice the amount of phones that were being manufactured.

By the time Craig and his colleague got to the listed address, Spirit Phones and the trusting Allen had disappeared, naturally. So they went back to Geoff and read him the riot act. But, on instruction from Val, they didn't revoke his licence. They wanted him around for the next set of visits.

If her boys were hiring talent that matched this description, Val was going to let them keep it. She had the time for a small, tight smile. Little bleeds. All over the shop. She'd learnt it from her boys, after all.

~

Once they restarted the burn, August and the jump across banking platforms became their primary focus. The vans moved back and forth on the M25, the money started running again. And then the visits started again. Customs officials, always in pairs, dropping by for friendly chats, shutting down one office in the chain for a couple of hours while they went over the paperwork again and again, asking the same questions again and again.

Aziz didn't worry about it. His first impressions after the raid became more distant with each passing day. The status quo had returned. It was the velocity that his own life had acquired. The machine was now running itself.

On 24 July he was pulled into a conference with JD and Sumit. Most of their conferences now happened somewhere between Chelsea and Tottenham Court Road. There were plenty coffee shops with tables outside. There were pubs that got loud enough. They had St. James Park and Hyde Park for the really long ones. And JD had fallen in love with the Royal Festival Hall as a rendezvous point.

When Aziz arrived, JD and Sumit were nursing pints. Aziz was momentarily surprised. JD drank enough to scare anybody. But Sumit never drank before work was done. They were in the middle of a long discussion in Hindi. JD's was very good, Sumit's—as with most Bengalis—was atrocious. Both the pronunciation and the gender attribution were phenomenally dodgy. When they saw him, JD waved and beckoned. Aziz had expected to be walking again, although a pause in any form was welcome. While VAT ran on in the background, he'd become as big a burn.

'Get a drink, bruv.'

Aziz studied JD carefully. He seemed better than the last time Aziz had seen him, although he'd lost a little weight. He no longer wore the vacant stare of the completely bombed and Aziz credited it to the raid. JD looked his sharpest in months. Maybe he was laying off the drugs a bit. Maybe he was on a stronger dose.

Aziz shrugged. Then he relaxed and ordered a coffee. JD raised an eyebrow.

'It's not propriety,' Aziz said. 'If I drink beer, I'm going to fall asleep right here.'

He looked it too. There were dark circles under his eyes and he'd lost weight. He was beginning to develop trouble sleeping on flights, and he spent half his time in the air.

All three of them lit cigarettes, waiting for the coffee to arrive. Smoking habits had gone the way of the burn—mindless escalation. They didn't know how much they were smoking any more, just like they didn't know exactly which models they were running. That would have been unthinkable a year ago. Now they simply calculated average prices. Two hundred and twenty pounds, that was their mean. The boys took care of the rest.

Aziz thanked the waitress as she placed the coffee before him. As soon as she was gone, he turned to JD.

'What's up?'

JD nodded. In the early days they would have simply talked for a while before someone brought up business. The schoolboy rush was gone. This *was* business.

'We've got to get a jump on the banking. We have to move off-shore *now*.' JD looked across the table to Sumit.

'It's getting hot, Aziz,' said Sumit.

'But weird. And in small ways,' agreed JD.

Aziz looked from one to the other. He sipped his coffee.

'So, what is it?'

'It's not major.' JD paused. 'But the dogs are throwing the trails back at us. It's a bit like the security protocol.'

Aziz frowned. 'It's built around confusion, right?' Aziz reached for his Zippo on the table, but stopped short of touching it. 'That's what they're doing. Making it confusing.'

Aziz turned to Sumit. Sumit carefully slid his pint to his left, like he didn't want to knock it over when he spoke.

'The dogs were asking around one of the 'A' companies this morning.' Aziz eyed the tabletop as he listened, working it out for himself. 'A' company. One of the idiots then. The 'B's and the 'C's had the clever soldiers. 'A's were offices manned by dribblers because they were nothing more than a rubber stamp.

'They suddenly tracked back to a deal that went down

three weeks ago. All the paperwork's in order but they fucked with him a lot, trying to nail the invoices and the delivery times—back and forth—and the release notes for the Forwarder.' Sumit stopped. For a moment, Aziz thought he might not continue, but he knew from hundreds of these little debriefs that Sumit was just getting to the ugly bit.

'They jumped through four deals, but the questions are getting quicker and quicker and at the same time they're going through the paperwork faster and faster, like it's all in order and this is simply formality. Then one of them jumps in after they've said that everything's okay, points at a wholly different transaction and goes simply "How did you make that delivery?"'

Sumit paused again.

'Well?'

'The man tells him, "My car. I did it in my car." The idiot didn't even look at the invoice.'

Aziz looked up.

'How many units?'

'Thirty thousand.' JD smiled. 'Thirty thousand. In his— what does he drive again, Sen?'

'Mondeo,' said Sumit, staring at the table himself.

'Thirty thousand units in a Mondeo,' said JD softly, his lips pursed as if to whistle.

Aziz drained his coffee and turned back to Sumit, who looked up and shrugged.

'After that, good cop bad cop,' he said.

Aziz nodded. Sure. One questioned him about the logistics of transporting thirty thousand phones in a Ford

Mondeo while the other stepped outside and called the Forwarder. Who in turn would have gone to town about the correctness of his own paperwork work and the fifteen vans—documented—that would actually be required to transport thirty thousand units.

'Why didn't you call me?' he asked Sumit. Sumit gestured to JD.

JD shrugged. 'Storm in a teacup,' he said. 'Jassi called Mike and he called me. We straightened it out. Guy's obviously a retard, we said, and look, the paperwork's grand.' He sighed deeply. 'But it's a foot in the door, A. It's the little chink that they've been looking for. *Their* little loophole. And now their burn. It's only going to get worse.'

'So what do you want to do?' Aziz asked.

'Pull us out, mate. Then we can go and get some new talent. And if you put the banking out of reach, we can do it right.'

Aziz thought hard. Customs was going to isolate them bit by bit and then dismantle them at their leisure. Because bit by bit was the only antidote to the system that they had created. As one long trail, it was still as good as anything anyone had ever seen. Bit by bit, under the right pressure, things would start to cave. Someone had spotted it.

With that, all his fears from the raid came rushing back. JD was right. They had to move. He nodded.

'We'll do it next week. First week of August. No more fucking Mondeos.'

But, by then, a soldier had gone missing.

∼

When he thought about it later, JD realized that the whole thing must've fallen together in about three weeks. The raid went through to the end of July. The lessons were learnt very quickly. It was a fabulously improvised play, one that almost had his stamp on it.

The Principle were still with the commercial banks. Check. They'd witnessed the big raid and the little raids. Check. They'd seen how one office could shut a single chain down for a few hours, and that damage control put the chain in cold storage for a whole day. Check.

The Principle had put their smarter soldiers at the tops of chains, allowing them to control the flow of dummy mobiles and real phones, letting them make decisions.

There were cracks you could wiggle into, if you saw them quick enough.

They were at the end of the month, the end of a cycle that had been interrupted by the big raid. The burn had been quick and violent after their week of inactivity. Money was pooled through the chain because it had been their final surge before they transferred to electronic banking. They would lose another week, so they compensated for that as well.

The time was ripe for a takedown, JD thought to himself.

~

Customs came calling again on 31 July. Brian's chain, supplied by the same Forwarder that they all used, ASF Logistics, and a different 'A' company, completely unrelated. The Principle were expecting them. They knew the raids were becoming part of their routine—the spot-checks, flags on the borders, the stamping of the stock, sometimes in ultraviolet ink. They started selling the stamped stock down legitimate channels, waiting for a fresh supply to run through the carousel again. They began to generate paperwork to justify the presence of junk stock in the warehouses. Customs became a series of traffic lights. You could still get where you were going, but they put a dent in the momentum.

On 2 August, a hundred thousand pounds that had been dumped into the 'B' company from a set of 'C's over the past seven working days simply exited the loop. And the ex-mechanic who had been running the company had disappeared.

Jassi called on the third mobile just past five on 2 August.

'A hundred Ks disappeared.' His voice was tight. 'And I can't raise the guy. His phone's off.'

'Where?' asked JD.

'It's gone from the 'B' account, Brian's chain. Strike Trading. Two withdrawals today. Four o'clock. And then eighteen past.'

After the three-fifteen transfer cutoff, then. JD looked at the wall. His first instinct was to call Mike, because the soldiers were Mike's. He picked up his mobile and then put it down again. Something didn't add up here.

The laptop with the schedule was in front of him, but the imminent shift to electronic banking meant that every single deal, every plant and every loop through the Principle's chain, was bright in his mind. He had already written this show.

And if he had written the show, why were the alarm bells ringing?

Because of the raid, Brian's chain was stuffed up to the gills with cash. Everyone was on a CHAPs transfer, the standard for all their current accounts, twenty-four hours for payments to clear. But this 'B' company was scheduled to clear all dues to the 'A' in the chain tomorrow morning.

Why the fuck, when the soldier knew that payments were due tomorrow morning, would he steal at the end of today?

JD had tweaked the accounting with Jassi without telling anyone else. Not even Mike and Aziz. Like with the hard disk, he didn't know why. On the mornings he was relatively straight, he thought it was paranoia. But that didn't stop him. It was the safety that he built into the system. And you built safety in because, somewhere, you were uncertain about the money sitting in the accounts.

Because you were uncertain about the people with access to that money.

JD was fairly certain that his doubts were limited to the idiot brigade at level 'A'. The Principle had worried about visions of glory from day one. But that didn't explain why he had kept the fact from everyone but Jassi.

JD had Jassi spend an hour three times a week checking the local balances with the ATM cards, and the Dubai accounts online. This was their version of Aziz's electronic banking pilgrimages. It didn't matter if they were in the middle of a quiet week, or whether they were in the middle of a blizzard of takedowns. They *found* the time. They thought it necessary.

Then why?

'Motherfucker,' JD breathed softly. The play made sense to him right away. Someone was running with the same logic as launching on the day Mad Cow hit. They'd all learned to move with chaos.

'What do I do?'

JD realized that Jassi was close to panicking. This was the first internal fuck-up and his arse was on the line. And Jassi knew that JD was already thinking too hard about something as nominal as a hundred grand.

'Calm down. This is no time to be a little cunt.' It was also no time to be gentle. Jassi had to be bullied out of falling apart.

JD closed his eyes and lowered his head, phone pressed to his ear. In his head he was *pelting* through corridors that were almost purely white, looking for angles.

Everything, when it came down to it, was about attitude. It was the sum of a man. Of a machine. Of a country.

Would you risk the wrath of Mike Hamilton for a hundred grand?

It was a snap decision.

'Wait,' said JD.

'*What*—I…' Jassi breathed hard, once. 'Okay.'

'Good boy. This is what I want. Dump everything you have for tomorrow. Tell Aziz that I need you running something for me. I want you in front of a computer, and I want you to step out every half hour tomorrow and check the balance.' JD paused, then spelled it out. 'Check the transfers. Online. And check the ATM balance. If there's nothing by one in the afternoon tomorrow, call me. And Jassi?'

'Yes?' The shock was gone. Jassi was guarded and careful. He was smart enough to have realized that JD was, essentially, setting a trap. This could get very, very ugly very quickly.

'If you even breathe about this to anyone—*anyone*—I'll kill you myself.' JD let Jassi spend a few seconds alone with it. 'Tell me you believe me.'

'I believe you, boss.'

JD held on for another minute. Something seemed to satisfy him. He hung up.

~

JD stayed over at the warehouse that night for the first time in months. He paced the office, smoking continuously, looking at his paperwork over and over again. He had a bad feeling about this that had nothing to do with the internal hit. The hundred grand that he'd hedged earlier that afternoon wasn't a big deal. What it represented was. He hoped he was wrong. But this was his curse, like his memory.

JD woke early. The Principle were still in the middle of the final, massive surge before shifting to electronic banking and they were counting down the last four days. They were shipping three hundred thousand units before they ducked out. JD moved Rich over to Jassi's spot in the line-up and simply waited. The paper trail ran that morning, and the money marched, and the vans moved like a swarm in and out of Hounslow, a steady rumbling of men and machines.

One o'clock came and went, and JD told Jassi to keep looking until he told him to stand down, all the way to five o'clock. His dread settled heavier, anchoring him to the desk. It was like being a witness to an accident that was about to happen. He couldn't look away. Time slowed to a crawl. He thought he knew what to expect but he kept hoping that he was wrong.

They stopped booking orders at two-thirty. By three, the invoices and confirmations began to flood through the fax machines. Just another day at the office.

At three-twenty, the 'A' company in the chain he was watching chimed in with an invoice from the 'B', declaring full and complete payment. The payment had come in too late for a further transfer today. On a Friday. JD buried his head in his hands briefly. Anticipation had become reality. Then that too passed, and by the time he looked up again he was chilled to the bone.

Jassi called not three minutes later. Four point nine mill had been transferred out of the 'A' company—Cell Box Trading—above Strike Trading in the chain. The time on the transfer was four minutes past three. The final move, then. JD had been expecting it, and he simply swung around in the chair and called Mike.

But he still held on to the last, dirty secret.

~

When Mike pulled in forty minutes later at the address it had taken JD all of five minutes and two phone calls to find—'Give him time, Mike, give him fucking time,' JD had told him—an Indian kid by the name of Pradeep Sodhia was trying to stuff a hundred thousand pounds into a duffle bag, realizing, very late, that the fifty-pound note had some huge disadvantages.

As usual with these things, Mike was in no rush. He walked up the stairs to the second-storey bedsit and knocked on the door. There was no response. Mike shrugged. That was what he would have done. He knocked again.

'Oi!' he called. 'Anyone there? It's the pipes! I have the master key!' The statement didn't make any sense, but it didn't matter. He heard hurried steps.

Mike stepped back softly. There was no tension in his body. His hands were still in the pockets of his jeans.

The steps paused. And then, very cautiously, the door opened slightly and the kid looked through the crack.

Mike kicked just under the knob—it wouldn't do to break the door—as hard as he could. It was a big fuckoff clearance from the goal-line. The chain snapped and the kid went sprawling backwards into the living room, blood filling the white of his right eye.

'You're a recent enough recruit,' said Mike as Pradeep stumbled into the badly sprung sofa. 'It's all right, I understand. A lad can dream, can't he?'

Pradeep put his hands over his eye and fell sideways onto the coffee table littered with car magazines. He was breathing in great gasps and he was already crying a mixture of tears and blood.

Mike walked into the room. He turned and shut the door

softly. Then he crossed over to where Pradeep was curled up, facing away. Mike turned him over onto his stomach.

'Please.' The word was almost incomprehensible.

'Please don't steal my money,' Mike replied. 'I think that was more or less implied when I hired you.'

Mike twisted Pradeep's left arm behind his back, grabbed his collar and dragged him to his feet. There was a second's pause as Mike looked around the room for the first time. Aiming carefully, he drove Pradeep across the four steps to the wall that separated the two rooms. He jerked him left and smashed the broken eye socket into the side of the doorway.

The kid sagged and then blacked out. Mike let him fall, crumpled against the doorway. He stepped over him and went into the bedroom. The bed was covered in stacks of fifty-pound notes. Mike nodded. He walked to the kitchen and washed his hands. Then Mike propped Pradeep up against the door and started slapping him lightly. One eye fluttered open the fourth time he hit him. Pradeep recoiled. Mike stood up.

'Are you going to yell?'

Pradeep shook his head. The eye was huge.

Mike waited for moment. He sighed and tossed the towel to Pradeep.

'Good.'

~

By the time Mike got back from his errand, Aziz, Sumit and JD were grouped around the table at the old warehouse. It

would be the last meeting there. And when Mike completed
the party, it would be the last time that the four of them were
in the same room together. Jassi stood guard in the loading
bay, his first job after having been promoted.

JD took one look at Mike and knew that he knew. The
realization was painless, like sliding a razor through his wrist.

Mike tossed his keys onto the table, something JD had
almost never seen him do. He sat down and looked around
at no one in particular. He ran a hand through his hair,
grimaced, and breathed out once. Then he was Mike again.

'He had a hundred K. In cash. Fucker was trying to stuff
it in a duffle bag.'

There was silence. Almost five mill was still unaccounted
for. That would come. That's why they were there.

'Where is he?' asked Aziz.

'Does it matter?' Silence again. 'I put him in a hospital,'
Mike finally offered.

Aziz frowned and then began to ask a question but JD
shook his head.

'He means that he fucked him up and then put him in
the hospital himself,' JD explained. 'It's an old party trick of
Mike's. Full service sort of the thing.' He tried to smile, but
there was no way it was going to happen.

Mike watched JD, expressionless, for a moment. Then he
got up and started to make himself a cup of tea. He didn't
ask anybody whether they wanted one. JD realized just how
angry Mike was, that he was taking it personally. Pradeep was
just business, but whatever he'd done to that kid wouldn't
even qualify as a preamble to what he'd do next.

JD suddenly found himself scared to be in the same room with Mike.

There was no way out of it any longer, so he just started talking.

'Four point nine mill disappeared from the account of Cell Box Trading, the 'A' company in Brian's chain, a couple of hours ago.' His voice was flat, even. There was a hollow ringing in his head, like someone had stuck a tuning fork in there and he had no idea how to get it out before he lost his mind.

'The thing is…' he said. 'The thing is. The… this morning, Cell Box acknowledged full and final payment from Strike Trading. Almost twenty-four hours after the hundred K had disappeared from Strike.'

'You were watching?' Aziz had a thin, humourless smile on his face.

'I was watching.'

'Full and final payment. Minus a hundred grand,' Aziz said. It wasn't a question.

'Full and final payment. Minus a hundred grand,' repeated JD.

Aziz nodded. 'And we wouldn't have clocked it. On a Friday. If you hadn't been watching.'

JD said nothing to that.

'It's like the fold,' said Sumit. 'The rip-off is complicit. And it's hidden from us because there's collusion.'

The room was very still. Mike stood near the doorway, drinking his tea. No one else moved for a long time. It was like a death in the family. One of them was, after all, missing from this conference.

Aziz lit a cigarette. He exhaled and watched the smoke curl away.

'Brian,' he said quietly.

Aziz went for the Zippo and JD realized that for all his poise, Aziz felt as fucked up as he did. He could barely look at Mike now. This was Mike's to deal with.

'What are we going to do, boys?' Aziz was really asking the question. He honestly didn't know.

There was a fraction of a pause and JD thought that he had a chance, a small one but worth a try—for all the years and all the rampages, for all the good times and all the games, and for the lives they'd shared.

'Maybe...' he began. 'Maybe, if... maybe...'

Mike turned from the door. There was nothing in his face. 'What do you think we're going to do?'

~

Aziz and JD picked Brian up at five-fifteen from Hounslow.

'There's a thing,' JD had told him on the phone. 'And then there's another thing. You know.'

Brian knew. They'd been working like this for years, much before the VAT game. Either the job was too urgent or it was something that couldn't be said on the phone. There wasn't any hint of a problem.

They went in a secondhand Jag that Mike had picked up, JD driving. Aziz ran the conversation. JD felt respect and revulsion in equal parts. Aziz had so many faces that it made him a monster. There was no part of him that you couldn't doubt once you saw the other parts.

It was a normal Wednesday. Aziz and Brian talked football—the season was only weeks away—and they talked girls, business, comparing notes and figures, discussing the easy burns. JD had managed the briefest of greetings. He thought that if he looked at Brian for too long, then Brian would simply know. He hardly spoke. That was okay. He was the weird one, people expected him to be lost in his head sometimes.

They got on the M25. That was normal. They all knew this route like the backs of their hands. They were headed east for Folkestone. This was the van route, the conveyor belt on which the phones ran.

JD had his instructions. He pulled into Clacket Lane Services, sliding into a parking space next to a parked M5. He didn't even turn off the ignition. Mike stepped out of the M5 to their right and took two steps across to the door behind JD. For a moment, the open door of the M5 framed Sumit's worried face in the driver's seat and then it was gone as Mike swung the door shut. He settled in the Jag and JD locked them in.

Mike was looking straight ahead, at the back of the driver's headrest. Aziz had stopped talking. JD turned to look at Brian and smiled briefly. It was the only apology that he could offer. If Brian hadn't known the moment he saw Mike, he knew it the second JD had locked the doors.

They were back on the M25. They'd learned the trick from the Russians. Now they were the Russians. There were no exits, no slowing down, nothing until the Chevening Road junction, Junction 5.

Mike had said that he wouldn't need any longer than that.

They sat in silence until JD had them back up to seventy. Aziz was looking out of the window to his left, head leaning back, like JD had done a million years ago when Brian had been such a crucial part of the Schillachi, where everything had begun.

When Mike finally spoke, he was still looking straight ahead.

'Why?' he asked.

Brian just blinked a few times and his mouth hung open. JD felt like they had just woken him up from some wonderful dream, and that he couldn't quite make sense of the real world he'd just come back to. That would have been four minutes ago, when anything could still have happened.

'I'm sorry,' is all he said. It wasn't a plea. It wasn't anything.

In the rear-view mirror, JD saw Mike turn and look at Brian for the first time. It's mine, JD heard in his head. They're not getting their hands on it. Not on mine.

Brian returned the gaze and then looked down at his hands.

'You guys are putting away, what? Ten bar a month? Each?' Brian shrugged and let out a snort. 'I've been making about two pounds a phone on a third of the units we move.' He sniffled, his face going red.

'I make six hundred thousand pounds a month,' he said. He sneezed into his hands and laughed. 'Depending on the size of the burn.'

Mike began to speak and Brian cut him off.

'It's better than before, Mike. I know that. But it's not the same league. And I—I put in the same work. And then the raids started and we were moving to electronic banking, and I thought, you know…' Brian didn't finish the thought. He smiled and flipped his palms out. 'What are you going to do?'

'It's not the smartest thing-' he started again. Mike interrupted him.

'It's not, you know.' Mike's voice was meditative. 'Not when you wire the money to your wife's account in Sheffield.' He almost turned to look at Brian. Then he shrugged and looked out of the window.

'That's the kind of thing a man who drives vans for a fucking living might do.'

Brian was silent. He looked at the rear-view mirror once, trying to catch JD's eye. He looked at his hands and nodded once.

'I just thought we might get away with it,' he said.

'You could have come to us. Told us you wanted more.' Mike said it like it was still an option, like the betrayal could ever be forgiven. To JD, that was the worst part of all.

'I could have. Yes,' Brian said. He wasn't defiant. It was a statement of fact. 'I could have done a lot of things.'

JD didn't know what else Brian could have said. And he was never sure whether begging for mercy would have helped. Instead, Brian's calm acceptance seemed to finalize Mike's decision.

That's what JD would tell himself. That he knew Mike had decided what was going to happen before he ever got into the car was something JD never thought about. Never in the waking hours.

For the next thirty seconds there was only the hum of the engine, the Jaguar doing seventy miles an hour on the M5. Then Mike nodded to himself and swung his left hand out, smashing the bridge of Brian's nose. There was a howl of pain from the back seat, but JD and Aziz stared straight out the windshield and the car kept going. Other noises came from the back—wet, muffled sounds. The car didn't swerve an inch.

'JD,' Mike said.

JD reached across with his left hand and undid the locks. Tears were running down his face, but he kept his eyes on the road.

Mike reached across Brian, opened the door, and pushed him out of the car. Brian was gone in less than a second. The wind pushed the door shut. Mike leant across again, opened the door again and slammed it shut more securely.

'Loop around back onto the A20,' he said. 'We'll ditch the car and report it.'

And then he closed his eyes. About five minutes later, JD saw him start to tremble and shake in the back, his eyes still closed, but twitching badly under the lids.

Which was just as well, thought JD. Because he couldn't stop crying.

3.4

All JD could do was turn up the volume until he went deaf. He coked up and dove into a freefall. That first night, he was passed out on the floor for sixteen hours. He woke up to discover that his nose had been bleeding slowly but steadily through the night, and that a PC was on his doorstep, investigating a noise complaint.

He still had his charm. He switched it on, sent the PC away with promises of better behaviour. And then did it again the next night, and the night after. Just like the burn. He built a wall of noise around him, and he was the only participant at a wake of one. He wasn't just mourning Brian, or the shred of innocence he could still have admitted to until he'd thrown the lock on the door. JD was saying goodbye to the game, because he knew it was dying a slow death in front of him. Their luck had gone bad, permanently, on the M25.

The Principle made the jump to electronic banking and the world rolled over faster than ever. They worked in fierce bursts, upping the rate to three or four deals a day. The three original members of the Principle continued to drift outwards. The process had become mechanical. And all the little raids kept the soldiers on their toes.

Over the next two months, JD started delegating his responsibilities to Jassi. He was still the counter when the deals moved, but with electronic banking he was going into work maybe twice a week. The rest of the time, he kept to himself, scoring occasionally, playing videogames and surfing the internet. And he drank, always. The ten mill came through like clockwork every month. Beyond that, he was just trying to lose the taste in his mouth.

With booze and coke and time, it stopped being about the darkness and shock of helping to murder his friend over money. It turned into what Brian had done to him. He'd been betrayed, and so had everything he'd believed in as well. JD took that idea and built a place in his mind with it. Then he moved in.

It took JD a while to realize that the other two, even Mike, were beginning to consider him a flight-risk. He was high-strung, probably a full-fledged alcoholic, and he had finally become unpredictable. It didn't take him long after that to realize that he didn't really give a fuck either way.

~

When Customs finally stalled in the middle of August, Val began to work quickly. She could see her window about to slam shut. Her team had been living on small successes for the past two months and with the pressure building from upstairs, Wexler's patience finally began to give.

Where was the big bust going to come from? They needed it. Already, there were two Parliamentary Affairs committees, and the beginnings of a Select Committee in the EU. Customs were rapidly losing their place in the VAT spotlight.

But the panic was mostly about the figures. Thanks to Val's team, everyone now knew where to look. And the third-party payment figures were worse than even she'd expected. Based on the current projections, they were looking at two and a half *billion* pounds missing by the end of the financial year.

Forces above her pay grade had named the VAT scam 'Missing Trader Intra-Community Fraud'—MTIC. Val had already been to a series of meetings where the word 'exceptional' was being thrown around a lot. MITC was exceptional in its scope, its execution and, most importantly, in its design. Val preferred what her team had been calling it: The carousel. It captured the schoolboy, magic-trick nature of the thing. But at least they finally had some official attention. They were shutting down banking with the government's total support. Banks weren't even opening accounts if the parties had anything to do with the mobile phone business. They were stamping as much of the stock as possible. They had stepped up checks and raids. They had legalized IMEI tracking and made it mandatory, though her team told her that generating IMEI numbers was easy enough. The domestic movement of money had slowed to a crawl.

Yet they continued to bleed.

The money trail was now simply passing through the country. The reclaim generating part of the scam had moved overseas, routed out of the Cayman Islands. Although Val had expected the move, it was still as frustrating as hell. Because her boys had now hidden themselves even further. Customs could only cover the same ground over and over again. And with the timing of the small raids, Customs had become predictable.

When Val was sure that Wexler was going to pull the plug on her team, turning their data over to the boffins in the Exchequer, she went back to where she had begun. She copied the very first set of files from the remittance defaults to her own computer. She worked steadily over the space of a week and a half. If there was anything, it was going to be here. It didn't matter if what she was doing was, technically, illegal.

Customs hadn't cracked the code yet. There seemed to be a solution to everything they came up with. And that bothered Val because the nature of the crime had to leave a trace of something, somewhere. They needed a single moment, the instant of the crime. Without it, they were stumbling in the dark.

She looked at the entire case as if she was trying to write a history of it. She tried to look at it in hindsight, to find the causes, the roots, the context that had allowed it to be born.

She had first known because of the initial spike. And then she had watched that initial spike grow into the problem that was now in front of them. The beginning, then. How did the scam start? The third-part payment model, the carousel, was too complex for anyone to have come up with as their first version of a system.

At first, the scam was simply a remittance failure. Then,

collusion. A nexus at the importer–retail level that hid them almost completely. And here, Val was sure, someone had read what was happening and made the connections on a larger scale. The same process could be repeated all the way down the line, into the UK and out the back door. Except that every company in the chain was filing for VAT reclaims. And if you put the structure together, you were suddenly making ten or twelve times the money.

The scam caught like wildfire because her boys were recycling the product. There were no real costs. They were banking pure profit.

Customs now understood this, and they were trying to make sure that the product wasn't recyclable any more. Yet the profits stayed exactly where they were, and the reclaims came in like clockwork. All the while, Nokia was telling them that far more phones were being bought and sold than they'd even produced. It was a controlled, systematic inflation to keep the reclaims climbing. But how? Where were the phones coming from?

Val dipped her head slightly. It was remarkable. And so simple. Her boys' fingerprints were all over it. A simple thing taken to its most logical conclusion.

Every time Customs ran a major raid, they were waiting until the dust settled, flogging *all* of the stamped stock and then running dummy stock until they balanced their books.

Dummy stock.

She had missed the dodge because she wasn't looking for it. She had been looking for a crime and her boys had played it straight. And when Customs started looking at the straight channels, her boys were playing crooked.

Every possible loophole was built into their system. But if her boys were running something even occasionally criminal, Val was going to find that one instance and then work backwards. The complexity would tumble if she could undo one knot and make a single arrest that stopped one of the paper trails completely. The sheer amount of money would make the chain collapse, as it had done with their first set of closures.

Even if their raids had become predictable, Val needed more of them.

Three days later, Wexler shut her down. Her team lost all of its authority and they were playing babysitters to the Exchequer's taskforce. Wexler had given her the power and it was his to revoke.

By the end of August, Customs had outlived their significance. There had been no breakthroughs in two months. The government was trying to keep the situation quiet while they were trying to police it, because they because they couldn't stop VAT reclaims without stalling the whole bloody EU economy. They'd just keep wandering in circles for years. They'd keep busting the little guys while the real players simply got stronger and stronger.

In her office, Val considered ploughing through on her own. She'd known all along it might come to that. Successes came and went, but there were always the patterns. She still had her lunch hours, and her bench in the park every morning.

She wondered where she should begin. She smiled.

If you want to catch a thief…

This was her last crusade with the old-boy network. She scribbled a word on her pad and then underlined it. Call it the kitchen sink.

Reg. Old Elton. At least that was a place to start. She didn't know if the meeting would lead anywhere, but she would get to smoke two filthy rollups and chat about the old days. And then, like everything else in this lovely scam, she would simply have to see where it went.

~

The world is going Tipnis, JD thought to himself, crying a little. By the time he'd gotten to Mike's, the first tower of the World Trade Center had collapsed.

Aziz had waited for his partners for three days while they stayed camped in front of the TV at Mike's. They had ordered in and simply waited, not knowing what to do with themselves any more.

Aziz was the most distant, the least affected. What it really meant to him was that his life was going to get less convenient. Foreign bank accounts would be policed harder. And the Muslim name, regardless of actual fact, was going to make his incessant travel even more difficult. It wasn't fair, but people would make their choices. The world was going to return to fundamentals. Eat or be eaten.

On the third day, Aziz made his choice. He had waited for his partners, and they had asked for more time, for things to settle, for them to get their heads around what had happened. Aziz saw no merit in the argument. They had nothing to get their heads around. Instead, sixty people were waiting on them.

Aziz commandeered Jassi and set the burn in motion. Once the Principle had switched over to electronic banking, it was possible for one man to run the show. You just needed enough laptops, and a really quick internet connection. They ran four deals on 14 September and it worked like a charm. The run was almost enough to suggest to Aziz that he didn't really need the other two any more. Almost.

JD had been a headcase since Brian had left them, but he and Mike had been running the system flawlessly. It lasted a moment, the temptation to cut and run, but in the end pragmatism prevailed. He still felt some loyalty towards the other two, and Mike was still the most capable board-runner he'd ever met. He kept the soldiers in line. The percentages were in favour of leaving the system just as it was. Besides, Aziz preferred three targets to one. He was already making almost as much money from his outside, legitimate, interests every month. He didn't need anyone's extra attention.

Once they were done, Aziz packed Jassi off to JD with the spreadsheets and waited for the explosion. When JD called, he was ready for him.

'Are you out of your mind?' Aziz had expected wild anger, but the question was cold and flat. If JD was wired or drunk, or both, you'd never know it from his voice.

'Get your head out of your ass, Jai,' Aziz said calmly. 'I waited three days for the two of you. The burn doesn't wait.

You know this. You used to know this. And once we went FCTB, one man can do it. That was the point, wasn't it?' The question might have been a threat.

JD waited. When he spoke again, his voice was still sharp. 'Bruv,' he said. 'The security protocol's based on the three of us. You can do whatever the fuck makes you hard these days. But the safety's built on three players. You're trying to see how far you can actually go before the whole thing comes crumbling down. That's your drug, mate. Don't push it here, though.'

Aziz closed his eyes. How did they get here so quickly? It hadn't even been a year since Dubai. But he was tired, and he was starting to get angry.

'How's the paranoia working out for you, Jai?'

Silence. Aziz waited, and then decided that he'd had enough.

'Come back to work. Then we'll worry about system failure. Because I *will* spin VAT whether you're here or not. The question is how you look at your contract, whether *you* need to be here, whether the system needs you to be here. And then we'll talk.'

Aziz considered his next statement, deciding there was nothing left to lose.

'We'll talk when you're not half-wrecked,' he said. 'When you're not sniffling like a six-year-old girl and working your jaw like a typewriter. Talk to me when you're off the shit, *bruv!*'

He was shouting by the end, panting as the blood rushed to his head. He wasn't entirely sure he'd done the right thing, or what he'd do next.

Aziz looked around. He was lucky that the hospital corridor was deserted. Even so, a nurse had emerged from the station at the end of the corridor. She briskly made her way across to him. Aziz fixed his gaze on her, trying not to look at Tasleem , who'd opened up the door he'd been sitting opposite and stood there, framed by the soft neon light, watching the end of his conversation with JD.

Aziz had a brief, vivid mental image of himself throwing lever after lever in his head with increasing desperation, because none of the fucking switches would catch. He clenched his jaw and narrowed his focus down to its absolute, brutal best. He felt like he was rocketing down a long, smooth slope without a single handhold. Darkness yawned down there. It almost had him. And then a cog caught somewhere.

He looked up at the nurse with an apologetic, dazzling grin.

'I'm really sorry,' he said, getting in before she'd had a change to reprimand him, or throw him out. His voice was soft, gentle, like silk. The final yell had roughed up his voice and he used it to his advantage. He sounded broken, hurt, genuinely apologetic, as if something had just caught him off guard. And once he had the grin out, he knew that he wasn't going anywhere.

'I know it's a hospital. Look, my gran's in that room. I'm really, really sorry. Look,' he said, holding up his phone, 'I'll get rid of it.' He got up and deftly dropped his phone into a waste-bin. It was his basher. And with JD in cold storage, and the burn running off laptops, he could pick up a phone tomorrow morning. It didn't fucking matter. He held out his hands and grinned like a schoolboy.

The nurse let out a horrified gasp.

'It's okay, you didn't have to—'

'I'm really sorry,' said Aziz. He meant it too. He could feel waves of black coming at him from somewhere deep in his head. The week was taking its toll and he wanted this woman gone. 'Don't worry about the phone. Really.'

The nurse left, after eliciting promises of better behaviour. But he'd knocked the fight out of her by dropping the phone into the bin. He watched her go and turned to Tasleem .

'Do you think she'd feel differently if she knew that about half the cell phones sold in this country pass through your warehouse?' Tasleem sounded amused. 'Are you all right?'

Aziz gestured weakly. It didn't matter.

'How is she?' Nusrat Daadi had slipped into a coma on 5 September. She'd been on life support for the past four days. Aziz had been splitting shifts with Tasleem and Meera. His friend and partner, meanwhile, was sitting around, watching CNN and funding Columbian cartels.

Tasleem shook her head.

Aziz realized that rage was part of the river of black running through his head. He stepped into his grandmother's hospital room and slumped against the wall. She lay on the bed. She had shrunk to half her size. He'd fought for a room with a large window, but she hadn't opened her eyes in nine days.

Aziz was very close to tears and he fought for some semblance of control. He breathed in, once, harshly. He gulped down the canned air in the room. He held the breath until he thought his heart would explode. He breathed out in a long hiss, not wanting to disturb the old woman's rest, refusing to consider the word *comatose*. He breathed in again.

He felt a hand on his forehead. Cool, like a compress. And then he felt a hand on his chest, just above his heart. The hand rose with his chest, and fell with it, as if it were trying to help in containing all the mundane, precious little secrets that threatened to spill out.

Aziz didn't know how long they stood like that, bringing him back to life. When he opened his eyes, Tasleem stood in front of his, her hands pushing back against him, holding him up. She looked at him. She leaned in and kissed him. Softly. He felt like he'd turned his face up to the first rains of the year. The kiss was a promise. He closed his eyes without being aware of it.

When he opened his eyes, Tasleem was looking at him with her half-smile.

'Well, we ought to have once. Before. Just to make sure.'

'Marry me,' he said.

She raised an eyebrow. The smile got wider.

'I thought that was what we were doing, Mr Basrai.'

Aziz didn't know what to say. He was suddenly embarrassed.

'How quaint,' said Tasleem. She grinned. 'We're an arranged marriage that became a love story.' She slipped her hand into his. Their fingers intertwined naturally, without thinking about it.

'Yes,' she said simply. 'Yes, I think I will.'

Aziz held her hand. She stood next to him, leaning against

the wall. He looked at his grandmother. He let his head drop
onto Tasleem 's shoulder.

~

The spreadsheets went to JD and he started showing up at
work again, mostly fucked up but somewhat functional. In
the silence that had now descended, no one told him about
Aziz's grandmother. And no one told him that the Principle
had cued the last burn on MSN Messenger. Even in the final,
desperate state before it all crashed, he'd have handed out a
right bollocking.

And then he would've trashed the laptops himself, with
a sledgehammer.

~

They had an uneasy calm for the next two months. The
carousel was a metronome, and minor Customs tricks served
as counterpoints. The Principle neatly sidestepped the IMEI
requirements by outsourcing the certification to a company
that they ran themselves. The ghost applied to everything;
it was now a lifestyle choice.

By the time the Principle entered 2002 the system had
become the Holy Grail that JD had always dreamt about—
self-perpetuating, self-aware, the perfect machine. By then,
it was the only thing that connected them any more. They
had money between them.

Each of the men had looked into the future and decided

for themselves what to do about it, and none of them told the others. Those moves were impulses that made sense to each of them in their own, secret ways as they looked for what they needed most.

They went looking for shelter.

JD had the last remnants of the office shipped out of the old warehouse. He let the lease expire and then he bought the building. He reinforced the doors, got deadbolts, wired each door to a keypad and had a new security system installed. He tore down the three rooms that he and Mike had built more than five years ago and turned the warehouse into an office he could sleep in. He powered it up, fired up the internet, and sat in the office for a couple of hours, wondering what he wanted to do. It seemed to him that he was building a really expensive vault that he could bury himself in. He shrugged and ordered the most comprehensive CCTV package he could find. For a moment, JD grinned the sunshine grin. If he was going the whole hog, he might as well *go* the whole hog. When he was done, he turned off the lights and locked up. He wouldn't see the office again for another ten months.

Although they didn't know it at the time, Mike went exact the opposite way. He had been on the hunt since August and, in early November, he had bought a four-bedroom house in Weybridge, tucked away in a gated estate called St. George's Hill. He was minutes off the M20, and twenty minutes from Heathrow. What Mike liked best was the fact that no one else knew that he had bought himself another property. He wanted a place that was free from work, untainted by friends—a place where not even JD would know to look for him.

Mike shipped two of his televisions and one large bed. He began to split his time between Chelsea and Weybridge. He was in London when he needed to be, and he was untraceable when he needed to be. It was forty minutes in full traffic, but, in truth, a world away. He prowled around downstairs, leaving the first floor largely unexplored and he took walks around the area when the mood took him. He had his horses and he had his football. He bought a microwave and stocked up on TV dinners. If he ever felt the urge, he drove down to the Hilton nearby for a drink.

Billy came by to visit occasionally. He and Mike would kick a ball about for hours, halfway between fun and a serious training session.

'Keep your head up,' Mike kept telling him. 'The moment the ball's at your feet, look up. You're not looking at the ball then. You're trying to see where it'll go. And it's the same with passing. You're passing to where the man will be, not where he is.'

The parallels weren't lost on Mike. Sometimes, when the kickabout got to that place where the ball was doing exactly what they both wanted it to do, where they could just about read each other's minds, the rhythm of that tap and return, the give and go, would get him thinking about Brian. He wasn't sorry, exactly. But he felt regret. He'd always looked after his own. Always. And his own had provoked him.

Mike gave himself another year. Because he knew his rage had continued to build. That was why he'd worked with JD all these years. In the way he'd kept JD from nailing his own hands to the table, JD had kept Mike from himself. Without that wild kid, things got bleak. The time had come to get out while he could.

It was only later that Mike realized both he and JD had come back to Heston, or closer to it, like filings pulled to order around a magnet. It had all been about getting away, but they were what they were. The universe didn't forget.

Aziz married Tasleem Malik on 19 October, barely a month after his grandmother passed away. They had come full circle since the engagement. There was no ceremony, no party, no social event. It was the two of them and their respective parents in a courtroom. They had a dinner for twenty-three people at a steakhouse. Mike and JD both attended. Aziz and Tasleem , in separate conversations, told Dr Malik that they'd do a grand reception in time, after a proper period marking Nusrat Daadi's death. Even Dr Malik knew that it was unlikely. But no one seemed to mind. The bride and groom seemed happy, in a generous, graceful way that felt like it would last.

A month and a half after 9/11, Aziz requisitioned the Principle's first private jet, a Citation 7-seater Excel. It cost them twelve million dollars. He'd had enough of immigration at most international airports with his name and his face, and the fact that he was born in Pakistan, and that he had been back every two years since he was ten. For a while, the jet became a joke for the Principle, a peace offering to JD. It was the last box they needed to tick on the schoolboy fantasy list. There was no mucking about with lines and lounges. They

drove out to Luton, drank a final cup of coffee while the
paperwork cleared and then took off. The process was the
same wherever they landed. You solved the problem of racial
profiling with the application of money. By the time he was
done, Aziz promised himself, he was going to buy peerage.

But the new order gave him migraines. No amount of
money could change that. Not the looks, not the questions,
not the fact that regardless of his accent and his passport—and
the fact that he was worth about ninety million pounds—the
colour of his fucking skin was going to be the thing that
tripped him. He couldn't control that one detail. He was the
same shade of brown as JD, but they were on different planets.
He knew now that it would never change. Not in his lifetime.

After he watched 7 October come and go, he simply went
with the percentages. He applied for a Pakistani Origin Card,
the closest thing to dual citizenship. Because Aziz was who
he was and because he knew who he knew, his application
was fast-tracked. And as soon as Aziz was sure that he was
going to get the POC, he started travelling to Pakistan on a
monthly basis. He began with a house in Lahore and then
began to build a base there, spreading his money across
continents now, creating a life and an identity that he could
kick-start in minutes.

Should it ever come to that.

~

After 9/11, Val watched the world unravel around her. Her
job remained the same, but resources ran dry. They were

watching the world prepare for war. Customs checks were being structured around the threat of terrorism. The façades were the same, but the internal machinery was changing fast. Besides, she knew that it would be impossible to raise Reg for the next month. His workload would have gone through the roof. Finally, in the last week of October, she was able to steal a meeting late on a Friday afternoon.

Reginald Henry, known mostly as Elton to anyone above the age of forty, headed Misc., a small department within the Metropolitan Police. Misc. wasn't the official name for the department. There wasn't, technically, a name for the department. In memos, it was mostly referred to as EX, after someone long ago had mistakenly thought that 'E' and 'X' were, respectively, the most common and the rarest letters in English usage. The name *should* have been EZ, but no one quite liked the ring of that. And EX captured the nature of the outfit since most of its active members were either very close to, or past, the age of retirement.

EX existed as a loose affiliation of former experts whose skills the police still found useful, although most of them were deniable. They ran the forgery division, the pickpockets, the kidnappers, the wiretaps, but their main purpose was gathering information, and creating networks. They were where the word on the street ended up. They also had access to the single largest association of ethical hackers in the UK, although most of the members of EX couldn't do anything with a computer besides turning it on, if that.

Reg was a career copper who had formalized the police version of the Old Boy network and nurtured it, strictly off the books, until it became apparent to everyone that reaction times would improve if phone calls were cut out of the equation and the mob of former specialists were given a bunch of rooms together. To Reg's colleagues from the Cold War days, the section was known as the Vatican because his gang of geezers were, in an odd way, the Swiss Guard. EX was an aging watch over the streets of the city.

It didn't get much attention, but Val was given to understand that it had been a crucial factor in the 25 October announcement that crime in London was at its lowest since 1981.

Dry, cynical and funny, Reg was one of Val's favourite people. He was a huge hulking bear of a man, hiding behind a thick black beard.

It spread around his smile when he saw her come in.

'Must be that VAT thing, then,' he rumbled. 'Finally beat Val down. Or are we simply getting old?'

'We *are* getting old, Elton,' Val said, returning the smile. Reg grunted. Then he roared from the desk for two cups of tea and began to roll them cigarettes.

'How busy are you, Reg?' she asked after the tea had arrived.

'It's been mental.' He shook his head, and Val knew that it was out of bounds. EX must have been on high alert since 11 September, and there was no let-up in sight. There wouldn't be for a very long time. 'What can I do for you?' he asked.

There was no bullshit among friends. So Val told him, laying the case out as briefly as possible. It *was* the VAT thing.

She told him of her suspicions about the three iterations of the scam. And that she thought that they were running dummy stock, beyond the obvious recycling of the product. That was the one criminal act she was sure of.

'I need a crack, a chink, something,' she said. 'I've got no leverage. Nothing to justify asking for resources.'

'Have you got anything for me to look at?'

Val pulled out three slim folders. 'This is—well almost completely off the books.'

Reg made a face. He was already stretched to the limit. If this was unofficial, then it made it even harder for him to commit anyone, even a single member of his team for a day. Val shrugged.

'I'm not asking for a miracle. I'm just asking for you to look if and when you can.'

'What did you get me? If they've gone electronic?'

'Addresses,' she said. 'And a sample of the bank documents from January to March.' The spurt that she had caused by asking for the attendance sheets. 'If there's anything, it'll be there. Because, after…' she left the thought unfinished.

'Because, after,' Reg mused. 'Because after, they vanish.'

Val had sampled the three companies that seemed the cleanest but continued to post unreal numbers.

At the top of the list was the Heston Principle.

Reg scanned through the folders quickly. The office continued to hum around them. When he was done, he gathered them up neatly and folded his hands over them.

'I can't promise anything, Val—wait.' He put up his hand, cutting her off before she could speak. 'I know you're going to say that's fine. But I can't even promise *when*, all right? It could be two months, it could be a year, it could be never. I can't do anything about that.'

Val nodded. There was nothing else she could do. The rest of the vigil was at her desk anyway, tracking transactions. This was her only planned visit to anyone outside her cubicle.

'Why these three?' Reg asked.

'It's just a feeling.'

Reg nodded. 'Call me if you have any feelings about any single one in particular.'

Val thanked him. She started to leave and paused at the door.

'Reg?'

He turned to look at her.

'By the end of the financial year, they will have stolen two-and-a-half billion pounds.' Val thought about how to finish the statement, how to underline the point. 'Stolen,' she repeated. 'They're clever, they're probably brave and they're clearly gifted young men. But they've been stealing. They're thieves.'

Reg looked at her for a moment longer and then nodded. After Val left, he leafed through the files again, and then put them away, allowing that part of his brain to run itself until he could come up with something.

~

The final meltdown was just stupid chance. For people who had made their careers out of having an answer for everything, it was quite ironic. It would have been a hell of a laugh had it been happening to someone else. JD was pulled out of orbit because there was a wedding in the family. He'd been doing his best to stay away the last few months, showing up at family occasions at strategic times and taking off again before anyone had a chance to get beyond small talk. This time, it was his cousin. And this time, he was the man.

'We're from the girl's side of the family,' his dad told him. 'And people know about you. They know you're a big man, a rich man. It helps. It makes us look better.'

JD had dismissed the idea outright. But his parents were relentless. He was worth a lot of money, he made the papers on a regular basis—he was their trump card.

He gave in because Pam called. Even with all the drugs and booze and a murder, he was an Indian kid at heart.

The wedding was one more of those semi-arranged gigs that were in vogue. Parents would allow their children to date, unaware of their rampant fucking, but they'd insist on the final call where marriage was concerned. And the match was always a community thing. The elements needed to be balanced and the partnership needed to benefit everyone concerned. In this scenario, JD was an invaluable trading chip. He gave the proposal weight. And he was not quite the most subtle of hints in case negotiations started going south.

When the meeting finally went off the rails, JD had time enough to reflect that, in spite of everything, it had probably been a situation tailor-made for Aziz. Aziz was better than anyone else in a social negotiation. It married his gifts. His diffidence, his respectfulness, his powers of persuasion. The hell of it was that Aziz would've probably done the meeting, too, despite the breakdown in communication. He would've done it for JD's parents. But JD hadn't thought to ask.

JD woke with the tuning fork full-blast in his head, which had become another ritual. His mouth was dry and it tasted like an ashtray. Cocaine was the only thing that got him through the day. And he had begun to smell. JD didn't know if other people smelled it, but the odour moved with him like a cloud. Sick-sour-sweet, like vomit and old sweat, the way alcoholics and wife-beaters smelled on the street where he had grown up. If the smell ever got bad enough, you might even see it.

He stumbled about the flat in SW3, squinting against the light. He was up earlier than he had been in months and he was worried it might not be safe to go out just yet. He could shower and shave and brush his teeth, but the really romantic part of slamming so much coke was the violent diarrhoea.

He crept to the CD-shelf, three entire walls of the study, and pulled out the Midnight Oil stack. For some reason, he had thought that the perfect place for his emergency stash was behind Christian Rock.

'Nothing personal, you understand,' he mumbled, and dropped half a gram of coke into a shot-glass as he trawled through the wreckage in the living room. He had cleaners and he had housekeepers but they couldn't keep up with him. He found a bottle of vodka on the table with a couple of inches left in it and poured some into the shot-glass. He stirred the mixture with his finger and tossed it back. He stayed where he was for a minute, letting the shakes work themselves out of his system. Then he showered and brushed his teeth, gave his stomach one cigarette's time to make up its mind, and left.

The first thing that bothered him was the house. JD's family was from the girl's side, so they made the trek to Southall. The living room was dark and heavy, and smelled too sweetly of incense. It was a close cousin to his own stench and he started to sweat.

He thought he noticed his hosts sneering at him during the introductions, but he couldn't be sure. He didn't even try to remember their names. They were servile and hostile and gracious. They demanded respect, they expected it. They infected the room.

JD stayed out of the conversation as much as possible and concentrated on little details in the room—the apples on the table, the magazines, the curtains that kept light out. Fried food that kept coming, along with cups of sugary tea. It was hot, claustrophobic, and he was becoming self-conscious about all the napkins he was using to wipe the sweat off his face. He had to concentrate on not running to the bathroom to empty himself out, one way or another.

He focused on the portrait of Guru Nanak, trying to keep the conversation from getting to him.

His own father, one of the hardest men JD had known, was bowing and scraping for these bloated, middle-class cunts. Yes. Yes, anything you say. Yes, we're lucky that the boy wants the girl. Yes. Yes to interruptions after every third word. Yes to little insults and insinuations, the demands getting bigger with every exchange. His family was agreeing to requests, and then ridiculous conditions, and finally taking orders.

JD knew his role. He was to keep his mouth shut, ignore any provocation that he might or might not hear. He was there as a symbol—he knew of what, and that annoyed him as much as anything—and he wasn't to react no matter how badly these people aggravated him. When JD had asked why there should be any aggravation at all, his father had simply gestured. That was the way things worked. Girl's side. Closed loop. No way out.

JD tried his best but it had been months, maybe as far back as February, since he'd really felt anything. He had doped himself up and had only occasionally left his flat to watch the world happen. Now he was furious, and it felt good, and he had to shit.

'Why don't you just let them be?' he asked coolly. The groom's father had been banging on about the need for both the groom and the bride to accept the impositions that both families would place on them leading up to the wedding.

The room fell silent. JD's father flashed him a warning look but JD ignored it. He'd been angry at a lot of things for a lot of years, and the asshole standing in front of him had everything to do with it.

'They know each other. They've *known* each other,' he said, switching to English as he gained traction. 'And they're old enough to make decisions without the rest of us haggling like we're in some filthy little Bangladeshi market.'

The groom's father cleared his throat. 'Son, it's simply a question of tradition. I know you young people—' He'd pulled out some English of his own, but JD didn't let him finish using it.

'Are we talking tradition, Uncle?' JD let the last word dangle, making it deliberately insulting. 'Let me know.'

'I don't know what you mean.' And he didn't. But the room was getting uglier.

'The fridge? That's tradition? The new car? For the new couple? That's tradition? The ratio of your guests to ours? That's tradition?'

'You don't understand—'

JD stepped on that one, too.

'I understand. Everyone understands. It's about money. And it's about your position as the boy's father. Substitute for money. I'll tell you what, Uncle. I'll equalize it.' He reached into the pocket of his jeans, still sitting, and pulled out his credit card wallet. He made a show of flicking through the cards—he knew the one he wanted.

He flicked the Amex Black on the table.

His mother closed her eyes briefly. She was the only one. Everyone else was either looking at the card or at JD. Even the old man knew what the card meant.

'Anything you fucking want, Uncle. Put it on the tab.' JD paused. 'Think of it as a new fucking tradition.'

His father managed to jump in and pull the situation back. They explained JD's outburst away as fatigue, and the pressure from the business, and a sense of humour that no one understood. JD even managed to apologize to the old man. He had seen his mother's face and realized that he had gone too far, that despite the apologies, there was no coming back.

When they left, JD was the leper. Every one of the eight people who had made the trip in three cars avoided him. They wouldn't even look at him. Still, he discovered, he hadn't done enough just yet.

'Why did you take it?' he railed at his father. 'You? Of all people? Why did you sit there and take it?'

His father refused to answer.

'Talk to me!'

'Jai.' He heard his mother's voice and JD turned to look at her. His head rocked back as she slapped him. The slap was measured and calm. Her face was terrible. There was no pity in her gaze. It was absolute.

'You have forgotten who you are.' Chaste Punjabi. She slapped him again. 'And we could have fixed everything, *everything*, even the card. If you hadn't used that word.' She paused. Her eyes never left his face. 'Fucking.' The word cost her—it took effort to get the pronunciation right. She had never uttered that word in all her life. 'Fucking,' she said again. She slapped JD a third time.

Then she turned and went and sat in another car. After a moment, his father followed her. And then the rest of the group drifted away from him, one by one.

JD stood there on the pavement watching his family drive away. His first thought was to turn around and charge back into the house. Of course they were watching from the windows. He wanted to grab the old fuck by the throat and kick a hole in his skull. The old fuck had managed to get between him and his mom. And no one, not even JD's father, had managed to do that.

Until today.

~

That night, JD gathered four of the soldiers. He didn't want to see either Mike or Aziz. They would've both heard about the afternoon's events by now. They were closer to his parents than he was these days. So JD found a few boys with the proper appetites and went on the final bombing run.

The last of the forty-thousand-pound bills. Three clubs, two fights, enough vodka to drown a rugby team. By the time they were done, they could barely walk, much less drive.

At eighteen minutes past twelve that night, they crashed the car into a building.

Joe Tarr, of the Ferrari, fought the airbags that had surrounded them, like they were in an inflatable castle for kids.

'Where the hell are we?' he managed. JD finally got the door open and fell onto the cobblestones. He peered about and got to his feet. Yup. The silhouette was unmistakable, even at night, through a blizzard of booze.

'Fucking Marble Arch, man.'

'Marble Arch?' Indistinct from inside the car. '*The* Marble Arch?'

They started giggling like idiots.

'Officer,' one of them suggested. 'Who even knew that thing was there?'

'We're tourists, guv!' offered another.

'Can any of you fucks walk a straight line?' JD asked.

The fit of giggles went hysterical at that. This was psycho-good. This was one for the ages. They had driven *into* Marble Arch. They might as well have crashed into the Queen's carriage.

JD sensed a larger problem. Even with tears running down his face from laughing like he hadn't since forever, something nagged at him. From a distance, something reached through the drunken haze, through the happy cape he'd flung about himself, and tapped him on the shoulder. Small. Light. Incessant. It tapped out a message on his shoulder. There were almost out of time. They were minutes away from blowing the whole VAT scam sky high. Here, now, Marble Arch, *something*.

But what could it be?

JD was still cackling when he leant against the bonnet of the Merc they were driving that evening. And then he stopped laughing. His breath caught with a hitch. His heart began to gallop. His hands were on the bonnet and he could feel his heart through his palm, thumping like they should have been on the run four minutes ago.

There were two-and-a-half million pounds in the boot.

Sobriety came quick when he needed it, but not as quick as it used to.

'We can still handle this,' he told the soldiers. They weren't laughing any more.

'Joe, you stay with the car.'

'But—'

'You're the cunt who crashed us. We'll figure a way to get your licence back.'

He sent the other three away with the duffle bags. They'd all meet up a few blocks away and organize a pick-up. JD was the last to leave. He waited until the last second, trying to remember if there was anything else, but he kept drawing a blank. The sense of fatalism that had been growing since he'd stopped laughing had taken hold of him like a lead weight dropped into the duffle bag he was shouldering.

Who the fuck was he? And how did he get here? Where was the kid who lived for situations like this? Where was the kid who thought this was fun?

For a second he thought about just staying put. Let the dogs bust him and then tear the whole deal down. Burn the motherfucker down, start again. Because he seriously wasn't having any fun any more.

JD slapped Tarr across the face to stop him gibbering. 'Stay calm. Laugh. Be drunk.'

Things he used to be good at.

JD turned and went. He went in the opposite direction. Suddenly, he didn't want to ride with the plumbers any more. He found a cab, dialled the boys and told them to sit on the money. He leaned over on the seat and started to tremble. He wasn't sure if he was finally falling apart or if it had already happened. He thought of Brian with a vague sense of sorrow, of things lost, thrown away.

He thought of himself, of Mike and Aziz.

Then he went home and got loaded, because that was what junkies did.

For the next six months, JD went back to being a recluse, scoring to get up and scoring to get numb and mostly staying at home. Within two weeks of his casual leave of absence, Jassi had replaced him in the burn, visiting him each week to deliver the spreadsheets. Beyond the ten mill a month, he was now a stranger.

~

The Principle rode the wave, unchanged, all the way through to March of 2002.

~

The burn had become an abstraction. It ran best when it was worn lightly, like a work-shirt. The six months during which the Principle treated the burn like a coin-op process were their best months. Drop, push, release, wait. And every time, unerringly, the system delivered. The Principle stayed tight, on top of the paperwork. They waited out the little raids, flogged the stamped stock, upped the dummy runs, and balanced the books.

JD was largely forgotten. He was gaunt, wild-eyed, burning from a fever that neither Aziz nor Mike could diagnose. They had both tried, repeatedly, to see him, to talk him out of whatever it was he was doing to himself. He was paying penance. For what, they didn't know.

Brian had simply *left them*. And, besides, that was a long time ago.

Jassi had moved up to occupy his place at the top of the accounting chain. There was even a vague discussion about cutting JD loose entirely, paying him royalties per deal. Mike had tried to tell him that having the spreadsheets sent to his place every week was stupid.

JD fixed him in a hollow stare and Mike felt like he was talking to a dead man. 'You can do what you want,' he said. 'But don't forget that it's my system.'

That was the truth. And it made Mike and Aziz feel guilty in small ways. The whole thing had sprung from him and, somehow, it had ruined him. Meanwhile, they were doing better all the time. It was probably a little unfair. It definitely didn't matter.

It might have gone on that way for years, if Mike hadn't decided to buy a football team.

~

The four-star daydream cliché wasn't lost on Mike, but buying a football team seemed like the most logical thing he could do. This is where the money from the game intersected with the thing that he loved the best in the world. He wasn't a collector like Aziz, and he didn't know what the hell JD's rampage through his own mind was doing for him. The football team was an economical ambition. It allowed him a life-sized model to build on his experiments and hunches, and the things that he wondered about. Plus, most importantly, he was a fan.

Mike had already been through a gruelling three months since January. If he'd had a choice, he would've bought Crystal Palace in a heartbeat. But Simon Jordan had bought

Palace in 2000. The sale hadn't helped. Palace was fucking around in the Championship. And although the takeover had brought financial peace of mind, the fans never got anything like the turnaround they'd been looking for.

Mike had waited too long. Palace had been on his mind for almost a year, but it went off the market before he had the money to make a serious bid. Instead, he formed the nucleus around which an increasingly vocal group of wealthy Palace supporters began to attack the Jordan era.

But the guy wouldn't budge. The slagging match through the press taught Mike a few things. He began to understand the valuations of a club, and how public perception could affect that valuation, and how the media could be used in a bidding war. Mike had become one of the people that *The Sun* went to for their quotes on the Palace management. And there was a growing rumour that one-third of the Heston Principle was shopping for a football team. That was the closest the papers were ever going to get to someone like Branson buying a club.

Mike couldn't afford a Premier League Club, not any of the good ones at any rate, and he wasn't particularly interested in something with the profile of Portsmouth or the Hammers. Instead, he wanted to get in low, build the team from ground up and ride the joy into the Premiership. A project like that would be worth his time and money.

On 4 March, surrounded by a team of suited cut-throats that Sumit had thrown together, Mike launched an aggressive bid for Queen's Park Rangers, a club that had entered administration the previous year. Almost immediately, he found himself enjoying a really vicious PR fight with the current management in the papers and on TV. It helped that QPR had been miserable for years and Mike loved pointing it out in the press. He had learned something from Aziz—it really didn't matter if it was this team or the next. The *process* was the fun stuff. He finally had his rich man's hobby.

Aziz didn't like all the attention Mike was bringing the Principle, but it was his money and he could do what the hell he wanted with it. The three of them were no longer married to each other. At least that's what Aziz told himself.

The Principle had been running the third system for just over a year. The three of them were worth at least a hundred and twenty million pounds each. They had spawned twelve millionaires from within their offices. And they had paved the way for the rest of the cowboys.

The revolution was complete. They were now the institution.

~

Val rang Reg during her morning tea break on 5 March. They had spoken twice in the past four months. She had called him in December to wish him Merry Christmas, and he had told her he had nothing on the three folders she'd left with him. The second time they spoke, he said he still didn't have any information, but Val had sensed that he had stumbled onto something. The break probably wasn't much, but he knew something. Val heard it in his voice. But she knew he wouldn't give anything up until he was absolutely sure. So she'd let it go.

When Val saw *The Sun* on the morning of the 5th, and then saw the headlines on three other tabloids, she abandoned *The Guardian* and bought them all. She leafed through them slowly over her cup of tea. The stories were the same, but it was the three names, repeated again and again, that stayed with her. QPR. Mike Hamilton. The Heston Principle.

Val knew that the Heston Principle were her boys. All the pieces fit. She recognized the face in the paper from almost a year ago. She knew them, through the files, through every transaction for a year-and-a-half, and this was the signature. This was the prize they had allowed themselves. Even more than the private jet, this was the one that spoke to her and she felt that she knew them like they were her own children.

Val had to put down her cup because it had started shaking in her hand. If things had been different, these boys might have been heroes. They had come out of their backgrounds on a rocket ship, so far in so little time. But they had disregarded the rules. And the rules were her job.

She *might* be wrong. But she didn't think so. And Reg had asked her to call if she ever felt strongly about any of the three companies that she had brought to his attention.

When Val called him, Reg threw her by saying, 'I've got something for you.'

Val thought about who should go first. 'No,' she said. 'It can wait. I've got something for you.'

'Did you have a feeling then, Valerie?' he asked.

'I did.'

'Go on, then. The suspense is killing us.'

'The Principle. The Heston Principle.'

There was a brief pause. 'Is it because the kid wants to buy a football team?' Reg asked.

Val smiled in spite of herself. 'It may be. But it fits. I'm sure it does.'

Reg grunted. Val could hear him scribble something down. When he spoke again, his voice was sharper and she knew that he had opened up the folder.

'You've got a lot on them, Val. Anything else I should know?'

Val took a breath and held it. If Reg knew what she knew, then they were looking at the first real possibility of proof. Suddenly, out of nowhere, she had a target.

'Scan through the transactions. You don't have to study them. Just look at the patterns of their peaks and troughs. And then tell me what you see, if there's anything in particular.'

Val waited, her pulse running hard, while Reg went through the pages.

'What it is, Val?' he asked. His voice was tight and urgent—he'd seen something.

'Are you looking at the file?'

'You know I am.'

'Every time they start a cycle, every single time—the big transactions—what do they wait for?'

Reg swore gently. Val heard him go through the pages again. He stopped and spent a full minute on one of them. Then she heard him flipping through again, faster and faster.

'Bloody hell,' he breathed.

'It ties in, doesn't it?' she asked.

'Every time,' he said. 'Every single time. They wait for an external cue. They wait so that everyone's looking in another direction.'

'They started with a bang when the Foot and Mouth Crisis was on. Then just after the election. Then...'

'Nine-one-one, and through to Christmas,' Reg finished. She heard him sigh. 'Every time.'

'Now look at their activity after the raids,' Val said. 'It's cross-referenced in blue. Look at the activity after.'

'They wait for a week. Or ten days. They dump the stamped stock. And then go mad.'

'I'm betting it's when they go mad that they run high volumes of the dummy stock. That's how they balance the loss from dumping the *actual* stock. And once they have parity, it's back to recycling. It's there, right there.'

Reg was silent. Val heard him tapping on the file in front of him.

'We know what we have to do then, don't we?' he asked.

'We need small raids. A small set. And then we need to get photographs of the dummy stock with paperwork that shows exactly the opposite.' Val stopped. 'How in the hell, Reg? I've got nothing except the two trends. That's not enough to get Wexler to listen.'

'We might have something, Val,' he said. '*Might.*'

He was being playful now. Val pictured him smirking to himself.

'Go on, then,' she said. 'The suspense is killing us.'

Val could hear him stretch in his chair and sit back. He was taking his time, enjoying himself.

'Here's what you tell Wexler,' he said. 'You tell Wexler that Alex Holding Company, the only account they opened themselves, personally, is a front for the Russian mob. It was a single cash injection at the very start of this recycling thing— close to ten million, I think. It was their start-up money, the cash that got them up and running in the first place.'

Reg relished every word as he summed it up for her. 'Tell Wexler that the operating capital is either powder money or blood money, probably both. That should wake the prefects up. Don't tell the prefects about the Russians. Tell Wexler. That should buy you your raids. And then we'll go around and see these boys. Then we'll see how they buy bleeding Rangers.'

~

It took Val six weeks. Wexler wouldn't even listen to her until the end of March. And there was another two weeks of endless meetings, trying to make people understand what the hell was going on.

The final campaign, ultimately, sprung from Alex Holding Co. Val bartered the information to Wexler for the first set of raids. And the first set of raids were just to lay the groundwork and Customs had to be careful about how they did it. This was the only chance they'd had after a year-and-a-half scrounging for a major breakthrough, one that could bring the whole thing down. The operation was never about a single bust—Customs were gunning for a corporation, for a chunk of the web.

Val had to surrender complete control to Wexler. That was the only other thing she could offer. Because this was the one way that Customs could regain authority on the VAT scam. There was more at stake than the Heston Principle.

Halfway through April, Wexler sanctioned the first wave of raids. He went behind the backs of the Parliamentary Committee, three taskforces, and his own minister. It was his and Val's little secret. No one knew the specific purpose of the raids. Aside from the two of them and Reg, no one knew about Alex Holding Co., either. The VAT fraud taskforce had become their very own ghost agency.

Over the next two weeks, a total of fourteen Customs agents hit the Principle's entire loop from top to bottom, company after company, over and over again. The officers were annoying, unapologetic and insisted on massive amounts of paperwork. Every deal was vetted at least twice. The stock-boys in the warehouses at the Forwarders' got on a first-name basis with the agents. Customs stamped damned near everything they saw. Mostly, they just slowed the pace down to an agonizing crawl, messing with the averages.

If JD had still been in the same world as everybody else, he might have seen the countdown for what it was. He might have seen Val's flurry of little jabs slowly wearing the Principle down to the mat. Instead, Mike shrugged and dreamt of his football team, Aziz cursed at the agents, and both of them figured they'd make back the count in a week.

Val reined the Customs boys in on 30 April. On 7 May, on cue, the Principle came back with a roar, running four deals on the first day. On 9 May, EX staged a four-man operation of which no official record exists. Val was prepared to have to run the stunt more than once but, for the first time, she had matched percentages with her boys.

~

At half past one in the morning, a mail van pulled up in front of ASF Logistics in the freight cargo area behind Heathrow, one man driving, no passengers. It waited exactly thirty seconds. Then electricity in the estate died, almost as if someone had run a pair of wire-cutters through the power lines. This was primary. The Swiss Guard still had to get through the secondary and tertiary circuits, the hard lines in the building they were targeting. It was easy enough for these men, but the window was small. They had ninety seconds to get in. And eight to twelve minutes to get out.

With the darkness in front of the mail van, the second car arrived, pulling into the parking lot. The driver of the mail van got out and locked his doors, leaving the van on the street, and waited behind it. Two men got out of the other car.

They were both in their fifties and they moved with the unhurried speed of serious professionals. One of them took a customized ATM card from his pocket and swiped it through the primary alarm system. He slid it in a second time and left the card in the slot. The keypad beeped once, followed by two quicker beeps, as if the gadget was trying to ask what was being done to it. The display went blank for a second and flickered back to life, bright green numbers flashing across the screen as the hack program whittled down all the possible combinations.

Eight seconds later, all out of other options, the PIN began to blink. The first man punched the numbers in and the LEDs switched from red to green. He pulled the card out and stood aside. The man behind him stepped forward, holding something that looked like a CD case. He studied the keypad carefully, unzipped the case and pulled out a key. He finessed it into the lock and turned. The door to the warehouse opened with an electronic hiss. The man with the key stepped into the darkness. The other man turned and whistled once, softly. The figure behind the van began moving toward the warehouse, pulling out an object that Mike would have recognized straight away.

From a corner, under the street light, a hundred and forty feet away from the estate, Reg Henry watched. So far, so good.

The Swiss Guard repeated the process with the tertiary alarm system inside. The driver of the van simply waited. When the lights on the second system had gone green, the man with the keys climbed the stairs. He found what he was looking for behind the second door, the bank of recorders for all the CCTV cameras in the building. EX had cut the transmission to the security agency when it had cut the power, but high-value insurers always ran a separate bank of recorders on the premises for backup. He let himself into the room and unscrewed the back panel of the security console.

He found the wires he was looking for. He pulled out a flat circuit board the size of a credit card and clipped it to the wires carrying the data feed to the hard drives. He went back to the door and nodded.

The driver of the van used the industrial strength slim jim he'd brought with him to pick the lock on the mobile phone cage. He moved carefully, always replacing and returning boxes before moving onto the next stack. In four minutes, he had ten boxes loaded with junk mobiles, placed against the different piles they had been extracted from. Always context. It was Reg's motto.

Both men on the ground floor photographed the evidence—in close-up, and in relation to the warehouse itself. The man who had worked the ATM card was careful to include the driver of the van in almost every photograph. This was internal evidence, it wasn't meant for the courts. Glancing at his watch, the man outside the cage tapped the bars lightly. The man inside nodded and started replacing the boxes. Two minutes later, both of them slid out of the warehouse.

The mail van started and pulled away. The other man waited in the car, engine running.

The man upstairs waited until the van was clear. He returned to the console and pressed the only button on the circuit board. There was a whine as the whole rig died. The man counted down the thirty seconds as the entire security system in the warehouse rebooted. This *would* set off the alarm at the security agency, but the response time was four minutes at the very least. He needed just half of that.

He waited until the options appeared on the screen in front of him. He reset the clock to midnight, erasing all activity recorded in the last hour-and-a-half, and then reset all the recorders to timecode zero. That gave him ninety seconds as the system purged all its banks. This was the absolute unanticipated catastrophe in the design of the system. It was never meant to be rebooted once it had been installed.

The man moved quickly now. He took the stairs at a run, the final key in hand. He locked the cage and hit reset on both the keypads on his way out. He closed the main door to the warehouse, seconds ticking down in his head. The car was waiting for him, door open. Then they were gone.

Four seconds passed. Seven seconds passed. With a whirr, the cameras started recording again. The operation had taken eight-and-a-half minutes, beginning to end—a little bubble of time with no record of it ever having happened.

Reg waited until the power came back, two minutes after the second car had left. Then, as the van from the security agency came around the corner, he began to walk to his car.

~

Customs raided ASF Logistics the next morning. It was a quick, clean visit. The paperwork, after all, was immaculate. Everything present and accounted for, all the stock genuine and paid for.

~

Val let the old monster out of isolation at the meeting the day after. The time was right for Bad Val. She cut through the aura of victory that had consumed Wexler. They weren't anywhere *near* being done.

'It's not it, Peter. It's not the Grail.' She wanted to leave Wexler with no option.

Reg stayed impassive. He was one of the architects of what Val was about to propose. And he understood that Wexler would always have trouble contemplating a field operation at the scale it needed.

'We have proof, Val,' Wexler said slowly.

'Yes, we do. We do, Peter. But what is the proof good for?'

Wexler shook his head.

'If we go,' Val continued 'if we try and use this as the basis for arrests, what do we get? We get a Freight Forwarder. They'll set someone up to take the fall. And then, three months later, they'll be off and running.'

Wexler lifted his hand, but stopped short of rubbing his eyes. 'I see what you mean,' he said. 'But where do we go?'

'The proof's enough to go to the prefects and the minister. Tell them that we have concrete evidence of how these men are running the VAT fraud. Show them the damned photos. Get the authority back. Get us resources.' So much depended on Wexler buying the line. Otherwise the opportunity would fall out of their laps and get trampled in the stampede.

'What then?'

Val looked at him for a moment. 'The only way you'll stop them is if you do a straight bust. Top to bottom, all the way, simultaneously. Bust every stage of the process in the middle of a very large transaction, at the same time. It's the only way you'll prove collusion. It's the only way you'll get the entire community of thieves out there. Otherwise, deniability is built into the system. That's why they compartmentalized it the way they did.'

Val couldn't tell if she was getting through.

'All of them,' she added. 'Together. At the same time. Running junk stock.'

He didn't reject it outright, but she could see him doing the calculations she had already worked out herself.

'Val.' Wexler hesitated, running the math again. 'That's about three hundred police officers and six hundred Customs officers.'

Val sat back and grinned at him. 'That's why you have the evidence, Peter. To be able to talk the prefects into it.'

Wexler nodded. She had done her job. It was his turn. 'And if we get it?'

'Then we wait.'

Wexler frowned.

'Look at it, Peter. Look at the charts. *They* wait. They wait for something big to happen in the outside world. That's where all their big pitches start from.' She started to say something else and stopped herself. There wasn't anything more to add. 'We're going to have to wait until they launch something massive. If you want the whole chain.'

Wexler ran his hand across his head. And then rubbed his eyes. 'You're asking for a lot, Val.'

'If you want to be a hero,' Val said, 'it's going to take just a little more patience.'

'Patience? I thought I'd been the bloody model of the stuff.'

'Don't tell them about Alex Holding Co.' Reg surprised both of them. It was the first time he had spoken. 'Don't tell them,' he repeated. 'It'll open up a can of worms that you can't control. It'll blow up in your face. Whatever you do, don't tell them.'

~

Neither Val nor Reg knew the details. It was better that way. Wexler spent the better part of six weeks bringing his masters around. He begged, pleaded and cajoled. Occasionally, he walked out of meetings.

On 26 June, 2002 he tossed the directive onto Val's desk.

'We're a go. Green light. All the way from the Cabinet. All told, six hours to assemble, on your command.' He looked at her. 'It's your show. And I'm guessing we wait?'

'We wait,' said Val.

~

Customs and its affiliates, working together for this one deal, waited for three weeks. And nothing happened. Eventually—the Principle could have warned them—the anticipation of a big move was cancelled out by a drawn out period of sitting still. It had taken Wexler six weeks to form the army. Two weeks after that, departments from all over the map were asking to withdraw their men. No one actually said, shit or get off the pot, but the implication was clear enough.

Wexler and Val had the only row of their entire careers, yelling at each other across the office and Wexler had, for the first and last time ever, given her a direct order.

Whether or not there was an incident on the outside, Customs was going to provoke and then opera the Heston Principle. The Full Monty, everything, every last possible ounce of resource. On one day, at the same time. And Wexler and Val, even though they had written and produced the show, were now spectators. Val simply needed to call the first cue.

She held on until the last possible moment and then, for the only time in a year-and-a-half, Val made the first move. On 16 July, Val blitzed the Principle across the board, stamping stock in a frenzy. She'd have ten days at most to see how the Principal reacted and then—whether they were flogging dummy stock or not—Wexler's army would storm in.

They sat back and watched for the first signs of movement from the Principle, Wexler by Val's side. She hated that Customs had forced the last throw of the dice instead of waiting for the Principle to step into the trap. She simply hadn't had any choice.

Wexler had spent too much time and done too many favours setting up the raid to lose it just because people were getting antsy. The raid could make him an instant legend, but there were now factors and factions he couldn't control. On 12 July, with the prize slipping out his grasp, he had bartered Alex Holding Co. to the Metropolitan Police in exchange for two more weeks of waiting. He hadn't told anyone, not even Val. It was a massive gamble. For five days, there wasn't a blip on either side, not from the boys or the dogs. On 22 July, all hell broke loose.

~

JD woke on the morning of the 19th and, for the second time that week, coughed up a mouthful of blood. It was vaguely interesting. He thought he was done and turned towards the bedroom to fetch his cigarettes. That was when the *real* shakes hit.

It started as a twitch in his left eye. JD paused. He liked watching twitches work themselves out in the mirror, watching indisputable evidence of his body not responding to orders. But as he leaned towards the shaving mirror, the twitch rippled through the left side of his face and down his entire body. Suddenly, he couldn't breathe. And as he struggled for breath, he realized he couldn't stand.

He fell against the sink, his body locking up on itself. He had no control over his muscles. He caromed off the sink and hit the floor, smashing his head against the tiles, hands like arthritic claws under him, utterly helpless. There was a single instant of anticipation before the pain screamed through his synapses. He jerked and thrashed on the floor, still fighting to fill his lungs.

When the second wave came, he felt a strange heat everywhere and blacked out.

JD surfaced about an hour later. He wondered why he

was on the bathroom floor and the spell came rushing back. He remembered the heat and understood. His nose had been gushing like a fountain, and he had shit his pants. He felt like he had been stabbed a hundred times over by a rabid motherfucker who had pissed on him for good measure. The last realization was that the smell of piss was his own. He had voided his body without noticing.

What he wanted most was a drink.

He remained on the floor and started to cry.

It took him an hour to sort himself out. First, he crawled to the shower and sat under the hot water. After a while, he pulled himself upright and cleaned up—first his body and then the floor. He threw his clothes in the garbage and showered properly. By the time he was done, he knew the one thing that he needed to do. He got dressed and picked up his keys. He slunk out of the apartment, head low, not wanting to look at the bottles of booze as he walked by.

JD drove to his mother's house, the house that he had bought her. He parked on the street and sat in the car for a while. How in the hell? And how so quick? He shook his head and smiled. If he had to take his medicine, then this was the place to start.

His mother answered the door. She looked at him in silence. They hadn't seen or spoken to one another since his performance at the wedding meeting. Her face tightened, as if she were about to say something, but then she thought better of it. She turned and began to walk down the corridor.

'Come in. Take off your shoes. Wear the slippers.' All in Punjabi, thrown over her shoulder.

She gave him tea and sat next to him at the kitchen table. When he tried to talk, she hushed him. So he cried instead, leaning against her shoulder the way he had done when he was a child. And when he had exhausted himself, she turned his face to hers and gripped it with one hand. She forced him to look at her.

'Go somewhere. Sleep. Turn off your phone. Phones. Don't drink. Don't take drugs. I'll feed you. Go. And sleep. Then call me tomorrow.'

'Here? Can I stay here?' JD asked.

His mother shook her head. 'When your father comes home, he'll annoy you and then he'll annoy me. And then he'll drink and then both of you will fight. Go somewhere where no one will disturb you.'

JD nodded. She fed him chicken curry and rice and sent him on his way.

At the door, on his way out, JD turned to her.

'I'm sorry, Mom' he said.

She smiled at him. She shook her head and kissed his cheek. 'It'll be all right,' she said in English, surprising both of them.

JD left feeling like he'd done something right for the first time since… he couldn't remember. And without thinking about it, he found himself in Heston. He parked the car three streets away and walked into the old warehouse. He felt like he was returning to a place that had been sacred when he was a child, but forgotten, years ago. He settled down, unsure of what to do. He thought about what his mother said and switched off his phones. He supposed that he would surf the internet until sleep came. It was unlikely. His body would start demanding its regular dosage at some point. He was still thinking about what to do when he fell asleep.

For the next three days, JD lived at the warehouse, like he had done when they were building the game. He stayed off the booze, he stayed away from the drugs and he smoked as little as possible. He spent hours on the internet, mostly playing bridge. He walked out at odd hours and bought food from a takeaway place that Mike would have remembered well. He left the phones off. The burn had been running without him for close to six months now.

He slept for hours, through large parts of those three days, trying to remember his old self, and the way things had been. He was as honest with himself as he could be. It was the final reboot of that immortal memory, still sitting in Heston.

~

Mike, unusual for him, spent the weekend drunk at the house in Weybridge. On Saturday, he had told Aziz to fuck off. Aziz had been calling incessantly, wanting to run the burn fast and hard, starting Monday, because their averages had been pounded by the latest round of Customs raids. It was one of the many unpleasant things that Mike had learned about Aziz since they'd started working together without JD's counterbalance. For Aziz, every Customs hit was going to bankrupt them in a week. All of his millions and he was still an old woman when it came to watching over every last quid. What he needed was a smack in the mouth.

The QPR bid had fallen though on Friday, capping a hell of a week. First Customs interference, and then the team gone because Mike hadn't been able to win over enough people on the board. The failed bid drove him up the fucking wall because it had nothing to do with money or football. He just didn't speak asshole. On the whole, fucking crime made more sense because enough intelligent or capable people would listen to an idea that was better than the one they had. There would be another team—Mike would only be getting richer every month—but with August coming up, he was probably done until the off-season unless there was a club in administration. And that would be another set of bollocks entirely.

Mike shredded his files on Friday afternoon and dismissed the team around him. He called Sumit and told him to start shopping for other possibilities. He did okay until noon on Saturday, when Aziz had finally gotten on his nerves. He rang Jassi and told him that he was out of commission and that he was switching off the third phone for the weekend.

'And if you want to run the burn on Monday, as fearless leader will no doubt want to do… well, you've done it before. I'm not in until Tuesday. Tell him. And tell him that I'll call him. He's not to call.' Jassi said nothing. Over the past six months, he had become used to being the three-way intermediary. He wished Mike a pleasant weekend and hung up.

Mike watched sports and drank steadily for most of the weekend. He tried to raise JD a couple times to invite him to come see the new house that he wasn't aware of. JD's phones were off. Fair enough. Mike decided that he'd had enough to drink and went to bed early on Sunday. He spent Monday at home, just to piss off Aziz. Towards evening, Mike told himself that Aziz wasn't to blame for the fact that he hadn't managed to land the team. He would go in the next day like a good sport and run his share of the burn. It was his job.

He went for a run in the early evening. By the time he got back, he was exhausted and soaked through with sweat. He showered and ate and was in bed by nine-thirty. As he fell asleep, he reminded himself that he needed to switch on the third phone in the morning and charge it before he went to work.

~

When Aziz met Jassi at his office on Monday morning, he was strangely satisfied. Mike would be back, probably tomorrow, but he realized now that it didn't really matter if either of the other two ever came back or not. The last six months had been an accelerated exercise in isolation for Aziz and now here he was, the last man standing. The three of them had been stripped down to their fundamentals. Both Mike and JD were remarkable men, Aziz still believed it. But how special you were depended on how special you made yourself. He was still here, stronger, better, because he had remade himself as the game rolled on, just like he'd been doing all his life.

It had made him rich. The three original members of the board had pulled out a hundred and seventy million pounds each in the year-and-a-half that they had been running the burn. And Aziz had parlayed that money into three hundred million pounds, scattered across the globe, accessible from anywhere with the push of a button.

And it still wasn't enough. He knew himself well enough to know that it would never be enough. It was who he was. It would never stop. And he was fine with that.

When he walked into the office on the morning of the 22nd, he slipped into the familiar motion that was his drug of choice. He started to make the money work.

The system was now so streamlined that he and Jassi could run it off their laptops, sitting in the office. JD and Mike had been good for that much. Aziz was in a hurry to bring up the averages, so they flogged the stamped stock in four deals by one in the afternoon. By three, the dummy stock had re-entered the game, waiting at the warehouses for a titanic burn the next morning. They were scheduled to begin at nine in the morning.

Aziz was utterly calm. It had been a good day's work. He was looking at two more days of running this cycle and then they would halt for the next week. He and Jassi were done and out of the office by three-thirty.

He paused at the door before he switched off the lights. There was a time, less than a year ago, when he'd have been at work until ten or eleven at night. He'd been building the game and now the game had repaid that faith. There were things to do with that time, he had learnt. The theatre. Films. Just sitting around and exchanging stories about the day.

Aziz left, a small smile playing on his lips.

At seven in the evening, nine hundred agents from

Customs and the Metropolitan Police got the code red
from the desk of Valerie Stewart. The raid, across eighteen
companies and two national borders, was a go. They were
slated to run at eleven-thirty the next morning, and every
single officer was aware that they needed to stop the chain in
motion. They *had* to go together. That fact had been drilled
into their heads for weeks. They had to go like clockwork
because they were up against clockwork.

Val was pale and quiet at her desk. She had stayed on after
five for the first time in fifteen years.

~

The thing crime and policing have in common are blind
spots. Blind spots are the advantages. Blind spots are the
gaps. And gaps are the cause of craft. Craft, any craft, exists
to exploit the gaps, to bridge them. The Principle could
have told Wexler this. The blind spots are what allowed
them their amazing run. Val could have told Wexler this.
The gaps were what allowed her to track down the Principle
from nowhere. And Reg could've told Wexler. Sometimes,
those gaps couldn't be bridged—they seemed small but they
yawned too large.

But no one ever did.

The Metropolitan Police waited a week after the barter.
Alex Holding Co. interested them a lot more than the VAT
fraud. The Russians were the all-time target. So after a week
without any action from Wexler and the old woman in charge
of the investigation, the Met moved.

Two undercover policemen made contact with Federov's men on 19 July. They were looking for money to get into the mobile phone game, but they made it clear that they were up for anything with the Russians as long as it would turn a profit. The two men waited the requisite thirty-six hours before they were invited to a Sunday morning meeting.

No one informed them that they hadn't checked out.

They weren't allowed to keep their cell phones.

~

The phone rang once and disconnected. There was a space of seconds. The phone rang again and disconnected. The two rings, unevenly spaced, were enough. Mike opened his eyes and sat up. He could have gone back to sleep, but he'd had two early nights in row and was fresher than he'd felt in days.

He was also annoyed. It was two minutes to eight in the morning and everyone at work knew not to call before nine unless it was life or death. The rule applied for all three of them.

Damned frogs, thought Mike. Fuckin' Frenchy importers at the end of the chain always forgot that there was an hour between them.

Mike looked at the phones lying neatly side by side. After a moment, he frowned. His third phone wasn't switched on. Number One, his oldest number, was still showing the display. That had been the one ringing. The other two were dark.

Mike picked up the first phone and looked at it. Two missed calls. From the same number, probably a callbox. As he was looking at the phone, it rang in his hand.

'Hello?'

'Mike?' The voice was low and urgent, and very, very tense. Mike struggled for a moment to place it.

'Adam?'

They hadn't spoken in over a year. The last time Mike had seen Adam, they had exchanged nods at a Christmas party, close to where home had been.

But Adam was gone. The call disconnected again and Mike listened to the silence for a full three seconds, still holding the phone against his ear.

Things happened very quickly in his head. The situation was bad. Police-bad. Mike could feel it like a rotting tooth. He tossed the phone onto the bed where he could see it, flung the sheets off himself and ran to the bathroom. He didn't bother brushing his teeth. He dressed as quickly as he could and dunked his head under the tap. When he came up, he looked at his face in the mirror. It was here. Whatever it was, it was here.

Mike was pulling his shoes on, sitting on the bed, when the phone rang. The same number, two-and-a-half minutes after the last phone call.

'Here.'

'I have two minutes,' Adam told him. He sounded a little calmer, more contained, but he was practically whispering.

'Yeah.'

'Your Indian friend is dead.'

For a second, Mike couldn't breathe. He felt the floor shifting beneath him and it took all his focus to stay on his feet.

'JD?' he finally managed.

'No.' Adam was impatient. 'The other one. Sen. The lawyer.'

That was easier than the first shock, but heat rushed into his throat and cheeks. Adam's voice seemed to be coming from a long way away.

'Listen, Mike. It's the Russians. It was a mob hit. It was an execution at six in the morning.'

Mike already had a dozen questions but he didn't say anything—just listened, waiting for the rest of it.

'Someone tore apart your place in Chelsea. JD's too. Before they got to the lawyer.' Of course, thought Mike. We're one and two. Sen was the contact. And Aziz, fucking Aziz, didn't exist for the Russians.

'Fuck,' he breathed.

'Mike, there's more. Customs were on the scene four minutes after us. The Met must have put them on and it was important enough for them to be there. They took everything—his phones, his laptop, everything.'

Mike closed his eyes, laughing in spite of himself. He understood. Everything was blown. Everything. That's why Adam was in a callbox. Every number. The three phones. The contacts. The addresses.

Customs, with the full co-operation of the police, were staging an opera. And they were probably doing it this morning. That's why Customs were on the scene four minutes after the Met. And the Russians? Someone, somewhere, had uncovered the truth about Alex Holding Co. Mike didn't care how. That didn't matter. What mattered now was that Customs had proof, and that there was going to be the mother of all raids across the city. There was no one he could call. He couldn't even send a signal. Customs had all the numbers.

'Adam—' he began to ask. And that was when he heard someone at the front door.

The Russians were here.

~

Mike hung up. He looked at the phone for a second, switched it off and dropped it on the bed. He was lucky that he slept in the downstairs study, unlike most people, and he was lucky that he always drew the curtains at night. Those two things had bought him a minute. The Russians wouldn't have expected him to hear the door, and they weren't sure about the security alarm. After all, he was a rich man. The rest didn't matter.

His only other advantage was that they would want to question him. They wouldn't mind hurting him, and they would kill him after, but they wanted to talk to him first.

What else? One person or two? Eight on a Tuesday morning in St. George's Hill. People leaving for work outside?

One person. That was the gamble. And with that, he stopped thinking for the next eighty seconds.

Mike ran into the living room at a crouch. He grabbed the heavy cut-glass ashtray, emptied it onto the table and he snaked across the room, crouching between the door to the living room and the TV cabinet. The door led to the small hallway with the front door to the right and the stairway to the first floor on the left. It was twelve feet from the front door to the stairs—that's where the guy would go.

The curtains were still drawn in the living room and the light inside was muted. It felt like eight o'clock in the evening, late summer, when it was still beautiful out and you could sit by the side of a hill, take your shirt off and drink a pint of beer.

Mike stayed still, breathing evenly, trying to stay loose. The scratching outside the front door, low and insistent, stopped. Mike heard the man step back a pace. All was quiet for a minute. Then the man moved forward again and the scraping sound came back heavier, more insistent. Mike nodded. The man had stepped back, checking for the telltale signs of a security alarm. After that, he'd looked around to make sure he was clear. Now he was jimmying the lock.

It gave easily. The door swung open with a faint creak. If he had been asleep, Mike thought, there was no way he would have heard anything. A few seconds passed. The man stepped into the hallway. The Russian closed the door behind him carefully, stopped for a moment, then headed towards the foot of the stairs.

Mike waited until the man had crossed past the living room door—he wanted to be out of his line of sight. He coughed. Once. Deliberately.

Mike heard the footsteps pause. When they began again, they were much quieter, but quicker. He was moving towards the living room.

Mike's gaze was fixed on the door. It was all timing. Everything he had ever touched was timing. He was relaxed, measuring rhythm, waiting for the only beat that gave him a fighting percentage. He waited until he saw the gun enter the room, leading its owner.

Mike exploded out of his corner, his right arm going back like a discus thrower, the ashtray clutched in his hand. He had time for one step, and he launched himself off his right foot, lunging toward the man's stomach and bringing his right arm around. He had never seen anything with such crisp brilliance in his life. The arm continued to rise and, at the very last moment, when his momentum was at its peak, he let the ashtray go.

It rocked the man square in the face a split second before Mike hit his body. The gun fired once as the Russian was propelled back, the bullet grazing Mike's forearm, and fell from his hand.

The two of them crashed sideways into the doorframe and the living room wall. The man's body softened the impact, but Mike still felt the jolt all the way through his shoulder. Mike was sure that he'd dislocated the shoulder and that he'd popped a disc. The pain was unbelievable. He lay panting on the floor, unable to move, even though the man and the gun were lying on either side of him.

It was the gun that finally got Mike to sit up. His back was doing better than he thought it would, but he had dislocated the shoulder for sure. Clutching the shoulder with the arm that still worked, Mike looked at the man who had come to kill him.

The gun wasn't going to be a problem after all. If the guy wasn't dead already, he just needed a few minutes. Pieces of glass studded his face like glitter. What was left of his face. It was really more of a crude outline.

There was no nose, for one. There were bits of bone and teeth in the red mess. Little ribbons of flesh fluttered in the man's dying breath. But no nose.

Mike looked at the face in front of him and threw up.

He struggled to his feet and got moving.

~

He changed his clothes, screaming out loud because his shoulder was so bad. He forced himself to shower, staying under the hot water as long as he could. He ignored the dying man in his hallway.

The pain made it difficult to think. But kept at it until he had something like a plan. If they could do it in the next three hours, there was still a way out. The game was gone. But they could still get away.

He didn't let himself hope. He just strung it together like he always did.

He took his passport. He remembered to carry his first phone. The landlines were on that one. He couldn't recall any of the numbers from memory even if he wanted to. He pulled out a small black case that he'd had since before he started working with JD. He put on his black overcoat, hiding the bone that jutted out from under his shoulder, and put the case in the pocket. He was strictly left-handed now.

From the kitchen he pulled out a long, thin knife, then grabbed the gun off the floor in the hallway. The man collapsed against the wall let out a whine. Mike shook his head and clumsily frisked the man. He pulled a phone off the Russian. A Motorola.

'Not one of ours, then.' His voice was loud in the hallway but Mike smiled nonetheless. He flipped the phone open and checked the battery and the network. Both were good. It was a start. He had communication. Maybe. Just maybe.

The man whined again. The sound was thick, from behind a curtain of darkness. Mike looked at him.

'I'm sorry, bruv.'

He turned and left. He didn't look back.

It was eight forty-two in the morning and sunny. For a lot of people, it was going to be a lovely day.

~

Mike's own cars were no good. The numbers were on the scanners, if the Met was involved. And he couldn't jack anything in St. George's Hill, not in this condition. But he needed to move. If someone eventually came to look for his Russian, he was fucked. He cut across through the middle of the hillside, heading toward Cobham, going through the grass and the bushes and other gardens like fucking Rambo in the first one. He hurt like a motherfucker, but he could live with it. His only concern was to be seen as little as possible.

Halfway down the hill, Mike pulled out the gun. It took him a moment to figure out the catch. He pulled out the clip and began to eject the bullets as he walked, littering the path behind him. When he was done, he chucked the empty magazine into a clump of bushes to his left. He counted off two minutes in his head as he walked and then chucked the gun to the right of the path. When he was sure of where he was, he cut left. Three minutes later, he was on Old Avenue.

Mike walked fast, sweating under the overcoat and looking over his shoulder every so often. He wouldn't get a cab here. He knew where he was going. He pulled out the Russian's phone and started dialling JD's and Aziz's old numbers alternately. The dogs were probably listening, but this was a risk he had to take. The Principle still had a little time.

JD's phone was off. And Aziz's rang on and on. Prick. He wouldn't pick up because he didn't know the number.

'Fuck,' he muttered. His breathing was getting heavier.

Mike began to go faster, phone still jammed to his ear, putting out the last call.

~

It took Mike seven minutes to walk to the Hilton at Cobham. When he stepped into the parking lot, it was one minute to nine in the morning. He had no way of knowing then, but the shower he took after the Russian lost his face was probably the difference. In the end, the game came down to seven minutes.

Mike pocketed the phone as he crossed the lot. He needed both his hands for what he was about to do, even the dead one. He had a slim jim up one sleeve and the kitchen knife in the other. He went through the rows of cars looking for an automatic. He loathed automatics but that was pretty much beside the point just then. He settled on a middle-aged Honda. He waited another minute in the long driveway that led to reception, trying to gauge the scene. He looked like he was admiring the view of the lawn that lined the hotel's façade.

'Even if it kills me, bruv,' he sighed to himself. This time, he had to make the luck come on his own.

Mike winced and let out a quick gasp as he worked the jim between the window and the door. The knife in his fucked-up right hand held the lock in place, trembling and taking off paint. Mike didn't care if there was an alarm. He'd deal with it later. The lock slid up and the door swung open without a sound.

With one last look around, Mike slid into the Honda and closed the door. He placed the knife into the ignition slot delicately, pushed once and left it in. He leant back and kicked the knife with the heel of his boot. There was a high twang as the steel went past its breaking point and split in two. The pieces flew in two directions, along with the plastic assembly. He sat down, ripped out the wires and looked at them. He could've simply turned the rotation switch but he didn't want to risk the wipers being erratic, not in a stolen car in broad daylight.

Stooping forward, he ripped the cover off the wires with his teeth and twisted the two ends together. The car rumbled to life. He pushed the gear home and drove out, nearly losing the backend as the car misunderstood his foot on the pedal and downshifted. He twisted the wheel around, this time screaming in pain, and pulled the car back. He drifted back onto the road and found the M25. Traffic forced him further down the road than he wanted to go before he could pull over and start digging the numbers out of his own phone.

JD's phone was still off. But Mike got through to Aziz's landline at the office and spent another minute on hold before the secretary put him through.

It was nine twenty-three in the morning.

~

'Mike?' Curious, but calm and confident, as always.

'Listen. Make sure that if there's anyone in the room that you don't want there, then nothing you say pins you. Got it?' Mike spoke in a flat, emotionless voice. They needed to play this right.

Aziz swivelled in his chair and looked at Jassi. The call was routine, and the kid was absorbed in the two laptops in front of him. Aziz closed his eyes and saw a shattered shaving mirror. He shook his head once and opened his eyes. In his mind, he was already running again.

'Sure.' Polite. Not too inquisitive.

'Everything's blown. All the numbers, the third mobiles, everything. The Russians killed Sumit this morning and Customs picked up the full bag. Which means they'll launch simultaneous raids today, *now*. Stop the run. Walk away.'

Almost unconsciously, Aziz reached out for the Zippo lying on the table. He didn't strike it, or even flip the lid up. He let the silence spin out. He breathed out once and squeezed the Zippo as hard as he could.

'It's gone, Mike' he said simply. Jassi looked up from the laptop to Aziz. Aziz shook his head and rolled his eyes. Jassi nodded and looked down at the laptop again.

'How many units?' asked Mike.

'Thirty-six.'

'Dummy?'

'What do you think?'

'Walk away,' Mike said again. 'Take whoever's there and walk away.'

'Meet me,' said Aziz, and he was surprised that he'd said it. He was even more surprised to realize that he meant it. They were in this together. This was the stain that coloured them. It would colour them for the rest of their lives. But the money was still within reach, wherever they were in the world.

'Might as well,' Mike agreed. They still had a few hours. The dogs wouldn't post bulletins at the ID points until they realized that the Principle was on the run.

'Where?' asked Mike. 'Luton?'

Aziz thought about it. 'The other one.' Heathrow might have seemed riskier, but the crowds would be useful. And it was the closest airport. 'Give me about twenty minutes. I'll call—' he paused. 'Do you have a number?'

'The last fourteen missed calls on your original number.'

'Okay.' Aziz was about to hang up when Mike spoke.

'Aziz.' He was strangely hesitant. 'I… JD?'

Aziz bit down through the inside of his cheek. He tasted his blood.

'His phones are off,' Mike said. 'All of them.'

The silence was awful. In the space of that minute, Aziz's phone chimed twice. The stock was on the move, and it had reached its first set of destinations. It was almost half past nine.

'I leave it to you,' Aziz said finally. He didn't wait for an answer.

~

'Is there a problem?' Jassi asked after Aziz hung up.

Aziz sighed. 'Jai's fucked something up. It's not major, but the three of us need to fly out to the Cayman Islands right away. Get there before the banks close today.'

'Is there anything that I need to worry about?'

He really was a good kid, thought Aziz.

'No,' he replied.

'Do I finish today or wrap it up?'

If he ran the burn, thought Aziz, then that bought them time. It was that simple.

'Finish today. Run the loop. Then bank it and wait to hear from me.' Aziz spoke with little emphasis or inflection. He had sounded the same way in the Jag, talking to Brian. He thought further for a moment.

'Listen, if Mike calls back, tell him that we'll do Luton instead. We'll fire up the jet. Make it easier for everyone.'

And when the cops raid the office, which Aziz assumed they would, Jassi would send them to wrong airport and he'd have a hell of a time proving that he hadn't meant to aid in his boss's escape. Ah, well, Aziz thought, if I'm going to stab the kid in the back I might as well do it properly.

'Sure.' Jassi turned back to the laptops.

It didn't even take a minute for Aziz to clear out. He pocketed the phones, taking the time to scribble Mike's new number onto his business card. He slipped on his jacket and picked up the slimmer leather briefcase that lived in his office. It contained his passport, his POC, and all his bank documents.

He was at the door when Jassi murmured, 'Good trip, boss,' without looking up from the laptop.

Aziz didn't answer him. He just started walking.

~

Paul picked him up downstairs. Aziz asked him to head towards Heathrow Terminal Four and that he needed to pick up a phone on the way. This was a frequent request. They found a store in five minutes, and Aziz picked up a hundred pounds of talk time on a prepaid card.

He stood on the pavement while Paul waited at the curb and thought about the phone call he'd hoped he'd never have to make. The phone call he'd been putting off for over a year-and-a-half.

Aziz felt like he'd been suddenly pushed out of an aircraft. Things of great value were ripped out of his hands, off his person, claimed from inside of him. The sounds of the traffic were faint, like they were coming from a great distance. He felt some part of him wink out of existence. Forever.

He dialled his wife's mobile phone and held the phone to his ear.

'Hello?'

Aziz thought about hanging up, just to avoid the first word he'd have to speak. Then he breathed out and familiar ice water flooded through his veins. This was like that night in Oxford. Nothing more. Nothing less. Nothing worse. Just put one foot in front of the other.

'Hello?'

'What's wrong?'

Such a long fucking way, thought Aziz. One word, a single word, was enough to give him away. His first instinct was to say 'nothing'.

'I'm not sure,' he said. Aziz sighed, long and deep. He could hear the pounding of his heart in his ears. His pulse simply would not settle.

'Are you—'

'There's been a raid,' said Aziz, cutting across Tasleem's question.

Silence. Aziz waited. Waves and waves of shame coursed through him. He felt like he'd jabbed his finger into an industrial socket. He waited until he couldn't bear the silence. He opened his mouth with absolutely no idea of what he was going to say next.

'Is it Customs?' asked Tasleem .

Aziz could hear her moving. She was walking quickly. And then he processed her question. He began to ask a question of his own but she interrupted him again.

'Or is it Customs *and* the Met? Together?'

Aziz swallowed. He heard, or imagined, a dry click, like a pistol being cocked. Suddenly he had too many questions.

'How—'

'You think I didn't know?' Tasleem closed a door behind her. Aziz heard her sit down, heard a click that he recognized. She'd opened up her laptop.

'Aziz?' The question was sharp, like she was trying to cut through shock.

'I—' He fought for control. It took a couple of seconds. He eliminated the shame, dropped it to the pavement and turned away. 'I didn't know you knew,' he said.

'I know.' Tasleem heard the change in his voice and hesitated. 'Nothing changes,' she said. Her voice had become a low growl. 'You understand? Tell me you understand.'

'I understand.'

'Good.' Aziz heard her begin to type. 'You need to go today, *now*.'

'I'm on my way to the airport'.

'Okay,' she switched to speakerphone. Aziz could hear pages being turned. He also heard the dial tone from landline on her desk. 'This is what you do. First flight to Dubai is some time soon. I'll book that using my mother's credit card. You call your travel agent and book other flights using your credit card. I'll call you back.'

'Three tickets, Tasleem.'

She didn't bother replying.

Aziz called his travel agent. He asked for three tickets: Jai Singh Dewan, Mike Hamilton and Aziz Basrai. He booked them on the one-thirty to New York, and an afternoon flight to Colombo. All the bookings were first class, confirmed, and Aziz quoted his credit card number to make sure that they showed up whenever the Met searched for them. He had no intention of going anywhere but Dubai. Still, this was the best he could do.

Tasleem called back three minutes later. Aziz had time to register the fact that she'd called from a different number. The earliest available flight this morning was an eleven-thirty to Dubai. That was tight. They had no check-in baggage, and they had enough frequent flyer miles and they were flying first. It could be done.

'I'll have your Lahore ticket by the time you land,' she said. Then, incredibly, she laughed. 'I'll have to get used to wearing a dupatta around my head when I'm out of the house.' She paused. 'I'll see you in a couple of weeks. I love you. Fly safe.' With that, she was gone.

Aziz stood there for a minute. His world had been turned upside down. And he hadn't even begun to understand it. He rubbed his face once, with both his hands and got moving.

For good measure, once he got back into the car, he called their crew at Luton and asked them to be ready to leave in a couple of hours. If the dogs were going to look, that was where they'd look first.

The job-list taken care of, Aziz called Mike and briefed him. It was nine fifty-two. They had an hour and eight minutes to check in. Maybe ten minutes more. But that was it.

~

Mike drove slowly and aimlessly for about ten minutes. He was trying to stall for JD and still get to Heathrow in time. The Motorola was jammed between his ear and his shoulder, and JD was still unreachable. With nothing left to try, Mike finally pulled over and called JD's mom.

'What's wrong?' she asked.

Mike had to concentrate. The shock that had numbed the pain enough for him to get through the morning had begun to wear off. His shoulder was now a throbbing ball of misery and he thought that, in a while, he was going to rip it off just to get some measure of relief.

'I don't know,' he said, his voice thick. 'Maybe everything.'

'I saw him four days ago, Mike. He wasn't well, but he looked better. I told him to go somewhere where no one could disturb him.' She paused. 'I don't know if that helps.'

Mike thanked her and hung up. He was done, he decided. He was going to wait for Aziz's call. If he had an idea about where JD was, then he'd see. But for now, he was played out.

Mike hit the hazards and turned up the air-conditioning. He was sweating and his shoulder was radiating heat. He lent back in the seat and let the cold air flow over him. His mind was still working when he dozed off.

He woke with a start three minutes later. The pain got him up, but he was glad for the nap. The pause had cleared his head and he realized that he knew where JD was. It should have been obvious, it *would* have been obvious if he hadn't had to avoid an assassination attempt and try to save their asses—and single-fucking-handedly at that.

Mike was sure that JD was in the old warehouse in

Heston. Months ago, he had mumbled something about wanting to buy the place and the remark and what it implied had slipped by unnoticed while they changed offices.

The warehouse made sense. Of all the places that JD had, that was the one with the most history. It was the one with the most ritual.

On cue, the phone rang. Aziz. They were booked on three flights, all departing today.

'Which one are you taking?' Mike asked.

There was no hesitation. At least they had come that far. No more games, not between the three of them. 'The first one.'

'Figures,' Mike said. He looked at the clock on the dash. An hour and four minutes. Not enough time to get to Heston and back to Heathrow.

If only the motherfucker had answered the fucking phone. Fuck!

It was what it was. That was the motto, the spirit behind the game, all the games.

Mike hung up and gunned the engine. The car streaked off the shoulder and into the fast lane like a black blur.

~

Wexler was the only one in the office who knew about the lawyer and he had kept it to himself. He wrote the death off as probably unimportant. If he divulged the news, he knew that Val would pull the plug on the raid. It was an executive decision. The prize was worth the gamble.

He and Val had been asked to stay behind and monitor the raid from the department. Reg had dumped the equipment in Wexler's office because it was the largest room on the floor and the two of them had been there since seven in the morning, pacing around radios and phones like expectant parents. The tension had been getting to Wexler. He'd handled enough raids in his day, but nothing on this scale and nothing with such a big payoff at the other end. Being around Val didn't help. She was rigid and uncommunicative, completely withdrawn.

So it was a hell of a relief when he saw the counter begin to move on the dot of nine. And they both saw the massive opportunity in the size of the first consignment. Wexler got his hopes up when Val ordered the raid at nine forty-two. Enough vans were out on the roads, in traffic, and enough vans had turned around, bringing the same phones back to the warehouses.

The first set of reports started to trickle in at ten. Van after van, with junk mobiles amongst the stamped stock, on their way back from a supposed delivery, with two sets of paperwork.

Leave a small window in there, Val had told Reg. Let 'em call their masters.

The agents around the warehouses and the serviced offices waited for ten minutes after the vans got busted. Enough to let one driver make the phone call that would trigger the stampede.

Val pushed the 'Transmit' button on her walkie.

'Reg.'

Customs swarmed all the nodes built around the Heston Principle. It was spectacular. They had knocked the table clean. At almost every office, men who already knew that they were in the middle of the biggest Customs trap in living memory began to talk.

Wexler let out a single roar of delight, the only celebration he allowed himself. On his side of the fence, Wexler's department had just become the Principle.

Only Val remained unmoved amidst the cheers and the back-slapping around the office. She shook her head. 'We need the three of them. Otherwise, we're simply gathering crumbs. We need all three.'

They ignored her. She was old-fashioned, on her way out—the killjoy.

~

Mike told himself that it was okay, he was doing the sensible thing, until he got to the off-ramp. He was doing eighty-five in the fast lane and he began to drift across to the left, heading for the roundabout that would take him to Terminal Four. It was ten past ten and the world as they knew it had collapsed somewhere nearby.

He slowed slightly to make the turn.

His eyes flicked across the sign once, twice. He took his foot off the pedal and then indicated left once more.

He read 'Heathrow Terminal 4' again.

Despite the pain in his shoulder, he winced and tried to shrug.

Like JD was fond of saying, it was about intent. And intent, when you thought about it, was really about choice. Mike gunned the engine and slalomed right, leaving sixty feet of rubber behind him on the motorway. There was honking behind him and the screech of tyres. He had jumped three lanes and he hadn't even indicated.

He laughed out loud. His head was clear and some of the heaviness that had dragged on him since the morning had lifted. He tried to shrug again and the pain only got him laughing harder. It was what it was. That was all.

He found the next exit and swung back towards Heston, driving more reasonably now.

~

When Mike pulled into the lane behind the old warehouse, it was ten thirty-five. He ditched the car and began to limp to the office.

If he could pull JD out, then that was two minutes. And if they drove like mad bastards, they could maybe make Heathrow by eleven or two past eleven. They'd check-in on the phone and they just might make it onboard before the plane was scheduled to start taxiing from the aerobridge. Mike was so engrossed in the possible scenarios that he nearly missed the copper peering into the front door of the warehouse and talking to an intercom.

The sight was so incongruous that Mike almost didn't believe it. He'd been on the run since eight in the morning and here he'd almost walked straight into an officer. And when the fuck did the old office get an intercom?

Instinct steered him into the newsagents'. He waited impatiently, pretending to look at magazines while he watched the officer. It was no good. The cop was clearly trying to talk to someone. After a while, he hurried away. Mike knew the walk. He'd be back and he'd bring company.

Mike risked the pass the minute the copper turned the corner. He dragged himself across the street to the front door. It wasn't just an intercom. It was the dog's fucking bollocks. There was a security system as well and he could spot three cameras from where he was standing. He was fading fast. Even if they got out of this one, he thought that JD would have to drive them to the airport. He pushed the buzzer. Once, and then twice in quick succession.

Mike heard the click, but there was no communication. Whoever it was, they were simply waiting.

'It's Mike, you cunt.' He was losing his voice. He shook his head and took two short steps to the camera that was closest to his eye-level. He peered at the lens and then waved his good arm about. There was a sharp buzzer from within the building and the door slid open. Mike walked in, pushed the door shut and turned around.

JD, his third mobile against his ear, watched him with an expression of complete shock. He pulled the phone away from his ear, looked at it, and then looked at Mike again. He disconnected the phone and simply stared at Mike.

Mike was at a loss himself. He'd spent the last hour-and-a-half frantically trying to reach JD. And here JD was, answering the door while he was on the phone.

'What the fuck is going on?' JD asked. Mike ignored him.

'When did you switch your phone on?'

'At ten this morning. Like I usually do.' Mike shook his head. JD hadn't switched his phone on until two or three in the afternoon for the past six months.

'What the fuck is going on, Mike?'

'Who were you talking to?'

'Jassi. But I—'

'For how long?'

'Ten minutes, I suppose. Maybe a bit longer.'

Mike closed his eyes. In the distance, he heard the first of the approaching sirens.

'Sumit's dead. The Russians killed him this morning.' He said it as a matter of fact, his eyes still closed. He waited for a second, then looked at JD.

JD's eyes widened and Mike could see him putting all the pieces together in his head. Why Jassi was telling him about the monumental raid that had gutted them in less than half an hour. And why the ten-minute conversation with Jassi had resulted in the single copper's visit and now the approaching sirens.

The dogs had the numbers and they had been listening. They had the numbers from Sumit's phone. And Sumit was dead because JD and Mike hadn't been where they were supposed to be the night before.

JD's face crumpled like a little boy's and it was the worst thing that Mike had seen in the entire run. JD cried silently for a minute, standing there with his hand covering his mouth and breathing furiously. He was grieving and he was angry. Mike understood.

JD turned and threw his phone. It exploded against the wall, the pieces skidding across the warehouse floor. Mike looked at it because it was better than having to look at JD's face.

It was a fucking Nokia.

~

The final boarding call for the Emirates flight to Dubai was at five past eleven. Aziz waited until then. He sat with his hands clasped together in his lap, dressed in the only set of clothes he currently possessed in the world.

He had been calling Mike for twenty minutes, but he wouldn't answer. At ten fifty-five, T-Mobile informed him that the phone he was trying to reach had been switched off.

Something else bothered him. He had been reduced again, a refugee again, thrust into another culture again. And he'd dragged his wife down with him. Perhaps there was honour in staying back. But he knew that he would never be able to do it. The safety kicked in every time. He wished them well. He hoped that they had landed on their feet.

Aziz stood up and stretched his legs. The final boarding call was announced. While he waited for the last of the stragglers, he walked across to the window and stood there quietly. It was the last time he would see England. He was sure of it. The pain was dull.

There would, however, be other games, other partners, other friends. As a consolation, that would have to do.

Aziz touched his forehead against the glass once. He turned and walked through the boarding gate.

~

JD and Mike knew they weren't getting out. They could see the gathering procession outside, like the opening ceremony for a World Cup. Aziz had called incessantly from ten forty-five onwards. After ten minutes of listening to Mike's phone vibrate on the table, JD got up and switched it off. He was worried about Mike. Mike was starting to fade. He'd gotten paler and he was fighting to stay awake. JD had listened to Mike's morning and had been astonished at how hard he had tried to pull the three of them out.

It surprised him. The man sitting opposite him on the bed still surprised him, after all this time. Mike needed medical attention. He wasn't going to die or anything, but he was slowly losing consciousness. And Mike had somehow surrendered control to him. Getting to the warehouse, through what it had cost him, was all he could manage. Now it was JD's show.

Three times, officers had buzzed the intercom and three times JD had talked to them.

The first time he had asked why they were here. It was the standard response, the lessons from Cleartone still held true. The officer had been equally polite.

The second time, the demand for the two of them to

emerge and surrender had been more forceful. JD had agreed, but he had asked for half an hour or so.

'I've got someone in here who's been in an accident. We'll come out when he's a little better,' he had said. The statement didn't make much sense. The officer had pointed out that they had an ambulance on standby. JD had repeated his demand.

Twenty minutes later, a third officer, clearly senior, had demanded they surrender.

'I said thirty minutes. You got the lawyer. I've got ten more minutes coming to me.'

He shook Mike awake and looked at him. Mike was still sharp. He was in pain, but he was still sharp.

'Why'd they kill Sumit, Mikey?'

Mike thought it through and shook his head. 'I don't think they wanted to kill Sumit, not the coppers. I think that Customs traded them the Russian connection so that they could pull out the big show. The rest of it is Federov. We broke the contract because the coppers showed up, and Federov came to collect the penalty. We weren't there. Sumit was.'

Mike tried to shrug. 'Just information. Just a tradeoff.'

'It's not very fair, is it?' JD was fixated on this point. He could deal with everything else. Games came and went. But that someone's life could be thrown away as a trading chip, *that* he had trouble dealing with. Especially if it was the government.

'No. It's not fair,' Mike agreed. 'Not at all.' And he blacked out again.

JD settled on the floor opposite him, hands dangling between his knees, head down. He was staring at the concrete.

It came like it did in the old days. Empty one minute and then there, fully dressed, the next.

He'd grown up with these three myths, the three stories of their possible directions.

Sudeep Sen. Jimmy Tipnis. Aziz Basrai.

These were his heroes. Who was right? And who was wrong?

Where was the honour? Who'd stayed true? Which one?

The game wasn't done. There was time for one more play.

Did he *still* believe?

JD looked up and grinned the sunshine grin. He shook Mike awake more vigorously.

'Can you wait another twenty minutes?'

'Sure.'

'Stay awake, Mike. This, you don't want to miss.'

Mike pulled himself up and watched JD. He began to rummage through the pockets of the big black coat he still wore everywhere. He pulled out a packet of gum and tossed it to Mike. Mike caught it, left-handed and snorted laughter. He popped the gum, started to chew and threw the packet back to JD. JD started up the laptop at the desk and got the gum going to his satisfaction.

From his other pocket, he extracted a small hard disk. He connected it to the laptop and looked at Mike carefully.

'Better in here than out there, right?'

I suppose it keeps us away from the Russians,' said Mike. 'What have you got there?'

'Only everything we've ever done.' JD's eyes gleamed.

Mike got it in an instant and laughed. Fucking Aziz

would've probably needed some sort of long-winded explanation. He watched JD work with his customary blinding speed. His fingers flew across the keyboard, and in a moment, Mike was looking at a year-and-a-half's worth of paperwork—every name, every company, every deal, and all that money—being transferred to a website.

Mike knew enough about computers now to know that he was looking at a password-protected secure BBS. It was one of the ideas that JD had come up with when they were trying to create the security protocol.

JD reached for the landline beside him and paused. Mike saw a single tear run down the side of his face, the last one.

'Do you know what I was about to do?' JD asked.

Mike looked at him, surprised at the question. He smiled. The smile made him look tired and dangerous and beautiful. 'You were about to call Sumit to get you a number.'

JD nodded. He blew out a jet of air, picked up the phone and dialled directory assistance.

'I'm looking for the number for Board Magazine, please.'

They put him through. It was a short, clipped conversation, only about three minutes long. At the end of it, JD gave up the password to the person he was talking to.

'Sumitsen. One word. S-U-M-I-T-S-E-N.'

He listened for another minute and hung up. He looked at Mike.

'D'you want to share a cigarette before we step out and make the papers again?'

They smoked in silence, as they had done hundreds of times before.

'Think of it, Mike,' said JD after a while. He had a slow, dreamy smile on his face. 'We're—effectively—retired. And you'll be coaching the football team in prison.'

Mike snorted and then choked on the cigarette smoke.

'You're a strange man, JD.'

JD simply smiled back. He drew on the fag, jetted the smoke out of his nostrils and flicked the cigarette away. He walked over to Mike and helped him up.

'You all right?'

Mike nodded and put out his cigarette. He shrugged the overcoat around him so that it looked okay. As they prepared to step out, he asked the only question he had left.

'You got a name for the stunt you just pulled?'

JD grinned.

'It's called the Jimmy Tipnis, mate. The one where you blow it all up and start all over again in a better place.'

The boys stepped out of the warehouse at eleven forty-three.

~

Reg was the officer who had led the raid on Basrai's office, the nerve centre to the entire organization. And it was he—when he knew that Basrai, at the very least, was gone— who made Jassi answer the phone when he saw who was calling, and fed him the conversation in mime.

They'd had the numbers since six in the morning, although Val still didn't know about the circumstances that had unearthed the information, and Dewan had stayed on the phone long enough for them to be absolutely sure where he was. And while the cavalry moved up the road, Reg had sent the solitary officer to the warehouse to ensure that Dewan didn't run. The git had left the scene, but they had received the unexpected bonus of Hamilton.

The next ten minutes were euphoric. Even Val cracked a smile. The carousel bust had been a grand success, including two of the ring-leaders. By the time they got to the warehouse, the office was sure that they'd lost Basrai, but that was their only casualty. All in all, it had been a surreal morning. Every single call they had taken, every guess and estimation had played out perfectly.

Until the wait began.

The first two requests were met with stalling tactics although Dewan assured the officers that they would emerge soon.

The third request was met with a reference to a lawyer that only three people understood. It was unfortunate that the officer who had asked the question was Reg himself. He was on the radio barely seconds later, yelling, throwing the entire book at the department.

Val watched Wexler go very still. He refused to look her in the eye. She felt a wheel turn somewhere inside her, and suddenly things that were important even half an hour ago didn't seem so any longer. But she stayed in Wexler's office. She had bought the responsibility, and unlike Wexler, she wished to see it through to the end.

Two of the three ring-leaders emerged at eleven forty-three, fully co-operative. One of them, Hamilton, was immediately rushed to hospital. Everyone around her, even that smug bastard, was delirious when they finally emerged. Customs had turned the game around, and they had smashed through what amounted to a cartel. Val excused herself from the celebrations and walked to her office. She sat in her chair, cheek in hand, looking out of the window. It wasn't over. It didn't feel over.

Ten minutes later, the switchboard on the third floor came to life like Christmas lights. Phones were ringing off the hook and people were yelling down corridors.

Val only caught snatches of the babble, but she heard enough.

Dewan had posted the entire financial records of *every single deal* on a secure bulletin board on the internet and handed the keys, with full authorization, to a journalist.

Every dirty little secret was now public domain. The colossal amounts of money, every dealer—straight and crooked—and the massive retail and wholesale outlets that had jumped on the bandwagon. And the small fact that the Exchequer had been attempting to hide a loss of two-and-a-half billion pounds.

Customs were strangers again. In about an hour after they had broken through.

By twelve-twenty, the first news van was parked under the building. By one that afternoon, Customs and Excise were on the National, European and International News. By two in the afternoon, the VAT scam was the biggest financial scandal since the collapse of Barings.

At two-fifteen, the Exchequer announced the immediate

suspension of all VAT reclaims, subject to review. The Stock Exchange began to tank, and thousands of mobile phone retailers, both legitimate and otherwise, started lining the streets in protest.

The end of the carousel was the single incident that caused the merger of Internal Revenue and Her Majesty's Customs and Excise, resulting in the formation of Her Majesty's Revenue and Customs, three years down the line.

JD had brought the Old World down all across the EU. And he had done it as an afterthought. All because he had lost a friend—because the dogs had finally crossed the line.

That made sense to Val.

She roused herself at half past two. She had been in her office since eleven-fifty, leaving only to get herself two cups of tea. The memos had come thick and fast. Clearly, word had gotten out. She was the poster-child for the successes of the morning. It was ridiculous. She was three years away from retirement.

Val tidied her desk for a moment. She opened up the first drawer and pulled out the envelope that she had put there yesterday morning. The letter wasn't fresh. She had been recycling the same one for the last three weeks because they had been so unsure of their schedules. But there was nothing left to add, nothing left to take away.

She put the resignation on her desk and looked around the office. The only thing she took was the dog-eared note that Des had sent her. She slipped it into her bag and left.

No one saw her go.

PART FOUR

EPILOGUE

'Think you must have me all wrong
I didn't care, friend. I wasn't there, friend
If it's the price of a pint that you need
Ask me again. . .'
—From a Dead Beat to an Old Greaser
Jethro Tull

4.1

The young man checked the address again. Behind him, his father began to ask another question. The young man turned to look at his father. The look stalled the question.

'It's here. This is the place.' In Punjabi, delivered with belligerence. The young man had been increasingly belligerent over the past three days.

Neither of them had been to this quarter of Lahore often. Consequently, having heard enough stories, they had set off this afternoon with an extra hour in hand. They had both been to estates where '3's sprang up next to '17's, next door to '68's.

But Model Town, in all the ways that they had heard, was different.

Within the locality, and the locality was one of the most posh in the city of Lahore, there were further subdivisions. The two men were looking at a life they could only imagine. They were looking at well-maintained, immaculate houses. But they were also looking at space, more space than they could ever dream of. Space was the real luxury in this part of the world.

Rumour had it that the man they were about to meet owned three houses in a row. That he had converted them into a single property.

Regardless of the opulence before them, both men felt like they were in a ghost town. The streets were empty. It wasn't just the seclusion of the rich. Pakistan's exit at the hands of India at the Centurion the previous day was most likely the real cause, thought the young man. Losses to India at the World Cup left the country in a state of mourning. There had been some rioting in Model Town. A few cricketers maintained homes here.

The young man, Rizwan Kardar, turned to his father. He clutched a large plastic packet, one of the good ones from a garment shop that his mother had visited maybe two years ago. It contained his life up until this moment.

'What do you want to do?' He hated how he sounded. He was sneering because he was afraid.

His father looked at him helplessly. Waiting here, in the sun, on the corner of the street, was stupid. But they were a good forty-five minutes ahead of schedule, and he felt very strongly about walking into a potential benefactor's house this early.

Rizwan read his father's thoughts. His bitterness welled up. He was as helpless as his father and he was lashing out at the only visible target. He hated it because his father didn't deserve his behaviour.

'We'll go in.'

His father started to shake his head, but Rizwan ignored him. He was the reason they were here. He had caused this opportunity. It was the safecracker in Rizwan's head that had led them to this street corner, this far ahead of schedule.

And he would go into this meeting with his head held high. That was all they could afford.

'If he's what they say he is, he won't mind.'

And with that, Rizwan crossed the street and walked up the sidewalk to the black gate they had been staring at. He consulted the scrap of paper in his hand and rang the bell. His father stood next to him, head low.

~

Rizwan hadn't known what to expect, but he was prepared to hate whatever greeted them. What he *hadn't* expected was that he would be deeply impressed by the next twenty minutes.

The smaller gate next to the main entrance slid open the moment he rang the bell. A polite, uniformed guard was expecting them. He had their names on a piece of paper, spelled correctly. His name, Rizwan saw, was before his father's on the register. That was uncommon. Fathers tended to headline, at least in his experience. Also written next to the names was '1400'. The guard made no mention of the actual time. He simply buzzed the intercom and spoke into it softly.

A man who could only be described as a secretary appeared. He introduced himself as Mir. He shook hands with both of them and led them into the house. Rizwan had expected the typical servant class to welcome them. Instead, the three people that he did see were uniformed, and spoke English. They murmured 'Good afternoon' and passed on. There were no requests to take off their shoes.

It was as if he and his father had walked into a very exclusive hotel. Rizwan had expected something gaudy, wealth substituted for class. Instead, the house was, sleek, ultra modern, all lines and angles and black and white. And it was cold. He'd known it would be centrally air-conditioned, but the temperature went beyond normal comfort. The house was freezing. He had caught sight of a thermostat as they passed through the house and saw that the temperature was at sixteen degrees centigrade. The contrast to the temperature outside was so great that Rizwan almost expected to see his breath. The house seemed to be in a state of permanent winter.

Mir led them to the library. Split-level, with wooden flooring, it was twice the size of the home Rizwan shared with his parents and siblings. Rizwan counted four wall-mounted televisions and at least three computers. The upper level was clearly a study of some sort. The remainder of the space was given over to books, wall-to-wall, floor-to-ceiling. There seemed to be no real order. Fiction rubbed shoulders with volumes on company practices. And there were hundreds of law volumes. The room was silent, gigantic and intimidating.

They chose tea when asked, and it came five minutes later, delicate Darjeeling in a simple but very expensive pot. Rizwan and his father drank their tea in silence. There wasn't anything to do, so Rizwan walked around the room, looking at the books. He carried the plastic packet with him. It was his umbilical cord to the world outside.

Ten minutes later, another uniformed member of the staff let himself into the room quietly. He enquired whether they were all right. When they said that they were, he went up to the study and then went around the library with four remotes, switching on the televisions one after the other, all of them on mute. Each of the televisions was tuned to either a European news channel or a European business channel.

Rizwan looked at his watch. It was a quarter to two in the afternoon. He was a clever boy; that was the primary reason he found himself in this room with his father, waiting for this mysterious businessman. And something had dawned on him.

He lives on UK time, thought Rizwan. That's why the appointment was for two in the afternoon. It's nine in the morning for him. And then the thought was gone because the door opened and the man walked in.

'Mr Basrai,' said Rizwan's father. He stood up as he said it, hands together. Rizwan had a single moment of vivid hatred—this was feudal at its worst, it betrayed everything that he had fought for his entire life—and then that, too, was gone, blown away by the force of the personality that had walked into the room.

Aziz walked straight up to Rizwan's father. He folded the old man's hands into his own and shook his head.

'Sir. Please.' Aziz spoke in Punjabi. It wasn't perfect, but it was serviceable. 'Please.' He indicated that Rizwan's father should sit again. He turned to Rizwan.

Rizwan had spent sixty rupees the previous afternoon—money that he'd made giving tuitions around where he lived—logging onto the internet and reading up on Aziz Basrai. Much of the information was sketchy, including the reasons why he had fled England so suddenly the previous year, but there had been a surprising amount of publicity that had very little to do with his business activities. Rizwan was surprised by this because of the low-profile Basrai and his wife maintained since they'd settled in Lahore. Most people weren't even sure *when* they'd arrived.

But nothing had prepared Rizwan for what he saw. If it weren't for the accented Punjabi, Rizwan could have walked by Aziz Basrai and not recognized him. The suave businessman was gone. In his place was someone off the streets of Lahore. A Pathani suit and a taqiyah. And a beard according to the faith—long, with the upper lip clean-shaven. Then he spoke, and it only added to Rizwan's momentary bewilderment.

'Rizwan. May I call you Rizwan?' Aziz asked. He spoke in English. The accent was international. It felt like it belonged in a boardroom somewhere in the West.

'Of course.' Rizwan replied in English. His was good as well, and he was determined to showcase it. He was determined to prove that he didn't *need* Basrai.

Aziz nodded. A small smile tugged at the corners of his mouth but it didn't reveal itself. He invited Rizwan to take a seat, and waited until he'd settled down before he sat down himself.

'More tea?'

Father and son both nodded. Now that he had revealed himself, they were unsure of how to progress. They waited for the tea, which came promptly, along with another member of the staff, bearing three mobile phones and a desk calculator on a tray. Aziz put them down at the table and poured them all cups of tea. He looked at them and nodded.

'Sir, we—' Rizwan's father began. Aziz shook his head, silencing him. He looked at Rizwan for a moment. He turned back to the old man.

'I beg your pardon. But it's your son's interview. He should speak.' And with that, he leaned back and looked at Rizwan.

Rizwan was at a loss. He had expected the feudal trend to continue. Certainly, he and his father had been running around for two months, looking for scholarships, reduced to supplication of the crudest form. It had built in him a rage against the contradictory blessing of his own ability. He wasn't looking for a favour. Instead, he was looking at a partnership, or an investment. He believed that he'd earned that much.

And here, this man who was almost a myth, who had changed so dramatically, had reduced this to what it was at the very beginning: a business meeting.

Rizwan struggled with the words. He was aware of his father's mounting tension. He heard the gentle hum of the air-conditioners, like a giant, invisible machine running all around them. And he saw the challenge in the eyes of the man who was looking at him. This was a test.

Did he *believe* that he deserved the opportunity that this man was willing to provide him? The opportunity that had come knocking because this man had found him?

That was the test.

In the end, he went with the biggest thing on his mind because he had nothing else to say after the months of running around.

'I want to go abroad to study. I want to do my Bachelor's and then my Master's.'

Aziz nodded. 'And do you think you deserve it? Do you think that you're good enough?'

Rizwan nodded back. Aziz held out his hand. And Rizwan realized that, good or bad, this *was* a business meeting and that, good or bad, he understood this particular currency and he was glad to trade in it.

Rizwan unwrapped the plastic packet and silently handed over his life—the report cards and the scholarships, the gold medals and the special mentions, and every recommendation that he had picked up in his brilliant academic career. Things that had meant nothing in all the interviews thus far.

Aziz went through every one of them. The scan was rapid, quicker than expected, but Rizwan could tell that it wasn't cursory. The man was simply going through the reports like he would a balance-sheet, plumbing the bottom line.

Aziz was almost at the end of the stack when one of his phones rang. He peered over the stack and picked up the phone to check the number. Aziz checked his watch and looked at Rizwan.

'Sorry, I need to take this.'

Rizwan nodded, reeling from the fact that Basrai had the courtesy to apologize.

'Yes?'

Aziz listened to the person on the other end for a minute. 'I'll have to call you back in about ten minutes.'

He hung up and continued reading Rizwan's academic record. He finished a couple of minutes later, put the stack back together neatly, and returned it to Rizwan.

'It's very impressive.' Aziz looked at Rizwan. 'What do you wish to study?'

Rizwan had known the answer from the age of eight.

'Law.'

For the first, and only, time in the entire conversation, Aziz smiled. It lit up his face. He shook his head once. The smile stayed on his face.

'Good answer,' he said. He continued to look at Rizwan and sat up straight. 'Okay. Give me a little time. Let me see how we can help you out.'

He looked at both father and son and something occurred to him.

'I'll tell you this much. It looks good. You have a gifted child,' he said in Punjabi.

And that was that. The meeting was done.

Aziz watched them leave, exchanging greetings and deflecting gratitude. He waited, seated in the same chair, until Mir returned from walking his guests to the door.

'Give him the grant,' he told Mir. 'All the way through to the Master's, everything paid for, two trips home a year if he wants. Clothing, accommodation, food. No repayment required. Interest-free if the boy's insistent, and he's doing well enough.' Aziz paused, waiting until Mir finished taking it down. The pauses were a minor irritant. Unless Mir wrote things down, he would miss something. Gone were the days when a debrief could be a conversation, walking through tourists in Leicester Square. No notes there.

Aziz shook his head. He had his place. It was here, *now*. It was what it was.

'Tell the kid that the only thing I want is his term reports. That's all.'

Mir took the last note down and left, on his way to change a family's fortunes forever.

Aziz watched him go. He looked at his watch. It was two minutes past two in the afternoon, in Lahore. He picked up the phone dialled the number that he'd received the last call from. It connected. And rang. There was an eternity between rings, like the time spent here in Lahore after ten in the evening.

Someone answered. Aziz rose from the chair and began to make his way to the study. His laptop was already switched on.

'Hello?'

There was a short, quick sentence at the other end of the line.

'Okay. Tag the VAT on it.'

Aziz sat down at his desk.

'Bring it into the "C" company.'

He made an entry into the spreadsheet in front of him.

'Let's go.'

Acknowledgements

I would like to start by saying thank you to the wind beneath my wings, my wife, without whose motivation and encouragement I probably wouldn't have embarked on this journey of writing a book. She believed in me and felt I had a story worth telling.

I am truly and deeply indebted to so many people without whom this work would not and could not have been done. I would like to thank all those who contributed towards my research. I would like to thank my parents for their unconditional support and confidence in me. I must also take this opportunity to thank my mother-in-law who actually read the first, never-ending extended draft! This book would have literally been impossible for me to ever write alone, considering my busy schedule, if it wasn't for my good friend and co-writer Arghya Lahiri. He spent days and nights working on the book with me and I would bombard him with systems, chains and confusing tax loopholes. I am confident enough to say he is now self qualified to be a legal consultant for customs and excise! I would like to acknowledge Ian Spiegelman for taking a look at my book after I had spent four years on it and giving me his priceless contribution in making the book sharper, simpler and more complete! A big thank you to Markus Hoffman and Joe Regal from Regal Literary, my agents, who made it all possible. How can I forget the man who played catalyst in introducing me to Gregory Roberts. But it was Markus and Joe's faith in my work with their honest advice that kept me rolling out draft after draft till we had a version we were all satisfied with. As for why I wanted to write *How Not to Make Money* it is an ode to all the legal traders who got caught up in the VAT tax scam and lost out due to the speed at which this white collar crime grew, causing humongous losses to their businesses. It definitely established one fact—crime doesn't pay!

I didn't think I had the ability to write this book but faith and the urge to tell this story kept me going. Not to forget Meru Gokhale and Faiza S Khan from Random House who have been my support system and held my hand throughout the process of publishing. This book will be something I can tick off my bucket list and feel very proud of.

Look forward to your feedback, you can catch me directly on twitter@therajkundra.

A NOTE ON THE AUTHOR

Raj Kundra is a successful entrepreneur. He has invested in trading, mining, construction and the IPL cricket team Rajasthan Royals. This is his first novel.